HOLY TEMPLE

JIMETA

GOMBE

ORON

LOKOJA

KADUNA

BENIN CITY

TOMI ADEYEMI

CHILDREN
OF
VIRTUE
AND
VENGEANCE

HENRY HOLT AND COMPANY ◆ NEW YORK

Henry Holt and Company, *Publishers since 1866*
Henry Holt® is a registered trademark of Macmillan Publishing Group, LLC
120 Broadway, New York, NY 10271 • fiercereads.com

Library of Congress Control Number: 2018945013

Our books may be purchased in bulk for promotional, educational, or business use.
Please contact your local bookseller or the Macmillan Corporate and Premium Sales Department at
(800) 221-7945 ext. 5442 or by email at MacmillanSpecialMarkets@macmillan.com.

First edition, 2019 / Designed by Patrick Collins and Angela Jun
Map illustration by Keith Thompson
Printed in the United States of America

ISBN 978-1-250-17099-6 (hardcover)
1 3 5 7 9 10 8 6 4 2

ISBN 978-1-250-23036-2 (B&N edition)
1 3 5 7 9 10 8 6 4 2

ISBN 978-1-250-23037-9 (Target edition)
1 3 5 7 9 10 8 6 4 2

ISBN 978-1-250-25708-6 (Indigo edition)
1 3 5 7 9 10 8 6 4 2

ISBN 978-1-250-23244-1 (international edition)
1 3 5 7 9 10 8 6 4 2

To Tobi and Toni,
I love you more than I could put into words.

THE MAJI CLANS

IKÚ CLAN
MAJI OF LIFE AND DEATH
MAJI TITLE: REAPER

DEITY: OYA

....

ÈMÍ CLAN
MAJI OF MIND, SPIRIT, AND DREAMS
MAJI TITLE: CONNECTOR

DEITY: ORÍ

....

OMI CLAN
MAJI OF WATER
MAJI TITLE: TIDER

DEITY: YEMOJA

....

INÁ CLAN
MAJI OF FIRE
MAJI TITLE: BURNER

DEITY: SÀNGÓ

AFÉFÉ CLAN
MAJI OF AIR
MAJI TITLE: WINDER
DEITY: AYAO

....

AIYE CLAN
MAJI OF IRON AND EARTH
MAJI TITLE: GROUNDER + WELDER
DEITY: ÒGÚN

....

ÌMỌLÈ CLAN
MAJI OF DARKNESS AND LIGHT
MAJI TITLE: LIGHTER
DEITY: OCHUMARE

....

ÌWÒSÀN CLAN
MAJI OF HEALTH AND DISEASE
MAJI TITLE: HEALER + CANCER
DEITY: BABALÚAYÉ

....

ARÍRAN CLAN
MAJI OF TIME
MAJI TITLE: SEER
DEITY: ORÚNMILA

....

ẸRANKO CLAN
MAJI OF ANIMALS
MAJI TITLE: TAMER
DEITY: OXOSI

CHAPTER ONE

◆◇◆

ZÉLIE

I TRY NOT to think of him.

But when I do, I hear the tides.

Baba was with me the first time I heard them.

The first time I felt them.

They called out to me like a lullaby, leading us away from the forest path and toward the sea. The ocean breeze ruffled the loose coils in my hair. Rays of sun spilled through the thinning leaves.

I didn't know what we would find. What strange wonder that lullaby would hold. I just knew I had to get to it. It was like the tides held a missing piece of my soul.

When we finally saw it, my small hand slipped out of Baba's. My mouth fell open with awe. There was magic in that water.

The first magic I'd felt since the king's men killed Mama.

"*Zélie rọra o*," Baba called as I drifted toward the tides. I flinched when the seafoam washed over my toes. The lakes in Ibadan were always so cold. But that water was warm like the smell of Mama's rice. As warm as the glow of her smile. Baba followed me in and lifted his head to the sky.

It was like he could taste the sun.

In that moment he grabbed my hand; laced his bandaged fingers between mine and stared into my eyes. It was then that I knew, even if Mama was gone, we still had each other.

We could survive.

But now . . .

I open my eyes to the cold, gray sky; to the howling ocean crashing against Jimeta's rocky bluffs. I can't stay in the past.

I can't keep my father alive.

The ritual that cost Baba his life haunts me as I prepare to lay him to rest. My heart hangs with all the pain he endured; every sacrifice he made so that I could bring magic back.

"It's okay." My older brother Tzain stands by my side and offers me his hand. A shadow of a beard wraps around his dark brown skin; the new hair almost masks how tight his clenched jaw truly is.

He squeezes his palm against mine as the gentle mist transforms to a pelting rain. The downpour chills us to the bone. It's like even the gods can't help but mourn.

I'm sorry, I think to Baba's spirit, wishing I could say it to his face. As we pull on the rope keeping his casket tethered to Jimeta's rocky coast, I wonder why I thought burying one parent would prepare me to bury the next. My hands still shake with all the things left unsaid. My throat burns from the screams I force into silent tears. I try to keep it all inside as I reach for the jar filled with the last of our burial oil.

"Be careful," Tzain warns as the tremor in my hand makes drops of oil spill over the jar's rim. After three weeks of bartering to get enough to soak Baba's casket, the rippling liquid feels more precious than gold. Its sharp smell burns my nostrils as I pour the last of it onto our burial torch. Tears stream down Tzain's face when he strikes the flint. With no time to waste, I prepare the words of the *ibùkún*——a special blessing a Reaper must pass to the dead.

"From the gods comes the gift of life," I whisper the Yoruba. *"To the gods, that gift must be returned."* The incantation sounds strange on my lips. Until a few weeks ago, no Reaper had the magic to perform an *ìbùkún* for eleven years. *"Bèèni ààyé tàbí ikú kò le yà wá. Bèèni ayè tàbí òrun kò le sin wá nítorí èyin lè ngbé inú ù mi. Èyin la ó máa rí—"*

The moment magic breathes under my skin, I can't find my voice. The purple light of my ashê glows around my hands, the divine power that fuels our sacred gifts. I haven't felt its heat since the ritual that brought magic back to Orïsha. Since Baba's spirit tore through my veins.

I stumble back as magic bubbles inside me. My legs go numb. Magic shackles me to my past, dragging me under despite how hard I pull—

"No!" The shout echoes against the ritual walls. My body slams into the stone floor. A thud sounds as Baba follows, stiff as a board.

I move to protect him, but his eyes are frozen open in an empty glaze. An arrowhead sticks through his chest.

Blood soaks through his ripped tunic—

"Zél, watch it!"

Tzain dives forward, reaching for the torch as it falls from my hand. He's quick, but not quick enough. The flame extinguishes the moment the torch falls into the thrashing tides.

He struggles to light the torch again, but the fire won't catch. I flinch as he chucks the useless wood into the sand.

"What're we supposed to do now?"

I hang my head, wishing I had an answer. With the kingdom in chaos, getting more oil could take weeks. Between the riots and food shortages, it's hard enough to secure a measly bag of rice.

Guilt cages me like a casket, trapping me in a tomb of my own mistakes. Maybe it's a sign I don't deserve to bury Baba.

Not when I'm the reason he's dead.

"Sorry," Tzain sighs and pinches the bridge of his nose.

"Don't be sorry." My throat closes up. "This is all my fault."

"Zél—"

"If I had never touched that scroll . . . if I'd never found out about that ritual—"

"This isn't on you," Tzain says. "Baba gave his life so you could bring magic back."

That's the problem, I hug myself. I wanted magic back to keep Baba safe. All it did was send him to an early grave. What use are these powers if I can't protect the people I love?

What good is magic if I can't bring Baba back to life?

"If you don't stop blaming yourself, you'll never stop, and I *need* you to stop." Tzain grabs both my shoulders, and in his gaze, I see the brown eyes of my father; eyes that forgive even when they shouldn't. "It's you and me now. We're all we've got."

I exhale and wipe my tears as Tzain pulls me into a hug. Even soaking wet, his embrace is still warm. He rubs his fingers up and down my spine the way Baba used to when he wrapped me in his arms.

I look back to Baba's casket floating in the ocean, waiting for a fire that will never come. "If we can't burn him—"

"Wait!" Amari calls from behind. She sprints down the iron ramp of the warship that's been our home since the sacred ritual. Her soaked, white tunic is a far cry from the ornate geles and gowns she wore when she was Orïsha's princess. It clings to her oak brown skin as she meets us at the thrashing tides.

"Here." Amari hands Tzain a rusted torch from the captain's quarters and a fresh jar of oil taken from her own meager ration.

"What about the ship?" Tzain frowns.

"We'll survive." Amari passes me the torch and my eyes linger on the new streak of white hair pasted to her cheek from the rain. A sign of the new magic that lives in her blood. A harsh reminder of the hundreds of nobles across Orïsha who now possess streaks and magic like hers.

I turn away before she can see my pain. My stomach clenches at the constant reminder of the ritual that gave Amari her gift and the boy who broke my heart.

"Ready?" Tzain asks, and I nod although it isn't true. This time when he strikes the flint, I lower the torch to the rope. It catches in an instant.

I brace myself as the line of fire races down the rope's oil-soaked cords, shooting toward Baba's casket. My hand grips my chest the moment he goes up in flames. Reds and oranges blaze bright against the gray horizon.

"*Títí di òdí kejì.*" Tzain bows his head, whispering the sacrament. I clench my teeth and do the same.

Títí di òdí kejì.

Until the other side.

Speaking the sacrament aloud brings me right back to Mama's burial. To watching her corpse go up in flames. As the prayer passes, I think of all those who might rest with her in alâfia. Everyone who died so that we could bring magic back.

Lekan, the sêntaro who sacrificed himself to awaken my gift. My friends, Zulaikha and Salim, murdered when the monarchy attacked our festival.

Mama Agba, the Seer who spent her life watching over me and the other Ilorin divîners.

Inan, the prince I believed I loved.

Títí di òdí kejì, I think to their spirits. A reminder to carry on.

Our battle isn't over.

If anything, it's just begun.

CHAPTER TWO

◆ ◾ ◾ ◾ ◾ ◾ ◆ ⬧ ◆ ◾ ◾ ◾ ◾ ◾ ◆

AMARI

FATHER USED TO SAY that Orïsha waits for no one.

No man.

No king.

They were the words he used to justify any action. An excuse to excuse everything.

As the flames around Baba's casket burn before me, the sword I sent through my own father's chest hangs heavy in my belt. Saran's body was never recovered from the ritual grounds.

Even if I wanted to bury him, I couldn't.

"We should go," Tzain says. "Your Mother's message will be here soon."

I trail a few steps behind him and Zélie as we leave the shore and enter the warship we stole to get to the ritual grounds. The iron ship's been our home since we brought magic back weeks ago, yet the snow leopanaires engraved along its walls still put me on edge. Every time I pass Father's old seal, I don't know whether to cry or scream. I don't know if I'm allowed to feel anything.

"All aboard!"

I glance back at the captain's high-pitched call. Families line up across the dock, handing over gold pieces as they board a small mercenary ship.

6

Bodies cram below the rusted deck, escaping Orïsha's borders to seek peace across foreign waters. Each sunken face sticks another needle of guilt into my heart. While I heal and lick my wounds, the entire kingdom still suffers from Father's scars.

There's no more time for me to hide. I have to take my place on Orïsha's throne. I am the only one who can usher in an era of peace. The queen who can fix everything my father broke.

Conviction warms my chest as I join the others in the frigid captain's quarters. It's one of the few rooms on the ship free of majacite: the special ore the monarchy used to burn the maji and neutralize their powers. Every comfort that once filled the room has been stripped away, traded so we could survive.

Tzain sits on the bare bed, scraping the last grains of rice from a tin cup. Zélie rests on the metal floor, half-buried in her lionaire's golden coat. The massive ryder lies across Zélie's lap, lifting her head to lick the tears that fall from Zélie's silver eyes. I force myself to look away as I reach for my own meager ration of rice.

"Here." I hand Tzain the cup.

"Are you sure?"

"I'm too nervous to eat," I say. "I'll probably just throw it all up."

It's only been a half moon since I sent word to Mother back in Lagos, but it feels like I've been waiting an eternity for her to respond. With her support, I can ascend to Orïsha's throne. I can finally right my Father's wrongs. Together we can create a land where the maji don't have to live in fear. We can unite this kingdom and erase the divisions that have plagued Orïsha for centuries.

"Don't worry." Tzain squeezes my shoulder. "No matter what she says, we'll figure it out."

He moves to check on Zélie and my chest tightens; I hate the part of me that hates what they still have. Only three weeks have passed since

Father's blade tore through my brother's gut, and I'm already starting to forget the growl in Inan's voice. Every time it happens, I have to grind my teeth to keep the heartache in. Perhaps when Mother and I are reunited, the gaping hole in my heart might actually start to heal.

"Incoming." Zélie points to the silhouette moving in the warship's dark halls. I tense as the tarnished door groans open, revealing our messenger. Roën shakes the rain from his black hair, the silky strands clumping together in waves that fall along his square jaw. With skin like desert sand and eyes like teardrops, the mercenary always looks out of place in a room full of Orïshans.

"Nailah?"

The lionaire's ears perk up as Roën kneels, removing a thick parcel from his pack. Nailah nearly knocks Roën over when he unties the binds, revealing a glistening array of fish. I'm surprised when a small smile finds its way to Zélie's lips.

"Thank you," she whispers.

Roën nods, holding her gaze. I have to clear my throat before he rises to face me.

"Let's hear it," I sigh. "What did she say?"

Roën pushes his tongue into his cheek and drops his gaze to the ground. "There was an attack. No word's gotten in or out of the capital."

"An attack?" My chest clenches as I think of Mother holed up in the palace. "How?" I rise to my feet. "When? Why?"

"They're calling themselves the *Iyika*," Roën explains. "The '*revolution*.' The maji stormed Lagos when their powers came back. Word is their attack made it all the way to the palace."

I brace myself against the wall, sliding down to the grated floor. Roën's lips keep moving, but I can't make out the words. I can't hear anything at all.

"The queen," I struggle to speak. "Did they . . . is she . . ."

"No one's heard from her since." Roën looks away. "With you hiding out here, people think the royal line's dead."

Tzain rises to his feet, but I put up a hand, forcing him to stay back. If he so much as breathes near me, I'll unravel. I'll be less than the hollow shell I already am. Every plan I made, every hope I had—in seconds, they're all gone. If Mother's dead . . .

Skies.

I really am all alone.

"What're the *Iyika* after?" Tzain asks.

"It's hard to pin down," Roën says. "Their forces are small, but lethal. They've carried out noble assassinations all over Orïsha."

"So, they're out for royal blood?" Zélie's brows knit and we lock eyes. We've barely spoken since the ritual went awry. It's nice to see she still cares about me.

"It seems that way." Roën shrugs. "But because of the *Iyika*, the military's hunting maji like dogs. Entire villages are being cleared out. The new admiral's all but declared war."

I close my eyes and run my hands through the new waves in my hair. The last time Orïsha was at war, Burners nearly wiped out the royal bloodline. Years later, Father struck back with the Raid. If war breaks out again, no one will be safe. The kingdom shall tear itself apart.

Orïsha waits for no one, Amari.

The ghost of Father's voice rings through my head. I drove my sword into his chest to free Orïsha from his tyranny, but now the kingdom's in chaos. There's no time to grieve. No time to wipe my tears. I vowed to be a better queen.

If Mother is no longer here, fulfilling that vow now falls on me.

"I'll address the public," I decide. "Take control of the kingdom. Bring back stability and end this war." I get back on my feet, pushing my plans above my grief. "Roën, I know I'm in the red with you, but if I could just ask for a little more of your help—"

"I hope you're joking." All compassion disappears from the mercenary's tone. "You realize that no contact with your mother means you still owe me my weight in gold?"

"I gave you this ship!" I shout.

"The ship you're still squatting on?" Roën arches his brow. "The ship my men and I stole? I have families waiting to escape across the sea. This ship isn't payment. It's driving up what you owe me!"

"When I claim the throne, I'll get access to the royal treasuries," I say. "Help me set up a rally, and I'll pay you double what I owe. Just a few more days, and the gold is yours!"

"You have one night." Roën pulls up the hood on his rain cloak. "Tomorrow this ship sets sail. If you're not off it, you're going in the ocean. You lot can't afford the fare."

I intercept his path, but it doesn't stop him from blowing out the door. The grief I attempt to push down threatens to break as Roën's footsteps disappear under the trickling rain.

"We don't need him." Tzain comes to my side. "You can take the throne on your own."

"I don't have a gold piece to my name. In what world will anyone believe I have a legitimate claim?"

Tzain pauses, stumbling back as Nailah passes between our feet. Her wet nose sniffs the grated floor, searching for more fish meat. I think of the meal Roën gifted her and look to Zélie, but Zélie shakes her head.

"He already said no."

"Because *I* asked!" I nearly sprint across the room. "You convinced him to take a crew of men to a mythical island in the middle of the sea. You can persuade him to help us out with a rally."

"We already owe him gold," she says. "We're lucky enough to be leaving Jimeta with our heads!"

"Without his help, what other choice do we have?" I ask. "If Lagos fell when magic came back, Orïsha has been without a ruler for almost a moon. If I don't gain control now, I won't be able to take the throne at all!"

Zélie rubs the back of her neck, fingers passing over the new golden marks along her skin. The ancient symbols have been there since the ritual, each curved line and delicate dot shimmering like it was tattooed by the smallest needle. Though they're beautiful, Zélie covers them the same way she covers her scars. With shame.

As if the very sight of either causes her pain.

"Zélie, please." I kneel before her. "We have to try. The military's hunting maji—"

"I can't be expected to carry the plight of my people forever."

Her coldness catches me off guard, but I don't give up. "Then do it for Baba. Do it because he gave his life for this cause."

Zélie's shoulders slump and she closes her eyes, taking a deep breath. The pressure lifts in my chest when she rises to her feet.

"I'm not making any promises."

"Just try your best." I cover her hand with mine. "We've sacrificed far too much to lose this fight."

CHAPTER THREE

◆ ⬦ ◆

ZÉLIE

Jimeta's night rains wash away the weight of the day as Nailah and I leave the warship. The howling winds hit us with the sweet scent of brine and seaweed; all I could smell in those cramped quarters was burning wood and ash. Nailah's meaty paws leave imprints in the sand as we exit the wooden docks and enter Jimeta's winding streets. Her large tongue flops from her mouth when we run. I don't remember the last time we galloped with nothing above us but the full moon and open air.

"That's it, Nailah." I hold her reins tight as we make our way through the nooks and valleys of Jimeta's sandstone cliffs. The homes nestled within the towering bluffs go black as villagers put their lanterns out, preserving what precious oil they have. We turn a corner as sailors lock up the wooden lifts that transport them up and down the cliffs. My eyes widen at a new mural painted in red against a cave wall. The crimson pigment gleams in the moonlight, forming an *I* created out of an assortment of different-size dots.

They're calling themselves the Iyika. Roën's words run through my head. *The 'revolution.' The maji stormed Lagos when their powers came back. Word is their attack made it all the way to the palace.*

I pull on Nailah's reins, picturing the maji who painted this. The way Roën talked, the *Iyika* didn't sound like a band of rebels.

12

They sounded like a true army.

"Mama, look!"

A small girl steps into the street as I approach a cluster of battered tents. She clutches a black porcelain doll to her chest, its painted face and silk dress the only mark of the girl's noble heritage. The child's only one of the new residents to fill Jimeta's thinning streets, dirt paths narrowed by the rows of pitched tents that line their edges. As she walks further into the rain, I wonder what noble life the girl had before this. What misery she had to escape to get here.

"I've never seen a lionaire." She stretches her small hand toward Nailah's massive horns. I smile at the twinkle in the girl's gaze, but when she nears, I see the white streak in her hair.

Another tîtán.

Resentment curls in me at the sight. According to Roën's reports, roughly one-eighth of the population has magic now. Of those, about a third have the magic of tîtáns.

Marked by white streaks, the tîtáns appeared in the nobility and military after the ritual, displaying magic similar to one of the ten maji clans. But unlike us, their powers require no incantation to come forth. Like Inan, their raw abilities are quite strong.

I know their awakened magic must come from something I did wrong in the ritual, but the sight of them always makes my throat tight.

It's hard to see their white streaks and not see *him*.

"Likka!" The girl's mother runs into the rain, pulling a thick yellow shawl over her head. She grabs her daughter's wrist, muscles tensing when she spots my white hair.

I click my tongue and ride off, dismounting Nailah when I reach the end of the path in front of Roën's den. Her own daughter may have magic now, yet somehow she can still hate me for mine.

"Would you look at that." A raspy voice greets me when I near the entrance of the hideout where Roën's crew resides. I roll my eyes as the mercenary slides down his black mask, revealing Harun—Roën's enforcer. The last time the mercenary and I met, I threw him to the ground. Roën told me I broke his ribs. Harun hasn't approached me since that day, but now danger dances in his gaze.

"Tell me." He drapes a heavy hand across my shoulders. "What's brought my favorite maggot crawling out of the dirt?"

I throw off his arm and whip out my staff. "I'm not in the mood for your games."

He smiles as I size him up, revealing his yellowed teeth. "These streets can be dangerous at night. Especially for a maggot like you."

"Call me maggot again."

My scars prickle at the slur King Saran had carved into my back. I clench my staff when more mercenaries slink out of the shadows. Before I know it, five of them have me cornered against the cavern wall.

"There's a bounty on your head, *maggot*." Harun steps forward, eyes flickering over the new golden marks on my skin. "I always thought you'd fetch a nice price, but even I couldn't have guessed how high that price would rise."

The smile drops off his face, and I catch the glint of a blade.

"The girl who brought magic back. Right before our eyes."

With every threat Harun makes, the magic he speaks of bubbles in my blood. My ashê simmers like lightning gathering in a storm cloud, just waiting to be released with an incantation.

But no matter how many mercenaries appear, I won't let it out. I can't. Magic's the reason Baba's gone. It's a betrayal to use it now—

"What do we have here?"

Roën tilts his head, sauntering in from Jimeta's streets. As he approaches the entrance of the cave, a ray of moonlight strikes a patch of smeared blood along his chin. I can't tell whether or not the blood is his.

Ease drips from Roën's stance and his foxer smile, but his storm-gray eyes pierce like knives.

"I hope you're not having a party without me," he says. "You both know how jealous I can get."

The circle of mercenaries instinctively parts for their leader as he makes his way to the front. Harun's jaw clicks when Roën pulls out a switchblade and flicks it open, using the tip to dig out grime from underneath his fingernails.

Harun looks me up and down before walking away. His threat leaves a bitter taste on my tongue as the other mercenaries follow suit, peeling off until Roën and I are alone.

"Thanks," I say.

Roën pockets his blade and glances down at me, lines deepening in his frown. He shakes his head and gestures for me to follow.

"Whatever you have to say, my answer's still no."

"Just hear me out," I plead.

Roën walks briskly, forcing me to keep up with his long strides. I expect him to lead me into the mercenary den, but he takes the winding ledge around the cavern's back instead. The path grows narrow as we ascend, but Roën only picks up the pace. I press into the cave wall as white waves crash against the sea bluffs meters below.

"There's a reason I slogged through the rain to get to that ship," Roën says. "You seem to forget my crew doesn't love your angry little face as much as I do."

"What was Harun going on about?" I ask. "Someone's put a price on my head?"

"*Zitsōl,* you brought magic back. There's no shortage of people willing to pay to get you in their grasp."

We reach the end of the ledge and Roën steps onto a large wooden crate reinforced with iron planks. He motions for me to join him, and I hesitate, following the bundle of ropes attaching his shoddy pulley system to something above.

"You know, in my lands *Zitsōl* is a term of endearment. It means 'one who fears that which cannot hurt her.'"

I roll my eyes and step onto the moaning planks. Roën smiles as he pulls on the rope. A counterweight falls and the cart shudders when we rise, ascending like birds in the sky.

My fingers fly to the cart's weathered edge when our height allows me to see all of Jimeta's new tents. From the warship, I counted the dozens along the northern dock, but hundreds more run up and down the rocky coast.

In the distance, a long line of people trudge along, white-haired maji and dark-haired kosidán boarding a modest boat. It's hard not to feel responsible as families disappear beneath the ship's deck. I can't believe the chaos from bringing magic back has already chased so many Orïshans from their homeland.

"Don't waste your time looking down," Roën says. "Look up."

My lips part as I shift my gaze, taking in the views thirty meters into the air. This high up, Jimeta's towering cliffs are dark silhouettes jutting into the sky. Bright stars coat the atmosphere like diamonds stitched into the fabric of night. The view makes me wish Baba were still alive; he always loved to stare up at the stars.

But as we continue to rise, I glance back down at the people below. I almost wish I was boarding a ship with them. What would it be like to sail to the promise of peace? To live in a land where maji weren't the enemy? If I could leave all this behind, would it still hurt this much to breathe?

"Do you think they'll be better off across the sea?" I ask.

"I doubt it," Roën says. "It hardly matters where you are if you're weak."

The pit of guilt in my stomach hardens, squashing my fantasy. But that same pit turns to a flutter when Roën slides a hand around my waist.

"Besides, what soul could be better off that far away from me?"

"You have three seconds before I cut off your arm."

"Three whole seconds?" Roën smiles as the cart swings to a stop. It brings us to the highest ledge, opening up into a modest cave. I hug myself as I step inside, taking in the sculpted rock formations that create a table and chair. A few panthenaire furs make up his bed. I didn't think his home would be so bare.

"This is it?"

"What, you were expecting a palace?" Roën walks over to the only real furniture he has, a marble wardrobe filled with different weapons and blades. He removes a pair of brass knuckles from his pocket and lays them down on a rack. Blood still stains the polished rings.

I try not to picture the face Roën used them on as I search for the right words to make him give us what we need. I don't want to be alone with him for too long. Despite Roën's advances, I trust myself less than I trust him.

"We appreciate all you've done," I say. "The patience you've had with us—"

"Please tell me Amari fed you better lines than that." Roën starts to sit in his chair, but winces, reaching behind his neck. He pulls his shirt over his head and my face warms at the sight of his sculpted muscles, crisscrossed with new and old scars. But then I spot the gash below his shoulder.

I grab a stained rag from the floor, taking my chance to get close. Roën's eyes narrow when I wring it out in a bucket of rainwater before wiping off his wound.

"You're sweet, *Zitsōl*. But I'm not in the business of favors."

"This isn't a favor," I say. "Help us with the rally, and you'll make double what you already have."

"Enlighten me." Roën tilts his head. "What is double of nothing?"

"If the ritual had gone as planned, Amari would be sitting on the throne. You'd already have your gold."

Baba would be alive.

I chase away the thought before it can haunt me again. Thinking of what could've been won't help me convince Roën to say yes.

"*Zîtsöl*, charming as I may be, you don't want men like me or Harun by your side. You definitely don't want to be in our debt."

"If Amari doesn't make her claim to the throne, someone else will seize control."

"That sounds like her problem." Roën shrugs. "Why do you care?"

"Because . . ." The right words slip to the tip of my tongue. *Because she's what's best for this kingdom. She's the only one who can call off the military's maji hunt.*

But staring at Roën, I don't want to lie.

Somehow, it feels like lying to myself.

"I thought things would be better." I shake my head. "Magic was supposed to make things better."

Speaking the truth aloud makes me feel like I might break. The truth makes my heart ache.

"Baba's death, the tîtáns, the hunted maji," I sigh. "All these people fleeing their homes. It hasn't even been a moon since the ritual and it feels like magic's destroyed the entire kingdom. Everything's worse than it was before." I wring out the rag, wishing I could turn back time. "Now that it's here, I don't want it. I wish I'd never wanted it at all."

I exhale a shuddering breath and move to wipe away more blood, but Roën grabs my wrist, forcing me to look at him. His touch makes my skin hum. This is the first time since that night on the warship that we've truly been alone. Back then, we stood beneath the yellow moon, sharing nightmares and scars.

The way Roën looks at me now makes my skin crawl, but it also makes me want to draw close. It's like his stormy eyes pierce through my shell, seeing me for the mess I truly am.

"If you don't want magic anymore, what do you want?"

His question makes me pause. All I want is the people I've lost. But the more I think, the more I remember Mama's embrace. The warmth of death's escape.

"I want to be free," I whisper. "I want to be done."

"Then be done." He pulls me in close, studying me as if I'm a knot to be unraveled. "Why ask for my help when you can cut your losses and call this the end?"

"Because if Amari's not sitting on that throne, it was all for nothing. My father will have died for *nothing*. And if that happens . . ." My stomach clenches at the thought. "If that happens, I'll never be free. Not with that kind of guilt."

Roën stares at me and I can see the objections rising to his tongue. But he seems to hold them between his teeth as I cup his chin, wiping away more blood.

He looks down and I see the tally marks that run up his arm, the worst of all his scars. He once told me that his torturers carved a new line every time they killed a member of his crew before his eyes; twenty-three tally marks for twenty-three lives. Deep down, I think those scars are the reason Roën left his homeland. The reason he understands me better than anyone else.

"I don't give second chances, *Zitsöl*. This would be your third."

"You can trust me." I stick out my hand. "I promise on Baba's life. Help us finish this and you'll collect in gold."

Roën shakes his head, but relief rushes through me when he puts his hand in mine.

"Alright," he says. "We'll leave tonight."

CHAPTER FOUR

· · · · · ◆ ◇ ◆ · · · · ·

AMARI

THE NEXT MORNING, my voice echoes in the cramped captain's quarters. As the warship nears Zaria's shores, I struggle to write the speech that will convince the people of Orïsha to back my claim to the throne.

"My name is Amari Olúborí," I declare. "Daughter of King Saran. Sister to the late crown prince."

I stand in front of the cracked mirror, attempting to feel the power embedded in those words. No matter how many times I speak them, they don't feel right.

Nothing does.

I pull the black dashiki over my head and toss it onto the growing pile of clothes on my bed. After weeks of living with what I could carry on my back, the excess gathered by Roën's men feels foreign.

It brings me back to mornings in the palace; to biting my tongue while servants forced me into gown after gown under Mother's orders. She was never satisfied with anything I wore. In her amber eyes, I always looked too dark. Too large.

I reach for a gold-tinted gele on the floor. Mother was always fond of the color. I nestle the gele along my temples and Mother's voice rings through my ears.

That's not fit to wipe a leopanaire's ass.

My throat dries and I set the headdress down. For so long I wanted to shut her out. Now I don't have a choice.

Focus, Amari.

I pick up a navy tunic, squeezing the silk to keep the tears in. What right do I have to grieve when the sins of my family have caused this kingdom so much pain?

I slide the tunic over my skin and return to the mirror. There's no time to cry.

I have to atone for those sins today.

"I stand before you to declare that the divisions of the past are over," I shout. "The time to unify is now. Together, we will be . . ."

My voice trails as I shift my stance, inspecting my fragmented reflection. A new scar spills onto my shoulder, crackling like lightning against my oak-brown skin. Over the years, I've grown used to hiding the scar my brother left across my back. This is the first time I've had to hide Father's.

Something about the mark feels alive. It's as if his hatred still courses through my skin. I wish I could erase it. I almost wish I could erase him—

"Skies!" My fingers flash with the blue light of my ashê and I wince at the burn. I attempt to suppress the navy glow that shimmers around my hand, but the room spins as my new magic swells.

Midnight-blue tendrils shoot from my fingertips like sparks from a flint. My palms sting as my skin splits. My scars rip open at the seams. I gasp at the pain.

"Somebody help!" I shout as I stumble into the mirror. Crimson smears across my reflection. The agony is so great I can't breathe. Blood trickles down my chest as I fall to my knees. I wheeze though I want to scream—

"Amari!"

Tzain's voice is like shattered glass. His presence frees me from my mental cage. The pain fades ache by grueling ache.

I blink to find myself on the tarnished floor, half-dressed with my silk tunic clenched in my hand. The blood that smeared across the mirror is nowhere to be found.

My scars remain closed.

Tzain covers me with a shawl before taking me into his arms. I brace myself against his chest as my muscles turn heavy, winded from the burst of magic.

"That's the second time this week," he says.

Actually, it's the fourth. But I bite back the truth when I see the concern in his gaze. Tzain doesn't need to know it's getting worse. No one does.

I still don't know how to feel about these new gifts. What it means to be a Connector; to be a tîtán. The maji had their powers restored after the ritual, but tîtáns like me have never had magic until now.

From what I can tell, the tîtáns come from the nobility: royals unaware of their maji ancestry. What would Father say if he knew his own children carried the blood of those he hated most? The very people he regarded as maggots?

"Gods," Tzain curses as he inspects my palm. The skin is red and tender to the touch, dotted with yellow blisters. "Magic's not supposed to hurt. If you'd just talk to Zél—"

"Zélie's not even using her own magic. The last thing she needs to see is mine."

I tuck away my white streak, wishing I could just chop the lock from my hair. Tzain may not notice the way Zélie looks at it, but I always catch the snarl it brings to her face. For so long, she had to suffer because of her gift. Now those that hurt her the most wield that magic themselves.

I can understand why she despises it, but at times it feels like she despises me. And she's supposed to be my closest friend. How will the rest of the maji feel when they learn that I've become a tîtán?

"I'll figure it all out," I sigh. "After I'm on the throne."

I burrow back into Tzain's neck, running my fingers against the new stubble along his chin.

"You trying to send a message?"

A sly smile rises to my lips. "I think it suits you. I like it."

He runs his thumb along my jaw, igniting a surge almost as powerful as my magic. I hold my breath as he lifts my face to his. But before our lips can meet, the ship groans into a sharp turn, jostling us apart.

"What in the skies?" I scramble to my feet, pressing my face against the smudged porthole glass. For the past three weeks, all it revealed were gray seas. Now vibrant coral reefs shine through turquoise waters.

Zaria's coastline fills the horizon as the warship navigates the ivy-covered cliffs jutting out of the ocean. A lump forms in my throat at the number of villagers gathered on the white sands. There are hundreds of people.

Maybe even thousands.

"You're ready." Tzain comes up behind me, sliding his arms around my waist.

"I don't even know what to wear."

"I can help you with that," Tzain says.

"You're going to help me pick out clothes?" I arch my brow and Tzain laughs.

"I've spent a lot of time looking at you, Amari. You're beautiful in everything you wear."

Heat rises to my cheeks as he looks at the pile of rejects on my bed. "But no tunics today. You're about to be Orïsha's queen."

He turns me toward the suit of armor I wore to the ritual grounds when we brought magic back. It's still covered with the blood of every opponent I cut down with my sword. Father's blood stains the front, darkest along the royal seal.

"I can't wear that," I exclaim. "It'll terrify people!"

"That's the point. I used to see that seal and my chest would clench. But when you wear it . . ." Tzain pauses and a smile like sugar comes to his face. "With you behind the seal, I'm not afraid. I actually feel safe."

He rests his chin on the top of my head, grabbing my hand again.

"You're the queen, Amari. Give everyone a new face to picture behind that seal."

CHAPTER FIVE

ZÉLIE

When the warship's ramp plunks into the wet sand, the people of Zaria don't cheer. They don't move. They don't blink.

The people only stare.

Nobles line the path to the rally site, black hair occasionally marked by the white streaks of tîtáns. Magic-less kosidán gather behind them, soldiers and military officers milling through their masses. I find my people standing at the fringes, white hair barely hidden under large hoods.

The stillness of the crowd holds the weight of this moment, this chapter of history we create. I can't believe that after all that's passed, we've finally made it here. *My gods,* I think to myself.

We're really doing it.

"I can't feel my legs." Amari comes to my side, imposing in her suit of armor. Bloodstains still coat the royal seal. A helmet covers her dark hair, perfectly placed to hide her white streak.

I don my own stolen breastplate, sliding my staff where the past owner's sword would have gone. I feel like I'm about to vomit, but she doesn't need to hear that.

"You've faced worse." I pat her shoulder. "You can face this."

Amari nods, but her hands still shake. I haven't seen this terror in her since we were strangers in Lagos's marketplace. Back then she was only a runaway princess. I was just a poor fisherman's daughter. She crashed into my life and now the entire kingdom will never be the same.

"You can do this." I ignore the pain it brings me to look into her eyes. But with her streak tucked away, it's easier to see her face and not the one of the brother who broke my heart.

"Father and Inan prepared their whole lives for this role," Amari says. "I've barely had a moon."

"Yet you've already given more to this kingdom than any man or woman who's come before you. I wouldn't have been able to bring back magic if it wasn't for you." I grab her hands and lace her fingers through mine, giving her another squeeze. "The gods chose you. They're choosing you the same way they chose you to steal that scroll."

Though I smile, it hurts to speak the words. If the gods chose her, then they chose for me to suffer.

They chose for me to lose Baba.

"Do you really believe that?" Amari looks away. "Even though I'm a tîtán?"

Her question makes my lips tense, but it doesn't matter how I feel about her kind. The cost of my scars, the price of Baba's blood—once Amari's queen, it'll all mean something. When she's queen, I won't have to carry this weight. I'll finally be free of all this pain.

"I know it." I lean in. "This is destiny. The gods don't make mistakes."

Amari hugs me with such force, I stumble back. I laugh and wrap my arms around her waist. I forgot how nice it feels to hold her like this.

"Thank you," she whispers into my braids, voice straining with the threat of tears.

"You're ready," I whisper back. "You'll be the best queen Orïsha's ever seen—"

"Don't forget the most important part." Roën interrupts our embrace, sauntering up with a cigarette tucked between his teeth. "Once you're queen you'll be in full command of your royal treasuries."

"As if you'd ever let me forget." Amari rolls her eyes. "Are your men in position?"

"We've cleared the path." Roën gestures down the ramp before shooting me a wink. "Ready when you are, my queen."

Amari exhales and shakes out her hands, muttering her speech under her breath. "My name is Amari Olúborí. My *name* is Amari Olúborí."

As she paces, I put two fingers in my mouth and whistle. In seconds, the sound of claws scratching against the ship's metal floors surges toward us. Nailah gallops from my quarters, skidding to a stop before me.

"What're you doing?" Amari's brows lift as I unlatch the belt keeping Nailah's saddle and reins in place.

"Giving you an entrance fit for a queen." I cup my hands to help her up. "You're the Lionaire. The least you can do is ride one."

* * * * ◆ ◇ ◆ * * * *

A COLLECTIVE GASP spreads through the crowd as Amari descends the iron ramp on Nailah's back. Even I marvel at the sight. Behind me, Tzain blinks away the tear that wells in his eye.

Shining rays bounce off Amari's suit of armor, glimmering every time Nailah moves. With her hands wrapped around my lionaire's horns, she looks like more than a queen.

She looks magical.

"Stay sharp," Roën whispers in my ear. "This isn't a coronation."

I follow his gaze to a thin soldier in the crowd, his hand wrapped tight around the hilt of his sword. He pushes through the nobles and kosidán along Amari's path, sunlight bouncing off his breastplate's royal seal. With a nod from Roën, Harun intercepts the guard, dragging him away before he can close in.

"I don't understand," I say. "I thought we only had to worry about the *Iyika?*"

"Not everyone was happy to find out their queen still lives," Roën explains. "The military knows she's a maji sympathizer. Most liked her better when she was dead."

My body tenses and I glance up, hoping Amari didn't see. Though the other soldiers don't grab their swords, they don't exactly bow before their new queen. Pairs patrol the crowd on both sides of the white sand path, nodding to each noble tîtán they encounter. But they watch the maji with beady eyes, hands hovering above the majacite blades in their swords.

The military's hunting maji like dogs. The new admiral's all but declared war.

Roën's words return as I look back to my people at the edge of the crowd, too afraid to get close. Though the hot sun beats down from above, most hide beneath patterned cloaks. Our gifts have returned, yet my people still cower.

"Almost there." Roën nods to a large sand dome a few dozen meters down the coast. The structure sits along the flowing tides. Waves foam white as they crash against the rectangular pattern carved into its sides. The towering dome is so large, it almost blocks out the sun.

"It's perfect," Amari whispers from above. A flash of joy lights her from within, but it flickers out when we near the smudged streaks of red along the dome's side, the smeared paint still showing the shadow of an *I*.

Amari catches my eye and I give her ankle a supportive squeeze. "Don't worry. No members of the *Iyika* are getting past me."

"Jagunjagun!"

I glance down to find a young maji with large ears and a mole on his chin. Unlike the others, he stands at the front of the crowd, hood obscuring his small white coils. Though he whispers the Yoruba for "soldier," he doesn't seem to refer to the royal seal on my breastplate. I smile at him, and his eyes become so wide I worry they'll fall from his sockets.

Baba wanted this for him, the realization sets in as we pass. *Him and everyone like him.* No more hiding after today. It's time for my people to stand in the sun.

Amari stops Nailah at the cracked archway of the dome's entrance and slips into the sand. She takes a deep breath before stepping forward.

I guard her close as we enter the rally.

CHAPTER SIX

AMARI

When we enter the dome, the sight is so brilliant it steals my words. There are so many people, more than I've ever addressed at once.

A sculpted mural fills the dome's sand walls, carved bodies intertwined in dance and song. A large opening in the dome's side allows a view of the sea. The tides kiss the sand at our feet.

"Wow," Tzain mutters under his breath, walking by my side. I lift my head to the sunlight spilling in from the large oculus in the ceiling. It bathes the crowd below in its warm rays, illuminating a wooden stage erected by Roën's men.

The sea of people parts as I march toward the platform in the center of the dome. They part for me the way they parted for Father.

Strike, Amari.

I hear his voice as I ascend the steps of the stage. In Father's eyes, this was never my destiny, yet it's almost like he trained me for this day. He was the one who taught me I must cut through every opponent in my way, even if that opponent was someone I loved.

Fight, Amari.

I take a deep breath, squaring my shoulders and lifting my chest. I made Father a vow when I drove that sword through his chest. Now it's time for me to secure my throne or lose it.

"My name is Amari Olúborí." The declaration booms against the curved walls. "Daughter of your fallen king. Sister to the late crown prince."

Someone moves toward me in the crowd and my pulse spikes; I brace myself for their attack. But when the young kosidán kneels, my lips part.

I'm not prepared for him to bow.

"Your Majesty." He dips so low, his head touches the sand. His bow starts a wave throughout the dome as more people fall to their knees. A warm wave radiates through my skin as others bow along Zaria's coast.

There's something sacred in the way they arc. Something I want so desperately to deserve. I left the palace a scared princess on the run.

Now I'm one speech away from taking the throne.

"Two moons ago I sat at a palace luncheon as my father murdered my best friend. Her name was Binta, and she was a divîner whose only crime was the magic that coursed through her skin." I clear my throat, forcing myself on though the pain of that day returns with each word. "My father forced Binta to awaken her gift against her will. Then, when her powers revealed themselves, he killed her where she stood."

Murmurs of dissent pass through the crowd. A few tears, some shakes of the head. In the back of the dome, a group of maji push their way in. Across the room, two burly soldiers exchange glares.

Our peace feels as fragile as glass, but I cannot shy away from the truth anymore. The maji have been silenced for far too long. If I don't speak for them, who will?

"You may not have known Binta's name before this moment, but I know you know her story. It is the tale countless Orïshans have faced, an unjust persecution that has plagued our divîners and maji for decades. For generations the story of Orïsha has been the story of divide. A story of violence and persecution that must end *today*."

The timbre in my voice surprises me; I can almost see it ripple through the dome. Someone shouts in agreement, and others join in. I blink as more cheers erupt.

The small show of faith emboldens me as I walk the length of the platform. The Orïsha I dream of is within my grasp.

Then I see a member of the *Iyika*.

The rebel stands in the middle of the room, a thick scar running down her left eye. Unlike the other maji in the dome, her forest of white coils is on full display, spilling onto her soft brown shoulders. Red paint stains her hands, the same color as the paint smeared outside the dome's walls. Though she stands still, the snarl on her face tells me everything I need to know.

She doesn't want me to take this throne.

Sweat gathers beneath my helmet as I scan the crowd, looking for more rebels like her. I reach to make sure the metal still hides my streak, but looking back at the maji forces me to pause.

She doesn't hide from my sight. She doesn't conceal who she is. Why should I?

Strike, Amari.

My fingers tense as I grab my helmet, preparing for what I might cause. Revealing my transformation is far from the smart move. But if I cower and hide the truth, I'm no better than Inan.

Be brave, Amari.

I take one last breath. My white streak tumbles free when my helmet hits the ground.

"She's one of them!"

"The queen is a tîtán!"

Gasps ripple through the crowd. A handful of maji push toward the front. Unrest builds in the dome as soldiers dive in after them.

My voice withers as Roën's mercenaries form a ring around the stage, but the dried blood across my breastplate reminds me of my strength. I am the only one who can bring Orïsha together. I am the queen who can keep all of these people safe.

"I wanted to hide my truth," I shout. "My apprehension about what I've become. But the return of magic and the birth of tîtáns are living proof that we are finally returning to the Orïsha the gods have always wanted for us! We're so full of hatred and fear, we've forgotten what blessings these abilities are. For centuries these powers have been the source of our strife, but the gods ordained us with magic so the people of Orïsha could thrive!"

The commotion in the dome stills as people become ensnared by my words. Our peace may be fragile, but as long as they're listening, I have a chance.

"Think of how Grounders could farm our land. How teams of Tiders could cut the work of fishermen in half," I say. "Welders could erect new cities in days. Healers could ensure those we love don't perish from wounds or sickness!"

I speak to the rebel maji with a scar over her eye. The young soldier with a scowl on his lips. I paint each dissenter a picture with my words, seeing my dreams almost as clearly as the mural carved into the ceiling above.

"Under my rule, this will be a land where even the poorest villagers are fed, housed, and clothed. A kingdom where everyone is protected, where everyone is accepted! The divisions of the past are over!" I extend my hands and lift my voice. "A new Orïsha is on the horizon!"

This time when the cheers erupt, they're deafening. I beam as the sound echoes around the dome, the cries to unify powerful and loud.

"*Kí èmí olá ó gùn Ayaba!*" Someone shouts, a chant that travels throughout the crowd.

"*Kí èmí olá ó gùn Ayaba,*" Zélie translates. "*Long live the Queen.*"

33

My body feels so light I'm sure I could float above the stage. The crowd's chant reverberates inside me, awakening pieces of me I didn't know I had. It brings me back to that magical moment in Chândomblé, the wonder of the art Lekan brought to life. Now I see that same peace and prosperity. That same magic is within our grasp—

"Lies!"

The voice booms above the masses, its ice quieting the crowd in an instant. Heads turn toward the dome's archway. I grab my hilt as metal boots crunch through the sand.

I lock eyes with Zélie, and she nods, ready for the fight. But when the sea of people parts and the challenger comes into view, my blade falls from my hand.

Even with her hood raised, I recognize the slink in her step. The iron in her veins.

"Mother?"

My hands fly to my chest. A laugh escapes my lips.

I move toward her, unable to believe my eyes. But when she lifts her head, the hatred that burns in her amber gaze freezes me in place.

CHAPTER SEVEN

ZÉLIE

I DON'T NEED to read Amari's face to recognize the source of her amber eyes. Queen Nehanda shares her daughter's beauty, but where Amari is soft curves, this woman is sharp angles and severe lines. Like her daughter, Nehanda wears a suit of armor, but hers shines in gold. The polished plates curve over her chest, accented with serrated shoulder pads and sculpted gauntlets.

"What do we do?" Tzain whispers, grip tightening on the handle of his axe. Despite what Roën's intelligence said, Queen Nehanda still lives. The monarch glides across the sand, a deep purple cape flowing behind her with the ocean breeze. Her precision is deathly familiar.

It makes the scars prickle on my back.

"You survived!" Amari smiles, but Nehanda doesn't even spare her daughter a glance. As she takes in the room, she seems acutely aware of how the entire dome hangs on her very breath.

Aware of how a single word was all she needed to take a cheering rally into her own hands like the crack of a whip.

"Bold promises," Queen Nehanda finally speaks. "Elegant lies. But these aren't the words of a devoted leader. Only the vitriol of a power-hungry tyrant."

Her accusation lands like a slap to the face. Amari actually stumbles back. A wave of rumbles starts among the crowd, dissent trickling through like water from a broken dam.

"Mother, what is this?" Amari steps forward. "I thought you were dead—"

"You wished it upon me!" The queen cuts her off. "You sent maji and mercenaries for my head!"

"I didn't—"

"You tell these people their king has fallen, but you fail to mention the crime of regicide by your hand? You speak of your late brother without admitting it was you and the maji who killed the rightful heir to the throne?"

Horrified gasps pulse around us, echoing through the dome. Air that once held hope and promise withers under a new cloud of suspicion and disgust.

"That's not true!" Amari cries.

"You deny killing your own father?"

"No, I—" Amari's cheeks flush and she takes a deep breath. "The king died by my hand, yes, but I didn't kill Ina—"

She doesn't get a chance to finish. Whatever hold Amari had on her people evaporates.

"*Traitor!*" someone shouts.

"*Liar!*" another joins in. Their fury builds and crests like a wave intent on bringing Amari down. My hands shake as their rage spreads, spilling onto the maji sprinkled throughout the dome.

Amari holds up her hands, a feeble attempt to hold their fury back. The stance makes her look like a helpless cub in front of a den of snow leopanaires.

"Before you stands a traitor." Nehanda glides forward. "A rebel who allies with liars and thieves. An insolent child who has endangered us all with magic just so she can be queen!"

"Mother, please," Amari begs. "Let me explain!" But her voice cuts like wood where her mother's strikes like iron.

Amari's cries shrivel even further when the queen's guards enter the dome, distinguished by their golden armor and razor-edged swords. In the glare of their gilded seals, I see Mama's corpse.

I feel the heat of the flames that engulfed Baba's casket.

"I will not allow you and your maji insurgents to run this kingdom into the ground," Nehanda shouts. "You are under arrest for your crimes against the crown! Anyone who aids you shall be taken down!"

Panic ignites as her guards stomp forward, arming themselves with glass orbs filled with night-black liquid.

"What are they holding?" I shout at Tzain.

"I don't know, but we have to get Amari out of here!"

Tzain runs toward the stage, but he's not fast enough.

Nehanda fixes a golden mask over her face as her soldiers smash their orbs into the sand.

CHAPTER EIGHT

ZÉLIE

WHAT IN THE GODS' NAMES?

I step back, pressing into the wooden stage. The black liquid spreads across the sand like the tide, foaming and frothing until it takes to the air as a gas.

The dark clouds overtake the crowd, but nothing happens to the kosidán it hits. The tîtáns caught in its path merely cough.

It's the maji who scream like their nails are being ripped off.

"*Help!*"

A young maji scratches at his throat. His light brown skin sizzles and burns. He struggles to scream as he chokes on the black smoke.

In that instant it dawns on me, the true nature of this attack. The poison of majacite, but not in chains or swords.

In the air.

As a *gas*.

"Go!" I scream at Tzain and Amari, clawing myself onto the wooden platform. Fear strikes my core like a battering ram. My feet go numb as I climb.

The majacite cloud moves through the dome, its thick mass expanding like a storm. Shouts and panic fill the air as maji scatter, trampling over one another in their dash for the far exits.

"Don't let one rebel escape!" Nehanda thunders above the masses. "Orïsha must be protected from their madness!"

"Mother, please!" Amari yells, but Tzain yanks her off the stage. He grabs my arm as he charges through the people in our way, pulling us through the hysteria.

The queen's personal guard closes in from all sides, golden armor flashing as they run. Like Nehanda, their forearms gleam with matching gauntlets. Golden masks sit over their noses.

"Attack!" Nehanda orders, and I wait to see more majacite blades or glass orbs. But when the guards' hands glow green with ashê, I realize the reason behind their special rank.

They aren't just her personal guard.

They're her own legion of tîtáns.

Horror consumes me as the tîtáns' powers break free and they target a group of fleeing maji. Circles of sand harden around maji's feet like cement. Sand pillars shoot from the ground, striking my people in the back.

I scream with rage as Nehanda's tîtáns desecrate the magic of Grounders before my eyes. How dare they wield our own gifts against us? But when one tîtán soldier bares his teeth in pain, I realize that they don't understand the fragile magic they now have.

"Help me!" he cries.

People flee the space as the tîtán screams. The sand around him quakes with incredible force. His skin corrodes as the magic surges beyond his control.

In a flash, the green light explodes in his chest. The life fades from his brown eyes.

The tîtán falls into the sand, his corpse trampled in the fray.

"Zél, come on!" Tzain pulls me along, but I struggle to stay upright. The way that tîtán screamed, the way he lost control—I've felt that strain myself.

It's the power maji are forbidden to use. A power so great it consumes all who wield it.

It's the power of blood magic.

And somehow the tîtáns have it.

"Murderer!"

Amari screams as a noble grabs her braid and drags her back. Tzain dives after them, smashing his fist into the noble's chin.

"Tzain!" I try to stay close, but within moments they're lost in the crowd. Without my brother, the bodies in front of me become an unbreakable wall.

"Tzain, I need you!" I claw at those in my way, heart pounding in my chest. Tîtán soldiers charge from the front. The black cloud approaches from the back.

I try to forge ahead, but when the first tendril of majacite hits my neck, I can only scream.

CHAPTER NINE

◆ ◇ ◆

ZÉLIE

FOR THE LOVE of Oya.

The airborne majacite attacks from all sides. My eyes sting inside the cloud of toxic gas. Smoke burns my skin like a branding iron.

The poison sears the skin of my calf. Another cloud hits the scars on my back. As the majacite burns my lungs, I can almost feel Saran's knife carving through my flesh.

"Don't let the traitor escape!"

Nehanda's shouts continue to fill the dome. My vision blurs in and out of focus as she marches forward, shaking the curls loose from her golden helmet. I don't believe my eyes when a single streak of white falls along Nehanda's cheek. *It can't be. . . .*

The Queen of Orïsha is a tîtán.

The air shifts as Nehanda summons her newly awakened magic. The green light of her ashê spreads around her hands, but it doesn't stop there. Her magic glows inside her chest, so bright it casts her ribs in black silhouettes.

Emerald light crackles around the queen's body like lightning as she calls on a power I don't understand. She stretches out her hands and her legion of tîtáns freezes in place. My body shakes as Nehanda sucks the ashê from her soldiers' veins.

How is this possible? I try to make sense of the sight. Green wisps of ashê break through the tîtáns' skin like smoke, traveling into Nehanda's palms. The feat brings Nehanda's men to their knees. She sucks the very life from their trembling bodies. One soldier seizes in the sand before going completely still.

"You will pay for your crimes!" Nehanda marches forward despite the pain she causes her own people. She lifts her palms and her eyes glow with emerald light. With another shout, Nehanda punches her fists into the ground.

The earth splits open at her touch.

"Get back!"

Screams fill the dome as Nehanda's fracture cuts across the sand. People fall to their knees, unable to stand on top of the quaking earth.

Nehanda's attack slows the fleeing maji down, but her eyes widen as she loses control. The shaking builds with incredible force.

Then I hear the crack.

No.

My stomach clenches when I look up. The crack cuts through the dome's walls, spreading through the sandstone like a spiderweb.

Get up, I scream at myself as sunlight filters through the widening cracks. But despair freezes my legs in place. I can't believe it's come to this.

Everything we did. Everything we lost.

It didn't change a thing.

There will be no victory in Baba's death. I'll never be free of this guilt—

"Zélie, *move!*"

Roën dives from the side, ramming his body into mine. We roll across the sand, and he curses when a broken piece of the dome's wall lands on his hand.

"Roën!" I scramble forward on my hands and knees, choking in the majacite cloud. When I find him, he presses bloodied metal to my nose. I wheeze as a burst of clean air passes through the golden mask.

"Hold on!" Roën yanks me close as we barricade ourselves under a fallen slab. The dome rains down like hail. I flinch with each piece of debris that crashes against our defense.

Someone shouts my name and I stick my head out; Tzain and Amari gallop toward us on Nailah's bare back. When she spots us, Amari stretches out her hands.

"Grab on!" she shouts.

Roën and I latch onto her arms as they ride past. Amari grits her teeth, bracing herself against Tzain as we clamor onto Nailah's back.

Nailah releases a vicious roar, dodging the giant slabs that crash into the tides.

The dome crumbles in our wake as we ride away from the beach.

CHAPTER TEN

◆ ◇ ◆

AMARI

A THOUSAND QUESTIONS race through my mind as we ride through the rocky mountainside on Nailah's back. Behind us, Zaria fades into the night, a dwindling speck on the far horizon. Fires burn in the distance, flickering scars from Mother's hatred. By now, her guards will have searched the entire town. It won't be long before her forces scramble after our path.

How did this happen?

I bury my head in my hands, struggling to process the facts. My mother is still alive. Just last night, that would've been my greatest desire come to life.

We should be in each other's arms. We should be mourning Inan. Mother should be backing my claim to the throne.

Instead, she calls for my head.

Think, Amari.

My lips quiver as I wrap my arms around myself. If I close my eyes, I can see the rally in my mind. I *feel* the vibrations of the cheering crowd in my skin.

In that moment I had everything I wanted for this land. I saw peace and unification. Orïsha's sun was finally rising.

And in seconds, Mother set it.

"Over here."

My eyes snap open as Tzain takes a sharp turn, guiding Nailah off the rocky path. With Roën's instructions, we pull into a clearing in the forest, a safe zone I thought we'd never have to see. Moss-covered trees wrap around us, their thick branches shielding us from the world. Heavy footsteps and thundering paws echo past as more maji flee the rally, racing away from Mother's soldiers.

"Dammit," Roën curses under his breath when we come to a stop. He jumps off Nailah's back, muttering in Sutōrīan as he rummages through his pockets. He pulls out a cigarette and holds it between his teeth, but when he catches me staring, I look away. Without the royal treasuries, I still don't have a gold piece to my name.

How will I pay him for this?

"Zél, what happened?" Tzain moves me aside, sliding across Nailah's back to get to his sister. He tilts Zélie's chin, inspecting the harsh burns along her dark skin.

"It was the majacite." She stares at the golden mask in her hands. "The monarchy turned it into a gas."

Majacite?

I touch my face, peppered with cuts and bruises yet free of any burns. If the majacite did that to her, why didn't it do the same to me?

Tzain starts to ask more, but stops when Zélie presses a shaking hand to her mouth. I've never seen her look this defeated. This empty. This *sad.*

"I'm so sorry." I reach out to help her, but Zélie recoils from my touch. My hand falls limp as she trembles, fighting to hold back her sobs.

"Give her some space," Tzain whispers. A lump rises in my throat when he turns back to her. I slide off Nailah's back, leaving them alone.

My body feels like it might shatter as I break for the stump across the clearing.

Just when I get the chance to atone for my family's sins, they go and hurt the people I love all over again.

"That'll be six hundred gold pieces."

I glance back: Roën struggles to light a flint with one hand. His other hand remains wrapped in a ripped swatch of cloth, bloody bandages barely containing the mangled mess.

"Excuse me?"

"That's what you owed before your little coronation was interrupted," he says. "When Harun gets here with the rest of my crew, the price of that extraction's going to cost you double."

Twelve hundred gold pieces? I try to keep the shock from my face. "Do you honestly think now is the right time to quibble for your payment?"

"This isn't a charity, Princess." I grit my teeth as Roën mocks me with a bow. "Oh, where are my manners? Queen."

He blows smoke in my face and I turn away before I strike back. I cannot play Roën's games when Mother is out there calculating her next move. I picture the cold expression on her face, the golden mask that amplified her cruel beauty and grace. I still can't tell if she really thinks I killed Inan or if she just wants to paint me as the villain.

There has to be more; something beyond her blinding rage. Spectacle for spectacle's sake is simply not in her nature.

She wouldn't have made such a bold move if it weren't part of a larger plan.

"I'll get your coin." I turn back to Roën. "I just require time."

The mercenary shakes his head and exhales a long trail of smoke. "Time is the one thing you no longer have."

"Listen—"

"No, *you* listen." He bares his teeth and I flinch, stumbling back. In a mere second, he's a different person. It's never been this easy to see the killer hiding beneath his skin.

"Your mother will be the least of your problems if you don't pay me and my men. I have restraint," he growls. "They don't."

"Is that a threat?" I step forward, and Roën's gaze flicks down to my hand. Blue wisps of magic fall from my fingers like rain. The ashê burns my skin as it sparks.

I've never called on my magic before; it stings to wield it now. But a strange thrill runs through me when Roën backs down.

"It's not a threat." He shakes his head. "It's a promise."

The patter of approaching paws breaks the standoff between us. We look over, and I expect to see more fleeing maji, but instead Harun and the other mercenaries ride in on stolen cheetanaires. Roën turns back to me, pointing two fingers at my chest.

"Whatever happens next is on you. Remember that."

Before I can respond, he gives a sharp whistle that makes his men perk up like meerkats.

"We're moving out."

"With our coin?" Harun asks.

"Our precious princess doesn't have it."

"Surprise, surprise." The news brings a sinister smile to Harun's face. "But after that mess of a rally, I'm sure we can find people who'll pay double her debts."

Harun's words wash over me like an ocean of ice. With Mother's declaration, there'll be no shortage of people who will put a price on my head. People with the gold to pay.

"We can work something out." I stomp after Roën, pulse spiking in my chest. Armor that once made me feel so powerful now drags down my every step.

Roën tosses his cigarette aside as he marches over to the nearest cheetanaire. But when Zélie shouts after him, the muscles in his back tense. His steps turn rigid as she calls out his name.

"Roën, wait!"

Zélie slides off Nailah's back, but the impact is too much for her majacite-filled lungs. The moment she lands, she crumples into the dirt.

Roën's steps slow and he exhales, pressing his fingers to his forehead. I watch bewildered as he turns back to help her; metal drifting toward its magnet.

"I'm sorry," she whispers, tears brimming in her silver eyes. One spills out and Roën wipes it with his thumb, his unbandaged hand lingering on the side of her face.

They stare at each other, and it's as if we all disappear. Unspoken words pass between their eyes. Roën's shoulders slump when he rises to his feet.

"Me too."

With that, he walks away, mounting his cheetanaire. My stomach sinks as Roën and his mercenaries ride off into the darkness, disappearing into the dense forest.

When I can no longer hear the patter of their ryders' paws, I don't know who I should fear more. Mother and her legion of tîtáns.

Or him.

CHAPTER ELEVEN

AMARI

For a while, everything is still. No one speaks in Roën's absence. Deep down I know we need to put as much distance between us and Mother as possible, but I can't bring myself to move. Roën's threat hangs over my head, joined by Mother's declaration.

If all of Orïsha is hunting us, where can we possibly go?

"I'll figure it out." I force myself to speak the words, though I don't know if they're true. "I-I'll find a way to stop Mother. I'll get Roën his coin—"

"Take a beat." Tzain walks over, putting his hand on the small of my back. "You've been through a lot. You don't have to find the answers tonight."

I want to believe him. To hide in the safety of his arms. But the comfort of his touch doesn't erase the sound of Zélie's tears. Despite the pain that rips through my heart, all I want to do is take away hers. I slip from Tzain's grasp and kneel by Zélie in the dirt.

"I'll fix this," I whisper. "I promise. I know my mother better than anyone. If I can figure out her strategy, I'll know how to counterattack."

"Counterattack?" Zélie tilts her head as if I'm speaking a foreign language. "She sent a *dome* crashing down on our heads. How in Oya's name are we supposed to beat her?"

49

Zélie's voice shakes with a terror I wish I could defuse, but I don't know what I can say. I've never heard of a power like the one Mother wielded today. Even as a tîtán, it shouldn't be possible to rip the magic from someone's veins.

"Mother's magic may be strong," I speak slowly. "Perhaps stronger than any magic that's come before her. But every great power has a weakness. With time, we can find hers." I think back to the tîtáns she drained, wondering if that's where our answer lies. "If we build our forces and learn how her ability works, we can dismantle her advantages. We can make her surrender the throne."

"And if she doesn't?" Tzain asks.

When she doesn't?

I dig my nails into my scalp; I don't want to speak the words. Mere hours ago, I had the cheers of kosidán, maji, and tîtáns ready to become one. In seconds, Mother turned that unity into chaos.

If she stays in the picture, every maji will be killed. Countless Orïshans will suffer. With her on the throne, all this kingdom will ever know is war. I have to stop her.

Even if she is my mother.

I rise to my feet and extend my sword, hands shaking as I stab it into the dirt.

"If my mother refuses to back down, I'll take her out," I declare. "I'll end her war and ascend the throne."

An uneasy silence follows in the wake of my vow.

"What about the nobility?" Tzain asks. "All those soldiers and tîtáns on her side?"

My stomach churns at the thought of ending all those lives. I don't want to fight my own people, let alone tîtáns like me. There have to be hundreds aligned with her war on the maji. Maybe even thousands. If I attempt to take them all out, I'll be no better than my father. I'll just be another monster.

"Before my mother showed up at the rally, I had the kingdom on my side. Once I take her down, they'll fall in line."

"No, they won't." Zélie's voice brings a new chill to the windy night. "We've already lost this fight. The monarchy has magic now and they still hate us. It was never about magic at all!"

"Zél—"

"The answer isn't to kill your mother," Zélie cuts her brother off. "Kill her and another maji-hating monarch will just rise in her place. It's time to let this go. Be free. Leave Orïsha while we can still breathe!"

The yearning in her voice takes me off guard. I don't understand. It's not like Zélie to cut and run.

"I know the odds are against us," I push back. "But we can't abandon these people to Mother's reign. We have to save the kingdom. We don't have a choice—"

"Yes, we do." Zélie rises to her feet. "We *do*. We tried to save the kingdom. Twice. Now it's time for us to save ourselves!"

"I am Orïsha's queen," I say. "Their queen even if they don't want me. No matter how hard it gets, I don't get to run. It's my duty to serve and protect every person in this kingdom!"

Zélie looks at Tzain for help, but he crosses his arms.

"Zél, she's right. Baba died so we could fight—"

"Baba died for a lie!" Zélie slams her fist into a tree. "He gave his life for magic, and look who has it? Nehanda was stronger than any maji I've ever seen!"

Her voice rings through the trees as she forces herself to take a deep breath. Her anger breaks for a moment, allowing me to see the pain that swells under its surface.

"I'm tired of choosing the kingdom, the magic, the maji—everyone and everything but me. This is our chance to be free! It might be the only chance we'll ever have."

She looks at me and it's as if I have her heart in my hands. All I want to do is heal it. To take away her pain. But it's not just her pain I must erase.

I close my eyes, preparing for the wrath that I'll ignite. Orïsha waits for no one.

Not even the girl I love.

"Zélie—"

"For gods' sakes!" She throws her hands into the air, stumbling as she stomps off.

"Just take a beat." Tzain tries to calm her down. "We're too tired and hurt to figure this out now."

"No, we're not." The ice in Zélie's voice extinguishes the warmth in her brother's gaze. "That gas didn't hurt you. It doesn't hurt them." She nods at me, and I clench my fist.

Them.

That word stings worse than any of Mother's did.

"What happened to the gods' plan?" I ask. "What happened to always being on my side?"

"How can I be on your side when Baba died so your wretched mother and her tîtáns could rise?"

"That's not fair." My cheek burns from the slap of her words. She glares at me like I'm the monster. Like I shot the arrow that killed her father. "I've lost people in this fight, too."

"Am I supposed to cry for your bastard of a father?" Zélie asks. "Pity the weakling you called a brother? I can't look at my own back because of what your father did! Because of you and your family, both my parents are dead!"

Zélie limps to Nailah's side and pulls herself up even as her muscles shake with exhaustion.

"Don't compare your scars to mine, Princess. You'll lose every time."

"I'll lose?" I charge forward. "I'll *lose*? You had two parents who loved you till their dying breath. A brother who stands by your side. Both my parents tried to kill me with their own hands! I took the life of my own *father* to protect you and the maji!" My voice shakes with the tears that want to break free, but I don't let them fall. I won't let her win. I will not allow her to bring that out of me.

"I am sorry for everything my family's done," I continue, "but don't you dare act like my pain isn't real. You're not the only one with scars, Zélie! My family's hurt me just as much as it's hurt you!"

Zélie's face goes cold, and I stop in my tracks. I want to fix the chasm between us, yet every word we speak drags us further apart. She stares at me for a long moment, that horrible, empty look in her silver eyes. Then she turns and guides her ryder down, low enough so that she can mount.

"Zél, stop." Tzain walks after her. "This has gone far enough. We're all upset. We're *all* hurting. The last thing we need is to turn on each other!"

Zélie pushes her tongue into her lower lip as she settles on Nailah's back. "How quickly 'you and me' became 'you and Amari.'"

"Gods, Zél—"

"Did you hear me?" she cuts him off. "When my skin was burning and I couldn't breathe? Did you hear me scream your name, or were you too busy looking after Amari?"

Tzain's lips part. His forehead creases with shame. "That's not fair," he says. "You know that's not fair!"

"You two deserve each other." Zélie squeezes her thighs, commanding Nailah to rise. "Say hello to her mother for me. I'm sure she loves poor fishermen's sons just as much as she loves maji."

"I swear to the gods—"

"Yah!" Nailah shoots forward at Zélie's command, sprinting through the trees.

"Zélie!" Tzain runs after her, but within moments she's too far away to be seen. He digs his hands into his scalp before pounding his fists against the nearest tree.

"She'll be back," he mutters into the bark. "Just let her breathe."

I nod, but as I sink to the ground, I don't know who he's trying to convince.

CHAPTER TWELVE

· · · · · · ◆ ◇ ◆ · · · · · ·

ZÉLIE

Tears blur my vision as we race through the trees of the Adichie Forest. My hands slip from Nailah's horns. Without a saddle, I can barely hold on.

I grip with my thighs as the world passes by, a whirlwind of mountain cliffs and blowing leaves. I try to pretend Nailah's speed is the only reason I can't breathe.

Gods, help me.

I clench my teeth, fighting it all back. It's like everything I've done wrong surfaces at once, a sea drowning me in its current.

No, I think to myself. *Not them.* Believing in the gods is what's brought on this mess.

They're the reason Baba's dead.

Despair swells inside me as the terrain starts to dip. The earth beneath our feet slopes downhill. The forest trees start to thin. I clutch Nailah's fur, struggling to stay upright when her paws slip. But the thought of how the gods used me makes me want to let go and tumble into the dirt.

All this time I believed in the gods' greater plan. Their path when I couldn't see. But all they led me to were the scars on my back. The open wounds on my heart. The gods used me like a pawn and cast me aside when magic returned. I can't trust them to bring me anything but pain.

Mama, take me.

The new prayer forms, my heart breaking for the only thing I can still believe in. I think of standing in alâfia with her and Baba. The peace of death and being back in her arms.

She told me Orïsha needed me, that my work wasn't done. But bringing magic back only made things worse. The maji are worse off than before.

I close my eyes, muscles clenching at the memory of Queen Nehanda ripping the ashê from her tîtáns' veins. Magic was all we had to defend ourselves, and now our magic isn't even as strong as hers.

It doesn't matter what I do. It doesn't matter how hard I fight. The maji will never be free.

All that awaits us in this world is heartache.

"Mama, take me!" I scream the words, throwing my head to the sky. The whipping winds cut at the burns on my face. Blood mixes with my tears.

"Take me back," I whisper, burying myself in Nailah's coat. No more fighting against the monarchy. No more fighting just to *exist*. No more tears. No more strife. No more pain.

No more Tzain.

The thought creates a canyon out of the hole in my heart. It's almost enough to make me turn Nailah around and run back into his arms.

And Amari . . .

I breathe deep, wishing I could take back every word I screamed. I don't know how to tell her that it's not her fault. That I scream at her because I can't scream at Inan—

"Whoa!" I gasp as we break free of the forest. The silver moon hangs in the night sky, shining over the black silhouettes of the Olasimbo Mountain Range. The terrain changes without warning as the trees disappear, bringing us to a steep cliff that juts out over plummeting darkness.

Nailah roars and digs her nails into the ground to slow us down. Gravel and dirt fly as we career across the mountainside.

"Hold on!" I yank back on her horns with all the force I have. With a yelp, my lionaire tumbles onto her side. I cry out as the collision throws me from her back.

I claw at the sky as I fly toward the forest. My body smashes through wiry branches before slamming into a tree. I wheeze as my chest collides with hard bark. My ribs fracture with a loud crack.

Blood flies from my lips as my vision blacks out and I tumble to the ground. I curl into myself, lying there until my sight returns.

After a few moments, my cheek grows slick with licks from Nailah's tongue. Her wet nose nudges my face as the world fades away. For once, I don't try to hold on.

Take me back. I lift up the prayer once more. Mama was wrong to keep me on earth.

I'm far too broken to help anyone.

Mama, please . . .

I release it all, allowing the blackness in. But when I open my eyes, I see white.

I see dirt.

I see reeds.

CHAPTER THIRTEEN

.... ◆ ◇ ◆ ....

ZÉLIE

I DON'T KNOW if I'm trapped in a dream or a nightmare.

No chains bind me, but I can't move.

Crisp air fills my lungs, yet I can't breathe.

Gray, wilting reeds surround me, a haze of white peeking through like a blanket of clouds. Brittle dirt presses against my bare skin, falling away as I force myself up.

How?

The question pulses through my mind when I look around the dreamscape. The last time I was brought to this ethereal space, Saran's knife had just carved through my back. I kissed Inan through my tears.

Now there's no lush forest. No trickles of flowing water.

There's only me.

And *him*.

Inan lies in the dying reeds, far closer than I ever want him to be. I don't know if he's just in my head.

If he's still alive or dead.

But seeing him now is a hand squeezing around my throat. Another wrapping tight around my heart. It's mountains crashing down inside me as he stirs and lifts himself from the dirt.

I step back when he groans, muttering to himself in a stupor. His chest is bare, his skin dull, his brown body now thin. The white streak shines bright in his unruly hair, a curl falling between his amber eyes. He blinks slowly as he steadies himself, coming alive when he spots me.

"Zélie?"

My hands shake at the sound of my name on his lips. It's a different kind of knife. One that digs into the deepest corners of my heart and begins to twist.

This isn't happening. I shake my head. *This isn't real.*

But Inan stands here. He holds the scarred flesh of his abdomen as if it still leaks blood. His eyes widen, and I can almost see the memories coming back to him. The pain of his father's sword driving into his gut.

I reach for my back and my fingers graze the MAGGOT etched into my skin. We've fallen so far. The dreamscape used to be the one place in the world where we were free of our scars.

"They weren't supposed to shoot," Inan exclaims, his words rushing together. "You have to believe me. I ordered them not to!"

My hand snaps to my mouth. A sob I can't fight breaks out.

Each word he speaks makes the magic I suppress breathe through my skin. Though I push it back, I can't keep it down. I can't keep the memories in—

"No!"

The shout echoes in my head. Echoes against the sacred temple walls. This time I see its source. Not my brother, but Inan.

My body slams against the stone floor. Baba follows with a heavy thud.

The arrow pierces straight through his chest.

His warm blood pools at my fingertips—

"Please," Inan begs. "I thought I was doing the right thing."

It's difficult to hear him over the pounding in my head. My magic howls, crying out to strike him.

"I trusted you." My words are so quiet I don't know if he can hear them. I feel the pieces of my heart like broken glass. Pieces that broke because of him.

"I'm sorry." He shakes his head. "I'm so sorry . . ."

He reaches out his hand, and it all comes back: the scared little prince. Lips that promised me the world. Hands that caressed my skin.

"I'll make this right," he says. "I promise. Even if it costs me my life."

But he's made me promises before.

Then he marched Baba to his death.

"Zélie—"

I roar like a lionaire as my magic breaks free.

A fire I haven't felt since the sacred ritual ignites inside of me.

Mammoth trees shoot up from the earth, blocking out the light though there is no sun. My magic bleeds through the dirt. The dreamscape shifts, a mirror of all my hurt.

"Zélie, please!"

Black tree roots explode from the ground, wrapping around Inan's calf. They coil around his body like snakes, dragging him backward. I don't know how I control Inan's dreamscape, but I don't care. I glide forward as the roots bind him against a tree, circling his waist, his chest, his neck.

"Wait!" he calls out as I clench my hand. Black vines tighten around his throat, cutting off his words as he chokes. Blood drips down his back, oozing as the jagged bark scrapes into his skin. My own shoulders burn with an echo of his pain, but I don't care if it hurts me.

As long as it hurts *him*.

"*Zélie.*" Inan's eyes burn red as I tighten my fist. I squeeze the roots so hard he can't even gasp. I squeeze so hard his collarbones *snap*.

"Run," I whisper through my teeth. "*Pray.*" I bring my face right up to his, clenching my fingers so hard my nails draw blood from my skin. "When I'm done with you, you're going to wish you died that day."

With a final squeeze, his eyes roll back.

The dreamscape shatters as he falls limp.

CHAPTER FOURTEEN

·····◆◇◆·····

INAN

ZÉLIE, NO!

My eyes fly open. My hands shoot to my throat. My body convulses with grating coughs, fighting me as I choke.

I grip the nearest surface, trying to steady myself through the pain. There's nothing beyond the darkness.

Only the war in my brain.

Run. Zélie's voice rings through my skull. *Pray.* Her hatred anchors me in this moment. The vengeance she swore to claim. Though my lungs still gasp for air, I begin to see through the pain.

It didn't work . . .

Magic lives again.

The realization is like a sedative spreading through my skull. Though my head pounds, it numbs all pain. For an instant, every other thought dissolves.

I gave up everything to stop magic's return. I betrayed my sister and the girl I love. Father's sword plunged through my stomach.

Yet the poison still runs through my blood.

Count to ten. I curl my fingers, exhaling a slow breath. I sink back into the sweat-soaked pillow as the pain in my stomach returns. My hands shake when I reach down and find the thick scar left from Father's sword. The gruesome mark is still tender to the touch.

As I run my fingers over the raised skin, I see the snarl on Father's lips. Hear the growl in his throat. Rage burned through his brown eyes as he stabbed his majacite blade through my gut.

How did this happen? I search the fog in my mind for answers. When I fell into a pool of my own blood, I didn't think I would rise again. The last thing I can remember is Amari running to my defense, choosing to face Father herself.

I don't know how I ended up in the dying dreamscape. How much time has passed since that fateful day. What happened to my father and my sister. Where I lie now—

Ha-wooooooooo!

My head snaps up at the deep and thunderous howl. The alarm begins as a steady rumble, but in seconds it blares with the force of a thousand horns. The bed around me shakes with its vibrations. The siren makes my blood run cold. It sounds like terror and bloodshed and death.

It sounds like war.

What in the skies? I scramble out of the silk sheets, my limbs moving like water. I try to stand, but my legs give out. With a lurch, I slam into the ground.

I lift my throbbing head from a velvet rug as the horn blares. My body goes stiff when I come face-to-face with the piercing green glare of an embroidered snow leopanaire.

"What's going on?" I whisper, questions mounting by the second. My eyes start to adjust to the dim candlelight and I take in the crimson walls; the marbled archways and lush upholstery of Father's royal quarters.

I turn to the gold-paned windows as the alarm grows louder. Sharp screams echo through the thick drapes. Hairs lift on the nape of my neck as the sliver of night that peeks through the velvet folds begins to turn red—

"Your Majesty, please!"

The door slams open. Candlelight floods in. I stumble into the wall, blinded as a general and armored troops storm into Father's room.

"Quick!" The general runs to the bed. "We need to get him to the cellars!" But as the woman scrambles across the silk sheets, I realize that she's not a general at all.

It's Mother.

I hardly recognize her petite frame in the golden suit of armor. Her bone-straight hair now falls to her shoulders in frizzy waves. But strangest of all is the white streak that falls behind her ear.

"Where is he?" she shrieks, tearing at the empty bed. "Where is my son?"

Soldiers drag her toward the door.

Then she spots me against the wall.

"Inan?"

The color drains from her face. A hand flies to her open mouth. Tears well in her amber eyes and she stumbles back, doubling over as if she's been punched in the stomach.

"You're awake!"

I can't tell how much time has passed since we last saw each other. I feel lifetimes in our distance. She still has her bronze skin, her pointed chin. But the light in her eyes has dimmed.

"Mother—"

Before I can ask what's going on, two guards lift her by the arms.

"Put me down!" she commands, but her orders fall on deaf ears.

"Get them to the cellars!" a lieutenant shouts. In seconds, soldiers lift me as well. Mother screams for me as they pull her back, carrying her and racing down the stairs.

"What's going on?" I yell. "Who's attacking us?"

Outside the palace walls, the horn blares louder. The night sky continues to burn red. The world passes in a blur as the soldiers drag me from Father's quarters and carry me down the ivory stairs. But the more I see of the palace, the more answers I need.

Gone are the spotless marble floors. The slender vases that lined every hall. Servants and soldiers sprint across the cracked tiles. Shattered glass and crooked frames stain the barren walls.

When we reach the bottom of the stairs, I can't believe my eyes. The entire east wing of the palace lies in ruins.

Nothing more than mounds of rubble and broken columns.

This is a dream. I close my eyes. *A nightmare. Nothing more.*

But no matter how many times I blink, I can't wake up.

"What's going on?" I shout, but no one acknowledges me. I can't just run and hide.

I need to get answers myself.

I slam my feet down and throw my elbows back; the guards wheeze when I punch them in the throat. Their grips loosen and I break free, ignoring the way they scream as I sprint for the balcony.

A painful spasm erupts from my abdomen, but I force my shaking legs to run. I push the sandbags away from the balcony door, clawing for the handle.

How could this happen?

Even as I live it, it all feels impossible. The last time these walls were breached, I wasn't even born. Burners rampaged through the palace halls, killing every member of Father's family. It was that attack that made Father get rid of magic. He vowed that the palace would never be attacked again.

Father's old stories fill my mind as the last sandbag falls away and I push open the door. My hands fall limp at the sight.

Lagos is gone.

"No . . ."

I drop to my knees. It feels like the ground has been pulled out from under me. I don't recognize the carnage before me. It's like my city's been ravaged by war.

Gone are the pastel buildings of the merchant quarter. The colorful tents and carts of the bustling marketplace that sat at its border. Broken windows and blasted buildings lie in their wake. Helpless corpses line the streets.

Half the divîner dwellings are up in flames, filling the night with the stench of ash. The wooden walls that used to surround them are no more than measly stubs. Giant mounds of rubble stand in their place, a barrier of destruction closing my city in.

I grab my stomach, stumbling as it reverberates with pain. I can't believe this is happening.

I cannot believe this is my home.

Ha-woooooooo!

The alarm grows to its loudest blare yet and I finally understand its cause. A sphere of fire rises above Lagos's rubble walls, the red sun growing larger by the second.

Even from kilometers away, my skin prickles from the searing heat of its flames. The fire's crackle fills the air.

Then the red sun explodes.

"By the skies . . ."

My body turns to stone as countless balls of fire arc through the air. They explode when they hit the ground. It's like flames raining from above.

Screams ring through the night as the firebombs ravage Lagos all at once. A pair of flames rise over the destroyed palace gates. I try to back up, but my legs don't move fast enough.

"Get down!" someone shouts. Strong arms grab my shoulders, pulling me toward the balcony doors. The rasp in the guard's voice makes me pause. I catch sight of the burn scars along the soldier's neck as our perimeter turns red.

"Ojore?" I don't trust my eyes. I haven't seen my cousin since he left the naval academy.

He drags me inside, throwing me against the sandbags lining the wall. His armored body covers mine as the world is drowned out in a blinding flash of white.

BOOM!

The impact rattles me to the bone. Windows shatter with the force of the blast. Shards of glass rain down on our heads.

The palace quakes with the force, subsiding as black plumes of smoke roll in. I grab my ringing ears as my cousin covers my nose, pulling me to my feet.

"You alright?"

I nod, though my head throbs more than it did before. Any part of me that didn't already hurt screams with pain now.

"What in the skies was that?" I ask.

Ojore shields his nose, coughing as he drags me toward the cellar.

"The *Iyika*," he answers. "Welcome to the war."

CHAPTER FIFTEEN

* * * * ◆ ◇ ◆ * * * *

ZÉLIE

Light bleeds into the blackness of my mind, stirring me awake. I groan as I slip back into consciousness, my body moaning with pain.

My head throbs like a herd of rhinomes warring inside my skull. Fleeting images of the broken dreamscape fill my mind with each ache.

"Hold her down," a hoarse voice orders when I stir.

I blink open my eyes as blurry faces come into focus. Tzain closes in, blocking out the rays of morning sun. Seeing him brings back the memory of running away with Nailah; of crashing into the tree before I fell into the dreamscape.

"Tzain . . ." I try to sit up, but he forces me to stay down. Amari appears at his side, applying pressure to my legs though she won't meet my gaze. A young maji with high cheekbones and wide-set eyes kneels between them, slender fingers pressed to my chest. Thick white braids fall to the small of her back as her hoarse voice continues to chant.

"Babalúayé, ṣiṣé nípasè mi. Babalúayé, ṣiṣé nípasè mi."

Behind her, two more maji stand guard at the forest perimeter, eyeing the rising clouds of dirt in the distance.

"They're closing in, Safiyah," one maji calls. "Be quick."

"The queen?" I grumble, and the maji shakes his head.

"Her tîtáns."

The tangerine light around Safiyah's hands turns dark as she releases more of the ashê in her blood. The spiritual energy heats her fingertips, increasing the strength of her magic.

I feel the drain on my own ashê as a searing heat kneads itself into my chest. A needle of fire threads through my ribs. My muscles spasm with the sudden surge—

Crack!

I flinch as my ribs snap together like reunited magnets. My bones grind against each other as they heal. I have to clench my teeth to endure the burn. Though the pain is sharp, the pressure lifts from my chest; I relish the way my lungs expand. But as cool air comes in, my mind returns to Inan.

He's still alive.

I bring one hand to my neck, picturing the vines I wrapped around his throat. I don't know how he survived, but I feel his lifeforce in my gut. My eyes fall on Amari, and I wrestle with what to do next.

How can I tell her that her brother lives after I caused her all that pain?

"Safiyah, let's *go*."

Sweat drips down the Healer's brown skin as she removes her hands. Safiyah hangs her head back with exhaustion, taking slow, labored breaths.

"I'm sorry," she says. "But we have to keep moving. Nehanda's tîtáns have been rounding up every maji east of Zaria. Entire villages are being imprisoned in Gusau's fortress."

Gusau? I think of the village a few days east. I wonder if their maji are locked in chains. If they're carving into them the way they carved into me.

"Thank you." I rest my hand on Safiyah's knee and she smiles.

"My thanks goes to you, *Jagunjagun*. It's an honor to heal the Soldier of Death."

My brows knit at the title as she and the maji move back into the

Adichie Forest. No one meets the other's eye when we're alone. I force myself to break the tense silence.

"How'd you find me?"

Tzain nods to Nailah, curled at my back. "She came running to us in a frenzy. We flagged Safiyah down after Nailah brought us back here."

I frown at the shallow gashes in my lionaire's skin, marks where gravel and branches cut through her golden coat. Her front paw lies wrapped in bandages, swollen from a sprain. Though it hurts, I reach up and pet her snout. She nuzzles me back, rough tongue sliding across my forehead.

I direct her to Tzain and he closes his eyes, wincing as Nailah licks his face. "Is this your way of saying sorry?"

"It is if it's working."

Taking my cue, Nailah turns aggressive, slathering Tzain with wet kisses. He pushes her away, but he can't fight the smile she brings to his face.

"I'm sorry." I reach for his hand. "I know I was out of line."

"I swear on Baba." He shakes his head. "If you pull that dung again—"

"I won't." I lace my fingers through his and squeeze. "You and me?"

"You and me." He nods. "Even when you're an ass."

I grin, but it fades when Tzain glances at Amari. The bags under her eyes tell me she hasn't slept all night. Her face is still flushed from crying.

She looks away, running her fingers through the new waves in her hair. It grows curlier by the day. I wonder if her awakened magic is to blame.

"I'm sorry." I hang my head. Shame fills me from every horrible thing I yelled. "I didn't mean what I said. I was just upset."

Amari nods, but her lips still quiver. I expose my aching ribs.

"You can kick me if you want."

"Will that make us even?" she asks.

"No. But it'll be a start."

Though Amari still won't meet my gaze, a small smile settles on her lips. I reach out and grab her hand. It makes her eyes brim with tears.

I can almost see my apology ease the weight on her shoulders, but that doesn't change the war we're in. The countless soldiers and tîtáns who now oppose us. The powerful mother she might have to kill.

"Do you still plan to take down Nehanda?" I ask.

"I don't see another way." Amari's shoulders slump. "But this is my fight. I won't ask you to get involved again."

"We talked about it," Tzain informs me. "If you really want to leave Orïsha, we'll help you run. I may not agree, but you've suffered enough. I understand why you want to be free."

Free.

The word already feels like a distant memory. Even from the grave, Inan had iron chains around my heart. With him alive, those same chains burn like majacite.

Freedom doesn't lie beyond Orïsha's borders. Not while the little prince still lives. Still wins.

If I want to be free, I can't run.

I have to kill him.

"I'm not running anymore," I say. "If war is what they want, then war is what we'll give them."

Amari grips my thigh. She and Tzain exchange a glance.

"I don't understand," she says. "What changed?"

My muscles tense and I take a deep breath; I don't want to hurt her again. But she has to know the truth. The other member of her family she fights against.

"I think your brother's alive," I sigh. "And I'm going to be the one to kill him."

CHAPTER SIXTEEN

AMARI

I THINK YOUR brother is alive.

Days pass, yet Zélie's words remain trapped in my mind. They haunt me as we make our way through the Olasimbo Mountain Range, moving through the shadows of night. Blankets of fog sweep our feet as we hike up a dirt trail that will give us a view of Gusau's fortress meters below. I need to focus on freeing the maji trapped inside to build my army and face my mother, but all I can think about is Inan.

I don't know what to do if he still breathes. I know I cannot allow Mother to sit on Orïsha's throne, but do I need to free the imprisoned maji in Gusau's fortress if Inan sits there instead? If Inan is king now, will he still wage this war?

Watching Father drive a sword through my brother's gut was a wound I felt in my own heart. If Inan is truly alive, I don't want to fight him anymore.

I want to run into his arms.

"You're thinking of him again."

I blink as Tzain comes up beside me, his expression kind. He brushes a lock of hair behind my ear before tracing his fingers down my spine.

"How can I not?" I lower my voice, eyeing Zélie as she walks ahead. "If what she says is true . . . if Inan really lives . . ."

Just speaking his name aloud brings me back to every night spent alone after the ritual went awry. My sobs bounced against the cold iron walls of the warship. I cried so much, my sheets were constantly damp.

Despite all the pain he caused, I didn't know how to breathe without my brother in this world. What in the skies am I supposed to do if he's really back?

"Hold up." Zélie raises a hand, forcing us to stop. The branches rattle ahead. Zélie reaches for her staff.

My pulse spikes as the footsteps draw near. Their approaching shadows loom large. But when the three bodies round the corner, my heart breaks.

The shadows belong to children.

"*Arábìnrin*, do you have any food?" A young maji steps forward, the tallest of the trio. Their clothes are weathered and worn. I don't know if they're related, or only linked by their white hair.

Zélie reaches for her leather bag, but I beat her to the punch. I remove a strip of dried hyenaire meat from my knapsack. I can always hunt for more.

"Thank you, *Ìyáawa*." The girl smiles as she splits the meat between the three of them. I wonder if it was the rule of Father or Mother that left them alone on this path. Watching them walk away forces me back into the war, to our army waiting to be liberated meters below. Every day I don't bring this fight to an end, my people suffer.

Inan or not, I have to bring my mother down and take that throne.

"There it is." Zélie crouches along the cliff, the valley sixty meters below revealing our target. Gusau's fortress matches Gombe's in size, an iron prison along the farming town's borders. Surrounded by fields of cassava plants, the fortress casts a shadow over its guards. Soldiers patrol every meter of the torch-lit tower, flickering flames lighting their stern faces.

"Open the gates!" a guard shouts. My throat goes dry as the torch flames pass over his golden armor. I don't need to see beneath his helmet to know a white streak runs through his hair.

I tuck my own streak away as I count the other two tîtáns in their patrol. I wonder if any of them are as powerful as my mother.

"Look." Zélie points to a panthenaire-pulled caravan as it passes below our cliff. When it docks, chained maji are forced out. Their heads hang as they pass through the barred doors.

My stomach churns as I take in the burns and bruises along the maji's skin. Each broken face hits me with another wave of guilt. If I were queen, these people would be free. We'd be working together to build the Orïsha of my dreams.

"Magic's been back all of five minutes, and your family's already rounding us up." Zélie smacks her lips. The resentment in her voice makes my stomach tight.

"Mother works fast," I say. "That's why we need to work faster."

I know she hears the name that I do not speak, but I don't care what she believes. I know my brother; if he's alive, there's no way he would sanction this. He's been through too much to fight like Father.

We both have.

"Let's stake them out," I decide. "Learn their schedules and find the optimal time to attack. With all the maji raids, they've got to have more than they can manage. If we can free the maji, we'll have the start of our own army."

"Are you sure we're strong enough?" Tzain asks. "When we stormed Gombe, we had Kenyon and my agbön friends to back us up."

"You also weren't at war." A voice rings from behind. "This time, the military's prepared."

My blade cuts through the air and Zélie whips out her staff. But when the speaker emerges from the bushes, her hands fall limp.

"Roën?" Zélie steps back as the mercenary finishes his ascent up the dirt trail. He leans against a tree, moonlight passing over a new bruise on his cheek.

"Come on, *Zitsōl*," he says. "Did you really think getting rid of me was going to be that easy?"

"What in the skies are you doing here?" I charge forward, teeth clenching as I scan the forest. "How'd you find us? Who sent you? Where are the rest of your men?"

"At ease, Princess. You've seen my work." He holds up his hands. "If I wanted you captured, you'd already be in a leather sack. I've tracked you down to make amends."

"Liar." I close in, raising my sword to his neck.

"What are you doing?" Zélie whispers.

"You didn't hear the threats he made after the rally."

Roën's jaw clicks as he stares at my blade. "I'm going to give you one chance to put that down."

Despite his threat, I tighten my grip. Another push and I'll draw blood.

"Don't listen to a word he says," I declare. "If he's here, it's to knock me out and collect the bounty on my hea—"

I cry out as Roën grabs my wrist, forcing me to drop my blade. In one smooth motion, he twists my arm behind my back.

"Like I said." He pushes me to the side, taking my place at the edge of the cliff. "If I wanted to take you out, we wouldn't be having this conversation." He gestures to the fortress's borders, waving Zélie over. "The *Iyika* have already attempted jailbreaks. Now every facility in Orïsha is armed."

"Majacite gas?" Zélie asks.

"Perimeter's riddled with mines." Roën nods. "Triple the strength of what they used at the rally. Any maji would choke to death before they ever broke out."

"Then we'll get masks," I say. "We can find a way past the gas."

"Even if you could, the guards will kill everyone inside before they let one maji escape."

The color drains from my cheeks as his words sink in.

"That's impossible." I shake my head. I know this is war, but even Mother couldn't be that cruel.

"With Lagos choked off, the military can't afford to lose another city to the *Iyika*," Roën explains. "They certainly can't afford for them to gather more soldiers."

I stare at the twigs on the ground as my plan crumbles like sand. After our success freeing Zélie from Gombe's fortress, I was sure this strategy would work. Liberating prisoners for our army was the foundation of my attack, the start of my path back to the throne. But if Mother will kill every maji we try to break out . . .

Skies.

We haven't even struck, and somehow she's already won.

"That still doesn't explain why you're here," Tzain says, stepping between Roën and Zélie. "You expect us to believe you came all this way just to warn us?"

"Come on, brother." Roën smiles. "Where's the coin in that? I've come to collect a bounty from the only person in Orïsha who doesn't want you dead."

"I knew it." I step back. "I'm not going anywhere with you."

"Good. Stay here. Zélie's the one they're after."

Roën removes a note from his pocket and I see the red *I* that's been tagged across our path.

"The *Iyika*?" Zélie reaches for the parchment. "They're looking for me?"

"The lot hired me to escort you to Ibadan and paid in advance. So, you can come willingly, or I can break out that leather sack."

I snatch the parchment from Zélie's hands, studying the assortment of red dots. I think of the rebel who stared me down at my rally, the hatred in her scarred eye.

"The *Iyika* want to kill me and the rest of the monarchy," I say. "We can't go to them."

"Everyone wants you dead." Roën rolls his eyes. "I don't blame them. But why waste your time jailbreaking fighters you can't have when you can join the maji on the winning side?"

I give Zélie a pointed look, but she shrugs in response.

"What other choice do we have?" she asks.

Roën smiles at my defeat, waving at us to follow him as he takes the lead.

"Come along, Princess. Let's see if the *Iyika* want to kill you as badly as your mother and my mercenaries do."

CHAPTER SEVENTEEN

· · · · · ◆ ◇ ◆ · · · · ·

INAN

STARING AT MY REFLECTION, I don't know what to think. I don't recognize the stranger who stares back.

The broken boy meant to be Orïsha's king.

With all the weight I lost while unconscious, I drown in Father's crimson agbada. The royal silk still reeks of his sandalwood cologne. Breathe too deeply, and I can feel his hands wrap around my throat.

You are no son of mine.

I close my eyes, muscles spasming in my stomach. The sharp ache makes my teeth grind. It's like his sword is still buried inside. As I prepare for my first royal assembly, my fingers twist around the ghost of his sênet piece. I hate myself for missing it.

I hate Father more for giving it to me.

"Are you decent, Your Highness?" The oak door cracks open, and Ojore's bearded jaw sticks through. "I've heard the legends of what greatness lies beneath your robes, but I fear I'm far too pure to see it for myself."

Despite the pain in my side, my cousin never fails to make me grin. He laughs as I wave him over, smile bright against his dark brown skin.

"You're looking good." He slaps my shoulder. "Like a king. And look at that!" He pinches my face. "You've even got a little color in your cheeks!"

"It's not real." I push him away. "Mother made the servants use her powders and paints."

"Anything to hide that horrible face."

The warmth he carries into Father's frigid quarters stirs something in my chest. Tall, lean, and handsome, Ojore looks like a portrait in his new admiral's armor, but it doesn't cover the burn scars feeding onto his neck.

We haven't been together since he was my captain at the naval academy, yet he's still like the brother I never had. He seems to sense my thoughts as he slings an arm around my shoulder, joining my reflection in the mirror.

"The admiral and the king." He shakes his head, and I grin.

"Just like we planned."

"Well, not exactly like we planned." Ojore ruffles my hair, drawing attention to my white streak. Though he keeps his voice light, he can't suppress his disdain.

"You hate it."

"It." He looks away. "Not you."

I stare at the reflection of the jagged white line, the mark of my curse. Since I woke up, every time I reach for my magic it feels like someone's driving an axe into my skull. I don't know if it's because of the way Zélie hurt me in the dreamscape, or if my abilities changed after the sacred ritual.

But after all that's passed, I don't even know if I want to use my magic. How can I when it's the reason Father tried to wipe me from this earth?

"What about the títáns in your ranks?" I ask. "Mother wasn't the only one wearing a golden suit of armor."

"We're at war. Are we supposed to charge at their fire with our swords?" Ojore rubs his thumb against his burn scars, still scaly after all these years. "We may need the títáns to put those maggots in the dirt, but magic is still a curse."

I almost want to laugh; moons ago, I would have said the same thing. But even after all I've learned, I know nothing could make Ojore see magic another way. His mind was set the day Burners tore through the palace and scorched his parents alive. He was lucky to escape with just those scars.

"I thought they got you, too." His voice gets quiet and he stares at the floor. "When I found you on the ritual grounds, there was so much blood. Even after they stabilized you, I didn't think you'd ever wake up."

I think back to the dreamscape. The dying reeds. The gray haze. Perhaps if Zélie hadn't found me, I could've remained frozen in the dreamscape forever.

"I owe you my life."

"Oh, you owe me a lot more than that. When this war is over, I want a title. I want gold. Land!"

I laugh and shake my head. "You talk as if the end is in sight."

"You're back, my king. Now it is."

"Inan?"

I turn, not even realizing the door opened again. Mother stands in its frame, sunlight reflecting off her crimson gown. The beaded fabric drapes over her shoulders, forming a cape that falls to the small of her back. It glides as she makes her way into Father's quarters.

Ojore releases a low whistle. "Even in a war zone, my auntie's still got it."

"Hush, boy." Mother narrows her eyes, but smiles as she grabs Ojore's chin. Though not related by blood, Ojore might as well have been Mother's first son. She took him in after his family was killed, grooming him until he could rise through the ranks on his own.

"The assembly's gathered in the throne room." Mother shifts her attention to me. "We're ready when you are."

"But the cellar's the safest place——"

Mother cuts me off with a wave of her hand. "Your people will meet their new king as tradition dictates. Not cowering in the dark."

Ojore nods in approval. "You don't miss a beat."

"We can't afford to," she says. "The entire council will be watching, General Jokôye closest of all. You must prove yourself to them if you're going to command the army you need to win this war."

My throat dries and I swallow, wishing I had more time to prepare. I know it's up to me to free Lagos and Orïsha from the *Iyika's* wrath, but the problems feel far too great to solve. With the blocked roads, the dwindling food supply, the unknown seconds until their firebombs rage again, how am I supposed to stop them when I couldn't even stop magic from coming back?

"Now for the final touch." Mother's painted nails glisten as she snaps her fingers, making a servant enter the room. He carries a velvet cushion with Father's crown. The sight of the polished gold sends a painful spasm through my abdomen.

"I'll wait outside." Ojore pats my back before making his way out. "But you're ready. Your father would be proud."

Despite the way my insides clench, I paste a smile on my face. But it falls the moment Mother takes the crown in her hands, gesturing for me to bend down. The shining metal rises like a two-tiered cake, every ounce of the royal heirloom forged from gold. Diamond-studded designs swirl around an elephantaire—the original royal crest. A glittering red ruby sits at its top, so dark it looks like blood.

"I know." Mother's eyes grow distant as she stares at the crown. "If I could burn it, I would."

"At least you don't have to wear his clothes."

"I'll have new robes tailored when I can." She places the metal on my head. Her hard shell cracks at the sight. She presses her fingers to her lips and exhales.

"Skies, Mother, please don't cry."

She swats at me before straightening my collar. Though I hate how she fusses, I love how she smiles.

"Your father was far from a good man," she says. "But he was a good king. He protected this throne at all cost. As his successor, you must do the same thing."

She places her hands on my shoulders and turns me toward the mirror. With her head next to mine, the person who stares back starts to look more familiar.

"I don't want to be like him, Mother. I can't."

"Don't be your father, Inan." She takes my arm. "Be the king he couldn't."

CHAPTER EIGHTEEN

· · · · · · ◆ ◇ ◆ · · · · ·

ZÉLIE

"Hold up!"

I stifle a grunt of frustration and lean against a canopy tree at Roën's command. Nailah yawns and stretches out by my side, her injured paw still too fragile for us to ride her. We pause amid the thinning stretch of rain forest lining the mountainside near the center of the Olasimbo Range. Though we're more than a half-moon from meeting the *Iyika* in Ibadan, each delay feels like a lifetime.

"Don't give me that look, *Zitsōl*." Roën wags his finger in my face before walking ahead. "We're about to lose our cover. I need to stop and do a check."

I tap my foot as he takes the lead, making his way through the thinning trees. Rich greens surround us, coating every sloping branch and tangled vine. As the rain forest breaks, the grass-covered slopes expand, stretching beneath the mountain peaks. The hot sun shines down on them from above, rays bright in the cloudless sky.

"All clear?" I call after Roën. "Or should we wait while you pat down the sheep?"

"I'm sure these maji wouldn't have minded traveling with someone like me."

He steps away from a dip in the wild grass, and my chest grows tight.

Two maji lie at his feet, neither one much older than I am. Dried blood stains their worn tunics, darkest around the blade wounds in their chests. The burns along their skin point to the majacite Nehanda's soldiers must have used to stop them.

"Don't stare." Tzain nudges my arm, moving straight ahead. Amari follows after him, lightening my load by taking Nailah's new reins.

"From the gods comes the gift of life." I bend down. *"To the gods, that gift must be returned."* Though I don't want to feel magic's rush, I whisper the words of the *ìbùkún*, laying the poor souls to rest. My eyes sting as the memories of Baba's death resurface, but I push them down. Roën crosses his arms as I rise.

"That's the first time I've seen you do magic since the ritual."

I brush past him without saying a word, covering the maji with palm ferns before forging ahead.

"Really? This again?" He falls in step by my side. "Are we just going to pretend you didn't call after me when I left?"

"Are we just going to pretend you didn't leave at all?"

Roën pushes his tongue into the side of his cheek, a coy smile dancing across his lips.

"At least tell me what changed," he says. "I thought you wanted to be free."

I turn my focus back to the mountain path, stepping over the thick stones littered throughout the wild grass. At times my thoughts still drift to the seas. To the lands that could be waiting beyond all this pain. But each time, Inan's face returns, keeping me anchored to Orïsha's soil.

"My plans haven't changed," I say. "I just need to take care of something first."

"I see." Roën smiles. "I hope that something is savoring his last breath."

He winks and I glare back at him. I hate the way he cuts through my words. It's like when Inan would read my mind, but with Roën there's no magical cause.

"Why'd you really come back?" I ask. "You would've had an easier time selling us out."

"Honestly?" Roën cups my chin, stopping me in my tracks. Though I don't want to feel anything, his touch makes an ember flicker in my stomach. It's like when he brushed my cheek after the rally. I can still remember the scratch of his callused fingers. There was so much said in that simple caress. I don't know what to make of it now that he's back.

"When I heard what happened, I couldn't take it." He shakes his head. "I knew you liked me, but to ram yourself into a tree at the very thought of living another day without me?"

Roën laughs as I shove him away, mischief twinkling in his stormy eyes.

"You're impossible."

"Don't be embarrassed, love. You're far from the first woman or man to lose the will to live in my absence—"

"Zélie!"

Our heads snap to the left as Tzain's yell echoes through the mountains. The crack of splitting rocks fills the air. Hairs rise on the nape of my neck. Roën grabs my arm, but I take off in a sprint before he can hold me back. More shouts ring as my feet pound against the wild grass.

"Up there!" Amari points when I skid around the bend.

Almost a full kilometer up, a troop of guards looks down at us from the edge of a cliff. The sun glints off their golden armor. For a moment we all stand still.

I scramble back when three of the guards jump, skidding down the towering mountain ledge. The tîtán Grounders move like lightning, pushing through the gravel as if it were snow.

My pulse races as I take in their skill; they have far more control than the tîtáns who attacked us at the rally. They barrel toward us as the rest of Nehanda's soldiers fasten ropes into the cliff's side, holding tight as they slide to the ground.

"I got this!" Amari runs forward, blue light sparking at her fingertips.

"Amari, stop!" I think of the tîtán who perished before my eyes. "You don't know how to use your magic!"

Her skin sizzles as the blue light surrounds her hand. She shoots her palm forward, but instead of releasing her attack, it flares in her own face. Amari cries out in pain, falling to the ground.

There's no way out.

If I don't use my magic to attack, we die.

"Ẹmí àwọn tí ó ti sùn—"

Time seems to slow as the ashê erupts in my blood. Spirits condense in the air like grains of black sand. My arms shake from the magic that fights its way out.

The spirits race through my bones, rising from the earth in droves. But as my animations take form, I realize that they're not the only ones.

"Ẹmí àwọn tí ó ti sùn—"

My brows furrow as a gangly soldier in golden armor repeats my incantation. I feel the spirits that he calls into animations, but they don't rise as individual soldiers. The souls weave themselves together, bringing one giant monster to life. My jaw drops as the gravelly beast rises from the earth. It's so large its silhouette blocks out the sun.

Frozen in our confusion, no one moves as our animations stand still. The soldier walks forward and pulls off his golden helmet, revealing a full head of white hair.

"By the grace of Oya, it's *you!*" The boy's mouth hangs open as he stares at me. He can't be more than fifteen. Like his massive animation, he has ears far too large for his head.

"Your form could use some work," another voice rings, its speaker limping toward me. "But I am impressed. That was quite the incantation."

As the soldier removes her helmet, all the breath leaves my lungs. The Seer inspects the work of my animations just like she used to inspect my form with a staff.

"Mama Agba?" I whisper.

A smile spreads across her brown lips. Tears brim in her mahogany eyes as she opens her arms.

"I told you we would meet again."

CHAPTER NINETEEN

ZÉLIE

I DON'T KNOW if I've ever cried as hard as I do in Mama Agba's arms. The scent of fresh fabric bleeds through her suit of armor, wrapping me in the memories of home. Her embrace brings the crash of Ilorin's waves, the sharp smack of two oak staffs. Another sob breaks free as I cling to her, terrified that if I let go, this dream will end.

"*Pèlé*," Mama Agba whispers into my coils, resting her chin on my head. She rubs my back and lets out a small laugh. "It's okay, my child. I'm here."

I nod, but tighten my grip; as I hold her, the sensation of holding my own mother's spirit in alâfia hits me like a wave. I barely got Mama back before she slipped through my arms. I won't survive losing someone like that again.

"Look at your hair!" I laugh through my tears and touch the small white coils now sprouting from her scalp.

"A little warrior brought magic back." She smiles. "I no longer wished to hide."

As she speaks, I take in the mole on her chin, the new spots and wrinkles along her dark brown skin. Her limp is more pronounced than I remember, but she's real. She's actually here.

"Come along." Mama Agba kisses my forehead before rising to embrace Amari and Tzain. I wipe away the rest of my tears and observe the soldiers behind her. Each maji shares my white coils. Their rich complexions cover a beautiful spectrum of dark and light browns.

The young Reaper with the large ears and bright eyes steps forward, an incredulous grin on his face.

"What was that incantation?" I ask. "I've never seen a giant animation."

"All the Reapers in my family could do it!" He beams with pride. "Instead of making a bunch of animations, we weave them together to form one."

"That's amazing."

"You're amazing!" His teeth clench, and I jerk back. He falls to his knees and bows. "*Jagunjagun Ikú*, I beg of you, take me as your Second!"

"By the gods, Mâzeli." A maji with beads woven through her white braids laughs. "She just got here. Give her a minute to rest."

"Ignore them." Mâzeli grabs my hand, round eyes open wide. "I will serve you faithfully until I can take your place as elder of the Reaper clan. But by then, we will have fallen in love." His grip tightens when I try to pull away. His voice rises in pitch. "You will be the mother of my children. I shall serve our family till my dying breath—"

"Alright," Mama Agba cuts in, patting Mâzeli on the head. "The military patrols will pass through soon. Why don't we continue this conversation behind closed walls?"

"Is he always like that?" I whisper to Mama Agba as we start walking.

"Like all great Reapers in the making, Mâzeli is quite determined."

I smile, but stop when I see that Roën lags behind. A maji hands him a bag of gold, and something in my chest deflates when Roën doesn't follow the others into the rain forest.

"That's it?" I hang back. "You're leaving again?"

"The job's done. I need to meet up with my crew back in Lagos."

"Lagos?" I ask. "You're working for the other side?"

"There's a lot of money to be made in a war, *Zitsōl*. If you stop messing around with all this fighting, you can grab some for yourself."

I shake my head; I don't know why I expected more. "Do you stand for anything besides gold?"

"I'm standing in front of you, aren't I?" Roën leans in, so close I can see the faint freckles over his cheekbone.

"Don't worry." His lips graze my ear as he speaks. "Something tells me our paths will cross again."

* * * * * ◆ ◇ ◆ * * * * *

THE MAJI LEAD us off the main jungle trail, walking along a gushing river. The flowing water cuts the rain forest in half, dividing the dense greens. Beneath us, the hilly terrain slopes up and down as the scent of fresh earth and wildflowers grow. Mammoth trees fill our path, creating rich emerald canopies above.

I keep my hand wrapped tight around Mama Agba's as we dip under raised tree roots. Tzain, Amari, and I stay close, listening intently as she explains the *Iyika*'s origins to us.

"I still don't understand," Tzain says. "You founded the rebellion?"

"In a way." Mama Agba nods. "But it started as a defense. Your father and I were halfway to Oron when I had a vision of the three of you at the divîner settlement. We didn't arrive in time to stop the monarchy's attack, but we were able to find the survivors." Mama Agba leans on me as we step over a fallen log. "The two of us were leading them here when more soldiers attacked."

Her voice trails and I think back to the deaths of Zulaikha and Salim. Tzain and I exchange a glance as the pieces fall into place. This is the reason Baba ended up in Inan's grasp. The reason Baba died.

"I promise, we fought with everything we had," Mama Agba sighs.

"But your father didn't want us to get hurt. He offered himself up to the guards and they agreed to spare our lives."

The flames of Baba's casket burn in my mind as she speaks. Though we pass sunset blossoms, the stench of ash fills my nose.

"I am so sorry." Mama Agba shakes her head. "More than you could ever know."

"Don't be." I squeeze her hand. "It's not your fault."

The memory of Inan walking Baba to his death reminds me why I'm here. With the *Iyika*'s help, we can take Inan and Nehanda down. I can wrap my hands around his throat.

"After the camp fell, we realized that we had an opening." Mâzeli picks up in Mama Agba's silence. "No one else knew that magic was coming back. We used that knowledge to plan an attack."

"The night of the centennial solstice, we banded with other maji and crowded Lagos's borders," a petite maji jumps in. "The moment our gifts returned, we stormed the city. The monarchy didn't know what hit them."

Amari's face falls, but I can't keep the wonder from my eyes. I can't believe they trusted me to bring magic back; that my sacrifice actually allowed my people to fight.

"What was it like?" I ask.

"*Brilliant*," Mâzeli whispers. "We would've taken the palace if it wasn't for Nehanda. But now that you're here, we'll break through their defenses. With the Soldier of Death, this war is ours!"

His words ignite a cheer among the maji that continues as we come face-to-face with a staggering cliff. A tall Grounder steps forward when we approach.

"Elder Kâmarū," Mama Agba gestures, introducing all of us. A silver nose ring glints against the Grounder's dark skin. His thick white hair stands straight up in small free-form locs. One of his legs is sculpted from iron, attached halfway down his right thigh. I step back as he passes, but he stops to bow, iron knee touching the ground.

"The stories don't do you justice," he says, making my cheeks flush. Mâzeli steps between us.

"Kâmarū, I don't care if you're twice my size. Back off."

The Grounder smiles as he retreats, his nose ring glinting as he takes position. Kâmarū places his large palms against the mountainside, pressing hard into the rock.

"Remember to breathe." Mama Agba nods, a familiar tone of instruction in her voice. He closes his eyes and releases a deep breath. Then he begins to chant.

"Se ìfé inú mi—"

I don't move as the incantation rings. It's been years since I've heard the steady rhythms that mark all Grounder incantations.

An emerald glow surrounds Kâmarū's feet, traveling up to his hands. Sharp cracks ring as his fingers dig into the sturdy rock like hands digging through sand.

"Widen your stance," Mama Agba calls, and Kâmarū squares his legs. The plants covering the mountainside fall away as the thick tapestry unweaves vine by vine.

Kâmarū steps back as pebbles and dust fall. With a groan, the mountain stone slides apart like a collection of tiles. I hold my breath as sunlight spills into the new, narrow opening, revealing the entrance of a never-ending stairwell. Hope flickers like an ember in my chest.

The *Iyika* are far more powerful than we realized.

"Excellent work." Mama Agba pats him on the back. Her brown eyes shine with excitement, one I haven't seen from her in years. She steps away, gesturing for us to enter first.

"Go on." She pushes me onto the first stair. "Welcome to the rebellion."

CHAPTER TWENTY

▪ ▪ ▪ ▪ ▪ ◆ ◇ ◆ ▪ ▪ ▪ ▪ ▪

AMARI

"What in the skies . . ."

My mouth falls open as we exit the long tunnel. Three mountains stand in a triangle, their tops flattened into wide plateaus. They rise so high into the sky it looks like we float above a blanket of clouds. Each mountain holds an assortment of stunning temples and towers crafted from gleaming black stone.

"You built this in a moon?" Tzain squints, and Mama Agba releases a hearty laugh.

"The *Ile Ijosin* was created by the original elders centuries ago, the first leaders of the ten maji clans. I was first brought here when I served as elder of the Seers. This sanctuary is nearly as old as Orïsha itself."

I breathe in the lush vegetation, the sunset blossoms peppering the air. A gushing waterfall flows down the center of the three mountains, creating a natural bath where young divîners splash. In the distance, sharp cliffs rise like stone thorns, poking through the tapestry of clouds. The sight steals my breath. It's like the war can't reach us from the ground.

"Over here." Mama Agba gestures to the looming obsidian tower to our left. Its ten floors stack on top of one another like giant ornaments welded together. "We added a new infirmary, but it still holds the old meditation centers and gardens. But on the second mountain we're in the process of converting old towers to dormitories."

She points across the stone bridge connecting the two mountaintops. The second mountain is larger than the first, peppered with half-finished structures. As we move toward the dormitories, I'm struck with the memory of Zulaikha walking us through the divîner camp. With its colorful tents and shoddy carts, it was easy to see man's touch. This place looks like a kingdom crafted by the gods.

"Imagine sanctuaries like this across Orïsha," I whisper to Tzain. "Imagine cities built this way."

"When you're on the throne, we won't need to imagine anything at all."

His words make my heart swell, but they also remind me why I'm here. With the *Iyika*'s forces, I can take Mother down. Together, we can build a new Orïsha.

"Before I forget." Mama Agba grabs Tzain's arm, turning him toward the third mountain. The tallest of the three, the mountain forms the waterfall's base. Ten temples stagger along its spiraling cliffs, each one devoted to a different clan. "I was told if you arrived to send you to the Burner Temple. From what I understand, you played agbön against their elder?"

"Kenyon?" Tzain's face lights up. "He's here?"

We haven't seen his old agbön friends since we parted ways after the ritual. If it hadn't been for them, we wouldn't have been able to rescue Zélie when she was captured by my father.

"What about the twins?" Zélie asks. "Are Khani and Imani here?"

"Khani's the elder of the Healers." Mama Agba nods. "Imani serves as her Second. They were the ones who set up the infirmary on the first mountain."

"Let's go." Tzain steers Mama Agba toward the third mountain before she can change her mind. He waves us on. "I'll find you later!"

I smile at his excitement as Mâzeli takes charge of our tour. But as we move, I start to count the *Iyika* soldiers we pass, my thoughts returning to Nehanda and the war. The soldiers stand out from the divîners in their brassy suits of armor, the sculpted metal reminiscent of Mama Agba's tailored cuts. Metallic undertones shine through their sleek gauntlets and shoulder pads, ten colors showing each maji's clan.

Twelve, twenty-eight, forty-two . . . fifty-seven . . . seventy-nine. I always pictured a band of disorganized rebels behind the *Iyika*'s red mark, but the eighty soldiers are organized and ready for blood. This is far better than anything I could've hoped for. If I can get them on my side, I can end this war a lot faster than I anticipated.

"Jagunjagun!"

We stop as a beautiful, dark-skinned maji struts toward us. She commands attention with her shaved head. Three silver hoops run up her right ear.

"Kâmarū wasn't lying," she says. "You're quite easy on the eyes."

Her smile turns mischievous, accentuating her wide-set nose and full lips. She bows and touches her knee to the ground, allowing us to see the ornate sleeve of tattoos covering her right arm.

"Nâomi," she introduces herself. "But my friends call me Nâo, so we might as well start there." She slings her tattooed arm around Zélie's neck, pulling her from Mâzeli's grasp.

"What're you doing?" Mâzeli asks. "Mama Agba wanted me to take them on a tour."

"You can do that later. She needs to meet Ramaya and the other elders!"

Nâo drags Zélie off and I start to follow after them, but Mâzeli grabs my arm, forcing me to stay back.

"Are you sure you want to come?" he asks. "The elders aren't exactly fans."

His gaze drifts to my white streak and blush rises to my cheeks. Sweat gathers along my temples as I think of facing the maji who stormed Lagos.

"The elders run the sanctuary?" I ask.

"And the *Iyika*." Mâzeli nods.

"Then I don't have a choice. Take me to them."

CHAPTER TWENTY-ONE

INAN

Drums beat through the halls, loud, like rolling thunder. Their vibrations shudder through my skull as Mother, Ojore, and I wait outside the throne room doors. As I prepare to make my first public appearance as king, the great monarchs of the past watch from their portraits above.

I try not to think about the fact that if it weren't for this war, Father's portrait would hang there, too.

"You'll be brilliant." Mother smooths the creases along my shoulders and straightens my crown.

"I don't know about brilliant," Ojore teases. "Probably mediocre at best."

We grin at each other, but stop when Mother glares. "This is no time to joke. Proving yourself to the people will be hard enough, but above all else, you must prove yourself to the advisors."

I nod, remembering her earlier words. Without the support of the royal council, I won't have control of the army I need to beat the *Iyika* and win this war.

Mother motions to the tîtán soldiers standing guard outside the throne room and they salute before welcoming her in. As the oak doors shut again, I start to lose feeling in my legs. I always thought it would be Amari who prepared me in my quarters. Father who handed over the crown when his time was done. I wanted this for him.

I wanted to make him proud.

"Something tells me you could use this." Ojore digs under his belt, reaching into the pocket of his pants. I don't know what he could possibly have, but my eyes widen when he removes a bronze piece. Seeing the coin brings me back to the divîner settlement before magic returned, back when Zélie taught me a single incantation.

"What's this?" I asked when she handed me the coin.

"Something you can hold on to without killing yourself. Have at it and stop fidgeting."

"I found it on you after the ritual," Ojore explains. "Almost tossed it, but I never saw you touch a single coin in your life. Figured if you carried this into battle, it had to be important. You were always doing something stupid with your hands."

He drops the piece into my open palm, and my fingers close around the tarnished metal. I run my thumb over the cheetanaire engraved at its center. I'm surprised by how fast my throat closes up.

"You don't know what this means to me," I say. "Thank you."

"It's just a coin." Ojore slaps my back. "No need to cry. Now let's go. The people are ready to meet their new king."

With a nod from me, the soldiers open the grand doors. Sunlight spills through the widening crack. The chatter inside draws to a halt as I walk through the frame.

Row after row of people fill the vast hall. The throne room is so packed, I can't see the tiled floor. It seems half of Lagos stands before me. Dozens more wait outside the palace doors.

Skies . . .

The weight of their stares is like an elephantaire pressing on my chest. I can't believe they're all here for me. I can't believe their well-being rests on my shoulders.

"Presenting King Inan Olúborí," a lieutenant shouts. "The twentythird ruler of Orïsha!"

It's hard to breathe when the entire room bows, a wave moving through the crowd. But before I get lost in the moment, the sight of Father's former advisors keeps me on guard. They stand at the front of the crowd, forming a hard line before the throne. I slow my pace as I take them in.

"Your Majesty." General Jokôye bows, a petite woman with russet-brown skin. Though no taller than a broom, she commands respect as the leader of our army and the oldest of Father's royal council. Suspicion pierces through her brass spectacles as she studies me. I can't help noticing the new white streak running down the center of her signature braid when she rises.

"The general's a tîtán?" I whisper to Ojore, and he nods.

"Jokôye's a Winder now. She's been working with your mother to bring more tîtáns into our forces. She's even training them to work together."

I give Jokôye a small tilt of my chin, inspecting the other advisors at her back. Typically a council of seven, only five members still stand after the attack on Lagos. The thirty nobles that used to sit in the front row are now only eleven strong. They all wait in front of the floor-to-ceiling windows, Lagos's battered landscape looming behind them.

I will win your approval. I press my thumb into Zélie's coin as I ascend the marble steps of the dais that holds the throne. Ojore takes position to my left, offering protection. Mother stands by my side as I sit in the golden chair. I'm not a prince anymore.

I have to be the king my father couldn't be.

"I know these are harrowing times," I address the crowd. "I apologize for all you've suffered. All you've lost. The wounds I sustained from trying to stop the return of magic left me unconscious, but I'm here now." I squeeze the arm of the chair, scanning the mass of kosidán and tîtáns sprinkled before my eyes. "I have a plan to liberate Lagos and beat the *Iyika*. I promise to bring peace back to Orïsha!"

Cheers ring and my shoulders relax as I wait for the crowd to die down. I have to squeeze the bronze piece to keep the emotion from my face. At my side, Mother smiles.

"With the events of the past moon, there are more problems than I can count," I continue. "But I ask that you present those problems to me now. I will help you however I can."

"Excuse me." A soft voice rings from the back of the room. People part for the young woman who walks forward, a mother with two children. She passes the nobles and advisors at the front of the crowd with a crying infant pressed to her chest. Her other child, a young boy with sunken cheeks, clutches her patterned skirt.

"Your Majesty." The woman bows when she reaches the throne. From this distance, I can see the way their skin hangs from their bones. The horrible way their bellies protrude.

"I know it is not my place to ask," she says. "But we're living off scraps. If you could spare some food . . ."

Mother leans down, whispering to me under her breath. "The blocked roads have prevented food from coming in and the marketplace has been closed for weeks. It was destroyed in the *Iyika*'s first attack."

I nod, remembering the bazaar that was once full of scented spices and red meats. I inspect the crowd.

"Who else is in need?" I ask.

Hands lift throughout the hall and my chest falls. This is supposed to be the prosperous capital of my kingdom and yet in this war, my people starve.

"Captain Kunle." I turn to Father's tax collector, a balding man with bushy brows and ruddy cheeks. "How much food do we have in our reserves?"

"Around two moons' worth, Your Majesty. But that's meant to supply the palace. Any rations left over are distributed to the nobles and military officials."

"Divide its contents," I decide. "I want rations made for every civilian."

Nobles rise to their feet at my declaration. Shocked whispers pass through the crowds.

"Your Majesty, your generosity is admirable." General Jokôye steps forward. "But how do you plan to sustain the palace? The military? Yourself?"

"When I defeat the *Iyika*, the roads will reopen. I am aware of the risks."

"By the skies, we'll starve!" Jokôye shouts.

"Everyone will starve if we don't bring this war to an end." I stare her down, forcing her to stay quiet. "I want a mobile distribution center set up in the marketplace by the end of the day. That's an order."

Everyone stirs as my words echo through the throne room, but I squeeze the bronze piece, staying firm. Though the nobles' discontent swells, it can't overpower the tears that fill the young woman's eyes.

Mother squeezes my shoulder, and I feel the warmth of her pride. A smile comes to my face as a line forms before my throne.

"Alright." I wave the next villager forward. "What do you need?"

· · · · · ◆ ◇ ◆ · · · · ·

ONE BY ONE, my people come forward, presenting their problems over the course of hours: the bodies in the streets; the orphaned children; the hundreds displaced by destroyed infrastructure. With additional rations as incentive, new workforces spring up. We organize groups to collect the dead. Under my pressure, nobles open their homes to displaced villagers and parentless children.

That's it. I smile as a few tîtáns volunteer for Mother's forces. With every order, I feel my new rank. The strength I wield as a king. A moon ago, declarations like these were figments of my imagination. Now, with one word, they become law. Even those who oppose me can't oppose my rule.

"Your Majesty, if I may." General Jokôye walks forward, hands clasped behind her back. Though petite, her presence is mighty. Guards stand taller when she walks past. "I admire your benevolence, but these are bandages, not solutions. The *Iyika* are holding us hostage with their attacks. It's only a matter of time before they return to finish what they started."

The general's words are like thick clouds blocking out the rays of sun. The flicker of hope that shone in the throne room extinguishes under the realities of war.

"We can scout their location—"

"Impossible." Jokôye slashes her hand. "Every time we've sent a soldier into the forest, they've retaliated. And our scouts never return alive."

I pull at my collar as sweat gathers at my neck. "Then we'll launch a full-scale assault. Overwhelm them before they can strike—"

"To get our army out of Lagos would mean destroying the ruins that provide our only defense." Jokôye adjusts her spectacles. "Do you really intend to take that risk when we can't pinpoint the *Iyika*'s location?"

Her words are like razors slashing through my solutions. She doesn't bother to hide her disdain. The stench of disapproval gathers in the room.

"These are important questions," Mother comes to my defense. "Ones best discussed behind closed doors."

"Secrecy will serve no purpose when we're all dead. Until we eliminate the *Iyika*, all these efforts are in vain."

I flip the bronze piece between my fingers and gaze out the long windows. Father always respected Jokôye most for her honest tongue. All conversation stops as people wait for my response. I take a deep breath before rising from the throne.

"Given more time, I'll come up with a plan—"

Shouts ring from the main hall. I flinch as the sound of broken glass follows.

Though we can't see what's happening, the commotion might as well be the *Iyika* alarm.

Guards form a barrier around Mother and me as villagers dash for cover. Ojore sprints toward the noise in the main hall. The soldiers usher us toward the palace cellars. But before I take cover, I hear the assailant scream.

"Let me go!" she shrieks.

I double back, forcing my way through my guards. A broken vase lies on the tiled floor. Stale loaves of bread litter the main hall. The young thief struggles against Ojore's hold as he forces her to her knees. When he removes her hood, a head full of bright white coils springs free.

"Your Majesty, stay back." Jokôye removes her sword, holding it to the maji's neck. She gestures to the red insignia on the girl's chest that marks her as a member of the *Iyika*. "She's one of them."

"At ease, General." I raise my hand. "She's just a child looking for food."

"You weren't here when Lagos fell," Jokôye snarls. "When it comes to the maji, children might as well be fully trained soldiers."

Staring at the girl, I don't see the same threat. Her brown eyes crinkle with rage, but her breaths turn ragged as she hyperventilates. Mother tries to keep me by her side, but the bronze piece burns in my hand. I move Jokôye aside and approach the young maji, kneeling until we're face-to-face.

"I don't care if you're the king," the girl spits. "I'll burn you where you stand!"

"What's your name?" I ask.

She blinks in surprise before narrowing her angular eyes.

"My name is Raifa, and I will live to see a maji sit on that throne."

Jokôye charges forward at the threat, but I force her to stay back. I pick up the loaves on the floor, placing them back into Raifa's cotton bag.

"You don't have to steal," I tell her. "We're giving fresh food away for free."

"Inan!" Mother hisses, eyes shining with concern. Behind me, Jokôye's jaw ticks. Soldiers glare at my back. The approval I need diminishes by the second, but looking at the girl, I remember the promises I made to Zélie. I don't just want to be king.

I want to be the king my father couldn't be.

"Take this back to your people and spread the word." I hand Raifa the bag. "Let them know any defector who volunteers for the reconstruction efforts shall receive double the food rations."

The color drains from Mother's face. Her legs buckle as she finds her seat. The crowded hall erupts in anger as I hand Raifa to Ojore. He's the only one I can trust.

"Make sure she gets back to the forest in one piece."

Ojore clenches his jaw so tight I worry he'll crack a tooth, but he forces himself to bow. Rage builds as the people watch their admiral walk the rebel out the palace doors.

"Your Majesty, you spit in our faces!" Jokôye roars, inciting her soldiers' cheers. "These maggots have destroyed our home. They've killed the people we loved—"

"So have we!" I cut her off. "For decades. We strike them. They strike us. The cycle never ends!"

Mother's cheeks are so pale, she looks like she may faint. But she doesn't understand the things I've seen. No one knows the things I've felt.

"If you were a maji and your powers returned, what would you have done?" I address the crowd. "Their families were slaughtered under Father's reign. We sent half their people to the stocks! Until this moment, the maji have had two choices—fight against us or face persecution. With this decree, they will have another option. An opportunity for lasting peace they've never been afforded."

Though I look for support in the crowd, no one comes to my defense. The advisors keep me under cold glares. Any goodwill I built with the military slips away.

"You may not agree with my methods, but this is a chance for peace." I face Jokôye again. "We only survive if both sides put down their arms."

Jokôye shakes her head, but she doesn't push back on my rule. Father always valued her loyalty. If I could earn her trust, I know I would value it, too.

"What about those who won't join us?" Jokôye asks. "Those who shall spit on your offer?"

"Any maji who makes that choice will suffer my wrath. I promise, I will not hold back."

CHAPTER TWENTY-TWO

AMARI

I BRACE MYSELF as Nâo and Mâzeli lead us past the sanctuary's narrow dormitories and half-constructed towers. Bodies crowd along the second mountain of the *Iyika*'s base as word of our arrival spreads like wildfire.

"Out of my way!" Mâzeli revels in the attention. "Soldier of Death coming through!"

The title echoes around Zélie as we move, inciting whispers through the crowd. People stare at her as if she were a goddess. They look at me like I'm a bug.

I don't know if they glare because they know who I am or because of the white streak in my hair. I attempt to tuck it away as we pass under the vine-covered archway of the mountain's largest tower.

"The elder quarters fill the floors above," Nâo explains. "But we use the ground floor as the cafeteria."

"Thank the skies." My mouth waters at the scent of spiced chicken and fried plantain. Platters of jollof rice line the far wall; it's more food than I've seen in moons. But my appetite quells when Nâo leads us toward the table of elders in the back. Though they wear the same suits of armor as their counterparts, the five clan heads present radiate natural power.

"Council, allow me to introduce the future of the Reaper clan." Mâzeli charges forward. "The legend of the lands. The eventual mother of my three sons—"

"Mâzeli, shut up." Nâo hits the boy over the head before taking her place on an empty stool. "Elders, the Soldier of Death joins us at last."

Zélie tenses as every elder stops talking. All eyes fall to her. *"Jagunjagun Ikú"* echoes around the cafeteria.

I clear my throat, waiting for my introduction to follow, but it's like I'm not even here. Not one elder seems to care.

"Jagunjagun." A girl with a scar over her left eye speaks first. A few years older than us, she sits with her back against the wall, one arm draped over her knee. My lips part as I take in the forest of white coils that frame her light brown skin; the freckles splattered across her flat nose. I've seen this girl before.

The rebel from the rally!

She glared at me from the crowd, red paint staining her hands. From the way the others wait on her word, I can tell she's their unspoken leader.

"Ramaya." She drops to one knee. "Elder of the Connector clan. It's an honor to meet the soldier who brought our magic back."

"I didn't act alone." Zélie gestures to me. "I had a lot of help."

Ramaya's eyes flick in my direction, but she looks through me as if I was glass. My insides burn when she steps closer to Zélie, extending her hand.

"We look forward to having you on the council."

"Oh, I don't know about that," Zélie says. "I'm only here to win this war."

"Winning's just the beginning," Ramaya pushes back. "With your strength, we can annihilate Nehanda and her tîtáns. Once the monarchy's out of the way, we can place you on the throne."

"Wait, what?" Zélie jerks her head back and the two of us lock eyes. I don't even know what to say. I can't find my voice.

"Who better to lead us than the Soldier of Death?" Ramaya asks.

My throat dries as I step forward, a feeble attempt to insert myself into the conversation. But before I can get a word out, another elder blows past us.

"There's word from Lagos." The Tamer sits down, a thick girl with broad shoulders and rich curves. Sunflowers rest in her luscious head of curls. Small hummingbirds flutter around their petals.

The Tamer's pink-tinted armor glistens as she hands Ramaya a small parchment from the yellow hummingbird on her shoulder.

"You're kidding." Ramaya's face falls when she reads the note. "The prince is alive?"

Inan? I lean forward, attempting to see the black ink.

"I know." The Tamer rolls her eyes. "Killing these royals is like killing roaches." She locks eyes with Zélie and nods, tossing her white curls. "Na'imah," she introduces herself. "I would bow, but I don't bow to anyone."

"This doesn't make sense." Ramaya shakes her head. "Why would the king offer food and gold to any maji who defect?"

Zélie reaches for the note, but I beat her to the punch. Ramaya bristles as I scan the report, but even she can't dim the light of Inan's decree. My hand flies to my heart as I read his promises, his bold attempts at peace. It's more than I've seen from any monarch.

I knew he could be this kind of king.

"Zélie, look." I push the parchment in her hands, fighting the lump in my throat. "He's keeping his word!"

My mind starts to spin as I consider everything this decree could mean. I thought I needed power to take Mother off Orïsha's throne and build a kingdom that was safe for the maji. But if Inan's willing to grant amnesty to the *Iyika*, we may not need to fight.

If I could talk to him, we might be able to reach an agreement that satisfies both sides. With the right terms, we could get the monarchy and the maji to put down their arms!

"You've faced the king." Ramaya looks to Zélie. "What do you make of this?"

Zélie's face hardens as she stares at the note. My stomach drops when she throws it to the ground.

"If the little prince is offering food to the maji, there's poison in it."

"Zélie, no!" I whisper under my breath, but her words incite the other elders.

"He's good with his words, but you'd be a fool to believe any of them."

"What do you suggest?" Na'imah leans forward. "How do we strike back?"

"That food is all they have," Zélie says. "Burn it and let them starve."

"No!" I fight my way through, pushing until I can place my hands on their table. "Burn that food and you won't just endanger the people of Lagos. You'll escalate the war the king's trying to end!"

The entire cafeteria quiets down in the wake of my outburst. Ramaya blinks at me, as if surprised I can speak.

"Apologies." I clear my throat. "I haven't introduced myself."

"Oh, I know who you are." The ice in Ramaya's tone chills me to the bone. "Your mother is the reason we lost Lagos. Your father is the reason I have this scar." She rises from her seat and the others move out of her way. "What I don't know is why you think you have a right to even breathe in my presence."

My cheeks heat as all eyes land on me. There's not one warm face in the crowd. Only Mâzeli gifts me a sympathetic frown.

"I helped bring magic back." I square my chest. "I have magic myself."

"The abomination you call magic doesn't earn you a place at this table. It certainly doesn't earn you the right to have an opinion." Ramaya looks me up and down before turning back to Zélie. "I look forward to working with you on the council. We'll hold a Reaper challenge and make your ascension official tomorrow."

"What about the king's decree?" Nâo asks.

"I agree with Zélie. Give the order to our soldiers at the front. I want those rations burned by sunrise."

"Ramaya, wait." I try to grab her arms, but she stops me with a look.

"Speak at my table again and I'll rip out your tongue with my bare hands."

I inhale a shaking breath as she walks away, causing the other elders to follow her path. My lips quiver with everything I want to scream. I can't believe how easily they reject Inan's attempt at peace.

"What are you doing?" I turn to Zélie. "You could've convinced them to give peace a chance!"

"That offer wasn't peace." Zélie shakes her head. "It was bait. Inan's using food the same way he used Baba. He'll kill any maji who tries to claim it."

I open my mouth to argue, but I know there's nothing I can say. There's no convincing her to give my brother another chance after all those two have been through.

"Just stick to the plan," Zélie says. "We can use the *Iyika* to take your family down. The elders will warm up to you when they know you can be trusted."

"They'll never trust me." I stare at the stool where Ramaya sat. I can still feel the heat of her disdain; her hatred for what I am. "But maybe they can respect me . . ."

My voice trails as I look at my scarred hand.

"What are you thinking?" Zélie asks.

"I need you to help me with my magic."

CHAPTER TWENTY-THREE

INAN

MY HEART BEATS in my throat as Mother and I make our way down the merchant quarter to welcome the *Iyika* defectors. Our soldiers have wasted no time on repairs since the rebels' last attack. In just a few days, all the bodies in the marketplace have been cleared.

We step over the scattered debris swept to the sides of Lagos's streets to make room for the new ration carts. The stands have only been open since dawn, yet the line of villagers waiting for food still goes all the way to the divîner dwellings.

"Inan, are you sure about this?" Mother grabs the reins of my snow leopanaire, pulling me close. Behind us, soldiers usher the villagers into underground bunkers created by Mother and her tîtáns. "Jokôye put you on the spot. That maggot threw you off guard. You're doing great work, but it's alright to change your mind."

She voices the thoughts that've been bouncing around my skull all night. I have no idea if this will work. If this is truly what's best for Orïsha.

We ride past the remains of the divîner slums, and I don't know whether the destruction tells me to move forward or turn back. There was something beautiful in the rainbow shanties that surrounded my city. Now they're only mounds of rubble and ash.

I stop in front of a giant hill that used to house fifty shacks; now only sheets of painted metal twist out of the dirt.

"Did the *Iyika* do this?"

"No." Mother shakes her head. "I did."

A ferocity shines in her amber gaze, one I haven't witnessed before. Every attempt I've made to do magic has almost left me comatose, but Mother seems to command the might of gods.

"I didn't know I wasn't like the others until those maggots attacked," she says. "The new tîtáns harmed themselves with their abilities, but I was able to absorb their power. I wielded it with a strength no maji could match." Her voice rises in pitch as her conviction builds. "For so long we've been defenseless against the havoc the maji wreak, but now the gods have blessed us as well. We're powerful enough to annihilate them, Inan. The only way to achieve lasting peace is to cleanse the maggots from this land."

Her words make my fingers grow cold. To cleanse Orïsha of maji would be finishing Father's work. It would be another Raid.

As we approach the ruin walls shielding Lagos from the forest, the weight of the world presses down on my shoulders. I'm out of time. I need to make a choice.

"I can break through these ruins," Mother says. "But I cannot bring them back. Do you really want to risk our only defense for a few rebellious maggots?"

General Jokôye and the other advisors watch from a safe distance, but their disapproval hangs over me like the smoke in the air. If I'm wrong, we could all suffer. *But if I'm right . . .*

Raifa's sunken brown eyes sear their way through the noise in my head. The young Burner may have spit in my face, but like the rest of my villagers, sharp bones protruded from her sagging skin.

"We have to try." I exhale a deep breath. "I have to *try*."

This is my chance to bring the peace my father couldn't.

Mother purses her lips together, but nods as she dismounts in front of the ruin walls. At a sharp wave of her hand, her tîtáns form a circle around her, imposing in their golden suits of armor.

"Your Majesty, this is a mistake." Jokôye shakes her head as I join her and the other members of the royal council.

"General, I know how you feel, but the maji need peace as much as we do."

"They don't care about peace," Ojore mutters. "They want victory no matter the cost."

His hand travels to the burn scars on his neck and I glance up at the sky. *Please*, I send the prayer to whatever gods lie above. *Prove me right. Let them be wrong.*

All conversation halts when Mother summons her magic. The air twists around her as she opens her hands, igniting an emerald glow within her chest. Deep greens crackle around her golden armor like lightning and veins bulge against her neck. Mother stretches out her fingers, making the circle of tîtáns around her freeze in place.

"Skies," I curse, flinching at the sight. The tîtáns around Mother seize, grunting as she rips the ashê from their veins.

The soldiers fall to their knees when Mother's eyes glow green. With a grunt, she thrusts her hands forward and her power breaks free. Emerald light cuts through the mounds of rubble like a knife, carving the dirt wall into pieces.

We shield our eyes as the ruin wall explodes, a mess of twisted metal and debris flying through the air. My chest tightens when the smoke starts to clear. Seven members of the *Iyika* stand at the top of the highest hill overlooking Lagos.

Here we go.

Stillness descends as we take the rebels in. Dirt mars their faces and white coils. Frayed kaftans hang from their limbs. They don't look friendly, but their presence is enough. It's the first sign of hope.

The first sign this peace could work.

"Raifa." I raise a hand to the young Burner standing in front. She takes the first step forward. I mirror her approach.

"I'm glad you came."

Mother tries to keep me from stepping beyond the broken gates, but I push her away. If this is going to work, they need to see that I trust them. They must think I'm not afraid.

"It's alright." I wave the others forward. "You're protected under my orders."

Raifa doesn't say a word. Despite our distance, I can hear her labored breaths. But as she nears, she extends her hand. I smile at her resolve, extending mine as well.

Then I see the sparks firing at her fingertips.

"Protect the king!" Mother's voice turns shrill. In a second, chaos abounds. Soldiers drag me back as Mother's tîtáns storm forward, deploying every majacite bomb they have.

Shattered glass rings as their orbs break. Someone forces a golden mask over my face. My head spins as the poisonous gas coats the battlefield, making it impossible to see the action.

"Mother!" My scar burns as I wait for the blackness to clear. When the smoke thins, I break free, praying the bodies on the ground aren't any of my soldiers.

"Is everyone alright?" My voice cracks as I approach the maji lying in the scorched earth. The rebels are burned beyond recognition. Their skin sizzles as the majacite lingers over their corpses.

Though some of my soldiers sport new scrapes and bruises, all of my men and women still stand. Mother wipes a line of blood from her lips and spits.

"Filthy maggots."

"I'm sorry." I stumble back, struggling to stay on my feet. My body starts to shake as everything that just happened hits me. I thought I was taking the first step toward peace. I risked everything to be a different kind of king. But the *Iyika* didn't even make it into the city before they staged their attack.

Ojore was right; the maji don't want peace.

They want victory no matter the cost.

Mother's brows soften as she takes in my despair. She sighs and takes me by the hand. "You were leading with your heart, but you must realize that not every person in Orïsha deserves it."

I force myself to nod, squeezing the bronze piece to quell the tremor in my hand. "I won't make that mistake again."

"Wait." We look up as Ojore walks among the corpses on the ground. "There are only six bodies here. I counted seven on top of that hill."

I jog forward, stomach dropping when I realize which face is missing.

"Where's the girl?" I shout. "Where is Raifa?"

Confusion spreads as people search the woods, but I catch her lanky silhouette behind the broken ruin walls. She whips around when she hears her name, a golden mask fixed over her face.

Panic fills her large brown eyes and she looks to the single path leading back to the marketplace. It's then I understand her true target.

The others were just a distraction.

"Stop her!" I command.

Raifa rips off her mask, sprinting as fast as her thin legs will allow. Her white hair bounces along her back as she races past the divîner dwellings, reaching the ruins of the merchant quarter.

Soldiers defending the ration carts move into her path, but Raifa stretches out her hand. Sparks fly from her fingers as she shouts.

"Iná òrìsà, gbó ìpè mi!"

A tîtán tackles her to the ground, but her embers still take to the air. They grow brighter as they fly through the sky. Horror floods me when the flames reach their full size.

Five comets race toward the ration carts. People dive out of the way. My heart seizes when they strike.

In a flash, the rations go up in flames.

"No!" I fall to my knees and clutch my chest, struggling to breathe as our food burns. A rage that doesn't feel like my own floods me from my core.

Half of our rations.

Destroyed in seconds.

"This is only the beginning!" Raifa shouts, thrashing as more soldiers hold her down. She trembles when Ojore stomps toward her, but she continues to yell. "Your time is over! All of Lagos will burn! The Soldier of Death is coming—"

I flinch as Ojore silences her with his sword.

The Soldier of Death is coming.

I don't need to see a face to know who the title describes. Zélie swore she'd be my end. I just didn't expect her to attack so fast. I underestimated the resources and soldiers she had at her command.

"Are you satisfied, Your Majesty?" Jokôye seethes at my back. "Thank the skies for your ideals!"

Raifa's blood pools as soldiers try to extinguish the flames in the marketplace, but there's no salvaging the food that burns. Even as my body shakes with rage, sorrow fills my heart.

I take in the despair of my advisors; the fury of my soldiers. From afar, villagers start to exit the underground tunnels. What will they do when they see I've condemned them to be raided by the *Iyika* or starve to death?

"I'll fix this," I shout. "I promise."

I just wish I knew how.

CHAPTER TWENTY-FOUR

AMARI

MY THROAT BURNS as yellow bile splatters across the wild grass. Somehow it carries the sweet scent of fried plantain. The smell makes me nauseous again.

As Zélie and I train on the hilly terrain outside the *Iyika* sanctuary, I wonder what I'm doing wrong. No matter what I try, using my tîtán magic is like torture. My powers rage beyond my control.

"Maybe this was a bad idea." Zélie flinches, turning away when I start to heave. "At this rate, your magic will do more harm to you than anyone else."

I reach to wipe the bile off my chin, but it stings to lift my hand. Zélie shakes her head at the burns along my palm. The blistered skin turns red.

"I'm fine," I say. "I just have to keep pushing."

"Keep pushing and you could kill yourself. Is that really what you want?"

My arms shake as I turn over, lying on the grass. After hours of failed training, my lungs burn with each inhale. But every time I get close to giving up, I picture Ramaya's scar.

Speak at my table again, and I'll rip out your tongue with my bare hands.

The *Iyika* will never respect me unless I can prove my power. I need control of my magic if I want to win them over to my side.

I push past my pain and rise. But before I can summon my magic again, Zélie stops me.

"It's not about how hard you push," she sighs. "Follow me. I can explain."

I trail after her as we descend into the jungle's valleys, ducking under hanging vines and curving around mammoth trees. Creaking cicadas form the chorus of the night. Above us, baboonems leap from hanging vines.

Though my muscles ache, I enjoy the serenity of the space as we come to the flowing river along the sanctuary's dirt trail. Zélie points to a section of water filtering through a pile of thick rocks as she kneels.

"Think of this water as our ashê," she explains. "The spiritual energy in our blood. When maji use incantations, it's like lifting one of these rocks. The magic flows freely, allowing us to cast safely."

She picks up a rock and I follow the new path of water that moves through the natural dam. I imagine the lavender magic flowing through Zélie's body, filling her veins like a glowing spiderweb.

"It's like threading a needle?"

"Something like that." Zélie nods. "The energy that flows free isn't as powerful as yours, but it's precise. It can be wielded to do more."

Zélie pauses, scanning the rock pile until she lands on the largest. "As a tîtán, you're using blood magic by design. That means you have no precision. No control." She lifts the heavy stone and the water explodes, gushing through the new path. "It's the equivalent of releasing all the ashê in your blood at once. Magic like that is a result."

I stare at my scarred hands, starting to understand the source of my pain. All night, it's felt like a fire raging from within, burning me with each attempt I make.

"If my magic is a needle, then yours is a hammer," Zélie says. "Without control, you and the people around you get hurt. Release too much ashê and you won't just feel pain. You'll drown."

I pinch my lips together as I mull over her words. If what Zélie says is true, every tîtán is a danger to themselves. How many have already perished from taking their magic too far?

"But what about my mother?" I ask. "She channeled more ashê than any tîtán. Why didn't it kill her?"

"I don't know." Zélie takes a shuddering breath at the thought. "I've never seen power like hers. It's like she's something else."

I take a deep breath, rising back to my feet. I attempt to turn Zélie's explanation around, searching for a solution instead of a condemnation.

"If I'm using blood magic by design, then I just need control," I say. "We can fix that if you teach me an incantation!"

Zélie's nostrils flare and she steps back. Her shoulders grow tense. "Yoruba is sacred to our people. It's not just something you can learn."

"This is bigger than that." I wave my hand. "For skies' sake, we're at war—"

"Our magic isn't about the war!" Zélie shouts. "Our incantations are the history of our people. They're the very thing your father tried to destroy!" Her chest heaves up and down and she shakes her head. "Tîtáns have already stolen our magic. You can't steal this, too."

"Steal?" I tilt my head. "Zélie, what are you talking about? How else am I supposed to learn control?"

"You don't need control," she says. "You don't need to use your magic at all!"

"If I don't have my own power, who am I supposed to count on?" I extend my arms. "It took less than five minutes with the *Iyika* for you to stab me in the back!"

"Stab you in the ba—" Zélie stops, snorting to herself. "So that's what this foolishness is about. After everything he's done, you still want to trust Inan."

My cheeks heat and I turn away, hugging myself. I know there's no way to explain it to her, but I know my brother's heart. If he was offering that food, it had to be real. There was a chance for us to end this war, yet she destroyed it without a second thought.

"My plans haven't changed," Zélie says. "I still want to see you on Orïsha's throne. But I won't apologize because I'm no longer stupid enough to believe your brother's lies."

A hard silence settles between us, chilling the jungle air. I want to trust Zélie, but deep down I know our interests aren't aligned. At the end of the day, Inan is my blood. To her, he's just the bastard who broke her heart.

I can't leave this fight to Zélie anymore than I can leave it to Ramaya. I need my own power if I'm going to win this war.

"I wouldn't ask if there was another way," I sigh. "But my mother is bringing buildings down on our heads. I can't keep relying on my sword. It's your duty to fight for the maji, but as queen, I'm responsible for all of them. I have to take care of the kosidán who're running scared. The tîtán soldiers Mother's sucking the very life from. I'm responsible for the maji who hate my guts, and I can't help anyone until I have power of my own."

"Amari, no." Zélie steps forward, softening her tone. "This isn't all on you. It's not your job to save Orïsha."

"If I don't, who will?" I ask. "You said it yourself—you don't trust Inan to stick to his word."

I rub my tired eyes, trying to keep my pain locked inside. I think of every life my actions have ruined. Every person who's died because I'm not sitting on Orïsha's throne.

"I'm the only person fighting for all sides. I can't do that without my magic. If you don't want to help me . . . fine. I'll find someone who will."

I start to walk away, but Zélie grabs my arm. My eyes widen as her shoulders slump and she exhales a long breath.

"You'll help me?" I ask.

"On one condition," she says. "If I'm going to teach you an incantation, you have to use it against tîtáns. Not maji."

I nod, understanding the weight of her words. "I promise. I'll only use this against Mother and her forces."

Zélie's feet drag as we take position, but she raises her arms.

"Okay." She positions my hands. "Square your legs and repeat after me."

CHAPTER TWENTY-FIVE

·····◆◇◆·····

ZÉLIE

THE NEXT MORNING, it's a struggle to keep my eyes open. Amari made us train all night. We didn't get back to the sanctuary until sunrise. But as the other two Reapers in my clan prepare me for the elder ascension, I fight the urge to escape the safety of the sanctuary's walls. I just wanted to find a way to win this war.

I'm not ready to be an elder.

"Grab the clean water," Bimpe, the older of the two girls, instructs. The young Reapers flutter around me in ill-fitting sêntaro robes. Bimpe stands so tall, the hem ends at her knees. Patches of discoloration circle her eyes and mouth, creating a beautiful pattern on her brown skin.

Beside her, Mári swims in the thick black robes, still short at the tender age of thirteen. Whenever she smiles up at me, I see the adorable gap between her front teeth.

Their presence warms the weathered walls of the Reaper Temple, a sacred site. Painted tiles create a mosaic over our heads, purple and red swirls depicting the Reaper elders of the past. Tear-shaped lanterns hang from the domed ceilings, lavender light bleeding through their tinted glass. I stare up at them as Bimpe scrubs me from head to toe, replacing the dirt along my skin with lemon-scented oils.

"Have you thought about your Second?" Mári whispers, ignoring

Bimpe's glare. She pulls down her hood, revealing her two large buns. "Because if you haven't—"

Mári cringes when Bimpe slaps the back of her head.

"*Jagunjagun*, please ignore her," Bimpe says. "She knows not to bother you before your ascension."

I hide my laughter as Mári sticks out her tongue. When Bimpe walks away to grab a comb, Mári leans in close.

"I can make *four* animations."

"Four?" I raise my brows. "That's impressive."

"With your training, I'll learn to make more," she whispers. "Maybe ones even bigger than Mâzeli's!"

She snaps her mouth shut when Bimpe returns, but we exchange knowing smiles. I stay quiet as Bimpe works the iron comb through my hair. Mári slides thick gold rings onto my fingers. When I'm clean, they help me into a billowing red skirt, its train so long it glides across the stone floor. Bimpe grabs a matching swatch of deep red silk.

"Almost done," she says.

I try to ignore the way my scars lie on full display as they drape the fabric over my chest. They tie a thick bow in back to hide the horrible marks.

"These symbols," Mári breathes, hands hovering over the golden tattoos that start at the base of my neck. "Should we cover them?"

"Not completely," Bimpe says. "They're a part of her."

I bow my head as Bimpe takes the traditional collar away and fastens a gold band around my neck. Lines of glittering beads spill from the collar, falling over my chest and down my back. They brush the leather sandals strapped to my feet. With the beaded headdress they place along my coils, I look like Mama.

Like Oya come to life.

"Our work is finished." Bimpe bows, an action Mári mimics.

"You look incredible!" Her brown eyes shine. "Much prettier than Mâzeli!"

"Thank you." I smile as they bow again. But when they walk out the door, all the tightness returns to my chest.

The Reaper Temple sits at the top of the third mountain, yet I can hear the chatter of all the maji waiting at its base. I don't know how I'm supposed to protect an entire clan when I couldn't protect Baba. I can barely protect myself.

The ships I watched from Roën's mercenary den sail through my mind as I sit back down. I know being an elder will help me take out Inan, but with each passing day, the freedom I crave seems to slip further and further away.

"Wow."

I turn to find Tzain standing in the doorframe. He lets out a low whistle, a dazed smile on his face.

"It's like you're getting married."

"I basically am." I sink into his hug. "But instead of tying my life to one person, I'm shackling myself to an entire clan."

"Ay, come on now. Before the Raid you wouldn't shut up about joining the other Reapers."

"I was just a child. But now . . ." My voice trails off and I close my eyes, not knowing what to say.

"Too much has passed?" he asks.

"Too much has been taken away."

Silence descends as I sit back down, thinking of everything and everyone we've lost. Magic used to be the thing that made me feel most alive, but now it's impossible to wield it without thinking of everyone who's died.

I know I have no choice; I can't defeat Inan without the *Iyika*'s help. But to become an elder and take on this sacred role?

It just feels wrong.

"You're scared." Tzain kneels in front of me. "But there's no one better for this job. Say what you want, but I remember the way your eyes lit up after you and Mama watched that Reaper elder ascend."

The memory he speaks of comes flooding back in. I see Mama's beautiful dark skin; her crown of thick white hair.

The last time a new Reaper elder was chosen, we traveled all the way to Lokoja to witness his ascension. Mama squeezed my hand as the ritual started. Her palms always smelled of coconut oil.

I remember holding my breath when the ascension site lit up with a deep purple light, the sign of Oya's presence. Black smoke filled the ritual grounds, obscuring the new elder from our view.

"*What's happening?*" I whispered.

"*His ìsípayá,*" she whispered back. "*Every clan elder receives a piece of their god's wisdom when they ascend. The prophecy is meant to help them lead their clans.*"

"*I want an ìsípayá!*" I said, and Mama laughed.

"*Me too.*" She held me tight. "*One day we might get one for ourselves.*"

I didn't know what it meant to be an elder back then. I just knew that whatever Mama wanted, I had to have.

"You can do this." Tzain helps me to my feet. "I know it. You just need to prove it to yourself."

I nod and exhale a deep breath, looking back to the temple door.

"Okay," I say. "Let's go."

．．．．．◆◈◆．．．．．

A HUSH FALLS over the crowd of maji as Mama Agba steps into the stone circle at the base of the third mountain. Almost eighty members of the *Iyika* watch from the stone's borders, accompanied by the divîners in their clan. Mama Agba looks like a goddess in a tall, silver headwrap and matching patterned cloak. The shining silk glides behind her as she walks to the center of the circle, white paint highlighting her brow and tracing her cheekbone.

"The gods are smiling today," she addresses the crowd. "Your ancestors smile as well. Each time a new elder rises to lead their clan, we breathe life into what our enemies tried to destroy!"

Cheers echo throughout the crowd and I have to inhale to take it all in. It's a sight I wish I could carry to Baba's grave. For the first time, his death feels like it means something.

"Before the Raid, the role of elder was reserved for the most powerful maji in a clan," Mama Agba continues. "If one believed that title belonged to them, they had the right to challenge for the chance to prove it. Alternatively, an elder could recognize a new power and step aside. It has been brought to my attention that is what one of you would like to do now."

Mama Agba clasps her hands together and turns to the three Reapers gathered in the far corner. Though it's the smallest clan at the sanctuary, seeing that many Reapers in one place makes my throat tight. A few moons ago, there were no Reapers in Orïsha at all.

"Mâzeli Adesanya," Mama Agba declares. "Elder of the Reaper clan. You are faced with a challenger. Do you want to concede or accept?"

Mâzeli puffs out his chest as he walks across the bloodstone. A black silk robe hangs off his shoulders, its dark base accented with Reaper purples.

"I happily concede." He bows in my direction. "Who else could lead the Reapers than the Soldier of Death herself?"

His call makes hollers erupt throughout the mountain. The shouts should bolster me, but instead sweat gathers along my temples. It feels like the world presses down on my shoulders as I rise. Every footstep I take across the bloodstone stretches into an eternity.

I think of my fantasy of sailing away. I feel the burn of my scars. But as I meet Mama Agba in the center, I can't deny the hunger in my heart.

"Zélie Adebola." Mama Agba's voice thickens with emotion as I kneel before her. Her mahogany eyes sparkle with tears; I have to dig my nails into my palm to keep my own in.

"Ṣé o gba àwọn ènìyàn wònyí gégé bí ara rẹ? Ṣé ìwọ yóò lo gbogbo agbára rẹ láti dábòbò wón ni gbogbo ònà?"

Do you accept these people as your own?

Will you use your strength to protect them at all cost?

The burden of her questions expands in my chest as I look to the Reapers gathered around Mâzeli. Bimpe watches with fingers pressed to her lips. Mári frantically waves her hand, almost immune to the gravity of the moment. Though I've only known them for a few hours, they already feel like blood. Like home. Being around them feels more right than anything has felt in years.

"What do you say?" Mama Agba asks.

I square my shoulders and nod. For the first time since the Raid, I see our potential. The beauty in what we could become.

"Mo gbà. Mà á se é." My throat tightens with the weight of my vow. "I will protect these Reapers with everything I have."

Mama Agba wipes the single tear that falls from her eye before dipping her thumb into a canister of glittering purple pigment. She paints a crescent along my forehead and a sharp line along my jaw. The entire mountain is silent as she finishes her blessing with an intricate design over my left eye. I keep still as she surrounds my feet with offerings of cinnamon and sweetgrass.

"I know your parents are proud." She kisses my forehead. "As am I."

I smile, thinking of what they would say if they were here now. Mama would've become the youngest Reaper elder in history. Now that honor falls to me.

"Your hand, my child."

I extend my palm and she pulls out a black dagger.

"Let your vow be recorded in blood," she declares. "Before your people. Before your gods!"

Mama Agba makes a clean cut across my palm and slams my hand into the center of the circle. I lurch forward as the stone lights up. Magic heats the air around me as more than blood is pulled from my form.

Gasps echo throughout the crowd as my hand bonds to the stone surface. The purple light spreads like the threads of a giant spiderweb. Embers crackle around my head. Veins bulge against my skin.

With a flash, the light beneath me explodes in clouds of purple smoke. The fog is so thick that even Mama Agba disappears. The smoke swallows all sound.

The rest of the mountain fades away as my vision blacks out. My tattoos hum against my neck.

Then Oya lights up the dark.

My gods . . .

No matter how many times I witness her power, it always steals the air from my throat. I can't breathe as Oya swirls before me, larger than life itself. Her skirts spin in a brilliant hurricane of red. A deep purple light glows around her obsidian skin. A teardrop of ashê breaks from her hand, glowing brighter as it falls through the blackness.

Every muscle in my body tenses as I prepare for her gift, the sacred wisdom only an *ìsípayá* can give. It was a Tamer's *ìsípayá* that led to the massive ryders we use today. A Reaper's *ìsípayá* that gave birth to the first animations. The same hunger I had as a child consumes me now as I open my hands, waiting for mine.

The teardrop of ashê floats into my palms and my eyes light with its purple glow. My skin heats as the *ìsípayá* takes hold.

It starts with a purple ribbon of light, spinning from my chest like a thread. A ribbon of gold appears next, twisting out of the blackness. Tangerines and emeralds join the fold, each light weaving themselves together. They intertwine like the roots of a mammoth tree, creating a power so great it roars like a lionaire.

Questions fill my mind as I extend my hand, reaching out to touch the spinning rainbow of magic. But as my fingers approach its searing heat, the ribbons of light disappear.

I snap back into the present.

"*Ugh!*" I wheeze, pitching forward onto my knees. I hold up my shaking palm, but any sign of Mama Agba's cut is gone.

When the smoke clears, Mama Agba extends her hand. Pride shines through her brown eyes as she helps me to my feet.

The rainbow of my *ìsípayá* fills my mind as Mama Agba turns me to face the crowd. When she raises up my arm, my heart sings as the entire mountain roars.

CHAPTER TWENTY-SIX

INAN

As the sun sets on Lagos, I finally decide how to respond to the *Iyika's* attack on our rations. Right now we're sitting ducks, but if I could locate their camp, we could launch our own offense.

If I don't free Lagos from their grasp, we won't have a shot at winning this war. At this rate, they'll storm our broken walls or let us starve to death.

I have to act now. Before it's too late.

I wait until night falls. Until the sliver of candlelight turns to blackness outside Father's door. By the time all falls quiet in the palace, a half-moon hangs in the smoke-filled sky.

I crawl out of bed, replacing my embroidered robe with a tattered kaftan. A stolen canister of black pigment sits under my pillow. I pull it out and cover the white streak in my hair.

Hopefully this is enough. I shift, inspecting my reflection in Father's mirror. The last time I wore something so simple, I was with my sister and Zélie in the divîner camp. It all seems so far away, it feels like it never happened at all. Back then I was only a prince. Zélie wasn't the Soldier of Death.

This is only the beginning! Raifa's words terrorize my thoughts. *All of Lagos will burn!*

If I don't find a way to stop the *Iyika,* the fall of Orïsha will be my fault.

I crack open my window, inspecting the drop from above. Father's quarters sit on the fifth floor of the palace, but a series of balconies and railings stand below. I climb onto the ledge, holding the windowsill for support. If I time it just right . . .

"You'd better be sneaking out to meet a girl."

I jump at the deep voice, nearly tumbling from the windowsill. Ojore stands in my doorway, arms crossed with a sly smile on his face.

"If you are, I'll look the other way," he says. "You could use a nice lay."

"Then that's where I'm going." I look back out at the jump. "You never saw this."

"Oh, give me more than that." Ojore closes the door behind him. "You're about to risk death. At least tell me her name."

Though he jokes, Zélie's face fills my mind. I think of her mane of white hair. Her silver gaze. Her dark skin.

For an instant, I'm alone with her in the dreamscape's waterfall, too ignorant to understand what will come. But I don't get to sit with the memory before I remember the pain of her black vines choking me to death.

"What happened yesterday was because of me," I sigh. "Me and this girl. If she's leading the *Iyika* now, it's only a matter of time before they attack Lagos again."

"So what do you intend to do?" Ojore crosses his arms. "Smooth it over with a kiss?"

"The *Iyika* are in that forest. If I can find their location, we can attack. I truly think Mother's magic is powerful enough."

I try to jump, but Ojore grabs my arm, forcing me to stay back. "You can't go after them alone."

"I can't ask anyone to risk their life for me again." I shake my head. "Not after what I caused. The *Iyika* achieved a great victory yesterday, but they also suffered a great loss. No matter their numbers, their guard will be down. This is the best chance I have to locate them."

Ojore stares at me before releasing a heavy sigh. My brows furrow as he removes his brass breastplate, placing it next to my canister of black paint.

"What're you doing?" I ask.

"What do you think?" He grabs an old pair of pants off my floor. "Like I said—you're not going in alone."

• • • • • ◆ ◇ ◆ • • • • •

OJORE AND I TAKE OFF, moving under the cover of darkness. We duck past the soldiers stationed around the palace. The guards outside Mother's door.

When we make it into the marketplace, it takes a full hour to get past Lagos's broken gates on foot. We pick up speed when we finally reach the charred forest surrounding the capital, beyond the military's watch.

"All we have to do is find them," I repeat my plan. "Find them, and Mother can take care of the rest."

I look at my own hands, wondering if my power could ever match hers. Out of curiosity, I reach for my magic, but my skin burns with the faint blue wisps that fall from my fingertips. I grab my temple as the meager attempt causes a splitting headache.

"It still hurts?" Ojore observes me, and I nod. The more time that passes, the more I worry my magic will always be like this. Before the ritual I could stun my opponents. Now I only seem to stun myself.

"It was never easy," I say. "But it used to respond when I was in need. I almost grew used to having it around. It was like another part of me."

Ojore wrinkles his nose, and I wonder if I've said too much. But before I can say more, branches rustle to our left.

My heart jumps into my throat and I grab my sword, waiting for the maji to attack. But when a spotted hyenaire runs past, relief almost brings me to my knees.

"Skies." I press my hand against my chest, attempting to calm my racing pulse. I look back at Ojore, but he still hasn't moved. A faraway look plagues his eyes.

"Are you alright?" I ask. Ojore's free hand trembles by his side. It takes a few moments for him to fall back into himself. When he finally does, he turns away from me.

I feel the heat of his shame.

"You need a minute?"

"I'm fine." He starts moving ahead, but I grab his arm, forcing him to stay still. Moments pass in silence as I wait for him to recover. It's strange to see him this way.

The Ojore I know always rushes into battle.

He never seems afraid.

"I don't know why it had to be Burners." He closes his eyes. "I'm sure the *Iyika* have Reapers. Cancers. They could've attacked with anything but fire."

He touches the burns on his neck, and his face twists with pain. I can almost see the flames burning in his mind. Staring at Ojore, I wonder if this was part of Zélie's plan. Moons ago I brought the fire to her shores. I burnt her people. I destroyed her home.

This could be her way of paying me back.

"If you don't want to do this——"

Ojore holds up his hand, cutting me off. "They've tortured us long enough. It's time for those maggots to crawl back into the dirt."

The hatred that settles on his face looks out of place, so different from the grin I know. I open my mouth to say more, but Ojore forges ahead. I have no choice but to follow.

Another hour passes as the distance stretches between us and Lagos.

It feels like we're halfway to Ilorin before we finally hear chatter. As soon as it echoes, we stop in our tracks. My muscles tense as we crouch behind a tree, scouting the *Iyika*'s camp.

"There it is," I whisper, leaning forward to get a better look. A few dozen meters ahead, the rebels cook a hyenaire over an open fire. They all sport red-tinted armor as they pass around wooden plates.

From the strength of their attacks on Lagos, I expected to find dozens of maji, but only nine sit around the flickering flames. The same rage Raifa ignited in my core returns as I take in the faces of the rebels who've made my city burn.

"Where are the rest?" Ojore whispers. "I was told dozens stormed Lagos when magic returned."

"Maybe this is all they could spare. After all, they only needed enough soldiers to keep us trapped in the capital."

"Let's turn back." Ojore nudges me. "Your mother and her tîtáns should be more than enough to wipe them out."

We rise to our feet, but when we turn toward Lagos, two rebels stand in our path.

"Drop your weapons!" the older of the two barks, the flames in her hand illuminating her snarl. My lips tremble as Ojore and I exchange a glance. With no other choice, we drop our swords and raise our hands into the air.

"Send word to the elders," the girl orders. "Tell them we have the king."

"Why wait?" The other Burner steps forward. "Let's send them his head—"

Ojore lunges without warning, grabbing his sword from the ground. I flinch as he drives the blade through the rebel's neck. Blood flies as the Burner falls into the dirt.

"Daran!" The girl's shriek brings me back to life. I tackle her to the ground, driving my elbow into her temple.

"Attack position!" a maji yells from their camp, spurring the rest of the *Iyika* to action. My legs turn to lead as they form one circle, chanting in unison.

"Òòrùn pupa lókè, tú àwọn iná rẹ sórí ilè ayé—"

The magi lift their hands into the sky, igniting the red sun. It burns with a vengeance, so bright it covers the forest in its crimson light. The air scorches around us, almost too hot to inhale.

"We have to stop them!" Ojore tears across the forest, racing toward the flames. He runs like a man possessed as he reaches for the throwing knives clipped to his belt. No regard for his life. No fear of his death.

"Ojore, wait!" I sprint after him. Back in Lagos, someone sounds the *Iyika* alarm.

Ha-wooooooooo!

The siren blares, deafening despite how far we are from the city. Trees catch fire around us as the red sun grows. The flames sear my skin as I run.

Ojore grunts as he races, throwing two knives into a Burner's chest. A guttural roar escapes the *Iyika* leader's throat as her soldier falls. When she spots Ojore, her lips curl.

"Odi iná, jó gbogbo rè ni àlà rẹ!"

Ojore stops in his path as a wall of fire appears out of thin air. It builds in strength, flames lighting the horror on his face.

"Ojore!" I scream as time comes to a stop. The maji swings her hands back to attack. My mind goes blank.

Magic swells inside me, a surge beyond my control.

I raise my hand and my magic explodes with such force I hear the bones shatter in my arm.

CHAPTER TWENTY-SEVEN

INAN

A FULL HOUR passes before the monarchy's forces find us. Soldiers hold me down as the medic bandages my arm. Others erect a canvas tent over my head, blocking out the celebration at the destroyed *Iyika* camp.

I grit my teeth to cage my screams. The pain is so great, I can hardly breathe. My arm aches as if every single bone has been smashed to pieces with a hammer.

"Inan, keep still!" Mother rushes in, an array of colorful glass vials in her hand. She picks up one filled with a dark blue liquid and forces the bitter sedative down my throat. "We're still scanning their ranks for Healers, but this should help."

I grab on to her as she props me up, keeping my bandaged arm still. The sedative hits like a wall. I exhale as it clouds my mind and numbs the pain.

I sink into the cot, rough fabric soaked with my own sweat. I still don't understand what happened. My magic's never caused me so much pain.

I didn't even know what I was doing when I raised my hand. I just wanted it all to stop.

I didn't think I could stun every *Iyika* at once.

"Give the king space." Mother ushers everyone out before kneeling at my side. She shakes her head as she runs her fingers through my sweat-soaked curls. "I could kill you."

"I'm sorry," I croak. "We weren't supposed to get caught."

"You're the *king*, for gods' sakes! If you have a plan, you fight with soldiers. You fight with *me*!"

She presses our foreheads together, squeezing me tight. Her hands tremble at the base of my neck. She stiffens as she holds back her tears.

"Please, next time, let me be involved," Mother whispers. "I just got you back. I can't afford to lose you again."

I nod and close my eyes; my mind still burning with the memory of the flames lighting Ojore's face. But as it drifts, it takes me to the first time I discovered my power, stunning Admiral Kaea back in Chândomblé.

"Have you done that before?" Mother asks.

"Yes. But never that many people at once."

"Well, don't use it again," she says. "Let your subjects bear this pain."

"Your Majesty!" General Jokôye enters our tent; something resembling a smile on her face. She pushes her spectacles up her nose and bows. "I am relieved that you're alright."

Ojore follows after her, bandages over his new burns.

"I owe you one." He smacks my foot.

"You keep saving my ass. It's about time I saved yours."

"I had my doubts," Jokôye says. "But I am not afraid to admit when I am wrong. You've done an incredible job of subduing these rebels. With the liberation of Lagos, we can turn the tide in this war!"

I pull back the tented walls and peek outside. Our soldiers shout with celebration, pulling generous swigs from their flask.

In the center of it all, the captured *Iyika* kneel in the dirt. Each rebel is bound in majacite chains, heads covered with bags.

Staring at them, I want to feel my victory, yet something hollow sinks in my chest. Last time I saw maji with bags over their heads, it was Father leading the charge.

"Now, for answers." Jokôye straightens and puts her hand on her sword. "It's time to locate and exterminate the rest of these maggots."

She marches into their camp, waist-length braid bouncing against the small of her back. With a wave, she halts the celebration. The determination in her gaze makes a new coat of sweat break out along my skin.

"Remove the bags," she orders, and her soldiers step forward, ripping the bag from each maji's face. Crackling flames fill the silence as Jokôye walks before them, inspecting every rebel.

"You've been efficient in your destruction," she shouts. "Now it's time for you to pay the price. Tell me where the rest of you maggots are hiding and I promise—your deaths will be quick."

Some rebels hang their heads. Others try to hide their tears. But one Burner stares up at the moon, her white hair blowing in the night wind.

Jokôye stops in front of her, teeth grinding at the girl's defiance. I flinch when Jokôye lunges for the Burner's throat.

"I asked you a question."

The girl struggles, choking under Jokôye's tightening grip. My general lifts her into the air. The sight makes my stomach twist.

"Answer me!" Jokôye shouts.

The Burner gasps for air, but keeps her eyes fixed on the night sky.

"If I'm to die where we stand," she chokes out, "then I choose the moon over your ugly face."

Jokôye throws the Burner into the charred dirt. The maji coughs as air rushes back in. But the way Jokôye looks at her, I know her breaths are short-lived.

My scar throbs as Ojore hands the general a vial of black liquid and a hollowed-out needle.

It's like watching Father torture Zélie all over again.

I start to get up, but Mother holds me back. She digs her hand into my thigh to keep me down.

"Whatever you're thinking, stop," she hisses. "You already gave them a choice. You can't save everyone."

I know she's right, but nausea still rises in my throat. This doesn't feel like being a better king.

This doesn't feel like being a king at all.

"Do you know what it feels like to have majacite in your veins?" Jokôye's voice rises as she fills the needle to the brim. Its metal glints in the firelight. "First it blocks the illness you call a gift. Then it burns you from within."

Pressure builds like a bomb waiting to go off in my chest. Watching the girl, I see Zélie in chains.

I smell the way her flesh burned as Father's soldiers carved through her back.

"You have a good heart, Inan," Mother whispers. "It will make you a good king. But you will destroy yourself if you don't distinguish between those you need to protect and those you need to eliminate."

"But, Mother—"

"These rebels burned your city to the ground. They wanted you and your people to starve. They are the poison of Orïsha! If you do not cut off the hand now, eventually you will be forced to sever the entire limb."

I clamp my mouth shut, digesting her words. I know as long as these rebels terrorize us, every maji in Orïsha will be seen as a criminal. The *Iyika* have to go.

But despite knowing this, my insides twist as Ojore grabs the Burner by her hair. He yanks the girl's head to the side, exposing her neck for Jokôye's attack.

"Last chance to talk," Jokôye offers, but the Burner spits. The girl cries out when the needle pierces her skin.

She tumbles from Ojore's hand like a brick, body seizing in the dirt as the majacite kills her from within. Mother tilts my chin, forcing me to look away.

"You've done more good in a few days than other monarchs have done in their entire reigns," she soothes. "Stay the course. End this war so you can continue to do good for the entire kingdom."

I nod, but my eyes drift back to the girl's corpse. Jokôye reaches for another needle.

"Who's next?"

CHAPTER TWENTY-EIGHT

AMARI

I'M SURPRISED AT THE LONGING in my heart that follows Zélie's ascension to Reaper elder. The celebration goes for hours, taking us deep into the night.

I watch with Tzain as she's celebrated through the sanctuary's mountain, every maji and divîner clamoring for her attention. All the while, her three Reapers crowd around her like ducklings, never more than an arm's length away.

Even before Mother interrupted my rally, the support of the Orïshans didn't touch the boundless joy of these maji. I wonder what it would be like to be embraced like that. To actually have a place where you belong.

"I wish Baba could see this." Tzain smiles. "Mama, too. I haven't seen Zél laugh like that since before the Raid. Growing up, she was always happiest around Mama's clan."

I nod, beginning to understand what it means to be an elder. All this time I assumed it was like occupying the throne, but now I realize that it's so much more. It isn't simply a position of power. An elder forms the foundation of their clan's home.

Across the bloodstone, Ramaya sits within her circle of Connectors, more like a mother than a cruel general. A young divîner puts a lily in her forest of curls. Ramaya's scar crinkles as she smiles.

I look down at my scarred hands, wondering if I will ever be allowed to sit among them. It feels like I could be as strong as my mother and they still wouldn't accept me.

A sharp bell echoes through the mountains, quieting all celebration at once. The majority of the maji seem to know what it signifies, but Zélie and I exchange a look.

People go still as a Burner runs over the stone bridge, metallic red armor splattered with blood.

"What's wrong?" Ramaya rises.

"It's Lagos." The Burner slows to a stop. "Our soldiers are gone."

The Burner's words suck the air from everyone's lungs. Ramaya's thick brows furrow as she steps forward.

"What do you mean, gone?"

"The king struck back," the Burner pants. "He and the tîtáns decimated our camp. By night's end, they'll reopen their roads. They're already reestablishing military communication."

The mountain erupts in chatter as everyone reacts to the loss. What was once a scene of boundless joy suffocates under the changing tides of war.

This is their fault. I clench my fist, thinking the words I can never speak aloud. Where would we be if they'd taken Inan's offer? If they'd simply heard me out?

"Elders," Ramaya calls, drawing each leader to the center of the bloodstone. I rise and get close, trying to catch their new plan.

"What do we do now?" Kâmarū's iron leg groans as he nears. "It won't be long before they get reinforcements."

"There's still a chance we can overwhelm them if we strike fast." Ramaya turns to Zélie when she joins them. "What do you think? Do you feel strong enough to take on the queen?"

I force myself into the circle before Zélie can respond, drawing glares from every elder.

"To rush into an attack would be a mistake. If I can contact my brother, I can see if he's still open to peace—"

Ramaya pushes me so hard, I fall onto the stone. The mountain quiets at once. My cheeks burn as she gets in my face.

"Your brother just slaughtered our soldiers." Her scar crinkles with her glare. "Interrupt us again, and I'll send him your head!"

Zélie meets my eye, warning me to back down. But I can't stay quiet. If they couldn't take my mother down before, there's no way they can take her down now. They're plotting their own demise.

Tzain comes to my side, helping me onto my feet. Concern shines in his warm brown eyes as he guides me away from the circle of elders.

"Just tell Zélie what you want," he says. "She'll listen."

"No, she won't." I shake my head. "None of them will."

Watching them makes my chest grow tight. The elders are fighting for the maji. I have to fight for the entire kingdom.

"Where are you going?" Tzain asks when I step away from his touch.

"If they won't listen to me, I have to make them."

My legs shake as I walk back to the circle of elders. I take a deep breath to fortify my resolve.

This is for their own good. Even if they don't know it.

Ramaya breaks away from the other elders as I approach, but I stop her with my words.

"I'm tired of fighting to be heard," I say. "Ramaya, I challenge you to be the new Connector elder."

CHAPTER TWENTY-NINE

AMARI

IF THE MOUNTAIN was abuzz with excitement before, it's ablaze now. Reactions spread like wildfire, only dying down when Ramaya closes the distance between us.

"How dare you," she snarls. "You don't have a right to be in this sanctuary, let alone challenge to become an elder!"

"Am I not a Connector, too?"

"You're not a maji!" she shouts. "You're not anything!"

My skin grows hot as blue clouds of magic froth at my fingertips. Whispers travel through the crowd, a hum building against my challenge. I scan the faces of the twelve Connectors behind Ramaya; not one of them looks like they'll back my leadership. But I already conceded to their ways once.

Because of them, we've lost our leverage in this war.

"The decisions we make today will not only affect the maji," I declare. "Whether you like it or not, tîtáns have magic, too, and in this fight, you need as many as you can get. You don't have to elect me." I shake my head. "You don't even have to listen. But I've been fighting for you and your magic just as long as the Soldier of Death. I deserve a chance to fight for this!"

"You want to fight?" Ramaya raises her fist, but Mama Agba blocks her path. Her brow creases and she releases a heavy sigh, surveying the rest of the crowd.

"Amari, the magic of Orí runs through your veins," she says. "You have the right to challenge. But are you sure this is what you want?" The look in Mama Agba's eyes warns me to concede. But I can't back down now. The people of Orïsha need me.

"I'm sure."

"Then let us begin." Mama Agba turns to the crowd. "Clear the circle."

Endless shoulders brush against me as the rest of the maji move to higher ground. People perch atop the mountain's ledges, legs swinging over the cliffs in front of their clan temples. Looking up reminds me of being in the Ibeji arena, stranded on a boat, waiting to face my death.

Somehow back then it felt like I had more of a winning chance.

"What in Oya's name do you think you're doing?" Zélie says, breaking through the thinning crowd. She still looks like a vision in her glittering golds and red silks, a maji worthy of wearing her people's crown.

"Our hold on Lagos is gone," I say. "If no one listens to me, we'll lose this war!"

"The maji are not defined by this war!" Zélie hisses. "Being an elder means you have to lead your clan. How do you expect to do that when you don't know our ways? How can you fight for this when you don't know anything about the maji at all?"

Her words give me pause; I don't know how to convince her that I'm only doing what's best. I'm fighting for her just as much as I'm fighting for everyone else.

"You may not have to concern yourself with the war, but as queen, I don't have a choice. I have to put Orïsha first, no matter the cost."

I ignore the hurt in Zélie's face as I walk forward. From across the circle, Ramaya stands, face pinched with hatred.

Just strike first, I repeat to myself. *Strike first and you'll be one step closer to ending this war and taking the throne.*

"The rules of *ìjà mímó* are simple." Mama Agba's voice echoes through the silent mountain. "The battle ends at concession or death, but we are in no place to senselessly lose our best." She takes a moment, looking Ramaya and me square in the eyes. "Be fierce, but be restrained. Do I make myself clear?"

"Crystal." Ramaya smiles. Her curly ringlets blow in the night wind as she cracks her knuckles.

I ignore the pit in my stomach and keep my face hard, forcing myself to nod as Mama Agba exits the bloodstone.

Strike, Amari, I think to myself. *Prove them wrong.*

"Begin!" Mama Agba shouts.

"*Ya èmí, ya ara!*" My skin stings as a vibrant blue light engulfs my entire arm. Though it doesn't take away the pain, I feel the thread of ashê moving through the needle.

Gasps arise as I dart forward, my arm ablaze with magic. I fight with the way of the maji, but when I throw the comet of ashê, Ramaya leaps over it. I don't have a chance to throw another when her palms slam against my head.

I cry out, vision flashing white. She yanks me by the curls, throwing me to the ground.

I shoot out my palm and try to chant again. "*Ya èmí, ya—*"

Her fist collides with my jaw before I can get the words out.

"I despise the sound of Yoruba from your mouth," she hisses. She puts her other hand to my head, kneeling to the ground. "Let me show you what an incantation's supposed to sound like. *Iná a ti ara—*"

I reach for my sword, but its metal does nothing to stop her attack. A cobalt cloud roars from Ramaya's hand, searing into me. The cloud engulfs my mind like a match ignited in my skull. The scream that escapes my lips doesn't feel like my own.

"You see that?" Ramaya laughs as I thrash, a malicious cackle that echoes through the mountains. "I strike with magic, and the tîtán reaches for her sword!"

The pain intensifies with her words, each one like another bomb exploding in my skull. It feels like an eternity passes before the white spots leave my vision and I can finally look up.

"Ready to concede?" Ramaya stares at me from a distance, a smug smile on her lips. I can barely finish a thought. She hasn't even broken a sweat.

The look on her face says it all. For her, this isn't about staying clan elder. She doesn't just want me to concede.

She wants to see me crawl.

Strike, Amari.

Beads of perspiration drip down my temples as I push myself onto my knees. Though my limbs shake, I grit my teeth and rise to my feet. My heart pounds like thunder in my chest. My skin begins to heat. Blue wisps spark from my fingertips as I launch another attack.

"Ya èmí, ya ara!"

I lunge forward, arm outstretched. My fingers come within a breath of Ramaya's neck before she spins out of my range.

"Ya èmí, ya ara!" I try again, but she ducks and slams another fist into my cheek. My jaw erupts as I fall to the ground.

Ramaya laughs before a new incantation spills from her lips. *"Idá a ti okàn—"*

This time her cobalt blaze hits me square in the chest. Within seconds, I'm on the ground writhing beneath the painful stabs erupting through my sternum.

It's like my body's being crushed between battering rams; like my fingernails are being ripped from my hands. I cannot breathe under the agony she brings. I cannot even scream.

"Get up, Amari!" Tzain shouts from afar, but sound is muffled in my ears. I can hardly hear anything above the blinding pain.

All the while Ramaya stands back, watching the torture she inflicts. She doesn't feel the need to bring this fight to an end.

A snow leopanaire playing with her food.

"For my father." Ramaya's next blast hits without warning. "For my mother!" Another cloud strikes my limbs. "For my sister!" This time her magic feels like thousands of nails drilling through my bones.

"*Ramaya! Nìsó!*" someone cheers from above, and others join in. Her torment isn't enough for these people. Not when they want to see my blood spill.

"I don't care what you've done." Ramaya's attacks subside, a brief reprieve as she catches her breath. "If you want to help the maji, kill your vile family. Kill yourself."

She bends down so low her white hair brushes against my cheek.

"The maji will be better off without you. Orïsha will, too."

Somehow her words cut deeper than her magic. It's Father's blade ripping through my back. Mother using my rally of peace to attack.

"*Idá a ti okàn—*"

My heart beats so loudly in my head it blocks the rest of her incantation out. I feel Ramaya's hatred like the pain within me. A rage that will burn my kingdom to the ground.

I reach for the power in my blood, pushing though I don't understand. The gods gave me this magic for a reason. I will use it to save Orïsha, even if the maji hate me for it.

I scream as I dig my hand into Ramaya's hair and pull, driving my elbow into her temple. She stumbles back from the blow. I take advantage of the opening and knock her down.

I straddle her body as a cobalt blaze ingites in my hands.

The needle isn't working.

So I release the hammer.

"RAH!"

Ramaya's ear-splitting scream shakes through the mountaintops. My magic carves through her mind like a knife as I dig through her scars, opening them the way I opened mine on the warship.

I feel the rough hand of a guard around her neck. I see the father who died for pushing him back. I flinch from the crack of knuckles over her left eye. I feel the warm blood that spilled from the wound.

"Amari, stop!" Zélie shouts from afar, but I can't release my hold. My eyes flash with blue light. The bones crack in my arm as my magic spins out of my control. A never-ending flood of Ramaya's life fills my mind. Every shard of pain that rips into her being rips through mine.

I don't feel the hands that pull me back. I barely see Ramaya seizing before she collapses. Shouts I can't decipher ring out as Zélie's face breaks through the madness, her voice muffled by the pain in my head.

Beyond her, Ramaya's body lies unconscious.

I can't tell if her chest still moves up and down.

"Khani, quick!" Mama Agba yells.

Khani, the elder of the Healer clan, runs onto the bloodstone. Her white braids swing as she presses her hands against Ramaya's neck, feeling for a pulse though Ramaya's eyes stay frozen in an empty gaze.

After a long moment, Khani exhales. Her lips turn to a frown.

"She's alive." The Healer shakes her head. "Barely."

Tears come to my eyes. My hands start to shake. "I didn't . . . I wasn't—"

Zélie pulls me into a hug. She rubs her hand up and down my back, but I can hear the tremble in her breath.

"Don't look." She squeezes my shoulder. "Don't do anything."

CHAPTER THIRTY

· · · · · ◆ ◇ ◆ · · · · ·

ZÉLIE

MY FEET DRAG as I make my way to the elder quarters. The days since my ascension have blurred together. With all the new maji and divîners that've flooded the sanctuary since we lost Lagos, getting anywhere makes me feel like a salmon swimming upstream. We now have over two hundred mouths to feed, and most are still powerless divîners. Rations decrease as our dormitories swell.

Every day, new people arrive, sharing stories of the monarchy's raids on the maji. I don't know how we're going to strike back. It feels like we're constantly losing ground, ground the monarchy is hungry to take. Victory that once felt a battle away slips further away from our grasps.

"Z, you coming?" Nâo brushes my shoulder, distracting me from my concerns. The Tider's blue-tinted armor glints in the sun, the right arm sculpted to show the waves tattooed along her dark skin.

The other elders stand under the vine-covered archway outside the dining hall, waiting for me to go to the council room. They seem to look to me more now that Ramaya's in the infirmary.

"I'll meet you there," I call.

The scent of pounded yam and fried bean cakes fills the halls as I head up the spiraling steps of the elder tower. Eleven stories high, each new floor brings me to a different leader's quarters. The only structure on this mountain built by the original clan elders, its sea glass tiles make me feel like I'm sleeping in a palace. I run my fingers through the hanging plants forming a canopy along the ceiling until I reach Amari's new room on the fifth floor.

Stifled tears bleed through the obsidian door, but I force myself to knock. The tears quiet at once. The thud of heavy footsteps approach.

"Who is it?" Tzain calls.

"Me," I say. "We have an elder meeting."

The door cracks open and Tzain lowers his voice, leaning outside so Amari doesn't hear.

"Where've you been?" he whispers. "She's needed you."

"So have my Reapers." I push past him to enter Amari's new quarters. "Don't forget, she got herself in this mess."

I pause to take in her room; like mine, turquoise tiles line the floor. A curved balcony opens outside, providing a view of the waterfall near the bathroom door.

"Be sensitive," Tzain says. "She refuses to see a Healer."

Amari sits in front of the cracked mirror, face puffy and red. Deep bruises line her temples and jaw. Her right arm hangs in a makeshift sling across her chest. She struggles with a canister of soft brown pigment, dotting it over her bruises to conceal them.

"You know a Healer can fix that," I say.

"I already asked," she keeps her voice flat. "After the fifth one refused, I gave up."

My eyes widen, but I look away, pretending to inspect her brass tub. Healers are supposed to help everyone in need, regardless of their own feelings.

Amari continues to do what she can to cover her bruises, but she's clumsy with her left hand. My anger still boils at the surface, but I sit her down and force myself to help.

"Thank you," she says.

I stay silent, but nod in response. Amari glares at the wall, but every so often her armor cracks.

I see the sadness she holds inside. The loneliness she must feel.

She may have beaten Ramaya, but she's isolated herself in the process.

"I tried to visit her." Amari's voice shakes. "Ramaya. I wanted to apologize, but she still hasn't woken up."

A bitter taste settles on my tongue, but I don't speak. Ramaya's been unconscious since their fight. Even Khani's healing hasn't been able to revive her.

"Do you hate me, too?" Amari asks, and my fingers freeze above her cheeks. I almost hate her for asking this of me. But I trained her that night. I taught her an incantation. In a way, I feel just as responsible for Ramaya's coma.

"You promised me you wouldn't use what I taught you against a maji," I say.

"I know, but I didn't have a choice—"

"You always have a choice," I snap. "You just chose wrong." I shake my head, putting the canister of pigment down. "You chose to win at any cost. Like your father. Like Inan."

Anger sizzles in the air between us. It takes all my effort not to walk away. I try to block out the sight of her white streak, the reminder of her people and all the ways they continue to hurt those like me.

But before I can storm out, Amari hangs her head. New tears stream free, streaking through all the pigment on her face.

"I'm sorry, alright? I truly am." She wipes her nose. "I know I messed up. I know I lost control. What I don't know is how to make things right."

Her heartbreak cools my rage. I exhale a deep breath and turn her to face me. Of course she doesn't get it.

She's a títán.

A monarch.

"If you're going to be an elder, you need to understand that true magic isn't about power," I explain. "It's something that's a part of us, something that's literally in our blood. Our people have suffered for this. Died for this. It's not something you can just learn. You may have helped us get it back, but right now we're still being hunted and killed for the very magic tîtáns like you use against us."

Amari nods, wiping her tears as she digests my words. "I'll find a way to apologize to the elders and the Connectors."

"Good." I pick up the pigment again, dabbing the streaks along her cheeks. "It's bad out there. We need you."

CHAPTER THIRTY-ONE

AMARI

A WALL OF SILENCE greets me when I stand before the gilded archway of the council room. I haven't shown my face in days. I can only imagine the things they'll say. But instead of focusing on the glaring elders around the teak wood table, I take in the sacred space. Stained-glass windows bathe the room in rainbow light. Glassy stones form spiraling patterns along the wall.

"Wow . . ." I breathe, pressing my hand against my chest. A jolt like lightning passes over my skin when I walk in. According to Zélie, the entrance is enchanted, only allowing the elders of the past and present through.

Ten bronze statues encircle the room, monuments to the original leaders of the maji clans. I begin to understand the gravity of these positions when I sit in front of the rusted figure with Connector-blue robes.

If you're going to be an elder, you need to understand that true magic isn't about power. I mull over Zélie's words as we wait for the last elder to join us, studying the maji around the table. Some scrutinize me with a heavy gaze. Others refuse to meet my eyes.

Nâo pulls Zélie into a conversation. Kâmarū leans forward, resting an elbow on his prosthetic leg. Beside him, Na'imah plays with the pink butterflies in her curls. They take turns landing on her painted fingernails.

To her left, Dakarai, the elder of the Seers, catches one. A plump boy with a thick head of curls, he keeps his chest bare with the exception of the two thin chains around his neck.

"Come to my quarters after the meeting." Khani pulls my attention, inspecting me with a frown on her freckled face. Though I can't call Tzain's old agbön mate a friend, it's nice to sit with her again.

"My Healers may not approve of you," she says. "But they shouldn't have denied you treatment."

"Can you blame them?" Kenyon mutters. "Her people are the reason ours are dying."

The broad-shouldered Burner sits with crossed arms, staring at the patterned walls. I heard he hasn't spoken much since he found out the monarchy killed a quarter of his Burners outside the city walls.

"I'm sorry about what happened in Lagos," I say.

Kenyon grunts in response.

"Sorry I'm late," Folake says as she enters the room. The elder of the Lighter clan shines in her flowing yellow kaftan.

She smiles at Zélie as she takes the empty seat beside her. Her thick locs and cat-like eyes spark memories from our first meeting at Zulaikha's divîner camp. With her arrival, all ten elders are present.

"Where do we want to begin?" Zélie asks the table.

"How about we start with elders who are actually maji?"

I stiffen when the boy across from me takes his dig. Though we haven't met, I know him to be Jahi, the elder of the Winders. A small ribbon of wind whistles between his fingers. If I've heard right, he's seeing Ramaya. No wonder he doesn't want me here.

"Àgbààyà, leave her alone." Nâo smacks her lips. "She won, fair and square."

"Their magic isn't like ours," Jahi responds. "There was nothing fair about it."

"I'd actually like to speak on that." I rise, forcing myself to stand tall. I picture how Mother would react in this situation. Even when she didn't belong, she always had a way of carrying herself that made others feel small.

"I want to apologize," I say. "I didn't intend to lose control of my magic like that. I can only imagine how difficult that was to watch. But—"

"Of course there's a *but*." Na'imah snorts.

My nostrils flare, but I push forward. "I think what happened is a perfect demonstration of why it's in your best interest to make peace with the monarchy."

I expect the flurry of anger that erupts at my proposition. Some elders curse at me in Yoruba. Others just roll their eyes.

"What are you doing?" Zélie hisses under her breath.

"I said I would apologize," I whisper back. "But we're losing this war. This is still the best plan."

"You see how this is a trap, right?" Jahi looks around the room. "I bet she's been feeding her brother information. She's probably the reason we lost our hold on Lagos."

"You are the reason you lost your hold on Lagos," I push back. "My brother's offer for peace was sincere. You forced his hand when you destroyed their food. If you'd only listened to me then, we wouldn't be here now."

"Forget that," Kenyon spits. Actual smoke rises from the Burner's skin as his anger builds. "They injected majacite *into* my people. We're fighting back. We're strong enough to beat the tîtáns."

"No, you're not," I stress. "At least, not all of them. Ramaya was your fiercest soldier, and with barely any knowledge about my magic, I've left her comatose. How do you expect to fare against more tîtáns with that kind of power?"

"Z, do you agree?" Nâo speaks up, directing all eyes to Zélie. A prick of annoyance hits me at the way they all quiet down, leaning in to get her perspective.

"I don't want to admit it, but there's truth in what Amari's saying." Zélie nods. "The tîtáns operate on blood magic. They're reckless, but when they strike, they're fierce. If that was the only thing we were up against, we still might have a chance. But Nehanda is something else." Zélie's silver eyes grow distant for a moment and she releases a shaky breath. "At the rally in Zaria, Nehanda sucked magic from the tîtáns around her. She used it to split the earth."

"She did the same in Lagos," Kâmarū adds. "When she struck, her eyes glowed green. The magic was so strong, it shone through her chest. I don't know how we face that."

I stare at the scars covering my hands as a blanket of fear settles over the room. This is my chance. If the elders are ever going to listen to me, it's now.

"You had one key advantage when Lagos was under your control," I say. "But you overplayed your hand. Now Lagos's roads have been re-opened. Their defenses are being rebuilt. The military is whittling down your forces, while new tîtáns flood to Lagos to join their ranks." I shake my head. "Who knows how many you're up against now? How many have powers like my mother?"

"What're you suggesting?" Na'imah arches her plucked brows. "'Cause we're not about to concede."

"All I want is for the maji to live in a kingdom where they're safe," I say. "I thought that had to be with me on the throne, but there's a chance Inan will agree to that now. My brother is not like my father. War is not what he wants for Orïsha. Just give me a chance to contact him and figure this out. He owes me his life. I promise, he'll listen."

I hold my breath as they mull over my words. I can practically see the wheels turning in their heads. But one by one, eyes drift to Zélie. I try to smile at her, but she keeps her gaze on the table.

"Even if we want to seek peace, it would be foolish to expect Inan to do the right thing," she says. "The tîtáns are strong, but their magic is reckless. Just look at Amari."

Zélie gestures to me as if I'm an object instead of a human being. Blood rises to my cheeks as I sit back down.

"Amari overpowered Ramaya, but that's because Ramaya played games," Zélie argues. "If we're disciplined and trained, we can defeat any tîtáns we meet. We can even take on the queen."

"You don't know that!" I try to regain control of the room, but all my efforts are in vain. The maji are quick to overlook me now, energized by Zélie's false promise of victory.

"How are we supposed to train without incantations?" Nâo asks. "Before the Raid, the clans had hundreds. Now some of our clans barely have three."

Zélie rests her palms on the table, gaze growing distant. With a gasp, she reaches over to her leather bag, pulling out one of the black scrolls Lekan gave her at Chândomblé.

"Where'd you get that?" Kâmarū takes the scroll, thick brows scrunching at the sacred text. "All of these were burned in the Raid."

"Not the ones at Chândomblé."

"You want us to chase a legend?" Na'imah cocks her head.

"It's not a legend," Zélie says. "Amari and I have seen it for ourselves. There's a room filled with hundreds of scrolls from every clan."

Excitement buzzes as the elders consider what the library of scrolls could mean for us.

"If we could get those, we'd have an arsenal." Kenyon's eyes light up.

"Imagine what remedies they might have!" Khani exclaims.

"We can leave tonight," Zélie raises her hand, regaining control of the room. "The monarchy's still focused on rebuilding Lagos. This could be the perfect time to slip under their noses."

I watch as they begin to strategize, knowing nothing I say will change their minds. I thought being an elder would be enough to influence them, but I'm still on the outside.

"Don't worry," Zélie whispers to me. "I'm not saying a bid for peace is off the table. But let's get these scrolls first. We need new leverage against your mother in case peace doesn't work."

I nod, but when she walks off, my jaw clenches tight.

I wonder if she's just trying to placate me, or if she truly believes her own lies.

CHAPTER THIRTY-TWO

INAN

As I MAKE my way to the war room, I feel the change in the air. With the *Iyika's* Lagos operations dismantled a half moon ago, the smoke that's lingered on my city's horizon has finally begun to clear.

Once again, the sun shines down on us. Bright rays illuminate our efforts to rebuild. Food rolls in by the wagon. Not one villager hungers.

"Your Majesty!" The soldiers standing guard outside the war room salute when I approach. They move to open the black oak doors, but I stop them when I spot Mother across the hall. She calls off her guards, descending into the palace cellars alone. I frown as I follow after her.

She moves like she doesn't want to be seen.

I try to keep my steps from echoing as I descend the stone stairs. An expansive brick labyrinth with dozens of rooms, the palace cellar seems to hold all of my darkest memories.

Father used to take Amari and me here when we were children. He forced us to spar. I still remember the way her screams bounced against the stone walls when I took things too far.

Where are you? I look up, wishing I could connect with her now. Mother's convinced Amari's working with the *Iyika,* but that's not the sister I know.

Zélie may want to burn Lagos to the ground, but this is still Amari's home. She should be here by my side. Not all alone in the world.

"Where's the rest?"

I stop in my tracks as the husky voice fills the cellar's damp halls. The boy speaks Orïshan with a strange lilt, as if he isn't from this land. I peek around the corner to find Mother standing with two masked men clad in black. One wears a snake-like smile. The other has skin the color of sand.

I've seen him before. . . .

I rub my chin, trying to remember where. Something about the foreigner is familiar. I know our paths have crossed.

"You'll get the rest when you finish the job," Mother answers, handing over a velvet purse that clinks with coins. "The majacite was an effective start, but it's only the beginning. And the *Iyika* are still interfering with my plans—"

"We've got company."

I freeze; all three sets of eyes land on me. Mother's lips part in surprise. The mercenaries don't even bat an eye.

"You scoundrels," she hisses at them. "Bow before your king."

The foreign mercenary snorts in response, counting the gold in his velvet purse.

"What?" I walk forward. "You don't bow before the kings of other lands?"

"I don't bow before anyone I can kill."

He looks me up and down before turning back to Mother. "This'll work for now. We'll be in touch."

I expect them to make their way up the stairs, but instead they disappear down the cellar's dark halls. They move with confidence, as if they've traversed this labyrinth before.

"What was that about?" I ask.

"Your sister has worked with them," Mother explains. "I was seeing if they had any information on her and the *Iyika*."

"Amari?" I lean in. "Any leads?"

"The look in your eyes is the very reason I didn't want you involved." Mother grabs my arm, leading me toward the stairs. "I know she is your sister, but she is also an enemy of this kingdom."

"She's also the only reason I'm alive."

Mother doesn't say more until we reach the war room doors.

"Remember, your duty is to the throne. Protect it above all else."

* * * * * ◆ ◇ ◆ * * * * *

"Your majesty."

Every advisor stands when Mother and I enter the war room. Their abruptness catches me off guard. They don't sit until I give the command.

I smile to myself, taking my place at the head of the oak table. Ojore rises at my signal, moving toward the vast map of Orïsha that covers the far wall.

"I'm pleased to report that after the valiant efforts of our king, we've managed to turn the tides in this war," he addresses the room. "Since liberating Lagos from the *Iyika*, we've reestablished communication with our bases in the north. Assassination attempts are down, and not one fortress has been breached."

"Let's not rush to celebrate yet," General Jokôye jumps in, braid swinging as she rises from her seat. "While these gains are impressive, the *Iyika* still pose a significant threat. We still estimate anywhere between two hundred and five hundred soldiers in their forces."

"Where are we on locating their base?" I ask.

"Closer, but not close enough." Jokôye gestures to the mountains north of Lagos. "According to the fortresses in Gusau and Gombe, all their movements appear to originate from the Olasimbo Range. We've sent scouts, but none have returned. However, there are signs that the *Iyika* are on the move again."

Ojore walks back to the table, grabbing two pieces of parchment. "I'm sure you're all familiar with the former princess."

Ojore hangs an old wanted poster with a sketch of my sister's face. It's strange to see Amari that way. The soft lines don't capture how she's changed.

"Her primary accomplice is a maji named Zélie Adebola," Ojore continues. "Native of Ibadan, and then Ilorin. She was fundamental in bringing magic back. Maji across the kingdom regard her as the Soldier of Death."

I try to avert my gaze, but I can't look away from the illustration. It's like Zélie stares at me from afar, ferocity piercing through her silver gaze. Look too long, and I feel her vines around my neck. Her lips against my ear.

If I can't even be in a room with her illustration, I don't know what I'll do when we're face-to-face.

"Do we know where they're headed?" I ask.

"Our best guess is Lagos," Jokôye answers. "They eluded our forces after an insurgent rally in Zaria, but today they were spotted moving south."

"They're coming here?" The color drains from Mother's face. "We're still a half-moon from completing the new wall."

"What about the moat?" Captain Kunle dabs the sweat at his temple. "It'll take weeks before the Tiders can fill it!"

I put my fingers to my ears as panic fills the room. Something doesn't add up.

"Admiral, they're already south of Lagos. What would they gain by doubling back?"

"We believe this route gives them direct access to the palace." Ojore illustrates the winding path. "I've taken the liberty of moving more troops to Lagos's borders, but we're going to need significant resources to stop them."

I scrunch my nose, extending their path in my head. The line takes me straight into the Funmilayo Jungle.

Right through an ancient temple.

I slap my hands against the oak table, rising to my feet.

"I know where they're going!" I run to the map, tapping the old canvas. "There's an ancient temple for the maji located here. It has the capability to amplify their powers."

Mother's face falls. "If they retrieve what they're searching for, they could become too powerful to defeat."

"Not if we intercept them," I say. "If they're coming from the mountains, we're closer to the temple. Leave tonight, and we may be able to catch them!"

"Can you really face your sister?" Ojore voices the question no one else will. Gazes flick between me and Mother before finding any excuse to look away.

I walk over to the wanted posters, gazing at Amari's face. I think of how she challenged Father for me. If she hadn't intervened, I probably would have died.

"It would be a lie to say I could hurt my sister." I face the room. "But I can take her in. Especially when she and the *Iyika* pose a threat to the kingdom."

Mother's lips pinch, but she nods to me in respect.

"What about the others?" Ojore asks. "Do we aim to kill?"

I glance back at the posters, this time stopping on Zélie's face.

"Let's focus on taking them down first," I decide. "Once they're captured, we can figure out a proper punishment."

CHAPTER THIRTY-THREE

...... ◆ ◇ ◆ ......

AMARI

WIND WHIPS THROUGH my curls as we speed through the jungle on our cheetanaires. Thick vines sting when I fly past, but I still have to snap my reins to keep up.

The elders ride with a vengeance, Zélie riding fastest of all. I can't help feeling that the closer we get to Chândomblé, the closer we are to the bloody end of this war.

Think, Amari. I rack my brain as my ryder picks up speed. As soon as the *Iyika* get those scrolls, they'll want to attack. The battle will be brought right to Lagos.

If they're strong enough to beat my mother, I doubt they'll let me take the throne. At this point, it's more likely to go to Zélie. But if they're not strong enough to take down my mother . . .

A brick settles in my stomach at the thought.

If they're not strong enough to face Mother and her tîtáns, she'll wipe them out. Them, and then every maji in Orïsha.

The longer the scenarios play in my head, the fewer answers I have. I have to prove myself to the *Iyika.* Convince them to attempt peace first. If they'll let me contact Inan, there's a chance we can avoid this path of destruction—

"Amari!"

A panicked hiss snaps me back into the present. I blow past the horde of elders pulled off to the side as my ryder races through the jungle.

"*Èdà Oxosi, dáhùn ìpè mi!*" Na'imah's melodic voice rings, making a pink mist swirl around my cheetanaire's head. The cloud stops my spotted ryder in his tracks. I have to squeeze with all I have to keep from flying off.

"For Oxosi's sake, pay attention!" she says, beckoning her cheetanaire back to the group. My cheeks heat as I slide off, joining their circle.

"What's going on?"

Dakarai raises his hand, thick curls pasted to his forehead with sweat.

"We need to stop. I'm having a vision."

• • • • • ◆ ◇ ◆ • • • • •

No one makes a sound as we all gather around Dakarai. Usually barechested, the boy looks out of place with the silver-tinted armor around his large frame.

"Give me some space." He shifts, isolating himself by facing a tree. "I'm much better at seeing the past than the present. I can't concentrate with all of you watching."

Every maji turns away, seeming to understand his need for space. I do the same, but I can't help glancing over my shoulder as he chants.

Sweat gathers above the Seer's sparse brows as he summons his magic. The silver glow of his ashê spreads around his hands. A mystical window of stars forms between his palms.

Unlike Mama Agba's vision of the future, Dakarai's doesn't show a clear fragment of time. Instead his window shows translucent images in brief flashes.

"*Ní Sísèntèlé—*"

The Seer adjusts his hands like a compass finding its way north. The dense greens of the Funmilayo Jungle fade through his blanket of stars.

Thick clouds of fog pass through the emerald trees. But by the time the window reaches Chândomblé's temple, the images are so faint it's difficult to make out the newly constructed bridge.

"Can you make the vision stronger?" I lean in, squinting to make out the soldiers on the battlefield.

"I can try, but the further away I am, the weaker the picture is." A silver light glows around Dakarai's hands as he increases the amount of ashê in his palms. With the surge in power, the image starts to crystallize, allowing us to see what's ahead.

"Dammit." Zélie curses at the iron bridge that sits where the old one fell. It connects the southern ledge of our mountain to the one holding Chândomblé's sacred temple.

More than two dozen soldiers stand guard at the bridge's base; nearly half of them are tîtáns. Battle tactics run through my mind, but they all crumble when I recognize the petite frame of the general who stands outside Chândomblé's entrance.

"Zélie," I warn.

"I know," she replies.

Even under the golden mask, it's impossible not to recognize the sharp angles of Mother's face. I knew our paths would cross again. I just didn't think it'd be so soon.

But if she's here, there's a chance Inan isn't far behind.

"Can you see anyone else?" I ask.

Dakarai attempts to increase the range of his vision, but nothing else appears in his celestial field.

"I'm sorry." He shakes his head. "But if there are that many on the bridge, it's safe to assume there are soldiers surrounding the entire temple."

"Then what are we waiting for?" Kenyon blows past us, putting his red-tinted helmet back on. "I don't care how many there are. I'll burn them all."

"Last time we faced Nehanda, she sent an entire dome crashing down on our heads." I run after him. "We might not be strong enough to defeat them."

"Speak for yourself. I'm not weaker than some tîtán."

"You're definitely not stronger than my mother!" I grab Kenyon's shoulder, forcing him to wait. "Besides, they knew we were coming. We don't want to alert them that we're here."

"Then what do you propose, Princess?"

All eyes drift in my direction and I pause; this is the first time they've ever turned to me for answers. Maybe this is my chance.

Do this right, and I can prove myself to the *Iyika* while keeping the body toll down. And if Inan's inside, getting into that temple could be our only way to speak.

"Soldiers on the bridge," I mutter to myself. "Mostly likely, soldiers around the perimeter . . ."

I kneel down to the ground, sketching out different scenarios in the dirt.

"I have an idea," I say.

"A good one?" Kenyon pries.

"It's an idea."

The Burner exhales a heavy sigh, but with no other options, he leans in.

"Okay, Princess. Let's hear it."

CHAPTER THIRTY-FOUR

. . . . . ◆ ◇ ◆ . . . . .

ZÉLIE

I RUN MY THUMB over the scars along my wrist as we wait for everyone to get in position. Amari's plan requires a nimble team. Less than half of us can make the trip. But as everyone prepares to set off, only one thought fills my mind. There are dozens of soldiers on that mountain.

One of them could be Inan.

Oya, strengthen me. I exhale the quiet prayer, tightening my grip on the stiff leather of Nailah's new reins. I try to remember how it felt to squeeze the breath from his throat, but all I can feel is how I don't feel him.

This close to the temple, it's impossible not to live in the past, to forget the days when Inan chased and I ran. With our connection, I used to feel his presence like the tang in the air before a summer's rain.

Now, I don't feel anything.

"Elder Zélie!" Tahir—our strongest Welder—calls out to me from afar. With light brown eyes and skin like pearls, his albinism makes him stand out from the crowd.

Though only fourteen, Tahir's prodigious talents have made him Kâmarū's Second. It's because of him and Mama Agba the *Iyika* have their innovative armor.

"Before you go." He expands my condensed staff, revealing its new and improved form. Instead of tarnished iron, the polished metal now shares the deep purple hues of my Reaper armor.

"It's beautiful," I breathe. "And you were able to make the alterations?"

Tahir nods, pressing a new button in the middle. I jump back when serrated blades extend from each end, piercing forward like daggers.

"You're a genius!" I spin the staff, marveling at his Welder's touch. Tahir beams and adjusts the rusted goggles that sit on his forehead.

"It's my honor, Elder Zélie. Really!"

I press my thumb against the akofena engraved in the staff's side, trying to draw strength from the swords of war. I stab one end into the dirt, imagining how it'll feel to dig the blade right through Inan's heart.

"You're the Soldier of Death." Mâzeli approaches from behind. "Why in Oya's name do you need that?"

"Because someone stabbed me in the back," I say. "If see him, I want to return the gift."

The smile falls off Mâzeli's face, pressing into a hard line. He picks at his ear as he looks down. "I'm sorry. I've never killed anyone."

"Why would you apologize for that?"

Mâzeli sighs, scratching the back of his neck. "'Cause if I had, then I could help you. I wouldn't be so afraid."

"It's okay to be afraid." I collapse the staff and attach it to my belt. "Everyone's afraid. I'm terrified."

My Second studies me with his big brown eyes, squinting as if I'm feeding him lies. "But you're the Soldier of Death."

"*Jagunjagun* is a myth," I say. "What you and I are about to do is real." He stands a full head taller than me, but I place my hands on his shoulders.

"Just stick by my side. I'll summon Oya herself before I let anything happen to you."

Mâzeli's smiles lights up his round face. Though my words don't take away all of his fear, his tense shoulders finally relax.

He exhales a deep breath as we make our way back to the others.

"Just know one day, it'll be me protecting you."

I smile at his resolve and pull at his large ears. "I look forward to it."

Our conversation draws to a halt as we wait behind Nâo. She rolls out her wrists and pulls her shaved head to the side, stretching out the *lagbara* tattooed down the length of her neck.

"Must you put on a show?" Khani arches her brow. Nâo grins and kisses her girlfriend's freckled cheek.

"Don't pretend you don't like to watch." No one else speaks as Nâo closes her eyes and spreads her arms out wide. *"Omi, tutù, omi mí. Omi wá bá mi—"*

The chill starts from behind, like winter's breath kissing the back of our necks. It creeps over my shoulders and crawls down my chest as the moisture in the air cools and expands.

Within seconds the thin layer of fog around us condenses into a thick cloud of white. It makes the hairs on my neck stand up, weaving itself into the dark night.

"Slow and steady," Amari instructs. "It has to look natural."

Nâo raises her hands and moves the blanket of fog east, spreading the white wall over the mountain's ledge and across the bridge. I reach forward and part the trees, watching the wall of white swallow our enemies. When it's spread far enough, Amari squeezes my shoulder.

"Let's do this."

· · · · · ◆ ◇ ◆ · · · · ·

TIME TICKS BY in an endless stretch. My breath hitches as I try to stay silent. By now, the fog is so thick we can't see more than a few centimeters in front of our heads.

A small flame in Kenyon's hand lights the path as eight of us make our way to the mountain's edge. Kâmarū and Tahir walk in the front, while Jahi, Dakarai, and Amari bring up the rear.

"Are you okay?" I whisper to Mâzeli. He nods, but holds clenched fists by his sides. His eyes dart back and forth, as if at any moment a soldier will strike.

For his sake, I try to pretend every crumbling leaf and snapping branch around us doesn't put me on edge. Jahi's quiet incantation rings out as he manipulates the wind at our feet, creating a vacuum that allows us to walk in silence.

"Here?" Kâmarū whispers.

Amari starts to answer, but her mouth clamps shut. I hold Mâzeli's hand tightly as footsteps groan along the iron bridge, only a few meters to our left.

"Go!" Amari hisses.

Kâmarū and Tahir join hands. A dull green light shines from the spaces beneath their palms.

"Se ìfé inú mi—"

The chant heats the ground beneath our feet. The footsteps near as the earth starts to vibrate. Mâzeli squeezes my hand and I hold him tight as we sink.

Our crooked ledge slides down the mountain in silence, a natural lift at Kâmarū's command. The further we descend, the more the fog thins, allowing us to see the green light glowing through the earth.

"Skies." Amari releases a sigh of relief when we come to a stop half-way down the mountainside. The soldier's footsteps fade from above, but we're still covered by the thick blanket of fog.

Tahir's knees buckle and he struggles to stand. Kâmarū props him up, allowing his Second to lean against his iron prosthetic.

"You're good." Kâmarū pats his back. "I can handle this."

The Grounder steps ahead, sweat gleaming off his dark skin. He chants under his breath, releasing a slow and steady rhythm.

As his magic builds, the mountain behind us erodes, glowing grains floating by our side. I almost scream when Kâmarū walks over the ledge of our cliff, but the grains swarm together, creating a step beneath his feet.

"No way . . ." Amari's jaw drops when Kâmarū moves again. He walks out onto the open air, the grains of earth condensing under his feet each time he moves. The glowing dirt hovers in the air like lily pads floating above water. Bit by bit, he makes his way across the divide, the floating steps taking him all the way to the other side.

"You're next," Tahir instructs, making the color drain from Amari's face.

"But I'm not a Grounder," she says.

"You don't have to be. We're using the incantation."

Tahir starts to chant behind her and Amari's hand shakes. She tests the magic by dangling her foot over the ledge, but it still summons the glowing grains.

"Skies, help me," she curses under her breath. Step by glowing step, she walks across the divide. The grains of rock rise to catch her every time.

Dakarai follows after her with his arms pressed to his side. Kenyon refuses to look down. When Jahi makes it across, I nudge Mâzeli forward.

"Let's go together," I offer.

I move toward the ledge, but Mâzeli's feet stay frozen in place.

"What'd I tell you?" I pull him along. "I promise, you'll be okay."

Mâzeli swallows and balls his fists, tiptoeing over the ledge. I follow close behind him, keeping my hands on his shoulders as we step across the floating earth.

"Almost there . . ." My voice trails off when I make the mistake of looking down. I can still remember falling into this pit myself, saved only by Lekan's magic. A giant skeleton lies between the sharp and pointed rocks. Gnats pick at the decomposing carcass.

My stomach reels when I recognize the horns. The memory of Lekan throwing Inan's ryder off the mountain plays before my eyes.

I snap my head forward and push ahead, grip tightening on Mâzeli's shoulders. I was powerless last time.

I won't let that happen again.

"Thank Oya!" Mâzeli plasters himself against the new mountain ledge, kissing a tuft of moss. Behind him, Tahir falls to his knees, struggling to steady his shaking limbs.

"I'm sorry," he pants. "I'm better with metal."

"You did great." Kâmarū helps him up. "You have nothing to apologize for."

"Get back to the other side when you can," Amari instructs. "If something happens and the troops try to cross that bridge, it's up to you to destroy it."

Tahir's mouth falls open and he looks up, studying the iron bridge like an architect. "What if you're not back?"

"Doesn't matter," Amari says. "If they catch the others, they could find the sanctuary. We have to protect it no matter the cost."

Though conflicted, Tahir nods, bowing to show his respect. Kâmarū bumps his fist before facing the mountain with a new chant.

"O ṣubú lulẹ̀. O ṣubú lulẹ̀—"

An emerald glow lights from his fingertips and he presses them against the jagged rock. I inhale a sharp breath as the stone begins to crumble. Kâmarū's magic erodes straight through the mountain.

The Grounder pushes forward until a tunnel begins to emerge, large enough for him to step inside. Amari nudges me and I follow after him, disappearing into the dark.

· · · · · ◆ ◈ ◆ · · · · ·

EVEN WITH KÂMARŪ'S MAGIC, tunneling through the mountain is slow and steady work. Eventually the others lag behind, preferring to walk with longer strides. Despite the temptation to hang back, I find myself drawn to Kâmarū's side. There's something calming in the way he works. Watching him, I can almost forget about the guards above.

"Do you even need to get inside this temple?" I ask.

Kâmarū glances back, thick brows knit in confusion.

"You've already mastered so many incantations." I gesture to his glowing hands, watching as the mountain crumbles like sand.

"My father was our clan elder," Kâmarū explains. "He wanted me to follow in his path. By the time I turned twelve, he'd already been training me for years."

I smile at the thought, picturing a pint-size Kâmarū without the thick white dreads or silver nose ring. It's easy to imagine him training through long days and cold nights, guided by a father who shared his angular eyes.

"You still remember what he taught you?" I ask. "Even after all this time?"

"After the Raid, practicing these incantations was the only part of him I had left."

My heart sinks in the echo of his words. In my mind, Kâmarū still whispers these incantations, but without the father he loves. Without the magic that was meant to run through his veins.

"He'd be so proud of you." I shake my head. "He *is* proud of you."

Kâmarū's dark brown eyes soften. "I like to think so, too."

As we walk, I think of the other elders and maji, what their lives might've been like before the Raid. Mâzeli's already told me how the monarchy took both his parents away. How his sister Arunima perished from grief.

The Grounder catches me staring and flashes me a smile, one so bright it knocks the wind from my chest. For the first time I realize that I could lose him, too.

"Does it scare you?" I whisper to Kâmarū. "Being responsible for so many?"

"Every day." He nods. "But that terror pushes me to be stronger."

I smile at his resolve, wishing I felt the same. But once we have these scrolls, I can teach my Reapers to defend themselves. I can teach them how to attack.

I tighten my grip on my staff, picturing Inan's face. Maybe when he and his wretched mother are dead, the maji can all feel free.

"We're here," Kâmarū announces.

Amari pushes her way to the front as the final bits of gravel fall away. They reveal a metallic stone that can only be the walls of the temple.

My fingers tingle with anticipation as we wait to break through. Amari's plan may have gotten us this far, but there's no telling what will happen once we're actually inside the temple walls.

"Everybody ready?" Amari turns back to the others, and they meet her with terse nods.

She closes her eyes and I can almost feel her prayer.

"Alright," she sighs. "Let's get those scrolls."

CHAPTER THIRTY-FIVE

AMARI

EVERY CHEST EXHALES as Kâmarū tunnels through the temple walls. Our footsteps echo against the cool stone when we enter Chândomblé's long and narrow halls. The last time we were here, the temple felt alive; it was as if I could touch the magic oscillating through the air. But this time, the entire mountain shakes. It vibrates like the new power flowing through my veins.

"Amazing." Mâzeli runs his hands along the gold-mounted torches fastened to the walls. They light as we approach, as if beckoning us to travel further. A steady drip still echoes through the halls. I can almost hear the rhythmic thud of Lekan's staff. *Thank you,* I think to his spirit.

Without his sacrifice, we wouldn't have magic at all.

"Which way?" I turn to Dakarai as he binds his frizzy curls.

"Relax your hands," the Seer mutters to himself. "Feel the weight of time."

I can almost picture Mama Agba by his side, whispering the instructions he repeats now.

"Bàbá olójó," he starts the incantation. *"Se àfihàn àsìkò—"*

Unlike before, his magic appears like silver sparks of flint striking a match. The hairs on my neck rise as the air cools around us, a chill traveling to the space between his hands.

The silver sparks writhe like smoke, giving birth to the swath of night that grows beyond Dakarai's palms. I breathe in as hundreds of suspended stars fill the long hall.

"It's so big," I whisper to Zélie. "So much stronger than before."

"It's the temple," she explains. "Our magic is stronger inside these walls."

One by one, each speck of light expands, creating a window to the past. We watch with wide eyes and full hearts as the first star grows, showing two sêntaros hand in hand.

"Bàbá olójó, se àfihàn àsìkò—"

Dakarai's magic pulls the memories out of thin air, creating a mosaic of the souls who have walked this very spot. Like ghosts, robed sêntaros pass by, white symbols traveling up their bare arms. Dakarai allows the other images to fade until there's only one left.

We marvel at the mamaláwo distinguished by her ornate headdress. Unlike her brothers and sisters, her robes are cut from an elegant fabric that flows like liquid silver across her dark skin. I step closer to inspect the image, but it disappears into thin air. Dakarai continues to chant, summoning the mamaláwo meters ahead.

"This one will show us the path to the scroll room," Zélie explains as we fall in line behind our Seer. We follow along as Dakarai's magic forms bread crumbs out of the past, creating a trail that leads us through Chândomblé's twisting halls.

"I recognize this." Zélie places her palm against a heart-shaped indentation in the gray stone when we turn into a new hall.

"We're close." Dakarai points up the stairwell. "If this is right, it should be just around this corner—"

The clank of metal soles stops us in our tracks. We look up the stairwell to find three new shadows, silhouettes growing as they near.

"Retreat," I hiss, backing down the stairs as fast as I can. The others rush to follow, but smack into each other. My stomach drops as Mâzeli pitches forward.

"Grab him!" I whisper.

Zélie extends her hand, but it's too late. Mâzeli hits the stone with a low thud.

The clanking footsteps come to a sharp stop.

"General Jokôye?" a soldier calls. "Is that you?"

He moves down the steps, carrying a torch that lights all of our faces.

For a moment, we all stand still, frozen in shock. Then the soldier grabs his horn.

"Run!" I yell. I dash the other way, and the maji follow my path.

"Where are we going?" Zélie shouts.

"I don't know! Away from them!"

My heart pounds as I break into the lead. The soldier's horn echoes down the stone hall. It's not long before more piercing tones bounce against the curved walls.

Every step we take brings us further away from those scrolls. If Mother and Inan knew we were coming, they might know what we're here for, too. Our failure could lead them to the library's very door—

Focus, Amari.

We descend another stairwell as the clanking footsteps behind us grow. I race forward when we turn the corner, but skid to a stop when a troop charges toward us.

A few of the soldiers wear golden tîtán armor and I see a flash of dark blue ashê. My skin tingles as the realization hits. The soldiers are Connector tîtáns like me.

"Get back!" I command the *Iyika*, and the maji clear the way as the blue light radiates from my hand. I only try to summon one strike, but a powerful wave washes over the hall.

My skin sizzles as the soldiers cry out, grabbing their heads when pain brings them to their knees. My magic seems stronger in the other tîtáns' presence, but I can hardly grasp what's going on as we run away.

We race up another stairwell, sprinting, though I don't know where we'll land. Dakarai leads us up another flight of stairs, his broad chest heaving when we enter a particularly long hall.

"Up here!" the Seer instructs. We turn past a sharp corner when I see it—a dead end in an unsuspecting wall.

"Wait!" I double back and put my hands against the metallic stone. I don't need Dakarai's magic to remember Lekan standing in this very spot moons ago.

"This is it!" I shout. "The scrolls are behind this wall!"

"We don't have time—" Zélie reaches for my arm, but I pull away from her touch.

"We're too close to leave them behind!" I yell.

The soldiers' shouts near as Kâmarū reaches the dead end. He places his shaking hands against the stone, but despite the way his fingers glow, he can't break through. I don't know if it's because he isn't capable, or if all the magic he's channeled thus far has taken its toll.

"We need to buy him time!" I whip around as the soldiers close in.

You can do this, I think to myself. *You took down Ramaya. They're just men.*

Magic stirs in my chest, buzzing as it extends to my hands. I think of the needle and the hammer, not knowing which I'll need to unleash.

"Ya èmí, ya ara!" The chant slips from my tongue. But my heart stops when the first soldier rounds the corner.

By the skies . . .

"Inan?"

CHAPTER THIRTY-SIX

ZÉLIE

IT'S LIKE ALL THE AIR leaves the temple at once.

Sound bleeds from my ears.

All that's left is him.

I fight to feel the rage I summoned in the dreamscape. To call forth the new blades embedded in my staff. But staring at the little prince is like breathing mud.

"Inan?" Amari's question echoes through the vacuum in my mind. Her call draws her brother's eyes to her.

Then his gaze falls on me.

Run, my threat echoes through my mind. *Pray.*

I reach for my staff, but this close to Inan I can almost feel the fluttering sensation of his nails brushing against my bare skin.

We stare at each other as time starts to slip, forcing us back into the present. The shouts of the armies around us bleed in. Soldiers' swords break free of their hilts.

"Don't attack!" Inan shouts, but behind him, darkness rises. A general with a white streak down the center of her braid holds back a cloud of majacite gas.

Every soldier stops, but then Nehanda bursts into the hall. She points at all of us she screams.

"Eliminate the *Iyika!*" she yells.

"Mother, no!" Inan shouts, but he can't stop their attack. Their general throws out her hands, creating a wall of dark air. It blows the majacite down the hall like a cannonball, the black cloud racing toward our heads.

"*Atégùn Òrìsà!*" Jahi dives forward, sky-blue light wrapping around both his arms. With a grunt he throws his hands out and a cyclone spins from his palms.

The wind howls as it blows away the gas, making the soldiers fly back. Inan's feet thrash through the air. He grabs onto the mounted torch for dear life. Even the general slides away, unable to withstand the force of Jahi's winds.

"Zélie, we need you!" Amari grabs my wrists, her hair whipping in every direction. She places my hands against the wall and the hazy memory of Lekan doing the same sinks back in.

Please. I try to concentrate in the chaos. *Lekan, ràn mí lówó. We need to get inside!*

The wall starts to vibrate under my fingers, but I can't get it to do more. There's still something missing. Something I can't unlock alone.

"They're gaining on me!" Jahi shouts from behind, and my hair blows in the shifting wind. More tîtáns join their general in the hall, each throwing another gust of air.

As they all attack, Jahi's cyclone starts to die. My fingers shake when Inan plants a foot back on the ground. Nehanda's golden tîtáns round the corner, and the queen lifts her arms.

Lekan, please! I know you're still with me. I press my forehead against the hot stone. *Mo nílò ìrànlówó rẹ. Wá bá mi báyìí—*

A sharp heat erupts along my neck. I gasp as my tattoos begin to glow. The golden light spreads to my fingers, searing into the wall until a seam breaks down the middle.

"Go!" I squeeze Mâzeli into the scroll room. The rest of the maji follow as the walls widen. Jahi backs in last when his cyclone dies for good.

"Stop them!" Nehanda shouts. All at once, the soldiers charge. My head spins as I place my palms on the stone. It vibrates as the wall starts to close.

One soldier breaks in front of the pack with his sword outstretched. Amari yanks me back when he lunges forward.

With a crunch, the closing wall cuts through his arm like wood.

We all flinch as the severed limb bounces against the scroll room floor. The hand still clenches the sword's hilt, drops of blood raining down upon it.

My legs go numb and I fall to my knees. Sweat drips from every pore. We've made it in.

But how in Sky Mother's name are we going to get out?

CHAPTER THIRTY-SEVEN

INAN

IT'S LIKE MY SPIRIT hangs above my body, suspended in a fragment of space. Seeing Zélie stops time.

Perhaps it always will.

I run my hand against the unassuming wall; there's not even a crease to indicate where the slabs slid apart. But I can hardly wrap my head around the magic at work when everything inside me is still coming apart.

She's here. . . .

That fact should fill me with fear. But with only a wall between us, all the words I want to say muddle in my chest: incomplete sentences within a mountain of unfinished letters.

I thought whatever connection Zélie and I shared was broken. Damaged beyond repair. But the way she looked at me . . .

Skies.

It's been so long since I inhaled her sea-salt scent.

"Your Majesty!" General Jokôye runs down the hall, Mother and Ojore at her heels. The sight of them makes my scar burn. After this, they won't want to hold back.

I was ready to attack, yet one look at Amari and Zélie and I could barely utter one command. I don't know what to do next.

Who I need to protect.

"Are you alright?" Jokôye pants.

"I'm fine." I nod. "But the *Iyika* got inside."

"Surround the room." Jokôye turns to the soldiers. "If they tunneled in, they may try to tunnel out. Chidi, take care of Emeka. Get him to a medic."

I look away as two soldiers approach, lifting the soldier who lost his forearm. The poor boy's screams hit my ears like knives. I squeeze the bronze piece tight.

With only seven fighters, the *Iyika* have left dozens of our best strewn across the floor. We only have forty soldiers left. I don't even know if we can take them.

"Summon all of our forces," Jokôye shouts. "I want every single tîtán stationed outside this door."

"No holding back," Mother yells. "Strike to kill!"

"General, wait." I stop them both before their orders can hold. "I still want the *Iyika* taken in alive."

"With all due respect, Your Majesty, we can't afford to exercise restraint." Jokôye gestures down the hall, and I'm forced to take in the blood of my soldiers. In the corner, a medic tends to the soldier whose arm was severed. Even with distance and sedation, the boy's moans echo through the twisting halls.

"I empathize with your struggle," she continues. "But the *Iyika* risked their lives to retrieve what's in that room."

"She's right, Inan." Mother grabs my shoulder. "We can't allow them to obtain it. They may become unstoppable."

My stomach throbs with a pain so sharp I have to lean against the wall. Deep down, I know they're both right. I can't allow the *Iyika* to leave this temple alive.

Duty over self. Father's voice rings through my head. *Duty above all else.*

But last time, I chose him; him and Orïsha, when Amari and Zélie risked everything to choose me.

"If they die here, this war will only escalate, and we'll never locate their base. Take them in *alive*." I turn to Jokôye. "That's an order, General. Not a suggestion."

Jokôye's eyes flutter close. I can almost hear the crunch of her biting her tongue.

"Soldiers, get the king to the back of the hall. I don't want him here when the wall opens." She fingers the white streak in her braid before placing her hand against the crooked wall.

"Be ready to apprehend the rebels at a moment's notice. This was their only way in. That means it's their only way out."

CHAPTER THIRTY-EIGHT

ZÉLIE

KENYON'S FISTS SLAM against the walls of the scroll room, a thud reverberating through the metal shelves. The Burner hits it again and again until Kâmarū grabs his wrists and forces him to stop.

"Keep it together," the Grounder shouts. "We're never getting out of here if we fall apart now."

Kenyon breaks free of his hold and slams the wall again. "We shouldn't be in here at all!"

The Burner's anger does little to hide the terror I know we all feel. I want to say something, but it's hard to focus over the ringing in my ears. I don't know if the noise is from seeing Inan or the chaos of making it into the scroll room. I reach back for the tattoos on my neck. The swirling marks are still hot to the touch.

"Jahi!" Dakarai shouts. I turn as the Winder falls to the floor, body shaking from the toll of his cyclone. Dakarai kneels to check him out.

"That tîtán," Jahi pants. "The way she moved . . ."

Gods, I shake my head.

We're doomed.

"Mâzeli, are you alright?" I turn to find my Second still standing in front of the spot where the wall slid apart. The soldier's bloody forearm lies on the floor.

"Don't worry." I wipe the splatter of blood from his cheek and force him to turn around. "I'll get us out of here. I promise."

I place my fingers along the wall's cool metal interior, temperature falling as my magic fades. A tingle erupts when I lay my palm flat. The same sensation used to crawl up my skin at Inan's touch.

"Did you hear Inan?" Amari's voice shakes. "He told them not to attack—"

"That bastard came here with half the godsforsaken military!" Kenyon snaps. "He's not here to make peace!"

"Everyone shut up!" Mâzeli's high-pitched voice rings over everyone else's. His hands still shake, but he stands his ground, silencing us all. "We got in here despite the odds. We can figure a way out. But we need to stick together and collect these scrolls!"

He takes in the sacred library, prompting us all to do the same. The last time I was here, I was flung over Tzain's shoulder; the rush of newly awakened magic masked my other senses. What I thought were walls of gold are actually a reflective substance I've never encountered. It lights the room with a soft orange glow, like the color of sunsets melted into a glassy stone.

"If my father could see this . . ." Kâmarū releases a low whistle, sitting on the ground. Shelves that stretch to the domed ceiling encircle us, each filled with thin, brightly colored scrolls.

Mâzeli inspects the case with the Reaper baajis, running his hands over the gaps that once housed the scrolls Lekan gifted me. But even with those gone, dozens of incantations fill the shelves.

With these scrolls, the *Iyika* could become an unstoppable force.

"Kâmarū." Amari kneels by the Grounder's side, concern creasing her forehead. His eyes drift in and out of focus as he presses a hand to his heaving chest. "If we wait for you to recover, could you break through this substance and tunnel us out?"

"It's not earth or metal." He shakes his head. "I've never felt anything like this."

Amari runs a hand through her disheveled hair before turning to Dakarai instead. "Can you use the same incantation to find a path out the front entrance?"

"I suppose." Dakarai treads with care. "But it'd be hard to do with the soldiers—"

"Don't worry about them," she cuts him off. "Everyone, fill the bags with as many scrolls as you can. Kenyon, burn the rest."

"Amari, you can't!" I whip around, blinking as the ringing sensation in my ears grows louder. My tattoos hum at the sight of her. I shake my head as my vision blurs.

"These are sacred incantations," I explain. "Histories of our people that will be lost to time!"

"This is war." She meets my impassioned words with a cold stare. "These are *weapons*. Do you really want to leave these sacred incantations in the monarchy's hands?"

Her words sting, though I know she's right. A solemn air fills the room as we look at the hundreds of scrolls, silently calculating how many will have to burn.

"How do we know which ones to choose?" Mâzeli asks.

"Just make sure you take the same amount of scrolls for other clans," Amari says. "No matter who's present, all the maji need these weapons."

She removes her leather sack and walks to the Connector shelf, but pauses when nobody moves.

"What are you waiting for?" Amari circles her hand. "Let's get the scrolls and get out of here!"

Though a few bristle at her orders, Amari's conviction brings a calm to the chaos. One by one, we all follow her, filling the bags as if troops weren't waiting beyond the wall.

"Whatever you feel about Inan, don't act on it today." Amari comes to my side. "If not for me, then for Mâzeli's sake. Getting out of here will require your full attention."

I clench my jaw and brush past her, walking toward the center of the room. How dare she try to tell me what I can or can't do?

It doesn't matter if being this close to Inan makes my heart beat like a caged hummingbird. When these walls part, I have to thrust my new spear through his chest. I don't have a choice.

"Zélie, promise me!" Amari grabs my arm and her touch makes the room spin. I reach for the nearest shelf as I stumble. Sweat leaks from my skin.

"Are you alright?"

I try to nod, but my head throbs. The pain makes my knees weak. I fall forward as my tattoos flicker with golden light.

"Zélie!" Amari shouts.

Bodies crowd around me, but I can't see them through the blinding pain. I grit my teeth as my tattoos heat, searing like branding irons pressed into my flesh.

Steam rises from my skin, and my body starts to shake. My hands go to my throat as my tattoos glow. In a flash, the sunset walls of the scroll room go black.

No one moves when an explosion of light escapes from my mouth.

The beam shoots from my lips like a snake breaking free from its cage. It coils around my head, so powerful I can't breathe.

A pulse of air radiates around my body and sends everyone flying into the walls. Amari slams into a scroll case so hard it crashes to the ground.

"*Jagunjagun!*" Mâzeli shouts as the golden beam changes the room around us. Deep blues and purples swirl like night bleeding through the glassy walls. Glowing stars fill the air.

I wheeze when the golden glow ignites in my chest, so stark it paints my rib cage in black silhouettes. My back arches toward the ceiling as my feet leave the ground.

"Hold on!" Amari scrambles up from the floor, running across the scroll room. She climbs onto a fallen shelf as I rise. The golden light floods out of my eyes.

Amari reaches for my hand, but the moment our fingers touch, a cobalt light ignites in her chest.

"Zélie, what is this?" she screams, losing control as her feet dangle in the air. Though she fights, she rises by my side like she's been plucked from above by an invisible hand.

Cosmic energy leaks into the space between us, rainbows of smoke twisting through the air. With Amari's touch, hundreds of voices fill my head, voices I haven't heard since the sacred ritual.

Àwa ni omo re nínú èjè àti egungun!

A ti dé! Ìkan ni wá . . .

As the incantation thunders in my head, dozens of heartbeats ring in my ears. They pulse harder and faster, growing as my tattoos spread along my skin. It's then that I see the cobalt ribbon of light twisting from Amari's chest.

My eyes bulge as I remember my *ìsípayá* and all the colorful threads of power weaving together. The same sight appears before my eyes now, but instead of a rainbow of color, Amari's ashê is all navy blue.

The cobalt ribbons intertwine before her body, creating a sphere of energy so powerful its light flashes through the room. Blue ashê crackles around Amari's form like lightning. Its glow shines through her amber eyes—

In a breath, everything disappears.

Pain rattles through my body as I fall to the floor with a heavy thud. Amari hits the ground across from me, flashes of blue sparking as she falls.

I groan and grab my shoulder, rolling to the side as the soft orange light of the room reappears.

"*Jagunjagun!*" Mâzeli rushes over. "Are you okay?"

In seconds, the library returns to normal. There's not one sign of the chaos I just unleashed.

"What was *that?*" Dakarai asks.

"I don't know." I shake my head. I look down at the golden tattoos still glowing on my skin. No longer confined to my neck, the swirling symbols now spread across my shoulders and down my arms. I feel their searing heat all the way down my back.

As they glow, everyone's hearts beat like drums thundering in my head. The louder they pulse, the more I can see the ashê glowing under each maji's skin.

"By the gods . . ."

I blink, bewildered at the sight. Ashê moves through everyone's veins like blood, traveling a path intertwined with their skeletons. Emerald light flickers beneath Kâmarū's heart like a flame. Mâzeli's deep purple glow shimmers through his dark skin. But when I look to Amari, I can't believe my eyes.

Her navy light surges through every limb of her body like a torch.

"What is it?" she asks.

I can't find the words. Ashê radiates from her heart like a star. It's so dark with power it's nearly black. With this much ashê running through her, Amari shouldn't be able to survive two minutes, let alone two moons. I reach for her hand, igniting the navy glow in her chest again.

"What are you doing to me?" Amari gasps when the navy light rises to her eyes. Cobalt waves drift through the glassy walls as her magic swells.

As the scroll room changes again, I think of the blue ribbons of light that spiraled from her. The vision Oya showed me in my *ìsípayá*. That day,

I didn't know what I was looking at, but I understood the vast power all those intertwining threads of light had.

I let go of Amari's hand, turning to the other elders as it all clicks. Suddenly everything makes sense. The source of Nehanda's vast strength.

"This is what Oya showed me during my ascension," I breathe. "I think I know how to beat the queen."

CHAPTER THIRTY-NINE

· · · · · ◆ ◇ ◆ · · · · ·

AMARI

"I DON'T UNDERSTAND." Mâzeli reaches for Zélie's hand, but nothing happens. Her tattoos dim as Kenyon, Jahi, and Kâmarū take turns trying to cause a reaction.

But when she touches my hand again, the cobalt glow ignites in my chest. I rest my fingers against my sternum and I can feel it: the vibration as my magic swells.

"I can see it," Zélie says. "Your ashê. There's so much swirling around your body, more than one person could form alone." She studies me, seeing something the rest of us can't. "I think you might be able to absorb tîtán magic like your mother!"

"What?" I squint. That doesn't make sense. The way Mother moves, the way she casts—even at my strongest, I've never come close to that kind of strength.

"Zélie, you were with me on that hill." I say. "My magic doesn't work like that."

"How do we know? You've barely spent any time around other tîtáns!" She drags me to the parting wall, forcing my hands open. "When Nehanda attacked at the rally, the other Grounder tîtáns were around her. She sucked their magic into her palms."

I start to pull my hand away, but stop when I feel something beyond

193

the wall. My magic swirls in my chest, sending shivers through my bones.

"Can you feel it?" Zélie asks, but I'm not sure if I can say yes. The pulse of distant heartbeats trickles into my ears when I press my hands against the closed wall.

Three . . . four . . . five . . . I count the different rhythms in my head. They grow louder the more I concentrate.

"Just try," Zélie coaches me, putting her hands on my back. The navy light glows in my chest before softly shining out of my eyes. It builds in strength, coloring the world before me in shades of blue. I breathe deeply and concentrate on each heartbeat I sense beyond the wall.

"That's it." Zélie lowers her voice. "I can see the magic growing inside your core."

My skin starts to burn as my fingers spark with dark blue light. I grit my teeth as my magic swirls.

"Just a little more," she pushes me. "Open your hands."

I stretch out my fingers and gasp.

Wisps of blue ashê drift through the glassy walls.

"By the skies . . ." I step back, staring at the magic that drifts into my hands. It nips at my skin, but the pain is warm. It almost feels *good*.

"That should be impossible," Kâmarū breathes. "For any maji or tîtán!"

"They're not tîtáns," Zélie says. "Oya tried to show me in my *ìsípayá*. They can absorb the powers of tîtáns who share their magic type. They're more like cênters." She creates the term.

"Skies," I curse, realizing the implication behind her words. "If I'm like my mother . . ."

"Exactly." Zélie nods. "With enough Connector tîtáns, you could dominate her the way you overpowered Ramaya!"

I stare at the magic in my hand, flickering around my skin like a blaze.

I didn't know how I would defeat Mother. What leverage I could use to end this war. But with this ability, I see the path to victory. The path to the throne. I never needed an army or the maji.

I only needed my own gift.

I close my fist and look back at the wall, imagining the army on the other side. I attempt to visualize their next move, picture how to counter their strikes.

"Can you open the wall again?" I ask Zélie, and she nods. "Then everyone, keep gathering scrolls. I have a new plan."

· · · · · ◆ ◇ ◆ · · · · ·

"EVERYBODY READY?" I call, and the others respond with tense nods. Zélie takes her place at the wall as we make the final arrangements. Kenyon positions himself on the other side of her.

You're getting out of here. I exhale, clenching and unclenching my fists. *You don't have a choice. You finally have the power to end this war.*

Jahi grunts as he pushes the last shelf against the far wall, creating our barricade. I join him in the narrow gap, holding my breath as I wait for Zélie to open the wall.

"I may have misjudged you," Jahi says. "You're not half bad."

"Let's see how you feel when we make it across that bridge."

I crawl forward and peek out of the triangular space until I can see Zélie's face. She places her palms flat against the stone wall, almost frozen stiff as she waits for Kenyon's incantation.

"As soon as that wall opens, you run," he says. "If you don't, you'll burn."

When Zélie nods, Kenyon holds out his hand. My muscles tense as the incantation flies from his lips.

"Ìlànà iná, hun ara rẹ pèlú mi báàyí—"

I shield my eyes as two streams of scalding fire shoot from his palms.

They intertwine like ribbons, wrapping around themselves until they form a sphere at Zélie's back.

The air sears as the blaze grows, the ball of fire hanging in the air like a sun. As black spots form along its surface I shout.

"Open the wall!"

Zélie closes her eyes. The tattoos on her neck flicker as they light up. I hold my breath as the golden glow spreads to her fingertips before cutting through the metallic stone.

She dives for an iron case as the invisible seam splits down the wall's center. With a crack, the entrance erupts. Soldiers' shouts bleed in from the hall.

"Take them in!"

The general's shouts are muffled under a blast of howling wind. My hair ruffles as the gust builds, two cyclones of air shooting down the hall.

Time slows as the cannons of air speed toward Kenyon's growing blaze.

My hands fly to my ears as the cyclones meet the flames.

CHAPTER FORTY

$\cdots\cdots\blacklozenge\diamondsuit\blacklozenge\cdots\cdots$

INAN

EVEN FROM THE END of the hall, the explosion rattles me to my core.

Unbearable heat sears my skin.

Black smoke fills the air.

"Jokôye!" I cough through the smoke and charred pieces of parchment that fly through the air. But Ojore drags me back. My eyes sting as he pulls me away from the fight.

"Don't let them escape!" Mother points at the seven figures who charge through the black clouds. As the smoke clears, I see the blanket of bodies on the floor. Jokôye lies unconscious, leg twisted in half.

Mother runs forward, igniting the emerald glow in her chest. But Amari doesn't back down. My eyes widen when a navy light flickers to life behind her ribs.

Magic swirls around Amari's body like a typhoon, spreading through every limb.

"Ya èmí, ya ara!" she screams.

Blue light radiates from her hands in waves, pushing through the soldiers in her way.

Mother cries out, arching backward in pain. She grabs her head as she falls to the floor. Her golden mask skitters across the stone.

My chest clenches as Amari raises her hand to me, but when we lock eyes, she doesn't strike. Even as our armies collide, I see my sister. I see my blood.

"Amari!" My steps falter as I try to slow, but Ojore drags me around the corner. I struggle to stay upright as he pushes me up a flight of stairs. We race down a long hall, my pulse spiking as the rumble of the *Iyika* grows near.

"In here!" Ojore pushes me into a cramped room, pressing a hand to my mouth. Sweat drips down my face as the *Iyika*'s boots thunder toward us. I flinch when they pass.

Ojore doesn't move until their footsteps die for good. I peek out of the room to see the *Iyika* disappear up another flight of stairs.

"Skies." Ojore trembles, bracing himself against the stone wall. Though I try to breathe, my throat tightens the farther away Zélie gets. Her spirit tugs at mine. It's as if she's still anchored to my soul.

I attempt to pull her into my dreamscape, but when my magic sparks, a splitting pain erupts in my head.

"Are you okay?" Ojore grabs me as I double over, and I nod. But even in this temple, I can't move into the dreamscape.

"Stay here," Ojore orders. "I'm going back for the others."

I hold the bronze piece tight as he turns to run back for my mother and Jokôye. When he disappears around the corner, I look to the stairs again.

I ignore every voice that screams at me to stop as I sprint after Zélie's sea-salt soul.

CHAPTER FORTY-ONE

◆ ◇ ◆

ZÉLIE

"Zélie!"

My muscles tense as Inan's voice echoes up the stairwell. I look back to find him standing in the hall. A crimson trail leaks from beneath his hairline and down his jaw.

The char of the explosion mars his breastplate. He wavers as he unfastens it and throws the armor to the ground. His voice escapes in a grated rasp.

"I just want to talk."

Those five words are all it takes for me to snap. My fingers wrap around my staff. My vision flashes white as I charge at him.

The temple blurs behind Inan's amber eyes. Shouts die under the roar of his lies. If it weren't for him, I wouldn't have my scars.

Baba would still be alive.

"I don't want to fight," he says, raising his hands in surrender. I bare my teeth and throw my weight forward.

"Then stand still and die!"

The air clings as my staff collides with the hard metal of his sword. The familiar collision reverberates through my skin, propelling me to strike again.

My body moves beyond my control, the memory of Baba's blood

consuming all thought. Yet in my blows, I feel the echo of Inan's touch. His breath. His kiss.

"Zélie, please!" he shouts. "We still want the same things! We can end this fight!"

As my staff collides with his sword again, I remember the fantasy of our Orïsha. The kingdom we were to rule together.

I swing my staff at his neck, yet he only brings his sword up to defend himself. I can't tell if he's too injured to fight, or if he can't attack because it's me.

Despite his hesitation, I hold on to my rage, stoking the fire in my core. He has to pay for what he did. If it weren't for him, tîtáns and cênters wouldn't exist at all.

I shift my weight, twisting Inan's sword from his hands. Before he can react, I extend my blades. My spear slices through his side.

Inan cries out, pitching into the wall. Crimson blood leaks from between his fingers, dripping onto the floor.

Now's my chance!

My nostrils flare as I drive my knee into his gut. He wheezes and falls to the ground. Pressure builds in my chest as I straddle him.

"Zélie, please . . ."

Magic nips at my skin, but I ignore it to position the blade in my staff above his heart. I don't want my powers for this. I want to feel him take his last breath.

"I'm sorry," he chokes out the words. His warm blood seeps onto my skin. A lump forms in my throat. Moons ago it was Baba's blood on my hands instead of his.

"I'm not." I speak the words, needing them to be true. Because when Inan's gone, my scars won't hurt. Baba's death will be avenged.

When he's dead, I'll be able to breathe again.

I'll finally be free—

"Jagunjagun!"

Mâzeli's voice stops time.

I whip around, praying he's farther away than he sounds. Mâzeli speeds down the stairs, lips trembling as he lifts his shaking hands.

It's only then that I hear the footsteps behind me. I turn to see an admiral charging forward, his sword poised to cut me down.

"Ojore, no!" Inan throws me off of him, reaching for his blade. I prepare to defend myself, but Inan uses his sword to block his admiral's attack.

"What're you doing?" Ojore yells. I wonder the same thing. But with Mâzeli in danger, I don't have time to think.

"Come on!" I grab my Second's arm, pulling him down the hall. I glance back to see Inan collapse, unable to stand with the wound in his side.

"I need a medic!" The admiral's shouts echo as we run up the stairs.

I squeeze Mâzeli's hand as I struggle to hide my tears.

CHAPTER FORTY-TWO

INAN

I WINCE AS OJORE ties the last bandage around my abdomen. With the help of another soldier, he moves me onto a canvas stretcher. The two grunt as they lift me up.

I pretend to keep my eyes closed with pain as we move through the sacred halls. Without the threat of the *Iyika*, the only sounds around us are the moans of the wounded and the voices of medics who move to help them.

What were you thinking?

My heart thunders in my chest as I glance up at Ojore. He hasn't said a word since my sword met his, but I know it's only a matter of time. *If he tells Mother what I did . . .*

I squeeze the bronze piece, banishing the thought. I'm the king.

It's his word against mine.

"Inan!" Mother rises when we exit the temple grounds. She pushes off the Healer tending to her half-treated burns.

"What happened?" she snaps at Ojore. "You're supposed to protect him with your life!"

"Mother, he did." I rush to his defense. "Ojore stopped a blade from going through my heart."

Mother's face falls and she throws her arms around Ojore's neck.

"Skies, boy. How many times will we have to thank you for saving his life?"

Ojore locks eyes with me, jaw clenching tight.

"No thanks necessary," he says. "I'd do it anytime."

I swallow and avoid his gaze. I don't know how long he'll let my lie stand, but at least my secret's safe for now. I can't explain what happened in the temple; I barely understand it myself. Zélie looked at that boy and somehow it was greater than my pain.

I couldn't stomach the thought of being the reason she lost someone else.

"You need to get to safety." Mother ushers us along. "The others are waiting across the bridge."

"What are you doing?" I ask.

My fingers grow cold as she hooks her golden mask over her nose. "This place only serves our enemies."

"No!" I jerk up, wincing at the pain that shoots up my side. "This temple may be the oldest Orïsha has. It holds the stories of our past!"

Though Chândomblé wasn't created for me, I feel its pulse like the beating heart of this land. I remember wandering its hallowed grounds in search of Zélie's path moons ago. Kneeling before the portrait of Ori. This temple was the one place that could quiet the noise in my head.

"You can't," I say. "I forbid it."

Mother purses her lips. I can almost see her swallowing everything she wants to yell.

"This is a den for rebellious maggots," she hisses. "Not some historical sight."

Ojore eyes me, but I don't back down.

"The *Iyika* came here for power," I say. "We can use the temple to seize some for ourselves!"

"Inan, look around you." Mother shakes her head. "Look at what they've done."

She points behind me and I see the endless trail of bodies being carried out. Though most of the soldiers head for the Healers, there are those who no longer breathe. The sight of every new corpse that piles up before the bridge lands like a punch to the gut.

Jokôye passes us on a medic's stretcher, still unconscious. Someone's reset her leg, but blood leaks through the bandages. My chin quivers at the sight.

Would she have gotten hurt if I hadn't wanted Zélie and Amari taken in alive?

"You do not serve the maji," Mother continues. "You do not even serve these lands. Your duty as king is to protect the throne. The throne and the people who bow before it."

I exhale, knowing I have no other choice.

"Destroy it," I order, though it hurts to speak the words.

My chest falls as Mother marches forward with her tîtáns that still stand. As she walks past the carnage in her path, I know she's right. Our enemies are gaining ground. We need to eliminate every asset they have. But how long can both sides keep going like this before we destroy Orïsha?

Mother's tîtáns form a circle around her as the last of the soldiers is carried away from the temple grounds. She opens her hands, igniting the emerald glow in her chest. Veins bulge against her neck and the ground begins to shake.

Her tîtáns seize as she sucks the power from their veins.

"More!" Mother shouts. The earth's vibration rattles my teeth as her tîtáns fall to their knees. The green light shoots out of her eyes and she punches her fists into the dirt. The ground cracks on impact.

The fissure speeds through the jungle, tearing up the earth in its path. Its rumble grows the closer it gets to the temple.

When it reaches the hallowed grounds, it's like a dozen bombs go off at once. The temple falls as the ground beneath it sinks into the earth.

"Skies," Ojore curses at Mother's power, shielding his nose. I cover my eyes as the rock explodes, debris clouding up the sky. Up ahead, a tîtán cries out before his body falls limp. He's dead before he hits the ground.

Mother's magic has taken everything from him.

I have to end this war. The thought echoes through my mind as I grab the wound in my side. The battles are spinning out of control. If we continue at this rate, the entire kingdom will be destroyed in the process.

I squeeze the bronze piece tight, searching for another way out of this fight.

If Zélie won't listen to me, I'll find someone who will.

CHAPTER FORTY-THREE

◆ ◇ ◆

AMARI

FOUR LONG DAYS pass before we make it back to the sanctuary. This high above the clouds the haven is at peace, ignorant of the chaos sweeping the lands at the mountain's feet.

By the time we step onto the first mountain, my legs drag like they're made of marble. The sanctuary lies in a calm silence, majestic towers painted in dark silhouettes across the indigo sky.

"*Yemoja, ẹ ṣé o.*" Nâo drops to her knees and kisses the wild grass with gratitude. I almost join her, but if I fall now, I won't be able to rise again. It feels like a sin to enter these hallowed grounds with the blood, dirt, and grime coating our weary bodies. My legs sway and I stumble forward, resting against the obsidian wall of the main tower.

"Need a hand?"

I look up to find Tzain's smile, and it warms me to my core.

"Were you waiting for me?" I ask, and he shrugs.

"I missed you too much."

I rest my head against his broad chest, finding refuge inside his arms.

"I missed you, too," I whisper. "It was strange being out there without you."

I don't know the last time I went into battle without Tzain by my side. It used to be the two of us who didn't have magic at our disposal, yet

I always trusted him more than I trusted anyone else. I squeeze him tight, attempting to close the space that's grown between us since I became a tîtán. I don't want it to increase now that I know I'm a cênter.

Behind me, Tzain catches Zélie's eyes as she dismounts Nailah. She waves at him with a smile before turning back to Mâzeli.

"Did you get what you wanted?" Tzain asks.

"In a way." I look back as the elders start unloading their scrolls, taking them to the council room. "After what we learned at Chândomblé, we have a fighting chance. I might even have enough power to face my mother and force the monarchy to surrender."

Tzain's muscles relax at the news, and he pulls me closer to his chest. "Then you can take the throne?"

I smile. "Then I can take the throne."

But as we stand wrapped up in each other's arms, his touch erases all thoughts of the war; of cênters; of the throne. Breathing in his sandalwood scent, I realize how much I want him. How much I want more.

"What is it?" Tzain pulls away, sensing my shift. I wrap my arms around his neck.

"What's it going to take for you to carry me to a bath?"

Tzain purses his lips in false contemplation, scratching his chin. Then without warning, he sweeps me off my feet. I laugh as he carries me across the stone bridge.

"It's that easy?" I ask.

"Of course." Tzain grins. "I live to serve, my queen."

Though he jokes, his words heat my skin. He's the only one who looks at me like I deserve that title. The one person who believes I can lead.

I raise my hand to his stubbled cheek and my gaze settles on his lips. I imagine what a few hours with him might entail. How his kiss might feel.

"Is there anything else I can help you with, my queen?"

My smile widens as he leans in. My heart speeds up in my chest as I dig my nails into his neck.

Our lips meet, and the rush is so strong it spreads through my entire body. A flutter erupts between my legs as I shift, pressing into him—

"Where do you think you're going?"

Our heads snap apart to face Jahi. My cheeks flush at the Winder's glare. I force Tzain to put me down.

"We have work to do." Jahi gestures to the line of elders making their way to the council room, and I groan.

"Can't we sleep?"

"Don't complain now," he says. "You're the one who wanted this job."

My shoulders slump and I turn to Tzain, wrapping my arms around him again. I feel his chest deflate as he slides his hands across my back.

"Another time?" I ask.

"Do what you need to do." His lips meet mine once more and I sink into the safety of his kiss. He squeezes my waist, sending shivers along my skin.

As I pull away, I wish I never had to leave his embrace. But Orïsha waits for no one. Not even him.

Jahi eyes me when I pass, but I ignore his glare.

"Wake Mama Agba," I order. "If anyone can get us answers, it's her."

$$\cdots \cdot \cdot \bullet \Diamond \bullet \cdot \cdots$$

NO ONE SPEAKS as Mama Agba studies the golden script along Zélie's skin. My shoulders burn from holding up the blanket that shields Zélie's scars and bare back from the other elders. Mama Agba pauses to scribble more sênbaría translations onto a brown parchment, the scratch of her reed brush echoing against the stained glass windows of the council room. A full hour passes before Mama Agba sets her brush down, ready to share what she's uncovered.

"I haven't seen markings like these since I studied with the sêntaros," she says. "The tattoos are the mark of the moonstone, a sister to the sunstone you retrieved from Ibeji."

"But the sunstone was destroyed in the ritual." Zélie tilts her head. "It shattered in my hands after I used it to bring our magic back."

"Unlike its sister stone, the moonstone is not one you can hold," Mama Agba explains. "It is a power bestowed by the gods. They must have granted it to you during the solstice."

Mama Agba waits as Zélie slips into a sleeveless kaftan, its deep purple fabric shimmering like wine against her complexion. When dressed, Zélie takes her place at the table, sitting in front of a bronze statue with amethyst crystals for eyes.

"The moonstone ignites by command," Mama Agba continues. "Few can summon its power." She rests her weathered fingers along Zélie's sternum before reciting the sacred words. "E tonná agbára yin."

Zélie inhales a sharp breath as the tattoos ignite along her skin. The delicate lines glow with golden light, so strong it shines through the wine-colored kaftan. Though not as bright as their shine in the scroll room, the sight still steals my words. Zélie looks like a goddess, bathing us in her golden glow.

"The moonstone has the ability to bind the lifeforces inside all of us," Mama Agba explains. "If you were granted this ability during the sacred ritual, it would explain the origin of Amari and Nehanda's abilities. It may be possible to use the moonstone to make more cênters like them."

"Wait, what?" I lean forward, mouth falling slack. More cênters would give us more power. We would have more leverage to negotiate the end of this war. "Would they be as strong as my mother?"

"The power might not exhibit itself the same way, but any maji who could hold that much ashê in her body would be able to perform great feats." Mama Agba nods. "A Tider could generate a tsunami with just a wave of her hands. A Seer in her prime might be able to see through any point in time. But pursuing great power requires great sacrifice." Mama Agba pauses, eyes settling on me. "You and your mother are cênters now, but didn't you have to sacrifice someone you love?"

My throat dries and I avert my gaze, back burning with the memories. "In a way," I say. "I killed my father on the ritual grounds."

Mama Agba exhales a deep breath and purses her lips. She removes her hand from Zélie's chest, and without her touch, the golden glow of the moonstone's tattoos dies.

"If you wish to create another cênter, you must be willing to make such a sacrifice," Mama Agba says. "A loss of that magnitude is the only thing that can come close to the power used to create the cênters during the solstice."

"What if I could find another way?" Zélie asks. "Use the moonstone to bind our lifeforces without killing someone we love?"

"Even if you could, the connection would not last," Mama Agba shakes her head. "A power that volatile would consume anyone it touched, and binding yourself to someone's lifeforce means binding yourself to their death." Mama Agba's eyes hang on Zélie as she grabs her staff and rises from her seat. "You are the elders now. It is not my place to tell you what to do. But you should know that there are weapons so great, they shouldn't be used."

A heavy silence hangs over us as Mama Agba exits the council room. Around the table, everyone seems to weigh her words; the cost of what it would take to become a cênter.

But in her explanation, I see our answer; our leverage; our peace. We have the power to win this war without losing one more soul. We can create the Orïsha we want to see.

"We went to Chândomblé to gain power over Nehanda, and now we have it," I address the room. "We could build an entire army with cênters as strong as my mother. With a threat like that, the monarchy would have no choice but to concede to us." I rise from my seat, picturing my brother's face when I tell him the power at our disposal. "Allow me to go to Lagos and meet with Inan. I know I can negotiate peace on our terms."

"Your terms," Kenyon scoffs. "Not ours. Our future isn't certain until we have a maji on the throne. No one in the palace will agree to that." Kenyon stands up, slapping his palms against the table. "With Zélie's ability, we have the power we need. Now it's time to use it and take Lagos down for good."

"Idiot." Nâo smacks her lips. "We'd have to sacrifice someone we love."

"Lives will be lost no matter what approach we take," Kenyon pushes. "At least this way sacrifices won't be made in vain."

"I refuse to spill maji blood." Kâmarū's voice shakes with a quiet rage. "If we can't win this war as maji, then we deserve to lose."

One by one, heads drift to Zélie, looking to her for the final say. I lock eyes with her as we wait, but she avoids my gaze.

"All I'm asking for is a chance to find out if peace is a viable option." I rise from my seat, kneeling before Zélie. "I know you heard Inan when he told his soldiers not to attack. For skies' sake, he risked his *life* so you and Mâzeli could escape!"

Her muscles tense as I grab her hand, but I don't back down.

"He still cares for you," I lower my voice. "I know you care, too—"

"No." She rips her hand away, balling her fingers into a fist. "We can't trust him. We can't trust any of them."

"Zélie—"

"I only asked for one thing when I joined this fight," she cuts me off. "All I wanted was to end Inan."

"He's my blood." I narrow my eyes. "You know I could never agree to that."

"Well this is my blood." Zélie gestures around the stone table. "The maji won't be safe until your brother's gone."

Her words cut deeper than she could know. It was only a few moons ago when she grabbed my hand and claimed me as her family. She claimed me as her blood.

"If you won't spare his life, then I won't fight for you." I cross my arms. "You need me on your side. I'm the only cênter you have."

"We can make our own," Na'imah glares.

"No, we can't." Zélie shakes her head. "Mama Agba's right. It's too dangerous. We're more likely to die trying to make the connection than to match their power, and it's not worth sacrificing someone we love."

She stares at me, and I can feel something fracture between us. There's no hiding it anymore.

We don't have the same plan to win this war.

"We don't need Amari." Zélie turns back to the elders. "We don't even need to become cênters. We went to Chândomblé to recover our scrolls and now we have them." Zélie gestures to the incantations piled against the far wall. "We'll train our maji until they're strong enough to face Nehanda and her títáns. And when that day comes, we'll end this war in the only way the monarchy will respect. The way that would make our ancestors proud."

"That's what I'm talking about!" Nâo claps, rising out of her seat. "Let's finish this our way, led by the Soldier of Death!"

My chest falls as the other elders jump in, enthralled by their future fight. I stare at Zélie and I know she can feel the heat of my gaze, but she doesn't meet my eye.

My chest slumps and I exit the room, unable to stomach the sight. I practically run out of the first tower, not stopping until I meet the cool night air.

Orïsha waits for no one, Father's whisper tickles my ear, reminding me of what I must do. I can't keep waiting for Zélie and the *Iyika* to see reason. No matter what, they only fight for the maji. I must fight for the kingdom.

"Orïsha waits for no one," I whisper to myself, balling my fists.

If the elders won't support my plan to win this war, I'll have to do it myself.

CHAPTER FORTY-FOUR

ZÉLIE

HIGH-PITCHED CHIMES BLEED into my ears, jarring me awake. Though I've only spent a short time swaddled within the mountain walls that cover the sanctuary, I already know what each unique tone means. Low bells commemorate the arrival of new maji. A twinkling melody signals each mealtime. But this piercing timbre is a recent addition. Chimes calling us to train.

I peel my head up from the ankara print on my pillow; a sliver of yellow peeks out from my balcony's ledge. I groan and bury myself under the covers. Only Mama Agba would make us rise before the sun.

As the chimes ring, the pit of guilt that's plagued me since Chândomblé settles like a brick in my stomach. How am I supposed to face my Reapers knowing I'm not fit to lead my clan?

It's been days, yet my mind won't stop replaying the memory of Mâzeli running down the temple stairs. I promised to keep my Second safe. To protect him with my life. But as soon as I saw Inan, I abandoned my vow to get my revenge. I was in charge of only one Reaper then. What would've happened if I'd led the entire clan?

There are so few Reapers to begin with; Oya doesn't bless many with our gift. If we're going to win this war and rebuild what the monarchy took, we can't afford to lose any of them. They need an elder they can actually trust.

A soft knock raps against my door, forcing me to lift my head. I half expect to find Mâzeli's oversized ears when the purple door creaks open, but a sweeping flash of silver peeks through instead.

"Mama Agba?"

I grin at the sight of the silver robe over her dark skin. The crimped garment flows behind her as she walks. It's like she carries a breeze within the silk's folds.

Before the Raid, past clan elders wore mantles like these, garments to mark their revered status. To wear this robe was as special as wearing the clan elder's headdress.

"*E kàárò ìyáawa.*" I drag myself out of bed, kneeling before her despite how my thighs burn. As my nose touches the ground, I think of how many times I should've done this. How many times we all should've bowed in her presence.

As a former elder, Mama Agba was supposed to be celebrated. Revered by all. Instead she spent years hiding who she was, wearing nothing but muted kaftans, while she stitched beautiful garments for nobles until her fingers bled.

"Get up, child." Mama Agba smacks her lips at me, but her mahogany eyes crinkle with emotion. She wraps me in a warm hug, and from the scent of cloves and *súyà* spices embedded into her silks, I know she's already put in hours in the kitchen.

"I wanted to catch you before your first training." She reaches into her bag and removes an imposing metal collar. The majestic piece stretches the full length of my neck with a base to cover my collarbone.

"It's beautiful," I breathe, touching its spectacular design. Dozens of triangular plates have been stitched together to form its skin, a unique mix of her seamstress skills and Tahir's metalwork.

"I thought about making headdresses, but with all the battle you're seeing, these felt more appropriate." Mama Agba gestures for me to turn around, but I stay still.

"You don't like it?" she asks.

I shake my head, running my toes over the mosaic tiles along the floor.

"I feel like I don't deserve to wear it. I don't think I'm meant to be their elder."

"Is this because of what happened at the temple?" Mama Agba rests her hand on my shoulder, beckoning me toward her. "Being an elder does not mean you won't make mistakes. It only means you keep fighting despite them."

"You heard what happened to Mâzeli?" I ask.

"Child, word travels faster in these walls than a cheetanaire in high sprint. I know far more than I want to about all of you." Mama Agba shakes her head as she turns me toward the mirror. "Apparently Kenyon's set his sights on Na'imah, but Na'imah set her sights on Dakarai?"

"But Dakarai likes Imani!"

"I *know*," Mama Agba sighs. "And that Cancer will eat him alive. It is one giant mess!"

I smile to myself as she reaches for the collar. I hope she hasn't heard whispers about Inan. Or whispers about Roën.

A flutter spreads through my chest at the thought of the mercenary, one I wish I could erase. Without the constant threat of battle, I find myself thinking of his pink smirk. I remember his callused touch. At times, I catch myself staring at the sanctuary's entrance, waiting for him to saunter back into my life on some half-baked mission.

But even he fades from my mind when Mama Agba places the collar over the golden marks on my throat. As I run my fingers through the thin grooves between each triangular plate, an unexpected swell fills my chest.

It reminds me of sitting in her reed ahéré after I completed my training, sipping tea before she placed the graduation staff in my hands. In a way, this feels exactly the same. Except everything and everyone in our world has changed.

"Zélie, if you were not meant to be an elder, your ascension would have been rejected," Mama Agba says. "Oya gave you an *isípayá* to mark you as worthy. You wouldn't have seen anything if she did not think you were the best person to lead this clan."

I chew on her words, thinking of what Oya showed me. If I close my eyes, I can still see the purple ribbon of light spinning from my chest like a thread, intertwining with a ribbon of gold. The power they created felt just like the one I sensed in Amari.

Back at the temple, I was sure it was a symbol of the cênters. But all of Amari's threads were only cobalt blue. If I looked at Nehanda's, I'm sure I'd see only emerald greens. Where were the purples? The golds? The tangerines?

"Mama Agba." I turn to face her. Even in my head, the question waiting on my lips sounds ridiculous. But I don't know how to account for the colors of light I haven't seen. "Is it possible to combine different magic?"

"Well, the very nature of the cênters—"

"Not like that," I interrupt. "Is it possible to combine different *types* of magic? The magic of people not in the same clan?"

Mama Agba's eyes go wide and she steps back, brows creasing in thought. "Why do you ask?"

"In my *isípayá*, I saw different colors. I saw purples mixing with golds. It was a rainbow of color," I explain. "A rainbow of power."

"I see." Mama Agba purses her lips. "Combining the same magic is rare enough, but to mix different magics . . . to my knowledge, it has only been done once before. It is the very reason Orïsha has majacite at all."

My mouth falls slack as Mama Agba tells me the tale of the Grounder and Cancer who combined their magic, a connection so powerful and explosive it created majacite deposits throughout the land.

"The two maji were killed on impact," Mama Agba explains. "But we still feel the effect of their connection today. The deposits they created are what the monarchy have mined for over a century."

"Could it happen again?" I ask.

"In theory." Mama Agba shakes her head. "If a connection like that could be sustained, if its wielders could survive, there is no telling what could happen. A Grounder and a Burner could raise volcanoes from the earth. A Reaper and a Healer might even be able to raise the dead."

I nod, thinking of the potential at hand. A power like that is difficult to comprehend. It feels even mightier than the gods.

"But Zélie, to go that route—"

"I know," I assure her. "It's still not the plan."

A gentle chatter rises from below as the maji leave their dormitories, and Mama Agba and I move to my balcony. I watch as groups traverse the stone bridge to the third mountain, crossing over the natural baths to meet at their clan temples.

Mâzeli leads Bimpe and Mári, his large ears easy to spot in the crowd. Mama Agba smiles as we look down on them. She rubs her hand up and down my arm.

"Do you still remember your *isípayá*?" I ask, and Mama Agba exhales. A soft smile settles on her face, so bright it lights the room.

"I peeked into the beyond," Mama Agba breathes. "I kneeled on the mountaintop. Sky Mother welcomed me with open arms."

"It sounds beautiful," I whisper.

"It was." Mama Agba nods. "It's been decades, but I can still remember that special warmth. That love."

Mama Agba straightens my collar and removes my headwrap, shaking out my coils before leading me out the door.

"You are the person your Reapers need, Elder Zélie. The only person you need to prove it to is yourself."

• • • • • ◆ ◈ ◆ • • • • •

By the time I make my way to the third mountain, most clans are hard at work. With the exception of the Reapers, every other clan has at least a dozen maji who can fight.

The maji gather in front of their clan temples, training while divîners watch. As I pass them on my way to the Reaper tower at the top of the mountain, the little confidence Mama Agba instilled in me begins to melt.

"Not like that," Na'imah instructs, shaking her head so hard that a shower of orange flower petals fall from her curls. Dragonflies orbit her head as she repositions a maji's hands around her cheetanaire's temples. "Feel the connection before you begin the incantation."

The Tamer nods and closes his eyes, face stern with concentration. Small monkeys skitter across his back as he chants, some hanging from his neck and ears.

"Èdá inú egàn, yá mi ní ojú rẹ—"

A soft pink light ignites behind the Tamer's eyelids, growing in strength. When he opens his eyes, the cheetanaire does as well. The same pink light fills the ryder's thin irises.

The Tamer's mouth hangs open as he gazes at the world through the cheetanaire's eyes. It's like their heads are controlled by the same source. The two even blink in unison.

On the ledge above them, Folake leads a demonstration for the Lighters, her long white locs tied back. She stretches out her slender fingers, gathering something I can't see.

219

"The trick is to feel the light like something you can hold in the palms of your hands. Once you can feel it, the incantation is easy. *Ìbòrí òkùnkùn!*"

Folake claps her hands together and in the blink of an eye, darkness descends over the Lighter Temple. She summons a blackness deeper than any I've ever experienced, like all the stars were plucked from a moonless night.

The blackout lasts only an instant, but when light reappears, every maji's eyes are open wide.

That was amazing, I shake my head. I hope I can be half as good.

"Reapers ready!" Mâzeli's high-pitched voice travels beyond the engraved stone of the Reaper Temple. He stands before our clan in the grassy terrain out back, making Bimpe and Mári chant in harmony.

"Ẹmí àwọn tí ó ti sùn—"

"Ẹmí àwọn tí ó ti sùn!"

"Mo ké pè yin ní òní—"

"Mo ké pè yin ní òní!"

My chest flutters with awe as my Reapers conjure animations in unison. Though each spirit holds a unique shape, the animations rise as one, blooming from the grass like a garden of calla lilies.

"Hold them steady," Mâzeli calls. "Maintain size!"

Mári's animation falls apart while Bimpe's grows large, but the way they work together reminds me of the Reapers I knew before the Raid.

"Jagunjagun!" Mâzeli's face lights when he spots me leaning against the temple. He drops to both knees, bowing as if I were the queen.

"What are we going to learn today?" he asks. "Soul ripping? Spirit tethers? What about—*ow!*" Mâzeli cries out when Mári punches his arm.

"Shut your mouth and let her answer!" she hisses.

"Mári, I'm your Second! You can't hit me here!"

Bimpe giggles and I smile, remembering the laughter that would echo in Mama Agba's ahéré. Though real problems awaited us outside her woven reed walls, she still allowed us to have fun.

Listening to my Reapers now, I realize that this training doesn't have to be about the war. For once, we can celebrate our magic by practicing the incantations that have been passed on through generations. We can bask in the Reapers' return.

"Today we're going to learn an ancient and powerful technique." I hand Mâzeli the scroll I've selected.

"*Òjìjí ikú?*" Mâzeli's brows rise as he reads. "Shadows of death?"

"You can already conjure animations." I nod. "This technique will allow you to strengthen that skill while building another."

I step forward and cast in my head, bringing an animation to life with just a wave of my hand. As the spirit rises from the dirt, I remember training alone in the desert, trying to create an animation for the first time. A few moons ago I couldn't even move one grain of sand.

"Creating shadows is just like creating animations. But instead of channeling a spirit into the nearest element, you wield it in its raw form. The shadows can take any shape, but the more complicated the vessel, the harder it is to mold."

"Stories say your shadows are powerful enough to turn entire armies to ash." Mári's words make every Reaper light up, but the memory of wielding Baba's spirit makes a pit open up in my chest. When he tore through my blood, the shadows that exploded from my skin were more than powerful. They were death incarnate.

"What I did at the ritual was fueled by the connection I had with my father," I explain. "My magic was amplified from the sacred grounds and centennial solstice. It'd be difficult to wield that kind of strength again."

"Can you try?" Mâzeli asks, a request the others echo. They all stare at me with hungry eyes. I know they'll need a demonstration.

I brace myself for the memories of Baba that'll hit with this incantation, but as I prepare to chant, the sun finally rises over our temple. As the rays and shadows move over the mountaintop, I'm reminded of the last time Mama used this incantation. It was years ago, back when I still lived in Ibadan.

Tzain dared me to climb a mountaintop and Mama screamed when I leapt from a cliff. Who knows what would've happened if she hadn't conjured the shadows of death that carried me down into one of Ibadan's ice cold lakes.

A smile comes to my face as I walk to the front of our temple. Just ahead lies the perfect cliff. It juts out over the waterfall baths meters below.

"Pay attention!" I shout before I take off, sprinting for the ledge. The others yell after me as I run. I lift my head to the whipping winds.

A freedom I haven't felt since I was a girl wraps around me, propelling me on. Magic rises like a wave preparing to crest. With a final step, I leap from the ledge.

"Èmí òkú, gba àáyé nínú mi—"

My incantation falls away in the rush of air and I spread out every limb. For a moment, I get to soar.

"Jáde nínú àwon òjìjí re—"

As the water rushes toward me, it's like I'm six years old again. Baba and Mama are still alive.

No one I love ever has to die.

"Yí padà láti owó mi!"

The final words of the incantation make the air ripple around me. Spirits of the dead explode from my back. The purple auras of the shadows are so dark, they're almost black.

The shadows writhe through the air like sparks, coming together as my mold takes form. The cold spirits spread across my back and wrap around my arms, creating a glider that cuts through the sky.

Laughter erupts from deep inside me as I soar. For an instant, I rise above all my pain. I feel the freedom I've craved.

I soar until I land on the waterfall's bank with a lurch. The shadows disappear in wisps of smoke. I turn to find every Reaper cheering from the cliff, joined by other maji who observed the feat.

"Alright." I point up at Mâzeli. "Let's see if you fly or make a splash."

His face falls as he looks at the water. "But I can't swim!"

My grin turns mischievous and I shrug.

"Then the greatest Reaper who ever lived better get it right on the first try."

CHAPTER FORTY-FIVE

■ ■ ■ ■ ■ ◆ ◇ ◆ ■ ■ ■ ■ ■

AMARI

I BREATHE A sigh of relief when the twinkling dinner chimes ring. After a week of training, I expected the ice to melt between me and the other Connectors, but if anything, it's only thickened. I lift my chin as the maji stop mid-incantation, gathering their things to make their way down the mountain.

"We start at sunrise tomorrow," I call at their backs.

No one even turns around.

A sour taste settles on my tongue as I clean up the scrolls, revealing the ceramic tiles that create a Connector baaji on the floor. It doesn't matter what I do; as long as Ramaya lies in the infirmary, I'm still the enemy. If I wasn't a cênter, they might even attack me in her name. Every time someone masters another incantation, I half expect them to "slip" and throw it in my direction.

Focus, Amari.

I attempt to shake the stench of disapproval as I close the door to the Connector Temple. I unravel the cobalt scroll in my hand, struggling to piece together the sênbaría transcribed inside.

"Èmí ni mò nwá," I whisper the Yoruba. "Jé kí èmí re și sí mi."

My fingers spark with blue light as I close my eyes, trying to make the incantation come to life. When I first discovered the scroll to create a dreamscape a few days ago, I nearly tossed it aside. I didn't realize what I held.

I was searching for incantations that would help the Connectors in battle. The ability to create a special plane and meld with someone else's mind wasn't something we could use. But as I pondered the incantation, I realized the gods had given me exactly what I needed.

If I can create my own dreamscape, I can make contact with Inan without anyone finding out. We can finally talk without our armies at our backs and evaluate our chances for peace.

"Èmí ni mò nwá, jé kí èmí re ṣi sí mi," I repeat. "Èmí ni mò nwá, jé kí èmí re ṣi sí mi!"

I try to picture the space in my mind, to push my magic through my hands once more. But even in the silence of the Connector Temple, the incantation won't take. I throw my head back in frustration. I don't know what I'm doing wrong. The other incantations have been difficult to master, but no matter how many times I try to cast this one, it never comes.

Every day that goes by is another day the monarchy could attack. A day the *Iyika* could decide to march on Lagos. If I'm going to figure this out in time to stop this war, I can't do it alone.

I need Zélie's help.

"Skies." I struggle to swallow as I roll up the scroll. Despite our differences, Zélie's helped me learn the Yoruba I needed to train the Connectors. By this point, I've taken dozens of scrolls to her for assistance.

But if she figures out why I want to learn this one . . .

I shake my head and exhale as I walk out the temple's navy door. I just need help with an incantation.

That's all she needs to know.

"Watch out!"

I throw myself back as Mâzeli zips past. His large ears practically flap in the wind. The end of an incantation flies from his lips as he leaps from the nearest cliff.

"Yí padà láti owó mi!"

A lavender cloud erupts from his back, engulfing him as he falls. He screams with delight as the cloud begins to solidify, forming wings around his arms.

"I'm doing it!" Mâzeli stretches out his hands in triumph as he nears the landing at the waterfall's bank. But right as he's about land, the cloud disappears. He claws at the air before hitting the water with a loud splash.

"Dammit!" Mâzeli breaks through the surface, glaring at all who laugh. He slaps the water with his hands. "I don't understand. There were wings that time, I saw them!"

"More like feathers than wings!" Mári calls out as she glides down on shadows from the ledge above him, a triumphant smile on her young face. She wields her shadows with a particular finesse, practically floating to the ground.

"Mári, hush." Zélie walks into the water, beckoning for her Reapers to follow after her. "You're close, Mâzeli, but your ojiji are still too soft. Your shadows are light because the spirits are struggling to keep form."

I watch from my perch on the ledge above as the three Reapers form a circle around Zélie despite the setting sun. The two of us wear the same collar, but Zélie's seems to fit like a second skin. With the way her golden tattoos shimmer beneath the rippling water, I am far from the only person who stares. What I wouldn't give to have just one maji look at me that way.

"Amari!" Zélie catches my eye, waving at me from below. I force a smile as she sends her Reapers ahead. "How'd today's training go?"

"Better," I lie. "But I need your help. I was thinking of teaching this incantation tomorrow. Could you help me with the words?"

I walk down to the bottom of the ledge and hand Zélie the scroll when she exits the water, but her smile fades as she reads the sênbaría. "You want to teach them about the dreamscapes?"

"You say it like you've heard of that before."

"I have." Her gaze grows distant. I'm surprised at the way her face softens. "Your brother took me into one a few times. I never knew if it existed in his mind or mine."

"How did he get you there?" I lean in. "Could you summon it as well?"

Zélie starts to answer my question, but stops, pulling the scroll to her chest. "Why this incantation? What use will it be when we march on Lagos?"

My ears heat as I scramble for a lie.

"For gods' sakes." Zélie shakes her head. "Tell me you're not this stupid!"

"How is it stupid to want to contact my brother?" I ask. "To explore the possibility of peace? I know you hate him, but Inan saved your life—"

"It's what he *does*," Zélie snarls. "He'll do the right thing when it's easy, but when it matters most, he'll stab you in the back! You can't trust him, Amari. All he leaves us with are scars!"

"Is this because you don't trust him, or because you don't want to be honest with yourself?"

Zélie's eyes flash and she stiffens. "You'd better choose your words with care."

"You keep pretending all you want is to kill my brother, but I saw the way you two looked at each other at Chândomblé. I know there's more in your heart than rage!" I point at her chest. "If you want to lie to yourself about how you really feel, fine. But if you damn us to this warpath, you're putting innocent lives on the line!"

I reach for the incantation, but Zélie pushes me back. As I stumble, she throws the scroll in the natural baths, stomping it out with her foot.

"*Stop!*" I scream, running into the water. I try to rip the scroll from her foot, but I only rip it in half. Ancient ink bleeds into the water as I fumble with the fraying parchment. My hands shake as I look back up at her. "What's wrong with you? That incantation could've ended this war!"

"You said it yourself," Zélie pants, walking back to the bank. "In the hands of an enemy, those scrolls are a weapon. Don't try to communicate with your brother again."

Blue wisps of magic spark at my fingertips, burning my skin. How dare she do this to me? How *dare* she give me a command?

"I'm starting to think the reason you don't want peace is because you're getting used to the idea of taking my throne," I spit.

Zélie stops in her tracks. The muscles tense in her back. I watch as her fingers clench, but she doesn't turn around.

"Get back to training," she says through her teeth. "I don't want to hear about this again."

She steps onto the stone bridge, abandoning me for the second mountain. I don't understand why she can't see beyond her rage. Why don't any of the *Iyika* realize this is what's best?

My throat closes up as I reach down, attempting to salvage the soaked pieces of the scroll.

"Do you need a hand, Elder Amari?"

I look to the bank—Mama Agba greets me with a sad smile on her face. The tears I try to fight threaten to break free, so I stare at the rippling water until they disappear.

"Why is everyone fighting against me?" I shake my head.

"Come, child." Mama Agba waves me forward. "I may be able to help you understand."

I'M STILL SHAKING with anger as we make our way into the gardens on the first mountain. Mama Agba rubs her hand up and down my arm, forcing me to exhale.

"Breathe, child."

I take a deep breath as Mama Agba leads me through the entryway of the gardens. Located at the top of the main tower, they shine with a wild beauty, banana leaves in perfect harmony with the sunset blossoms hanging over our heads.

"Just ahead." Mama Agba gestures to a weathered bench in the back ravaged by vegetation. "That one has always been my favorite. The moss forms an excellent cushion."

As we walk the lanternlit path, I think of how the broken stone and unkempt greenery are so different from the manicured lawns of the palace. Overgrown vines weave themselves around the surrounding stone fixtures, creating natural tapestries around the old benches and cracked gazebos. They're nothing like the royal gardens where only the most perfect carnations were allowed to grow. Like everything else in the palace, they were strangled. Controlled.

"I used to sit here all the time." Mama Agba sinks into the moss as if it were a luxurious bath. "The temples were created for meditation, but somehow I always found the greatest peace right here."

I wait for her to release whatever scolding she must be holding back, but she allows the chorus of jungle cicadas to ring out in our silence. As it stretches, I realize she's not waiting to speak. She's waiting to listen.

I open my mouth, but it's hard to find the right words. It feels like I'm always fighting to be heard. I don't remember the last time I was able to have a simple conversation about this war.

"Is it wrong to fight for peace?" I ask.

"I think life is more complicated than right and wrong," Mama Agba answers. "I think you will never obtain peace trying to prove either one."

I sink back down and stare out at the gardens. Across from us, two Tiders sit in a stone gazebo. One kneels while the other uses a knife to shave her head. As thick tufts of white hair fall to the gazebo floor, I realize the girl's motivation. She's shaving her head to match Nâo's. She respects her elder so much, she wants to mirror her.

"I know my brother has made mistakes," I say. "More mistakes than most. But no one will ever understand what it was like to grow up with my father. Inan bore the brunt of his torture."

"You empathize with him?" Mama Agba asks.

"I understand him. All he's ever wanted was to be a great king. Even when he's wrong, he thinks he's fighting for the right thing." I pick at the moss beneath my arm and sigh. "I know if we talk, we can reach an agreement. We both want what's best for Orïsha. It's Zélie and the *Iyika* who refuse to listen."

Mama Agba purses her lips and I bite my tongue.

"I've gone too far?" I ask.

"I do not think you've gone far enough," she says. "You speak of this war as if it is the start, but the maji and the monarchy have been fighting for decades. Centuries. Both sides have inflicted great pain on each other. Both sides are filled with mistrust." Mama Agba runs her fingers along her wooden staff and closes her eyes. "You cannot blame Zélie for her actions any more than you can blame Inan for his past mistakes. You have to look beyond the surface if you truly want to achieve the peace you seek."

I nod slowly, meditating on Mama Agba's words. Though my anger toward Zélie fades, my desire to get into the dreamscape only grows. If the monarchy and the maji have been at war for centuries, this could be our only chance to end this fight for good. But how can I broker peace between both sides when every attempt I make gets struck down?

"Do you know the meaning of your name?" Mama Agba asks.

"My name doesn't mean anything."

"Every name means something, child. Yours means 'possesses great strength.'" Mama Agba smiles, the skin crinkling at the corners of her large eyes. "A few moons ago you were a scared princess on the run. Now you're an elder leading the maji through war. A queen poised to take her throne."

Her words force me to think of everything I've done, how far I've truly come. I thought victory would only be achieved once I sat on Orïsha's throne, but I suppose there is another victory in what I've already become.

"This all started the moment you stole that scroll. It was your courageous actions that brought us here at all. I know it's difficult, but give it time. If anyone can bring about peace, I know it is you."

She cups my chin and looks at me with such a warmth, I can't help but smile. I don't know when it happened or why, but I feel genuine love in her eyes.

"Thank you," I whisper.

"Thank you is unnecessary." She pulls me into a hug. "Your courage has given so much back to me. I am as grateful to you as I am to Zélie."

She rises to her feet and I move to join her, but she sits me back down.

"When I was younger, this was the best place in the sanctuary for me to explore the extent of my powers. It may help you, too."

"But I don't have an incantation." I scrunch my brows. "Zélie destroyed it."

"You're a cênter, Amari. For better or worse, you're not bound by incantations. You share a special connection with your brother. Clear your mind and focus on that."

I smile as she walks off. Her advice lifts a weight from my shoulders that I should have never tried to carry at all. I'm not a maji, and I never will be. I need to stop playing by their rules. Their incantations, their restrictions—they don't apply to me.

I stare at my hands, remembering the thrill that ran through me when I summoned my cênter powers and took Mother down in Chândomblé's halls. That moment was the best I've felt in moons.

The most I've felt like myself.

My skin stings as I call on my power, focusing on my core. Though no tîtáns are around to fuel my magic, I can feel it swelling from a different source.

Come on, Inan. I think of him as a faint blue light ignites in my chest. *I need you now more than ever. We're the only ones who can end this.*

As sunset turns to night, I settle on the bench, reaching for my brother in the dark. I don't know if this will work, but I won't give up.

I'll stay here for an eternity if it means I can finally end this war.

CHAPTER FORTY-SIX

◆◇◆

INAN

THOUGH I GRAB the polished table of the war room, the world keeps slipping away. The advisors' faces blur around me. Mother's whispers drown under the ringing in my ears.

Reality slips from my hands like a dream coming to an end. I attempt to keep the confusion from my face as I hear the voice again.

Inan—

"Pay attention." Mother nudges me, forcing me to sit up straight. I blink as I focus on Jokôye's presentation, a report of all her progress. Though she's never been one for smiles, a new venom has seeped into her words since our return from Chândomblé. She still struggles to move around the room with the iron brace around her leg.

"I've been training my tîtáns," Jokôye says. "All day. All night. The next time we face the *Iyika*, we'll be ready for their games. We'll annihilate those traitors where they stand."

She speaks the words I need to hear, yet they still make my fingers cold. Every day we get closer to the bloodbath I desperately want to avoid.

"Have you located their base?" I ask.

"We're getting closer." Jokôye marks a new oval on the map, zeroing in on the *Iyika*'s supposed location. "We tend to lose contact with our scouts once they enter this zone. But as we speak, my soldiers are finding new ways to scour the location. Our forces in Oron have been training a few tîtán Seers. When they have better control over their abilities, they may be able to give us the answers we need."

Once they do . . .

I rub my thumb over the cheetanaire engraved onto the bronze piece. There'll be no delaying Jokôye's forces. We'll throw everything we have at that attack.

"Continue training your tîtáns and bolstering Lagos's defenses," I command. "Notify me immediately if there's any more information on their location. Otherwise, you are dismissed."

Everyone rises, bowing before they exit through the door. Mother puts a hand on my shoulder.

"Get some rest," she whispers. "You look awful."

I nod, placing my hand over her own. Even as we speak, the world starts to blur again. That strange voice tickles my ear.

Inan, I need you. . . .

My lids start to close when Mother walks away. But then I feel a new presence at my back.

"She's right," the presence speaks. "You look like dung."

My body tenses at Ojore's dig. We haven't been alone since we returned from Chândomblé, since I stopped him from attacking Zélie with my blade.

I even sent him to oversee a special construction effort on Ilorin's coast just to avoid this conversation. I thought I had a few more days until his return. I still don't know what to say.

"You're back." I lift my hands.

"I am." Ojore nods. "Your soldiers are hard at work. Construction should be complete by moon's end."

"That's good to hear." I turn back to the table, sifting through the endless parchments. "There's another effort that needs your attention up north—"

"Are you going to send me all over Orïsha before you're man enough to talk?"

My cheeks burn and I clench the scroll in my hand. I don't know how to respond. Ojore closes the war-room doors before sinking into the seat beside me.

"Did you really think you could avoid facing me?" He tilts his head. "All this time I thought you were hesitating because of your sister. Family, I can understand. But a *maji*? The Soldier of Death?"

I wrap my fingers around the bronze piece, wishing I had a good answer. How can I explain something to him that I barely understand myself?

Even as he speaks Zélie's terrifying title, I long for the scent of her soul. She could've killed me in that moment, but she didn't. She held back despite all I've done.

"Before magic came back, that girl was in my way," I explain. "I wanted to kill her. I tried. But when I got the chance . . ." My chest falls as I recall that fateful moment in the forest after our siblings were taken. When my magic surged beyond my control, I saw every part of Zélie. I still remember the bitter taste of her terror. The warmth in her soul.

"She taught me that there are more sides to every story," I say. "She made me want to be a better king."

Ojore and I lock eyes and I feel the growing distance between us. Staring at the scars on his neck, I know he won't understand. He wasn't taught to fear the maji like me. They burned him themselves.

He presses a fist to his lips as we stare at the war-room map. But as we sit, the low ringing builds in my ears again. I grip the table when the world around me starts to blur.

"I know you're not your father," Ojore sighs. "I respect that you're trying to be a better man. But not everyone can be saved. You have to stop looking at these maji like they're the ones who need protecting."

I reach into my pocket and squeeze the bronze piece. "You sound like Mother."

"Well, like your mother, I have a vested interest in keeping you alive," he says. "On the battlefield, Amari's not your sister. This girl isn't someone you can love." Ojore rises from his seat and pats me on the back. "They're your enemies, Inan. They're the soldiers on the other side of this war. When we face them, blood will spill. Don't let it be yours."

He closes the door behind him and I rest my head on the table. I don't want him to be right, but he speaks the words I'm too afraid to speak myself.

For a moment, I long for the days of being a prince. Before magic. Before the throne. I may not have had power then, but things were simple. Now I fear those days will never return.

Inan . . .

The voice tickles my ear, louder now that no one else is here. The bronze piece falls from my palms as my fingers go limp. Sleep wraps its hands around me, pulling me into its blackness.

When it hits, a cool breath of magic passes over my skin. The world swirls around me as clouds of white float in.

It feels like I hang suspended in space, feet searching for ground that doesn't exist. But when I finally find it, I don't believe my eyes.

An endless field of blue lilies brushes against my skin.

CHAPTER FORTY-SEVEN

AMARI

"Brother?"

I yearn to say more, but the words don't come out. I've spent so long trying to get to this moment; I didn't think about what would happen once I was actually here.

With the rough beginnings of a beard around his jaw and the heavy bags under his eyes, my brother looks far older than his nineteen years. If it weren't for the streak of white running through his unruly curls, I might even think he looked like Father.

"Yours is different." He blinks at me, a half smile rising to his tired face. His eyes fall closed as he breathes in my dreamscape, tasting the cinnamon-scented air.

He forces me to take in the world around us, the magical space of my creation. A sea of deep blue flowers lie at our feet. A star-filled sky twinkles above.

Though I've never set foot in this space, somehow it feels like returning to myself. In here, the air is sweet. The light shines brightly though there isn't a moon.

Inan bends down, smelling a flower before the half smile falls from his face.

"Did you bring me here to kill me, or do you want to talk?"

237

He keeps a joke in his tone, but I see the way his fingers tremble. The way he expects everything and everyone to hurt him. He carries the same scars I fight to live above.

My eyes water as I take a step toward him. I break into a run when Inan opens up his arms. I think of how much I've missed him. How much I've wanted to hold him tight.

Everything that's passed between us flashes behind my eyes as I run. I see every way we've been hurt. Every face that we have lost. Binta. Admiral Kaea. Father. But worst of all, each other.

The moment I place my head against his chest, I don't know who weeps harder. Me, or him.

* * * * * ◆ ◇ ◆ * * * * *

BY THE TIME our tears dry, it's difficult to tell how long it's been. Even pain is different in this magical space. It doesn't hurt to cry.

We settle into soft mounds of dirt, picking at the flowers at our feet. So much passes between us, but none of it needs words.

"Are there flowers in yours?" I ask. Inan shakes his head.

"Just reeds." He holds a lily in front of his nose, plucking its petals off. "Zélie found a way to make forests and waterfalls, but I don't know how to do more. I can't even get back into mine. Every time I try, it feels like someone's driving an axe into my brain."

I'm surprised at the smile that rises to his lips. Even after all that's passed, she brings out a different side of him.

"How is she?"

I roll my eyes and look away. "She's determined to kill you. Completely blinded by rage."

"Believe me, I know." Inan peels up the hem of his shirt, allowing me to see the new scar across his side. "But when she's not out for my blood, how is she? How does she feel?"

I wrinkle my nose, attempting to see Zélie through another lens. We've been at each other's throats for so long. I miss looking at her as my friend.

"She has her clan now," I speak slowly. "Not many Reapers, but enough. Taking care of them makes her happy. They actually make her laugh."

"That's good." Inan sinks into the flowers, a softness filling his amber eyes. "She deserves to be happy."

"You say that like we don't."

"We're royalty," he snorts. "We suffer so everyone else can smile."

I hug my knees to my chest, hating the words he speaks. I'm tired of suffering because the people of this kingdom refuse to believe in peace. I know there's a world where we can make this work. An Orïsha where maji, tîtáns, and kosidán can live as one.

I still see the Orïsha of my dreams even if reality only gives me nightmares.

"They're training to annihilate you." I exhale a deep breath. "I keep trying to convince the *Iyika* that peace can work, but they don't trust the monarchy. They want to put Zélie on the throne."

"Zélie?" Inan shoots up, brows knitting together.

"They call her the Soldier of Death. To them, she's a living legend. But if that happens . . ." my voice trails as my chest grows tight. I want to believe that Zélie would do the right thing, but after all that's happened since magic came back, that feels naive. She has no interest in unification. Only annihilation.

"What are they after?" Inan asks. "What do they need to end the fighting?"

"Power." I picture the elders' faces. "True freedom. They want an end to the torture and the baseless persecution. A real place in this monarchy and a say in what happens in this kingdom."

Inan inhales, chest seeming to expand with each demand. He rubs his fingers together as he considers my words.

"That's it?"

I shrug. "More or less."

"Alright." He nods. "How do I give that to them?"

I grab onto his arm, eyes nearly bulging out of my head. "You're serious?"

"If that's what it takes to end this war," he says. "I want those things myself."

"I knew it!" I clap my hands together. Excitement floats like a balloon in my chest. But as soon as it rises, reality dawns. This still isn't enough.

"What's wrong?" Inan asks when my shoulders slump.

"It doesn't matter that we want the same things. The *Iyika* will never trust that your declaration is real." I shake my head. "As soon as they hear that I've talked to you against their orders, they'll be too enraged to listen to what I have to say."

Inan rubs his fingers together, brows creasing as he thinks.

"What if they don't hear it from you?" he asks. "What if they hear it from me themselves? I could draw up a treaty. Present it to their leaders."

My heart skips a beat as I realize the sincerity of his words. If the king himself offered a treaty like this, even Zélie would have to listen.

"You'd have to come alone . . ." I tread with care.

"I don't have a choice. After what happened at Chândomblé, the royal council would have me executed before they ever agreed to this."

"But how would you get out of the palace?" I ask.

"Ojore will cover for me if he knows I'm going to meet with you."

Inan holds out his hand and a tightness fills my chest. This is everything I wanted; the peace I knew we could get.

But as I stare at the lines along my brother's palm, Zélie's voice bleeds into my mind.

He'll do the right thing when it's easy, but when it matters most, he'll stab you in the back. You can't trust him, Amari. All he leaves us with are scars.

"What will happen to me?" I look up at him. "When you were gone, I prepared to be queen. What comes after peace?"

Inan sets down his hand, considering my words. "Mother is a fierce ally, but she's tainted by the past. Orïsha needs a queen who's willing to do whatever it takes to make amends."

My fingers fall limp as Inan opens his arms, extending the invitation.

"You mean it?" I ask.

"We'll rule the kingdom together," he says. "The way we should've from the start."

The weight of the world falls off my shoulders as I lunge forward, wrapping my arms around my brother. My heart swells to see him this way. I always knew he could be a magnificent king.

But as he hugs me back, a prickle erupts along my scars.

I pray Zélie allows him to breathe long enough for us to bring Orïsha the peace we both desire.

CHAPTER FORTY-EIGHT

ZÉLIE

WHEN THE SUN climbs onto the horizon, none of my Reapers speak. We watch from a cliff as it sets the sky ablaze, warm rays spilling over the hilly terrain outside the sanctuary. It lights the blankets of fog seeping through the mammoth trees, revealing the baboonems that swing through the jungle leaves. I study the path I want to take as the sun's rays reach our finish line.

"Over there." I point to the hill where Amari and I first trained. "First one to the top wins."

"That'll be me." Mári rubs her hands together. "Everyone else stay out of my way."

I smile at her resolve. The hill lies almost three kilometers outside the sanctuary's mountain walls. This'll be our greatest distance yet. After a half-moon of training, it's the perfect way to test their mastery over our new incantations.

"When I win, can I be your Second?" Mári asks.

Behind me, Mâzeli crosses his arms. Though he's gaining control over the incantation, he has yet to master the wings.

"Whoever wins gets to brag till the end of time," I offer instead. "These are the first Reaper races. Oya herself will sing the winner's praises."

All three of their faces light up and a flutter fills my heart. I remember looking at Mama Agba the same way when she would tell us stories of the gods.

I wait as they take position, prepping to recite the incantation. Bimpe cracks her knuckles. Mâzeli shakes out his leg.

"Be safe." I lift my hands. "Three . . . two . . ."

"One!" Mári shouts. She takes off in a sprint, afro-puffs bouncing as she runs. The others scramble after her as she leaps from the cliff.

"Èmí òkú, gba àày̌é nínú mi—"

Mári's shadows shoot from her hands, weaving together to form a glider at her back. The wine-colored shadows shift with the changing currents, allowing her to surf the wind.

Her laughter rings as she slips into the lead, nearing the grassy hill. But a strong gust of wind blows her off course. I have to navigate the flow myself as I take off.

"—Jáde nínú àwon òjìjí re. Yí padà láti owó mi!"

Below, Bimpe takes a different approach. Her shadows billow behind her in a large sheet, trapping the wind like the sails of a boat as she floats to the ground. When she nears the gushing river along the trail, she recites the incantation. The shadows of death dissipate in puffs of smoke, transforming to form a board under her feet.

"Take that, Mári!" Bimpe beams as she surfs the thrashing currents with her wiry frame. Her waist-length braids bounce against her dark skin as the shadows propel her through the water.

Incredible. I bring my shadows in, drawing closer to the trees to follow her path. I don't think anyone will beat her until I hear Mâzeli's shout.

"—Yí padà láti owó mi!"

He passes below, a blur arcing beneath the trees. His lavender shadows are still too weak to maintain their form, but he uses that weakness to his advantage. As soon as the shadows release, he casts again, molding the spirits into another rope. They wrap around the next branch and Mâzeli pulls, allowing him to shoot forward.

"Keep going!" I shout from above, eyes wide at the sight. Mâzeli swings from shadow to shadow like a gorillion swinging from jungle vines. The way he moves steals the rest of my words. I never thought to use the shadows of death that way.

When he lands on top of the hill, a swell of pride heats me from within.

"I did it!" He punches up his arms. "I'm the greatest Reaper to ever live!"

"No fair." Mári lands after him. "I thought we had to fly!"

My shadows dissipate as I touch onto the grassy hill. "I never said that."

Mâzeli stalks around the mountain with his hands on his hips and his chest raised. "I am the new Soldier of Death! No—call me its master!"

"You are no master!" Mári huffs.

I laugh as they bicker, wishing I could share their joy. At first I think of telling Tzain, but Roën sneaks his way into my mind. I can only imagine the trouble he'd get Mâzeli into once he saw how he could move. He'd probably try to induct the poor boy into his mercenary crew.

I smile at the thought as I turn to greet Bimpe, hugging her as she climbs the hill. But when I near the slope, I spot a white streak moving below.

Amari's lithe form passes between two large hills in the distance, seemingly unaware of our presence. She doesn't move like she's taking a stroll. She moves like she doesn't want to be seen.

"Lead the others back," I squeeze Mâzeli's shoulder. "I want to check something out."

"Is everything alright?" he asks, and I nod.

"I'll meet you back at the temple."

He bows before turning to the others, and I jump from the ledge. By now the shadows of death are second nature. I don't need to speak the incantation as they wrap around my arms, allowing me to glide to the ground.

What are you doing? I tail Amari, lifting up a thick web of vines to follow her path. We haven't spoken since I destroyed her scroll in the natural baths. According to Tzain, she actually expects me to apologize.

She must be making a run for Lagos. I pinch my lips together, holding back my fist. I could knock out her teeth for this. What's it going to take for her to realize the monarchy will never accept her bid for peace?

"Amari, stop!" I break forward, following her into a jungle clearing. She freezes at the sound of my voice. I grab her shoulder and whip her around.

"Where do you think you're going?"

The color drains from her cheeks, but she doesn't speak.

It's only then that I see the second streak of white waiting in the trees.

CHAPTER FORTY-NINE

◆ ◇ ◆

ZÉLIE

FOR A LONG MOMENT, shock steals my words. I don't know how to process what's before me. What it means for my clan. For the *Iyika*.

But when the shock fades, my body shakes with a hatred that reaches new depths. Magic bites at my skin as I throw up my hand.

"Give me one reason I shouldn't kill you both!"

"Zélie, no!" Amari throws herself in front of Inan, nostrils flared. But the sight of her only makes my magic surge. I aim my other hand at her chest.

"How could you betray us like this?" I yell, scanning the trees for more soldiers in golden armor.

"No need to search." Inan steps out of his sister's protection. "I came alone."

"Like hell you did." Being this close to him makes me feel like glass. My fingers tremble as I try to keep my hands steady. I don't know which incantation I should unleash.

Hearing his voice, seeing his face—it makes my chest ache. It takes me back to the dreamscape; to the feel of his hands around my back. I remember every promise he made. Every lie he told.

I feel every time he held my heart, only to crush it in his hands.

"Zélie, please," Amari begs. "Inan came here to offer a treaty to the council. He's prepared to give you and the *Iyika* everything you want!"

"His offers mean *nothing*." I bare my teeth. "The maji won't be free until every member of the royal family lies in the ground!"

"Including me?" Amari yells. "I am the daughter of King Saran. The daughter of Queen Nehanda. I am part of the same family, yet you've trusted me to fight for your people! Why can't you trust that I'm doing that now?"

"After this, I don't trust you at all!" I charge forward, making them stumble back. Shadows of death begin to build around me, wisps of smoke waiting for my command. I want to tear into them. I want to see their bodies crumble to ash. I can't believe that after everything, Amari would do this.

That she would put all my people at risk.

"Do you honestly think a battle at Lagos's gates is going to be enough to tear down the monarchy?" Amari asks. "Even if you win, think of your Reapers. Think of how many will die!"

"Don't you bring them into this!" My voice shakes as the shadows condense. But Amari raises her own hands. Blue light sparks at her fingertips.

Her silent threat is an arrow to my chest. A chain wrapping around my neck. I taught her how to use her magic.

Now she wields it against me.

"I'm fighting for you now," Amari whispers. "I'm fighting for Mâzeli and Mári and Bimpe. Even if you can't see it."

I clench my teeth as Inan takes a step toward me, moving though Amari tries to keep herself between us. But Inan doesn't let her act as a guard. He approaches me despite how my shadows froth and hiss at my back.

"You keep acting like you don't know me," he speaks up. "Like you don't know my heart. But I know you do. Zélie, I know because I still

247

know *you*. The louder you scream, the more you fight, the more I see you haven't changed." He shakes his head. "You're still that little girl. Terrified that the king is going to take away everything you love."

"The same terror he speaks of bubbles to the surface, but now it's so much worse. Back then, Tzain and Baba were all that I had left. All I thought I would ever have in this world. But now I have Mâzeli and my Reapers. Mama Agba and the clans. If I lose them now, I won't survive.

I won't be able to stitch the pieces of my heart together again.

"You know me." Inan's voice drops to a whisper. "You *know* this is real. I want to keep every promise I made to you, Zél. I want to build a kingdom where you laugh every day. A land where you feel safe!"

A slight quiver rocks his chin as he closes the distance between us, not stopping until my palm rests against his chest. His life lies in my hand, yet he still looks at me like I'm the only girl in Orïsha. Like I'm the only girl in the world.

Tears prick at my eyes, but I don't let them fall. I can't when I know the cost of letting him into my heart. Giving in will only lead to more scars.

"We've already done this dance," I breathe. "You've already promised me a new Orïsha."

"I wasn't the king before." He lifts his hands. "This time I have the power to keep my word."

Pretty lies. I close my eyes. *Pretty lies.*

I believed them once.

Then Baba paid the price.

"He's drawn up a treaty." Amari steps forward with raised hands. "One that gives you everything you want. This is how you can be free. How you can protect every person you love!"

I look back and forth between their amber eyes. I hate the part of me that wants to lower my hands. The part of me desperate to believe there could be an end to this endless fight.

"Moons ago it was you and Amari asking me to see reason when I was filled with hatred and doubt." Inan closes his eyes. "Think of all the lives we could've saved if I had been the leader I needed to be then. Think of how many maji you can save by being that leader now."

His words bring me back in time. I know the moment he speaks of. Right before Amari and Tzain were taken. Before we found Zulaikha and the divîner settlement.

"It's not fair to ask you to trust me," Inan says. "Not after all I've done. All you've lost. But if you really want to protect your clan, why not choose peace? Why not choose the only monarchs in Orïsha who will give you what you want?"

My chest rises and falls in the echo of his words. I think of Mâzeli's triumphant smile. The hunger in Mári's eyes. I imagine all the other Reapers I don't even know outside the sanctuary walls, just waiting to be a part of a clan again.

"Please." Amari lowers her hands. "At least allow the elders to read his treaty. That's all I ask."

I look back at Inan; to my hand against his chest. His heartbeat reverberates through my bones and I remember the times when that same pulse used to remind me of the tides. Of safety. Of home.

I exhale a deep breath and close my eyes, lowering my hands. The tears I've been holding inside break free as I step back.

"You're doing the right thing." Amari moves to embrace me, but I hold up my hand.

"I'm not letting either one of you past me until I see that treaty."

Inan's mouth falls slack, but he nods, reaching into the leather pack on his back. As he pulls out the parchment, something lifts in my chest.

For so long I've wanted to fight. To make him pay for everything he's done. But somehow giving in feels right. Every chain around my heart starts to lift.

If this peace is real . . . if it allows me and my Reapers to be free . . . Gods.

That would be everything.

"Here." Inan hands me the parchment, and I start to read. I feel him and Amari holding their breath as I comb over the words.

"It won't be enough to convince the others," I say. "But it'll be enough to bring you to the tab—"

A horn blares, catching me off guard. I whip around as it rises in pitch, ringing from the direction of the sanctuary.

"What's that?" Amari turns around and Inan's brows crease.

"I don't know . . ." his voice trails off. "I swear, I came alone!"

Shadows extend from my arm, weaving around a branch above me. I let them raise me up through the trees, up through the canopy. I pray the alarm isn't what I fear.

But as I rise, I see it: the black and gold of Nehanda's seal. Over a hundred velvet banners flutter in the jungle winds, marking an endless line of military caravans.

An ice I haven't felt since the night of the Raid chills me from my core.

The enemy's at our gates.

The war has come to us.

CHAPTER FIFTY

✦

AMARI

"You monster!" Zélie shrieks as she unwinds her shadows and descends back to the ground. She lunges with her staff for Inan, but stops when the *Iyika* siren blares again. Her face falls as she turns around. She flees through the trees. When she disappears, I collapse to my knees.

After saving his life.

After fighting Father on his behalf.

After all the time I've spent pleading with Zélie to trust him.

Tears burn my eyes as I curl into myself. I can't believe he did this to me. To Zélie!

"Amari, I swear." Inan reaches out. "This wasn't a part of my plan——"

His voice blacks in and out. I can't hear him over the sounds of war. Hundreds of creaking wagons speed toward us. A sea of velvet seals flap in the wind. I brought Inan here to make peace with the maji.

Instead he brought our demise.

"You have to believe me!" Inan's voice shakes. "Only Ojore knew! He promised he wouldn't tell!"

He'll do the right thing when it's easy, but when it matters most, he'll stab you in the back. You can't trust him, Amari. All he leaves us with are scars.

Zélie's words return, destroying me from within. I wanted her to be wrong. I thought Inan was the one person in the world I could trust, the only other person who shared the vision of a united Orïsha.

But there's no denying it now. No lie he can't tell.

He's truly Father's son.

He's been a monster all along.

"I-I'll call it off," Inan shouts over the blaring siren. "Just give me a chance!"

But staring at him is like staring into a void. I feel myself slipping away, losing the person I want to be to the person my family's forced me to become.

Inan and Mother are just like Father.

Orïsha won't be free of their tyranny until they both lie in the dirt.

"Amari—"

Inan's eyes bulge when I open my palm. His heartbeat pulses through my ears. It vibrates through my bones.

Blue wisps of magic leach from his skin as I suck the ashê from his veins. His slowing pulse reverberates through my chest. It would take nothing for me to stop it for good. To drain every essence of his life and never look back.

Strike, Amari.

My breaths hitch as Father's voice fills my head. I think of standing across from Inan in the palace cellar all those years ago. I held back and I got hurt.

I always get hurt.

Tîtán soldiers appear on the hilltop above, running through the jungle trees. I count almost three dozen among the first wave. More caravans pulled by panthenaires ride in behind them.

But the closer they get, the more heartbeats bleed into my ears. I feel the ashê of other Connector tîtáns like the rising heat of a flame. My power builds as I start to pull the lifeforce from their veins, too.

"We're done." I reach forward, putting my hand over my brother's chest. More magic feeds into my hands, charging me up as the first wave of tîtáns descend down the hill.

"You're not my brother anymore," I speak through my teeth. "You're dead to me."

Tears stream down my face as I throw his shaking body to the ground. The ashê of other tîtáns rumbles within me as I lift my hands.

When the first soldiers attack, my heartbreak strikes them in an endless blue wave.

CHAPTER FIFTY-ONE

ZÉLIE

HOW COULD HE?

I hate myself for even asking the question. Twigs and vines scrape my skin as I sprint back to the sanctuary. My throat burns with hoarse breaths.

I think of the look in Inan's eyes. The tenderness embedded in his words. He's gotten so good.

It's as if he believed his lies himself.

And Amari . . .

I can't deal with her betrayal now. Even as I run, the rumbling caravans gain ground. Three dozen soldiers ride in on panthenaires. Though they're still a kilometer out from the mountain barricading the sanctuary, I can't let the military get close. If Nehanda's with them, she'll bring the entire mountain down. The sanctuary and the *Iyika* will be buried in the rubble.

"*Jagunjagun!*" Mâzeli calls out to me from the line of Reapers that stand half a kilometer from the sanctuary. As I charge closer, I can see the terror shining through their brown eyes. For their sake, I try to look calm.

"What do we do?" Bimpe asks. "No one from the sanctuary has made it out yet!"

I want to tell them to run, but we can't just protect ourselves. All the elders are still behind that mountain. Right now, we're all the *Iyika* have.

"Mári, summon the elders," I command. "We need every maji who can fight to mount our defense. Bimpe and Mâzeli, stay close." I point to my Reapers as Mári disappears through the trees. "It's up to us to fend off the first wave."

I don't know where my calm comes from, but I don't question its source. Mári and Bimpe fall in line as we turn back, facing the scourge of charging soldiers. Dozens of them wear golden armor, the ashê of their different powers blazing around their gauntlets. I see the reds of their Burners; the oranges of their Cancers. I even see tîtáns who glow with Reaper lavenders.

"Focus," I shout when we enter the caravan's path. "Everyone circle up! Prepare to unleash the shadows of death!"

"*Oya, bò wón,*" I pray under my breath. "*Protect them.*"

My jaw clenches as we spread out along the dirt trail, three Reapers strong. I close my eyes and breathe deep, sensing when my Reapers do the same.

"*Èmí òkú, gba ààyé nínú mi. Jáde nínú àwon òjìjí re—*"

My body warms as the shadows swirl around me, twisting like ribbons of light. Different spirits circle my Reapers when they follow suit, their ashê fusing with mine.

"*Yí padà láti owó mi!*"

Our shadows bleed together like mixing paints, deep purples turning black with raw power. Our voices rise as the shadows take shape, condensing until they funnel into one giant arrowhead. With the final words of our incantation, we unleash our attack. The arrowhead shoots forward, a rush of wind blowing around us as it twists through the air.

"Look out!" a tîtán shouts. Time seems to slow as the caravan speeds toward us. Sound muffles to a low hum.

The first wagon skids to avoid the attack, sliding off the dirt trail as our shadows swarm. But the soldiers crouched inside don't stand a chance. The moment they meet our shadows of death, they crumble into ash.

I hear the beginning of screams, but the cries of agony wither into nothing. Our shadows cut through their path, taking out three transports in one blow.

"Zélie, look!" Mâzeli points behind us as more maji run into the fight. The sight of them spurs me on. Together, we can defend the sanctuary.

Though my chest heaves up and down, I charge down the warpath.

"Come on!" I shout at my Reapers. "Let's do it again!"

CHAPTER FIFTY-TWO

◆ ◇ ◆

INAN

"STOP THE ATTACK!"

Though I shout, my voice is little more than a hoarse whisper. My head spins from Amari's attack. I can barely stand.

As I stumble through the jungle, the world around me descends into a battlefield. Maji flee from their base in droves as my forces continue their attack.

"Wipe the rebels out!" a lieutenant shouts, sending another line of wagons speeding down the dirt trail.

A burly maji with a metal leg slaps his hands to the ground. Other maji in matching green armor follow his lead.

"*Odi àwọn òrìṣà—*"

Their magic seeps into the earth. Towering walls of dirt shoot into the air, hardening into stone. The wagons try to skid out of the way, but they're not fast enough. Wood and metal fly as the transports crash and explode.

Skies!

I take cover, bracing myself against a tree. Majacite gas leaks into the air, but a twisting cyclone from the *Iyika*'s maji blows it all back.

Though my soldiers lead the charge, the maji overpower their every maneuver. This isn't working.

Whoever mounted this attack is losing.

"Inan!"

Ojore's voice is a lifeline and a curse. He runs to me through the madness, wrapping my arm around his shoulder. Troops cover our tracks as a Tamer runs forward, a large girl with sunflowers in her curls. Clouds of pink magic fly from her hands, turning our ryders rabid.

Soldiers scream as they're flung from their panthenaires' backs. The ryders foam at the mouth. I look away when a rabid panthenaire sinks its fangs into its soldier's throat.

"How could you do this?" I shout. "I gave you a command!"

"I didn't have a choice!" Ojore pulls me forward. "I couldn't lie to your mother!"

"Mother ordered this?" My hands fall limp as realization takes hold.

"She said Amari would kill you the moment you met. She ordered us to save you from this trap—"

BOOM!

One of our wagons collides with a blinding gust of fire. The force of the blast knocks us to the ground.

"Get the king to safety!" Ojore orders as another round of soldiers descends. A tîtán lifts me onto a ryder, steering me away from the battle.

As we ride away from the front, I want to scream to call off the attack, but I know I can't now that the battle's begun. The *Iyika* hit us with everything they have. Even fighting at our strongest, we'll never be able to break through their defense.

This is the end.

I clutch my chest as we flee. At this rate, we're going to lose the war. All of Orïsha will burn.

A few kilometers away, Mother flags us down. She flings her arms around me when I dismount and squeezes me tight.

"Thank goodness you're alright!"

"I wasn't in danger until you attacked!" I pull away from her hug. "We need to retreat now! Or else we're going to lose this war!"

"Don't worry." Mother points to another transport in the distance. "Jokôye's forces are coming in. The *Iyika* end today."

CHAPTER FIFTY-THREE

ZÉLIE

"*Èmí òkú, gba ààyé nínú mi—*"

My throat scratches raw as magic rattles from my core. Shadows twist from my hands like snakes, lunging toward the ten soldiers who charge. They go down in one wave, shadows binding them to the jungle's mammoth trees. Mâzeli follows with an incantation of his own, raising a giant animation that knocks a dozen more tîtáns unconscious.

"We're doing it!" he shouts, smile stretching between his large ears. Across the way, Nâo and her Tiders drag five tîtáns into the gushing river along the sanctuary's trail. They create a whirlpool that drags the soldiers under the water's surface, drowning them as they spin.

Mâzeli and I pivot, preparing to cast again. Then the monarchy's horn blares.

Ha-woooooooooo!

The siren echoes through the rolling valleys, a blare that sounds like death. As the approaching troops come to a stop, the remaining soldiers fall back.

"They're retreating!" Kenyon punches his hands up, shooting a stream of fire into the air. The rest of the maji cheer as the soldiers flee, abandoning their caravans and majacite bombs.

I grab onto a tree root and lift myself up, climbing higher to watch them run. I look past the maji and wreckage in my path, searching through the dense greens of the jungle. I'm ten meters off the ground when I feel it—the vibration building in the air.

My stomach clenches as I turn, peering into the distance. A single cart rides down the dirt path four kilometers away, pulled by three snow leopanaires. Two dozen soldiers stand on the wooden transport, arms clasped behind their backs. The general we faced in Chândomblé's halls stands in front of them, thick braid falling to her waist.

Though each soldier wears golden tîtán armor, my tattoos hum at the sight of the general. When she and her tîtáns ride past the monarchy's retreating soldiers, it all makes sense.

The enemy's not running away from us.

They're running away from them.

"Retreat!" I scream. "Get back to the sanctuary!"

The *Iyika* meet me with confused stares as the tîtáns stop their cart a full kilometer away. The soldiers riding on top of it dismount in waves.

"What's going on?" Mâzeli shouts. I can't speak when the general raises her hands. At her command, the tîtáns form a circle around her. Her eyes glow with silver light as she opens her palms.

"She's a cênter!" I yell. "She's harnessing the wind!"

The vibration in the air transforms to a violent shake. The wind sucks everything forward, pulling at my clothes and the dirt and the leaves.

Chaos descends as everyone scrambles back toward the sanctuary. Paws thunder all around us as wild ryders gallop, trying to escape the general's attack. Na'imah uses an incantation to freeze a pack of wild tigenaires fleeing from the north, stopping them until the elders and maji can climb on.

"Go!" I shove Bimpe up the beast's striped coat. I try to shout more instructions, but the whipping air swallows my voice. In seconds, I can't even hear myself breathe.

A new terror grips my chest as I spur Bimpe's tigenaire forward before motioning for Mâzeli to take cover. I can't believe my eyes when I see the blade the cênter forms out of the sky.

The attack is unlike anything I've ever seen. Anything I knew could exist in this world.

The blade of air hurtles toward us, a massive scythe ripping through the sky.

It's as if she flings a twisting tornado at us like a boomerang. The howling storm shakes the air as it twists toward us.

The blade of air tears up the earth beneath it as it flies. The dense jungle clears away. The air turns heavy in its presence. I lunge for Mâzeli as it nears the forest.

"Get down!"

Sound returns when the blade hits the first mammoth tree in its path. The world explodes around us, a whirlwind of splintered bark and clouds of debris. We crawl under the web of thick roots as massive trees rain from above. I can't see beyond the cyclone of dirt. I can't hear beyond the howling winds.

How is she doing this? My body shakes as I try to protect Mâzeli. I know cênters can absorb the magic of tîtáns around them, but this magnitude is beyond comprehension.

Giant trees lie ripped from their roots. The damaged wagons that littered the dirt path are blown to smithereens. The jungle is completely unrecognizable. A whole kilometer of land lies in ruins.

Mâzeli trembles in my arms as the wind abates with a vicious hiss. Only a quiet breeze blows through the destruction, passing over the thin stretch of battered land that lies between us and the tîtáns. It won't be enough to shield us if the cênter can strike again. For all our scrolls and training, we can't face this kind of power. The cênter doesn't fight with the magic of mortals.

She fights with the might of a god.

"Is it over?" he asks.

"I don't know." From afar, I see the dozen tîtáns she drained for her first attack lying on the ground, their skin wrinkled and their cheeks hollow. They all lie around their general in a ring of death, skeletons protruding from their sunken forms.

But despite the fate that awaits them, a new wave of tîtáns circle around their general. The general loads them up like ammunition, preparing to absorb their magic.

"One more hit and she'll blow through the sanctuary's walls!" Mâzeli's eyes bulge. "We have to take her out!"

"How? We can't get close!"

I press my fists to my head when the cênter's eyes fill with silver light again. The steady hum ripples through the air. The winds begin to howl.

"There's one thing we can do." Mâzeli balls his fists, filling his chest with a confidence I know he doesn't have. I step back, looking at the tattoos along my skin.

The power of that cênter is one we can't face. But if we wielded that power ourselves . . .

"It's too big of a risk." I shake my head. "The connection could kill us!"

"If we don't use it, that cênter will kill us! We have to protect the maji, no matter the cost!"

The conviction in his big brown eyes brings a calm to the chaos. He's right. We don't have a choice. Our people are behind those walls.

My body warms as the magic of the moonstone stirs in my chest. Mâzeli's heartbeat starts to bleed into my ears. The violet light of the ashê beneath his skin appears before my eyes.

"Are you ready?"

He nods, lacing his fingers with mine. My tattoos glow with golden light as I whisper the ancient command.

"Ẹ tọnná agbára yin."

It's like a bolt of lightning crackling in the space between our palms. Mâzeli grunts as we're both lifted into the air, chests arcing toward the sky. Violet light shines from our eyes and our mouths. The same particles of light materialize before our hearts.

They stretch forward like ribbons, weaving themselves together as our lifeforces tether together. The air continues to thin, but I feel the power of Oya in our breath.

"It's coming!" Mâzeli shouts as our feet land back on the ground. The general's wind swallows all sound in its deafening silence. Trees snap in half as the blade of wind rebuilds. But as the cênter prepares to release her attack, purple light crackles around our hands.

"Ẹmí àwọn tí ó ti sùn—"

Our incantation rings in the absence of sound.

CHAPTER FIFTY-FOUR

ZÉLIE

IT STARTS WITH A SHAKE.

A shift beneath the earth.

The first hill explodes as monstrous animations twist from the dirt.

They claw their way out of the ground, each as big as a gorillion. Even at my strongest, I can only summon dozens of animations. In seconds, Mâzeli and I create hundreds.

"—mo ké pè yin ní òní."

Veins bulge against our necks as the tide of spirits rises. Dirt rains from their bodies when they charge, a tsunami of animations surging over the land.

The cênter releases her blade, blowing our monstrous animations to smithereens. But it's not strong enough to take out the whole wave. Her wind dies half a kilometer away.

"Keep going!" I shout. I feel Mâzeli's heart beating in my chest. My body burns as our ashê bleeds together.

The magic of the moonstone binds our souls, creating a force unlike any I've commanded before. Animations crawl onto the carts, ripping the soldiers apart. The tîtáns' screams ring as our soldiers attack. But the longer we push, the greater the strain. The more I feel our pain.

"Zélie . . ." Mâzeli's voice scratches through his clenched teeth. His screams turn sharp as strips of skin peel away from his arms.

The powerful ashê rips through our veins. It burns through us both. But despite how I want to let go, the Winder cênter still stands.

"Just once more!" I shout. *"Ẹmí àwọn tí ó ti sùn—"*

I grit my teeth against the pain. More hills explode into animations as we chant. The power of Oya races through our veins.

New spirits rise like mountains, closing the distance in mere seconds. The general wails as our animations descend upon her. An explosion of silver light flickers from beneath their earthly bodies as the general falls. When the animations move away, her corpse lies over the wreckage like a rag doll.

"We got them!"

I turn to Mâzeli, but he doesn't move. Blood drips from the corners of his mouth. His fingers fall limp.

"Mâzeli?"

The deep purple glow fades from his gaze. His eyes roll as he stumbles back. I see the strain of our combined magic, the great power that's eaten through his being.

His hands go to his chest and I feel his heart seize beneath my own ribs.

"Mâzeli!" I reach out for him when he falls.

But the moment his body collapses, my own legs crumble.

CHAPTER FIFTY-FIVE

· · · · · ◆ ◇ ◆ · · · · ·

ZÉLIE

"Khani!"

My voice is little more than a shriek as Kâmarū carries us into the infirmary. The Healers clear the area at once, making space to set our bodies down on the netted hammocks. Though I can barely lift my arms, I squeeze Mâzeli's hand with the strength I have.

The golden light of my tattoos flickers as his heartbeat slows, and my own slows with it. The moonstone still connects our spirits. Without a blood sacrifice, we can't sustain the connection.

"Oh my gods . . ." Khani's face falls when she runs over to us. Bloodstains coat her tangerine robes and white braids. She adjusts her spectacles before taking charge of the room. "Yameenah, water. Chibudo, fresh wraps. Obu, quick—I need all free hands!"

"Idán ti ẹjẹ, jí láti wo ọna rẹ láradá—"

"Ogbé inú, dáhùn ìpè wa—"

The swarm of Healers descends, their rhythmic chants bouncing against the ivy-covered columns. Khani and her Healers channel their ashê into us, placing their hands over our heads, our hearts, our stomachs.

But despite how hard they chant, our skin chills with every passing second. Our breaths turn slow.

"The connection," Mâzeli croaks. "You have to break it."

267

His waning lifeforce pulls on my own, an anchor dragging me under the surface. But despite the growing pressure in my chest, I won't give in. I don't care about the blood I cough up. I don't care how much it hurts.

The connection that's killing me is the only thing keeping him alive.

"We'll be okay!" I fight to speak. "Just hold o—"

Mâzeli starts to seize, making my own body spasm. The Healers struggle to hold me down as I thrash in the hammock. Despite how hard I pull, I can't draw breath.

"Mama Agba, I need you!" Khani shouts. The Seer's silver-clad body runs into the infirmary as my vision blurs in and out. Her wrinkled hands press against my chest. An ancient command only she can summon rings out.

"E túu sílè!"

It's like the same bolt of lightning that connected Mâzeli and me strikes my heart. My back arches as my tattoos shine bright. Then the light disappears for good.

My ears ring from the jolt. My stomach burns. But when I inhale again, my blood runs cold.

I can breathe, but I don't feel him.

"Mâzeli!" I grip my heart, falling to the floor as I tumble out of the hammock. His body still spasms beyond his control. His skin feels so cold.

"E tọnná agbára yin!" I grab his hand. *"Ignite! Connect!"* But despite how hard I try to bind our lifeforces, my marks only flicker. My magic stays dead.

"You're too weak!" Mama Agba grabs my shoulder, but I push her away. My vision goes black with rage. It's so strong, I can't see straight.

"What have you done?" My voice echoes through the infirmary. But then Mâzeli's seizing stops. My heart falls as he moans.

"Jagunjagun . . ."

His voice is so weak. A scratch of his usual shout. I have to clasp a shaking hand to my mouth to hold back the sobs.

"I'm here." I take his hands, kissing his cold fingertips. "I'm right here. I'm not going anywhere."

As the moonstone's marks flicker against my skin, I see the violet lifeforce around his limp body. Before it shone so brightly. Now it fades before my eyes. A star that can no longer burn.

Behind him, Khani lifts her hands and her face says it all. There's no saving him.

The damage is already done.

"The others." Mâzeli's lids flutter. "Did I . . . are they . . ."

"They're safe." I fight the knife in my throat. "Because of you, every-one is."

Shimmering tears pool in Mâzeli's brown eyes. I can't hold back my sob as he tries not to cry.

"I don't . . . I don't want . . ."

He starts to tremble and I can almost see the terror flooding in. I paw away my tears and force iron around my heart. I can't cry when he needs me the most.

"This is just the beginning." I stroke his head the way Mama used to when I was young. "You'll see your mother on the other side. You and Arunima will laugh again."

"Oya, too?" He squeezes my arm as tears spill onto his cheeks. I take his face into my hands and give him my brightest smile.

"She'll welcome her bravest soldier home with open arms."

He tries to nod, but his face twists with pain. He coughs up blood again.

"I'm not afraid."

"Good." I rest my forehead against his. "You're a soldier of death. You have nothing to fear."

Every word I speak is like a blade cutting me from within. It's the arrow they shot into Baba's chest. It's being forced to rip out my heart and bury it all over again.

"The Reapers . . ." he speaks through his labored breath. "Don't let them be sad."

His round eyes start to lose focus despite how hard he fights to keep them open.

"Mâzeli!" I squeeze his hands tighter as his grip fades away.

"Don't . . ." His eyes fall closed. "Be sad."

CHAPTER FIFTY-SIX

AMARI

MY THIGHS BURN as I race up the steps to the maji sanctuary. All around, I see what damage I've caused. The scars left from trusting Inan.

Though the sanctuary remains intact, injured bodies lie across the first mountain's stone paths and flat grass. Each elder's Second struggles to keep people from crossing the bridges as Healers tend to everyone who was injured.

"For Yemoja's sake!" Nâo curses when a Healer pulls a thick shard of bark from her thigh. Sweat pours down her shaved head. Bloodstains coat the *lagbara* tattoo on her neck.

In front of her, Kenyon lies unconscious, drawing slow but shallow breaths. Blood mats his white locs to his forehead as Na'imah shouts, struggling to revive him.

"Zélie?" I scan for her through the chaos, but she's nowhere to be found. I can't even find Mâzeli. None of her Reapers stand in the crowd.

"You." I grab a Healer's arm. "Have you seen Zélie?"

"They had to take her to the infirmary. . . ." His eyes go wide. "She and Mâzeli weren't breathing—"

I take off, sprinting to the main tower. I race past the bodies at my feet. I push through all the Healers in my way. Blood stains the stone steps of the tower, leaving a grim trail to the infirmary. I pray it isn't hers. If she's not alright, I'll never forgive myself—

"*No!*"

The howl stops me in my tracks. It doesn't even sound human. My skin crawls as it echoes through the hall, leaving me frozen outside the infirmary's swinging doors.

Everything in me wants to stay out, but I force myself to walk inside the ivy-covered room.

"Zélie?" My legs go weak when I spot her frame. But then I see the source of her pain.

Skies . . .

My hands fly to my mouth. Zélie hunches over Mâzeli's battered body, her arms wrapped around his neck. The boy who's usually bouncing off the walls lies completely still. Blood drips from the corners of his lips.

His gangly arms hang limp.

He'll do the right thing when it's easy, but when it matters most, he'll stab you in the back. Zélie's words echo through my head. *You can't trust him, Amari. All he leaves us with are scars.*

Guilt eats me from within as I stare at a scar I know will never heal. She tried to get me to see the truth, but I chose to trust Inan.

"Zélie, you must rest." Mama Agba approaches her, feet dragging with hesitation. Zélie's sorrow forms a ring around her. No one else dares to get close as she howls.

Zélie doesn't respond when Mama Agba calls her name again. But when our Seer lays a hand on Zélie's shoulder, Zélie snaps.

"*Don't touch me!*" Her shriek pierces my ears like shattered glass. She pushes Mama Agba so hard the elderly Seer stumbles into a column.

"He couldn't be saved!" Tears well in Mama Agba's eyes. "You would've died—"

"Then I die!" Zélie yells back. "I should've died!" Her hands fly to her chest as her face twists with pain. She digs her nails into her skin, clawing as if she could reach her own heart.

"I should've died." Her voice goes quiet and she falls to her knees. "I should've *died*."

The world feels like it's falling out from under me. Because of me, Mâzeli's dead. Because of me, we might have lost this war.

We may have chased Inan's armies off today, but they'll be back with stronger forces. There's no place for us to hide. Every advantage we had is gone.

Zélie's sobs grow feral, forcing Khani to step in.

"Sedate her!" the Healer orders. "Her body can't handle the strain!"

Zélie thrashes like a wild animal as the Healers close in. I have to run out of the room as their incantations ring. I can't take the sight of what I've caused.

I can't stomach the sound of her screams.

Her shriek rings through the swinging doors, and I clasp a hand to my mouth to stifle my tears.

I've ruined everything.

And I don't know if I can fix it again.

CHAPTER FIFTY-SEVEN

· · · · · ◆ ◇ ◆ · · · · ·

INAN

IT'S NEVER ENOUGH.

The simple truth is a sword through my abdomen. A spear in my heart. As I stare at the carnage outside the *Iyika's* base, my hand trembles around the bronze coin. This was supposed to be the place where we brokered peace. Instead, we can't even count our dead.

"I thought we had them." Ojore's jaw quivers and he has to look away. Mother takes him in her arms, shielding him from the slaughter. Bodies lie in the remains of the jungle. The rolling hills are now battered mounds of dirt. Every colossal tree lies ripped from its roots. Jokôye's body still hasn't been recovered.

I've been training my tîtáns. The general's last words to me return. *The next time we face the Iyika, we'll be ready for their games. We'll annihilate those traitors where they stand.*

I hang my head, crossing a fist to my chest to honor Jokôye's spirit. She gave everything to this kingdom. Everything to protect its throne.

The general was supposed to be our secret weapon. A force even Zélie couldn't beat. Her strength was the only reason I felt powerful enough to enforce peace, but what kind of peace could last when our enemy is capable of this?

"I don't want to be crass," Mother says to me. "But there is no time

274

to mourn. We can't give the *Iyika* a chance to regroup. If they retaliate in Lagos . . ."

Her voice trails off, but she doesn't need to speak the words. It only took moments for the jungle to become a wasteland. If this had been a city, thousands of civilians would've died in our fight.

"Duty before self," I whisper the vow. If Father were here, that's what he would yell now. This war has spun out of control. Soon there won't be an Orïsha left to protect.

I wanted to be a better king, but after all that's passed, there are no more options. It doesn't matter if I didn't sanction this attack. Any hope of peace lies with my dead on this battlefield.

Duty before self. I squeeze the bronze coin. *Duty before self.* The next time we meet, there will be no reconciliation. Only complete annihilation.

One victor shall stand at the end of this war. One ruler shall sit on my throne. I can't hold back anymore. I have to take out the *Iyika* no matter what it does to Amari and Zélie.

This war ends with me.

"Summon the rest of our soldiers." Mother turns to Ojore. "We'll lead another assault while they're down."

"No." I shake my head. "As long as they're united, they'll defeat us all. It doesn't matter how many soldiers we have." I close my eyes and try to visualize our next moves like pieces on a sênet board. "We need to weaken them beyond repair. Divide, conquer, and then force their surrender."

"How do we do that?" Ojore asks.

I look down at the bronze piece, picturing Zélie's face. For an instant, I thought we had a chance to move beyond all this pain. Now I know that day will never come.

"By using the one thing Amari and Zélie hate most," I answer. "Me."

CHAPTER FIFTY-EIGHT

◆ ◇ ◆

ZÉLIE

DON'T BE SAD.

Mâzeli's voice still echoes in my head. Silent tears run down my face, falling onto the bathroom tiles of my elder quarters. My ribs ache as I cradle my chest, struggling to draw breath. After three days, the world has still lost its color. Mâzeli's blood still stains my skin.

"Zélie?"

I freeze as Tzain's voice bleeds through my bedroom door. I clasp a hand over my mouth, trying to stifle my strangled breaths.

"The sanctuary assembly's starting," he says softly. "The elders are asking for you."

"I don't care." I look away. "Just go."

With the sanctuary's location exposed, everyone stays on high alert. But I can't see or do anything beyond how much I hurt. All we do is fight and fight and fight.

What's the point when our people only die?

"Don't be sad." I whisper Mâzeli's last words. "Don't be sad." My legs shake as I drag myself to my feet to face the copper bathtub that's spent hours waiting for me. I dip my fingers into the cool water, but the air around me thins. It happens every time I try to wash away the last remnants of him.

Dammit.

276

My hand flies to my throat as the guilt suffocates me. The bathroom starts to spin. It's like all the air's been sucked out of the room.

He could've lived. He should've lived. It was my duty to keep him safe. But I failed.

Now I have to live with the weight of my mistakes.

Soft knuckles rap against my bedroom door. A painful spasm erupts in my chest when it creaks open.

"Go away," I wheeze. I can't have Tzain see me like this.

I crawl across the floor, trying to shut the bathroom door. But before I can, a bandaged hand props it open. I don't know if I can trust my eyes when its owner walks through.

"Roën?" I whisper.

Black waves hang from the mercenary's head, clumping along his square jaw. He kneels on the tiled floor and places callused hands on either side of my face.

"What are you—"

"Don't talk," he interrupts. "Breathe."

My eyes water as I fight to inhale. I curl forward when another spasm erupts in my chest.

"Look at me." Roën brings my face to his, firm yet tender in his grip. But I don't want to meet his eyes. I don't want anyone to see how broken I truly am.

"Just look at me." His voice drops to a whisper. "It's okay."

It feels like pushing two mountains apart with my bare hands, but staring into his eyes, I manage to open my throat. Roën's touch softens as I inhale, sucking in a feeble, strangled breath.

"That's it." He moves his thumbs back, stroking the skin behind my ears. I stare at him, gasping until all the air in the room returns.

"What're you doing here?" I ask. The ache in my chest magnifies as Roën pulls me up and sits me down on the bathtub's edge.

"The elders summoned me. The lot of them pooled together every resource they had just to hire me to help."

He grabs a rag and cups my cheek, gentle as he wipes away the blood and dirt coating my face. I close my eyes and lean into him, inhaling his honeyed scent.

"He's gone."

My lips tremble as I speak the words. It sounds so strange to say it out loud. I only met Mâzeli two moons ago. I don't know how he burrowed himself into my heart.

"I never had a Second." Roën wrings out the rag. "But I had a partner. The day I lost her is still the worst I've ever had."

He keeps his voice even, but his words don't hide his scars. It's strange to see this much of him. To peer into the heart he pretends not to have.

"How'd you meet her?"

A small smile rises to his pink lips, but it doesn't last long. "She found me digging through trash. That girl practically dragged me out of the dirt. She'd probably still be alive if she'd just let me starve."

New tears well in my eyes and I have to turn away. I wonder where Mâzeli might be if we hadn't met. If I'd escaped across the sea. I never wanted this war. This clan. After Baba died, I didn't want anyone or anything.

I just wanted to be free.

"I have to get out of here." I shake my head, pawing away my tears.

"Out of the sanctuary?"

"Out of the kingdom."

It feels like a betrayal to utter the words, but I can't lie to myself. I was a fool to think that freedom lay on the other side of this war. The only thing I can count on is disaster and death. It follows me everywhere I go.

Staring at the red bathwater, I know I can't keep doing this.

"I can't keep burying the people I love," I whisper.

Roën's hand hovers over my cheek as he digests my words. He avoids my gaze, dipping the rag into the water before moving to the blood on my hands.

"Is that really what you want?"

I nod, and Roën looks down at the floor.

"If you really want to go, now is your best chance."

I tilt my head at his coded message. "How do you know that?"

"I can't say more."

As he brings the rag to my arm, I stop him by grabbing his hand.

"Talk," I demand. "What do you know?"

CHAPTER FIFTY-NINE

AMARI

I HAVE TO MAKE THIS RIGHT.

My chest aches as the entire sanctuary gathers on the third mountain. Though Mâzeli was the only maji killed in the attack, every space feels empty without his laugh. His death hangs like the gray clouds below.

The elders move to the center of the bloodstone. It feels like a sin to stand among them. Every day since the attack, I've waited for the truth to come out. For people to punish me for my mistake. But Zélie still hasn't revealed how the monarchy discovered our base. I don't know why she's protecting me.

"We have to make a choice!" Nâo raises her voice over the unruly crowd. "The sanctuary is exposed. It's too dangerous to stay here."

"Where are we supposed to go?" Na'imah asks. "No place in Orïsha is safe."

"We don't go anywhere," Kenyon shouts. "We fight!"

I look up as Tzain joins the last of the maji walking across the stone bridge. When he catches my eye, he shakes his head. I worry Zélie will never leave her room again.

I have to find a way to win this war. Now more than ever. If I can't, Mâzeli will have died for nothing. There will be no point to our pain and suffering.

"This started in Lagos." Kenyon riles up the crowd. "It ends there, too. We keep pretending we're defenseless, but we held off the royal forces with the moonstone. We know what we have to do!"

"Zélie won't use that power again," I tell them. "Not after what happened to Mâzeli."

"Why does she get a choice?" Kenyon asks. "Someone drag that girl out of her room!"

Tzain's nostrils flare as he breaks from the ring of people around the bloodstone and storms toward the center. I run to intercept his path.

"Don't." I put my hands on his chest. "It'll only make things worse."

"Have some compassion," he shouts over me. "She lost her Second."

"I lost a quarter of my clan!" Kenyon yells. "I didn't get to sit around and mourn!"

So many arguments break out at once, it's impossible to keep track. I close my eyes, attempting to block out the noise. We can't stay here, but we can't blindly attack. The next time our forces meet Inan's, we have to be precise.

Only one of us can survive.

"What're you thinking?" Tzain asks. I lift my hands and stare at the scars left from my magic. I can almost hear Father in my head, whispering the words he tried to embed in me as a child.

I've had the power to end this all along. I just didn't want to use it against the people I love. But now I have no place to run.

Orïsha waits for no one.

"If I can surround myself with enough Connector títáns, I think I can take Mother down."

"No." Tzain takes my hands. "It's too dangerous to face her on your own."

"Who else can challenge her?" I ask. "Who else can suck the life from Inan's veins?"

I close my eyes, replaying my mistakes. All these years I thought Father was a monster, but what if ruling this kingdom forced him to act that way? War is a race to the death, and right now Mother and Inan are winning.

I push past Tzain, walking into the center of the circle. I can't allow any more of our blood to spill. I need to end the war at any cost.

"I have an idea." I raise my hand, quieting the circle. But before I can speak, a voice rings out from behind me.

"Wait!"

All eyes turn to Zélie as she comes sprinting out of the elder tower. Her purple kaftan flies behind her as she runs. Blood still mats her white coils.

My face falls when she catches my eyes, but she doesn't linger on me before addressing the crowd.

"We don't have to fight." She holds up her hands. "There's another way out of this war."

CHAPTER SIXTY

ZÉLIE

My palms grow slick with sweat as I prepare to address the maji. The elders stand in a broken ring around me. Tzain moves between me and Amari.

My throat dries as I look at her, but I keep her role in our attack to myself. I can't deal with her now. I don't have much time.

I can smell the maji's bloodlust from here. Their desire to run right into battle. But the information I squeezed out of Roën creates a choice we've never had. For once, we don't have to fight. We can live beyond this warzone.

"The king isn't in Lagos," I shout. "He's hiding in Ibadan. The monarchy's expecting us to march on the palace and exhaust our forces in the wrong location. They plan to annihilate us when we're divided."

"What does that mean?" Nâo's forehead creases. "We go to Ibadan?"

"We shouldn't take the bait," I respond. "We should take the opening."

I ball my fists, steeling myself for their reaction. It would be so much easier to run. To slip away in the middle of the night. But the thought of Mâzeli forces iron into my spine. He would never leave the maji behind.

Neither can I.

"If the monarchy's forces are split between Ibadan and Lagos, we have a clear path to safety." I address the crowd. "We can break for Ilorin's coast. Sail beyond Orïsha's borders."

"You can't be serious." Nâo stumbles back. "You want us to run?"

"No." I shake my head. "I want us to *live*."

I'm not prepared for the flood of anger that is hurled my way.

"You're just going to let the monarchy win——"

"This is our home! Where would we even go?"

"What about the rest of the maji?"

How do I get them to see the truth? That there's more beyond this endless fight? What's the point of staying here if we know we can't win?

"I'm not leaving." Kenyon stomps forward, taking charge of the opposition. "I don't care if you lost your Second. Burners don't run."

"Then you'll die." I march up to him, meeting his fury head-on. "Who knows how many more cênters the monarchy has? After this last attack, they know exactly where to find us!"

"Then let them find us!" Kenyon shouts, a battle cry others rally behind. "Let them come to our walls again! Let them try to capture us!"

"Do you know what happens when they catch you?"

Silk brushes against my skin as I yank my kaftan over my head, exposing my back to the world. A collective gasp runs through the crowd the moment I reveal my scars.

My cheeks burn with shame, but I refuse to hide my pain. They have to understand that there is no winning this fight. Only bloodshed awaits us in a kingdom that will always see us as maggots.

"Our enemies have no honor," I say. "No restraint. When they find us, they will carve through our bodies. They'll destroy us from within." As I pull down the kaftan, I find Mári and Bimpe in the crowd. The sight of them pushes me on.

"I made a vow to protect my clan. This is the best way I know how. I can't keep fighting." I lift my hands. "I can't keep losing the people I love."

Heads hang in the face of my words. For a moment, the entire mountain stays silent. Even Kenyon backs away, returning to the circle of elders.

"But this is our home." Kâmarū steps forward, deep voice shrunk to a whisper. More than confusion, more than rage, he offers his heartbreak. I know he speaks the pain none of us want to face.

"When the elders built this place, it was only bare mountaintops." I look to the crowd. "It didn't become a home because they filled it with towers. It became a home because they built it together. This land, these temples—they're not what matters. As long as we have each other, we will carry Orïsha in our veins. No one can ever take that away."

I hold my breath as I wait for the elders' response. The whispers start to shift in the crowd. I can almost see the acceptance I crave.

But when Amari walks forward, her face lights up as a new idea takes hold in her mind.

"Zélie's right." Her voice echoes in the silence. "This is the only chance we might have to escape. But it could also be our chance to win."

"What are you doing?" I grab her arm, pulling her until we're face-to-face. My body still shakes at the sight of her, but I don't look away.

"Don't do this." I tighten my grip. *"Please."*

Amari presses her lips into a hard line. Her gaze settles on my hand. She exhales a long breath and closes her eyes.

"I'm sorry, but I can't abandon my home without a fight."

"Amari, no!" I try to hold on. "This bloodshed has to end!"

But she pulls herself out of my grip. The entire mountain hangs on her silence as she turns to face the crowd.

"For once, we have the upper hand," she yells. "We can work around their tricks. We don't need to march to Lagos and take down the entire army. We just need to take out the king!"

Her words run together as her excitement builds and she soaks in every gaze. I can almost see the glint of a crown in her curls.

"Why run?" She throws up her hands. "Why risk the dangers that lie in the unknown when we can avenge the death of Mâzeli and fight for our home?"

My body goes numb as Amari turns the tides before my eyes. Rumbles echo from all around. Even my Reapers latch onto her call for vengeance.

"Let us rise!" She punches her fist into the air. "Let's band together and end this war! Together we can win! *Gba nkàn wa padà!*"

The Yoruba is slick on her lips, but it does the trick. The cry ripples from maji to maji until the entire mountain shakes.

"Gba nkàn wa padà! Gba nkàn wa padà!"

I sink to the bloodstone as my ears ring with the sounds of war.

Gba nkàn wa padà.

Take back what's ours.

CHAPTER SIXTY-ONE

AMARI

THE NEXT FEW HOURS pass in a blur. Everyone comes together with new purpose, energized by the chance to win this war. With Zélie against our attack, command of the *Iyika* falls to me. My head spins as we sit in the dining hall, using every maji at our disposal to hammer out the final details.

"I say we take everyone who can fight and storm the village." Kenyon slams his fist on the table. "Nehanda's probably with the king. We'll need every maji we can get."

"You can't *storm* Ibadan," Na'imah retorts. "It's sequestered in the mountains."

"And if we storm the city, we lose our biggest advantage," I remind him. "We don't want Inan to know we're there until it's too late for him to stop us."

Out of instinct, I wait for someone to push back, but they accept my every point. Every elder takes a moment, brainstorming stealth-based alternatives.

"What if we only attack with the elders?" Kâmarū asks. "Most of their soldiers are still outside Lagos. We don't need a massive force."

I nod. "Sneaking in ten people will be far easier than sneaking in a hundred."

"Are we sure there will be ten of us?" Na'imah purses her lips and all eyes fall on the empty seat. I haven't seen Zélie since she walked off the bloodstone. I don't even know if she plans to fight.

Blush rises to my cheeks, but I force myself to move on. Would the *Iyika* follow my command if they knew Zélie's heartbreak was my fault?

"If we're only taking the elders to Ibadan, then our Seconds should guide everyone else toward Lagos," I decide. "We can keep them away from the fight while making Inan think we're taking his bait."

"I'll take care of it." Kâmarū rises and a small weight lifts off of my shoulders. After what happened to Mâzeli, I don't want any other maji in harm's way. At least this way, they'll stay safe.

"What about the villagers?" Khani presses. "They could still get caught in the fight."

"Or worse." Jahi stares at the table. "The king and queen could use them as shields."

My throat dries as a tense silence falls over us. I feel the part of me that wants to argue that Inan wouldn't sacrifice his people, but I no longer believe it. He and Mother don't care who they hurt. They'll kill anyone to win this war.

"We should consider alternative plans." Jahi speaks slowly, treading with care. "The same mountains keeping the king safe also lock him in a cage. We don't need precision to win—"

"We're not like them," I cut Jahi off before he can go any further. "We can take them out *and* keep the villagers safe. We just need an undetectable way in."

My gaze drifts back to the stool where Zélie should sit. She and Tzain grew up in Ibadan, but I can't imagine she'll help when she doesn't want us to go at all.

"Tzain!" I wave him over from across the dining hall. He takes a break from loading supplies with Imani, Khani's twin and our strongest Cancer.

"What's going on?" He looks around the table and I gesture for him to sit down.

"None of us have been to Ibadan, but we need a way to get in undetected," I explain. "Is there anything you know that could help us?"

Tzain's lips part; it's like a shadow falls over his face when he realizes who's missing. A bitter taste settles on my tongue. It feels wrong to put him in this position.

"If it's too much—"

"You're trying to win a war." He holds up his hand. "I'll do whatever I can to help."

We lock eyes across the table and my skin warms under his gaze. Tzain blows out his cheeks as he stares at the crude maps, searching for a way in.

"Here." He points to the lake north of the village center. "Zélie and I used to swim here all the time when we were children. Go deep enough and you'll reach the underwater caves."

"How far out do they go?" I ask.

"Find the right one, and you'll be able to sneak in from outside the mountain range. I can show you the way."

It takes everything in me not to fling my arms around Tzain's neck. The tightness in my chest begins to dissipate as the final pieces of our plan fall into place.

Kâmarū can tunnel us through the mountain. Nâo can take us through the water. For the first time since my rally went wrong, victory hangs just beyond my fingertips. All I want to do is lunge forward and grab it.

We all work together until every detail is confirmed. By the time we've solidified our plans, the sun has set on our final night in the sanctuary. A solemn air hangs over the dining hall as people prepare to say good-bye.

"What now?" Nâo asks.

"Summon Mama Agba." I rise from the stone table. "I have an idea."

. . . . . ◆ ⟨◇⟩ ◆ . . . . .

IT ONLY TAKES an hour to prepare the dining hall. Kâmarū creates a stone stage as Dakarai sets up bata drums. Folake and her Lighters make twinkling orbs float through the room like stars while the young divîners lay out the rest of the sanctuary's food. The sweet aroma of súyà and egusi soup drifts into my nose as I move through the crowded hall. The excited chatter dies down when Mama Agba limps to the center of the room.

"This sanctuary has stood nearly as long as the magic of our land," Mama Agba says. "It has seen every elder since the beginning of time. It has served as the beating heart of the maji. When the monarchy attacked, you defended these sacred walls. You have made every one of your ancestors proud."

Her words rouse a few cheers from the crowd. Mama Agba smiles to herself as she takes in the faces that fill the hall. Though I know not to expect much, my heart falls when I don't see Zélie in the room.

This is bigger than her, I remind myself. I can't fight for my friend over the fate of Orïsha.

"These past few moons have been far from easy. You have been pushed more than ever before. But because of you, we have a chance. Because of your spirit, we can still win this war. We will bring our people the freedom they deserve."

I close my eyes and imagine the sight, what our victory will taste like. When my family's gone, Orïsha will have a chance at peace. Perhaps the first chance it's ever had.

We've proven we can come together, and under our leadership, there will be a place for every maji, tîtán, and kosidán. We just have to pull this off.

One attack, and this kingdom is ours.

"Tomorrow our elders set out on a path to make sure no life was lost in vain. We shall honor each valiant sacrifice by creating a kingdom where those with magic can reign!"

In the back of the room, Nâo and her Second chant in unison. Using magic, they lift liters of palm wine from thick barrels and pour the sweet drink into tin cups. Tahir and the other Welders start to chant, distributing each cup through the crowd.

One floats into my hand just as Mama Agba raises hers in the air. When the dozens of cups meet her toast, I feel everything we've been fighting for. In my Orïsha, we will craft sanctuaries throughout the land. We shall gather and celebrate as one.

"You have done all you can to prepare. The rest lies in the gods' hands. Tomorrow you fight." Mama Agba tips her glass. "Tonight, you live."

CHAPTER SIXTY-TWO

AMARI

WITHIN HOURS, music and laughter bounce against the sanctuary walls. Palm wine runs free. Na'imah's rich melodies fill the dining hall as she sings. I smile to myself as I lean against a table, taking in the bodies that fill the dance floor. If I breathe in hard enough I can almost smell the sweet scent of hope that fills the air.

"Come on!" Nâo nudges me from the side, radiant in a long blue dress. "It's your party, for gods' sakes. Grab a cup of wine!"

She snaps her fingers and a Welder floats a tin cup into my hands. She knocks our cups together, throwing her arm around my neck.

"To victory!" she shouts.

"To victory," I repeat. I take a sip, enjoying the way the word tastes on my lips.

"If I decide to let you be queen, you'd better throw more celebrations like this."

Though she jokes, her words catch me off guard. Up until now, Zélie's the one they've wanted on my throne.

"Na'imah!"

Music draws to a halt as the loud scream echoes through the hall. I jerk forward, ready to fight, when Kenyon barrels his way through the crowd. His locs spill onto his bare chest. He falls to his knees before the stage.

"Na'imah, I love you!"

"For gods' sakes." Na'imah hides her face in her hands as the snickers ring through the crowd. "Kenyon, you're drunk!"

"I know! But it's still true!"

"Mo fí àwon òrìsà búra—" Na'imah stomps down from the stage as the music resumes. She starts to yell, but then Kenyon pulls a battered bouquet of sunflowers from his belt. Even she can't help but smile.

Nâo throws her head back at the scene, cackling with laughter. "You've done good work," she urges me on. "Have some fun."

I wait for her to disappear before setting my cup down. Father wouldn't drink before battle. Neither can I. More memories of him fill my mind as I drift through the crowd. I wonder if he would be proud of what I've done. The ruler I've become.

"I sense something . . ."

I stop as I stumble into a group of people gathered around Mama Agba. She sits in a colorful tent while Folake generates twinkling lights behind her head. People smile as Mama Agba lifts her chin, peeking out at the crowd through a poorly hidden squint.

"Why, I sense a great and powerful elder has entered my presence!"

Every eye falls on me and my cheeks heat. I try to move along, but others force me into Mama Agba's tent.

"Come, Elder Amari." She takes my hand in both her own. "Let me search what the stars have in mind for you!"

I can't hide my laughter as Mama Agba shakes and shimmies like the false prophets that fill Lagos's streets. Her hands arc in broad, sweeping motions, dancing around Folake's rainbow lights. Though she can't cast real incantations anymore without putting her health at risk, she gives us the next best thing.

"You have great battles ahead." Mama Agba nods. "Great victories, too! And, oh my . . . I'm seeing something else!"

"Tell us, Mama Agba!" a divîner demands.

"What is it?" I play along.

"I see . . . great love."

She winks at me as someone approaches from behind. I glance up and Tzain's smile steals the air from my lungs. Jeers ring as he takes my hand, leading me away from the crowd. Na'imah's soulful voice croons over our heads as we move to the dance floor.

"Òòrùn mi, ìfé mi, èmí mi—"

Khani harmonizes with the Tamer's rich tones. Together, they sound like songbirds. Tzain laces his fingers with mine and we sway, getting lost in the song. I place my head against his chest, disappearing into the warmth of his arms.

"I've missed this." Tzain dips his chin and kisses the top of my head. He places his hands along my waist, making my skin tingle when his thumbs brush a sliver of bare skin.

"I have, too," I whisper, closing my eyes. Dancing with him takes me back to the fields of the divîner festival, back when it felt like tomorrow was ours.

I look up at him and he stares at me with a tenderness I don't deserve. It's then that I realize I don't want to spend tonight with prophecies and palm wine. Tonight, I want him.

"What's wrong?"

I lace my fingers through his and pull him toward the door.

"Come on. Let's get some air."

* * * * * ◆ ◇ ◆ * * * * *

"WHEN YOU SAID *AIR* . . ." Tzain laughs as I push open the door to my quarters. I grin and take him by the hand, stepping into the cool breeze that passes over the balcony. We slip our legs through the bars, dangling our feet over the curved ledge. Staring out at the sanctuary makes something deflate in my chest.

"I'm going to miss this place." It's strange to admit after all that's passed inside these walls. Since the day we arrived, I don't know if there was a moment I didn't feel ostracized. But for all that went wrong, this place was still home. It kept us safe. It's where I found my voice. Where I found the path to my throne.

"There's been so much—" Tzain brings a fist to his mouth and coughs. "I just want to say I'm proud of you. I don't think you hear that enough."

My hands move before my mind can catch up. I grab the sides of his face, pulling it to mine.

"*Ow!*" I groan when his chin collides with the bridge of my nose.

Tzain grabs his belly and falls back with laughter. "*Skies*, my queen. I never pegged you for such an animal!"

"Shut your mouth!" I smack his arm as my ears heat. "How can I lead a battle if I lack the coordination required for one measly kiss?"

Tzain takes my shoulders and guides me down to his chest. "Here," he murmurs. "Let me help."

My fingers curl the moment his lips meet mine. I sink into him, tasting the sweet remnants of palm wine. But as he runs his hands through the waves in my hair, a pit of guilt sinks into my stomach. While we sit here, Zélie's probably floors above. Grief-stricken and alone.

"Where'd you go?" Tzain asks. I blink as he pulls away.

I pick at a hole in his tunic, not wanting to meet his eye. "Do you think Zélie will ever forgive me?"

"If my lips are on yours, can you try not to think about my sister?"

I smile as Tzain touches my cheek. "I'm sorry. I just hate knowing how much I've hurt her."

"She needs time," Tzain sighs. "Space. But you're doing the right thing.

Not just for her. For Orïsha. The kingdom you're going to build . . . it's something that needs to be fought for, even if she can't fight anymore."

He takes my hand and it erases the entire world. My stomach flutters when our lips meet. His stubble scratches my chin as I press into him. I think of how many times I've imagined this moment. Imagined being here with him. My pulse races as I slip my fingers under the hem of his tunic, but Tzain stops me, grabbing my wrists.

"Am I doing something wrong?" I ask.

Tzain shakes his head, staring at the lines in my palm. "I don't want you doing this just because you're scared."

"Scared of what?" I pull my hands back.

"Dying."

He looks the other way and I exhale. That word is a tidal wave, washing away every escape he brings. The battle ahead of us taints the air as we sit back up.

"I'm sorry." Tzain pinches the bridge of his nose. "I didn't mean to ruin the moment. But I can't let you do that. I care about you too much."

"You have nothing to apologize for." My heart warms as I press my nose to his cheek. "But you're wrong. I'm not scared. At least not right now."

Tzain tilts his head as I put my hands on his cheek, staring into the haven that lies in his warm brown eyes. I think of every moment we've had since we first met. The way he fought for me when I was only a princess.

"Tzain, I don't want to be with you because I'm afraid of dying. I want to be with you because I love you." I smile. "I feel like I always have."

With a courage that doesn't feel like my own, I rise to my feet. My fingers fumble as I remove my tunic and release the band of my skirt. He stares when both fall to the floor.

"Say it again," he demands.

"Say what?" I ask.

"You said you love me." He rises to meet me. "Say it again."

My smile spreads so wide it makes my cheeks hurt.

"I love you."

"One more time."

"I love you," I repeat.

"I don't think I caught that—"

"Tzain, I *love* you!" I speak through my laughs, giggling when he lifts me into the air. It feels like I'm floating as he carries me inside and lays me on the bed. He kisses me and every single restraint melts away.

"I love you, too." His lips brush against mine with every word.

The moment I feel his touch, I pray it never ends.

CHAPTER SIXTY-THREE

ZÉLIE

As I STAND outside the dining hall doors, I wonder why I bothered to show up. Inside, the halls are filled with drink and song. In the face of Mâzeli's death, it feels wrong.

It's hard not to hear his giggle through the crowd. To picture the way he would shimmy up and down the hall. He always lit up when someone cooked súyà for dinner. If he were here with me, he'd probably eat too much and throw up.

Don't be sad.

I close my eyes, wishing I could take his advice. I know he would want me to walk in. He would hand me a cup of palm wine. We would laugh and dance and he would declare his future as the greatest Reaper to ever live. He was so ignorant of how great he already was.

"You should join them."

I freeze at the sound of Mama Agba's voice. As her staff thuds near, my throat closes up. I haven't seen her since that day in the infirmary. I don't want to see her now.

"If not for yourself, go for your Reapers." Her words carry a new rasp. "They are still here, Zélie. They still need you to fight."

When I don't react, Mama Agba places herself between me and the door. I have to turn my head away. I still can't bear to look her in the eye.

"Can we talk?" Her voice shakes. "I have a special bench in the gardens."

"I don't care about anything you have to say."

"Zélie, I am *sorry*." Tears spill between the wrinkles in her cheeks. I hate how much it hurts to see her in pain. How much I want to take it away.

"There was no saving him," she pleads. "Without a sacrifice to bind your connection, you both would have died. I need you to understand—"

"I understand." I step away. "I know why you did what you did. But I know I could've saved him. I can't forgive you for taking away that chance."

"Zélie, please—"

I ignore the tightness in my chest as I turn my back on her.

"I should've died that day," I say. "Just pretend that I did."

Mama Agba sobs and it hits me in the heart. I've never heard her cry like that.

I nearly run away from her tears as I move up the stairs toward my quarters. Leaving my room was a mistake. There's nothing for me out here.

"You're back."

I look up to find Roën sitting outside my bedroom door. Two thick bags hang from his shoulders, clinking as he rises. He gestures for me to grab the smaller one.

"Let's go," he says.

I roll my eyes and brush past him. "I'm going to bed."

"No you're not." He follows me into my room. "I need your help."

"Roën, please. Not tonight," I beg.

"You get to ask for my help whenever you want, but the moment I need something in return, you're too tired?"

I glare at him and he smirks. "That's what I thought."

I frown as he slides the smaller bag over my shoulder. "Will you at least tell me where we're going?"

"Do you know what *Zïtsōl* means in my tongue?" He tightens the bag's strap before marching off. "'Beautiful girl who asks far too many questions.'"

· · · · · ◆ ◇ ◆ · · · · · ·

HOURS PASS IN SILENCE as we ride on the back of Roën's cheetanaire. The jungle humidity leaves us first, followed by the mountain rock. We gallop across the Opeoluwa Plains, heading north from the sanctuary. I hook my chin over Roën's shoulder, lifting my face to the biting winds.

"Can you please tell me what we're doing?" I yell.

"I see no point," he shouts back.

"Can you at least tell me if it's legal?"

"*Zïtsōl*, I never ask you all these silly questions."

I roll my eyes and bury my face into his back. Forget it. It doesn't really matter.

The farther away we get from the sanctuary, the better I can inhale. Mâzeli's absence doesn't strangle every breath. Beyond those walls, I can think of more than his death.

As we ride, I savor the break, not knowing when it will come back. I wonder if Roën always feels like this, unshackled from the weight of the world. From all those he's lost.

"Here we go."

I lift my head as Roën pulls on the reins of his cheetanaire. We stop along a thin stretch of the coast, meters before a rugged shore. Black waves crash against the shallow bluffs, foaming over the smooth and glassy rocks. The silver moon casts a path down the rippling water, beckoning me to come in.

"What's going on?"

Roën takes both bags and walks across the shore, guided by the rays above. A wind-powered boat sits anchored against the coast, filled with more supplies.

"How far are we going?"

"Again with the questions." Roën clicks his tongue. "It doesn't matter. Get in."

Though I don't trust him, the prospect of the sea is far too great to pass up. The last time I saw the shore, we were racing from Zaria's sands. My body itches to float above the rocking water. It only takes a few moments before we're off. The boat's hum intertwines with the crashing waves as we sail. I close my eyes and inhale the salt-filled air. I forgot how much I missed the sea. How close it made me feel to Baba.

Roën steers us until the coast is only a speck on the horizon. The wind turbine shudders as it comes to a stop. He throws the anchor overboard before removing his shirt and kicking off his pants.

"Is this a ploy to get me naked?" I ask.

"*Zïtsöl,* we both know I don't need ploys for that."

He unzips the smaller of the two bags and pulls out two strange-looking masks. As he works, I remove my tunic, leaving only the wrap fastened around my chest.

"Listen closely." Roën fastens the first mask around my head. "Bite down. Breathe in. Don't let go of my hand."

I stay still as he tightens the straps, running my tongue over the built-in mouth guard. It takes a few breaths before the oxygen begins flowing. The stale air dries my throat.

"Do everything I do," Roën continues before fitting the second mask over his head. "There's no time to hesitate."

Before I can ask a single question, he pulls his mask over his face. With a grunt, he throws one bag overboard and stretches out his hand. I don't get a chance to brace myself before we jump in.

I clench my teeth at the ocean's bite. It feels like crashing through a sheet of ice. Bubbles fly as water surrounds us. I squeeze Roën's hand, allowing the weight of his bag to drag us farther down.

My breath hitches when we slow to a stop and we hang, suspended in pure blackness. Roën guides my hands to the rusted chain connecting us to the boat above. From the way he squeezes my grip, I can almost hear him saying, "*Hold on.*"

I squeeze the chains as my breaths start to slow. There's a strange peace this far underwater. I take it in as Roën brushes my side, hands moving to the large bag. He unhooks the latch and I have to squint at the glow. Orbs of light float up from the opened bag, all connected in a spider-web of chains.

What is this? I tilt my head at the sight. The orbs fill the water above our heads, shining bright through the darkness. The spiderweb of light brings the ocean to life. I can hardly believe my eyes. A rush spreads through me like the first time I watched Mama do magic.

There's no place fish don't swim. Long eels with silver scales zip under our feet. Crabs with metallic shells skitter along the surrounding coral reefs. A giant sea turtle passes overhead, so close it swims through loose strands of Roën's hair. My breath shudders as I run my fingers over the reflective mosaic on its shell.

The sea turtle swims toward the spiderweb of light, joining the thousands of fish now circling above our heads. The sight is so majestic I nearly lose my grip on the rusted chain. I didn't know the water I loved could be so beautiful.

I try to catch Roën's gaze, but he stares off into the distance. With no warning, he snaps into action, removing a crossbow from his pack that's loaded with a flat hook instead of an arrow.

What's going on? I drift closer to him, trying to figure out what he's doing. He grabs my wrist and kicks down, taking us deeper into the blackness.

A speck of light shines in the distance, glowing brighter over time. But as seconds pass, I realize that it's not glowing brighter.

It's growing bigger as it races toward us.

I try to kick away, but Roën forces me to stay. It's difficult to remain still when he places the crossbow against his shoulder and takes aim. The beast cuts through the water like a cannon, so large it changes the ocean's currents. It lights up the sea with its approach. My heart thrashes when it nears.

For the love of Oya.

My chest constricts as the blue whale zooms overhead, so big I can't take it all in. The sight is so bewildering, I forget to breathe.

The blue whale fills an entire stretch of ocean, glowing like the bioluminescent plankton of Jimeta's coast. The light spreads from the tip of its nose to the flukes of its tail. It's like the fabric of night shines through its smooth skin.

The beast opens its mouth to feed, consuming the tornado of fish that swim above. It devours thousands in one bite. Then it begins its ascent.

Hold on!

I feel the words through Roën's grip. He hooks an arm around my waist as I wrap both of mine around him. With a jolt, he pulls the trigger of his bow, launching the flat hook through the water, and the projectile connects under the whale's massive flipper. A moment is all we have before the connecting cord yanks us through the water.

Every bone in my body rattles as we shoot forth. It's like being pulled by a thousand elephantaires. Water pounds against our skin as we fly through the ocean at unimaginable speeds. The whale's glow lights up the sea like the sun, illuminating more than any lanterns ever could.

Massive stingrays flash by. Rainbow scales crackle across the water like lightning. It all feels like a dream, one I never want to end.

I wheeze as we breach the surface. The whale arcs through the air, so large it blocks out the moon.

Roën's arms wrap around me as he lets go of our connection. The beast twists in a circle before crashing back into the sea.

"Brace yourself!" Roën yells over the roar.

The waves rip around us like a tsunami. I squeeze Roën tight as we thrash through the water. It feels like minutes before the ocean returns to its gentle tug.

As the water settles, I spot our boat floating half a kilometer away.

I rip off my mask with shaking hands, gasping for breath. A laugh escapes my throat and I grab my chest, kicking my legs in a circle to stay at the surface. The sea shines with the dying light of the whale's glow. I stare down until it vanishes, leaving us in the black water.

"That was incredible!" I scream. "The most amazing thing I've ever seen!"

Roën smiles as I yell. "That's usually what my lovers say about me."

I splash water at him and he laughs, true joy crinkling his nose. It catches me off guard. He almost looks like someone else.

"Why'd you do that?" I ask.

His smile softens and he drifts closer to me, touching my cheek.

"That." His fingers rest along the corners of my lip. "It's been far too long since I've seen that."

CHAPTER SIXTY-FOUR

* * * * * ◆ ◇ ◆ * * * * *

INAN

I STARE AT the maps and battle plans scattered across our table as reality sinks in. They're only parchment and black ink, yet they outline our road to victory. Our troops are stationed outside Lagos. Mother and I are out of harm's way. Every trap has been put in place.

This time we're going to win.

"Is everyone clear on their marching orders?" Mother takes charge in my silence. Her low voice echoes through the pyramid ahéré outside Ibadan's village center, clay padding insulating the stone from the cool mountain air. I stare at the fire burning in the back of the hut as the military officers nod.

"That's all for now." I wave my hand. "Send me updates when you make progress."

As they salute and exit the room, I walk to the fireplace. The heat of the flames warms my skin as I wait to feel a sense of satisfaction, a flicker of relief. But no matter how much time passes, I only feel numb. It's hard to believe that this really is the end.

"I shouldn't be here." Ojore comes to my side when the last officer walks out the door. "Send me back to Lagos. Let me be your boots on the ground."

"I already have boots on the ground," I say. "I need you here."

"Inan, it's not your job to keep me safe!"

"It is after what happened to Jokôye!" I whip around and get in his face, nostrils flared. "Orïsha will need you when this is all over. I will, too."

Mother puts a hand on Ojore's shoulder, breaking the tension between us. "There's still work to be done. Coordinate with the perimeter guards to make sure everything's in order."

Ojore blows out his cheeks, but manages to nod before marching into the night. I wish I shared his burning desire to fight.

I can't look at our battle plans without picturing Zélie and Amari on the other end. I don't want to beat them like this. Who knows if they'll even survive?

"That boy." Mother shakes her head and smiles to herself. She hands me a cup filled with red wine before lifting her own in a toast. "To protecting the throne."

We clink our glasses together and Mother takes a long sip. She exhales as she brings the cup to her chest.

"You're doing the right thing," she says.

I sigh and turn back to the crackling flames. "It doesn't feel like it."

"No cost is too great if it means finally ending this fight."

To that, I take a drink, savoring the rich liquid. "It feels like this war's been going on for years."

"In a way, it has."

Mother runs her painted finger over the rim of her cup. She stares out the square window, watching the families that line up in front of the village well.

"This war didn't start when magic came back, Inan. You are only seeing the end of a battle countless have given their lives for. By winter's dawn, we will have wiped the scourge of maji from this land. Even your wretched father couldn't achieve that."

"Mother, what are you talking about?" I grab her arm. "We're fighting the *Iyika*. Not the maji."

"We're fighting them *all*. We have been for decades. This war started long before the Raid. It began before you were even born."

Mother sets her cup down and wraps her hands around my own. The tone in her voice puts me on edge. I don't like the way her amber eye shine.

"Did your father ever tell you how close the monarchy came to unifying with the maji clans?"

I nod, recalling our talk on the warship before we reached the sacred island. It was the closest I ever felt to him. The only time I'd ever seen him conflicted about what it took to be king.

"That referendum would have changed everything," Mother hisses. "In no time at all, the maggots would've usurped the throne. This crusade began the moment I realized that I was the only person who could stop it."

"Stop what?" I tread with care. What in the skies is she talking about? "Burners assassinated the king. They're the ones who killed the referendum."

I wait for her to correct her mistake, but she only holds my gaze. "The throne had to be protected, Inan. No matter the cost."

I yank my hands back, eyes widening as realization dawns.

"You were the cause of that attack?" I whisper. "You killed all of those people just to kill the referendum?"

"I didn't tell those Burners what to do." Mother reaches after me. "I only showed our people what would happen the moment we allowed maggots to set foot in the palace—"

I press my hands to my ears, trying to block out the venom that drips from her mouth. The room starts to spin. My fingers go numb.

Those rebels nearly burned the palace to the ground. Father was the only member of the royal family to survive. If not for that act, he would've never become the king.

He wouldn't have retaliated with the Raid.

It could've worked. It would've worked. There was a chance for a better path.

But Mother destroyed that chance herself.

She's the reason we're still fighting now.

"Those Burners started a war!" I push my chair back from the table as I leap to my feet. "A war we are still fighting today! Thousands have paid the price! How can you live with yourself?"

"Keep your voice down!" Mother reaches for my arm again, but I back away from her touch. I search for regret in her eyes. An ounce of remorse.

I find none.

"All the blood on your hands . . ." I grab my abdomen as my scar throbs. "For skies' sake, Ojore was there that day. He had to watch his parents *burn* before his eyes!"

"Those people gave their lives so the true Orïsha could *live*." Mother shakes her fist. "When this kingdom is rid of the maji, there will be no pain. No war. You are the ruler who will make sure every sacrifice wasn't in vain!"

She puts her hands on my cheek, fingers shaking as she smiles.

"Remember what I said. No cost is too great if it means defeating the maji."

CHAPTER SIXTY-FIVE

·····◆◇◆·····

ZÉLIE

BY THE TIME Roën and I make it back to the sanctuary, I can barely keep my eyes open. Any celebration has long since ended, leaving the maji who couldn't make it to their beds passed out across the grounds. We tiptoe by sleeping bodies tucked into the corners of long halls and curled under tall stairwells. Far below, Nâo and Khani still sway by the waterfall, at peace within each other's arms.

"*Hökenärīnusaī.*" Roën gestures to my bedroom door. He drags behind me, forever-vigilant eyes falling to a soft close. The night's adventure has more than taken its toll, but despite our hours together, I still don't want him to go.

"What does that mean?" I ask.

"Welcome back."

"*Höke-närī-nusaī,*" I repeat, making his sleepy eyes widen. "Am I messing it up?"

He shakes his head. "It's just been years since anyone sounded like home."

His words wash over me like a cool breeze as I lean my shoulder against the door. *Go in,* I think to myself. *Let this be the end.* But when Roën nestles against the wall, I find myself standing still. He reaches up, fingers brushing my ear as he plays with a wet coil of my hair.

"Are you coming with us tomorrow?"

I nod, though I wish it weren't true. "I can't send Tzain in there alone. Amari will eat him alive. And even if Mári and Bimpe don't want to follow me, I took a vow. I failed to protect Mâzeli from this war. I have to do what I can to protect them."

Roën traces his fingers down the slope of my neck and his touch erases every other thought. His caress sends a shiver through my chest. I dig my nails into my palm, fighting the part of me that wants to sink into him. I still can't believe what I saw tonight. Everything he did just to make me smile.

After Baba died, I didn't think anyone would care about me like that again.

"You know, you're not half as heartless as you pretend to be."

"I wish that were true." Roën trails his thumb across my collarbone, bringing it to my lower lip when I frown. "You were hoping to hear something else?"

I exhale and look away. "I fell for a monster once. I can't do that to myself again."

My stomach clenches as he cups the back of my neck, drawing me closer to him. His gaze drops to my lips and I find myself holding my breath.

"Your mistake wasn't falling for a monster, *Zìtsōl*. It was falling for the wrong one."

"Are you supposed to be the right one?"

Roën smiles, but it doesn't hold any joy. "I've never been the right anything."

Something in my chest deflates when he meets my forehead with a soft kiss. He releases me and turns around, walking down the hall.

Let him go, I will myself. I already know the pain of giving my heart to someone I can never trust. But with each step he takes, everything inside me wants him to stop.

"Roën, wait." I speak the words though they make my hands shake. I walk toward him, fighting the part of me that wants to run the other way.

"Stay with me." I reach for his hand, grazing his fingers with my own. "Be with me. Even if it's wrong."

I gasp as Roën's cold hands grab the sides of my face. His body presses against my own, lips meeting mine as my back hits the wood of my door. He doesn't kiss me like I've lost pieces of my heart. He doesn't kiss me like we're marching into battle. He kisses me like he's never going to let go.

Like we have all the time in the world.

"*Zitsōl.*" His forehead presses against mine and his honeyed scent fills my every breath. The thought of Inan crosses my mind, but it's not enough to hold me back.

All we had were lies and broken promises. Dreams we could never achieve. With Roën there are no facades. Only reality.

My door swings open as I surrender to his touch. To the feel of his lips against my ear. He makes me lose myself in his arms, stealing the air from my lungs with every caress.

"Is this okay?" he whispers.

My breath hitches as he squeezes my waist, hands lingering at the hem of my tunic. I nod and mirror his actions, my own fingers traveling up the sculpted muscles of his abdomen.

"Keep going," I whisper, urging him on. My skin burns at his touch. I breathe in as he pulls me close, fingers trailing up my back—

In a breath, a searing pain shoots through my skin. My own screams echo in my head. My scars prickle beneath Roën's hands.

I flinch and push Roën back, hyperventilating as the world unravels around me. Though I fight it, I see Saran's face. I feel his knife digging into my flesh.

"Did I do something wrong?" Roën tries to touch my hand, but I pull it back. I scramble to the far wall, putting as much space between us as I can.

Everything I fight forces its way out, spinning out of my control. I hear Mâzeli's voice. I feel Inan's touch. I smell Baba's blood as it pours out of his chest.

"I'm sorry." Roën steps away, fear creeping over the confusion on his face. I feel the part of me that wants to explain, but I keep it inside. The last time someone was this close to my heart, he didn't just stab me in the back. He took the people I love. He left me with wounds that will never heal.

"You should go," I whisper.

"What's going on?" Roën's brows crease. "Talk to me. We don't have to do anything. *Zitsōl*, that's not why I care about you—"

"Well, I don't care about you!" The words sting coming out of my mouth. But I know it's all I have. The only weapon that can keep Roën away.

"You're just a mercenary." I shake my head. "Just a monster for hire. At least Inan was a king. At least he *believed* in something!"

The look on Roën's face cuts deeper than any other blade I've experienced. For once, I don't see his armor. Only the boy who let me in.

"I don't care about you." My breath shakes with every word. "I never could. Just go."

His face turns to stone as he walks out the door. When it closes behind him, I hug my chest, falling to the floor. I clasp a hand to my mouth, trying to stifle the sound of my sobs.

The silence around me burns more than the memory of the scars on my back.

CHAPTER SIXTY-SIX

······◆◇◆······

AMARI

WARM RAYS HEAT my back, jarring me from sleep. I mumble Tzain's name, reaching for him as I rub my eyes. My nose wrinkles when I look around, searching for the tiled walls of my elder quarters. It's as if I've been stolen in the night.

All that surrounds me now are reeds.

"What in the skies . . ."

I run my fingers over the stalks, the feathery leaves tickling my hand. Tall daffodils sprout between the reeds, peppering the endless field with yellow.

I cannot figure out where I've gone. It feels far too real to be a dream. But then I sense another presence.

My heart stops when I hear his voice.

"We need to talk."

The sight of Inan is like a fist driving through my gut. It knocks the wind from my chest as he raises his hands in surrender, brown lips turning into a frown.

"It's Mother," his voice shakes. "Amari, if you knew the things she's done—"

"What about what you've done?" I scramble to my feet. "Do I look foolish enough to fall for your tricks again? How dare you summon me after attacking our base!"

"Look at me!" Inan storms forward. "Look into my eyes! If I had ordered that attack, why would I have gone out to meet you? Why would I waste time talking to Zélie if I knew Mother was about to turn that land into a war zone?"

I open my mouth, but his words force me to pause. He looked just as confused as I was when we first heard the sanctuary's horns.

I thought it was all part of his act.

"I know you can't trust me." Inan shakes his head. "I know 'I'm sorry' will never be enough. But being queen means you don't get to rule by your emotions."

I narrow my eyes. "Why did you bring me here?"

"You win." Inan's hands go limp. "I *concede*. I can't keep fighting knowing what I know. I don't want any part in this war."

What's going on? My mouth falls open as my mind spins. I can't believe a word he speaks, but real pain shines in his eyes.

"You'd really give up the throne?" I ask.

He winces, as if the very word is a curse. "For the good of Orïsha, I'd give up anything."

I clench my jaw, legs shaking as I step back. I don't know what happened, but I know he speaks the truth. Sacrificing for the good of Orïsha is all my brother knows how to do.

But when he holds out his hand, I think of Zélie's father. Of her battered body sobbing over Mâzeli's corpse. This is how Inan gets in. How he always wins.

He's gotten so good at lying he doesn't even know when he's lying to himself.

"Let me go."

"Amari, please!" Inan chokes out the words. "Everything that's happened . . . it started with Mother. But it can end with us!"

"This kingdom doesn't stand a chance of surviving until you and Mother are gone for good." I cross my arms. "I don't need you to win this war."

"Yes you do." He brings his hands to his gut, gritting his teeth with pain. "You'll never beat her. You can't. For Mother, no sacrifice is too great."

"I will *win*," I growl. "And when I do, I will make up for everything our family has done wrong. I will be Orïsha's greatest queen. I will change the entire kingdom!"

I ball my fists, chest heaving up and down. "This is the last time I'll ask. Let me go. Now."

Inan lowers his head and it's like he shrinks before my eyes. The sight of him makes my throat tight. I look away before I start to cry.

"I never wanted it to be this way."

I close my eyes as the dreamscape fades.

"Neither did I."

· · · · · ◆ ◇ ◆ · · · · ·

With a gasp, I shoot up, clutching Tzain's agbada against my bare skin. He snores by my side. I lie in my quarters again.

My heart thrashes in my chest as Inan's words run through my mind. *You'll never beat her. For Mother, no sacrifice is too great.*

"You're wrong," I whisper under my breath. They both are. Victory hangs just beyond my fingertips. It's so close, I can taste it. I just have to push harder. Be bolder. Outsmart every angle.

To beat them, I have to be ruthless.

I have to be willing to fight like Mother.

I move slowly as I slip out of bed, not wanting to wake Tzain. I throw an old tunic over my head and enter the hall, my footsteps echoing in the silence as I run up the stairs.

Mother and Inan were right to use those villagers as shields. Even if word got out about their location, their presence ties our hands. But if those villagers were out of the way . . . if they weren't a factor at all . . .

The new plan takes shape in my mind as I bang on Jahi's door. A curse bleeds through before it creaks open.

The Winder squints at me through the hall's lantern light. "We better be under attack."

"It's about Ibadan. We need to adjust our plan."

Jahi steps back, opening his door. "Are the other elders coming?"

"No." I step into his quarters, picturing Inan's face. "They have their plan. This one stays between us."

CHAPTER SIXTY-SEVEN

⬩ ⬩ ⬩ ⬩ ⬩ ◆ ◇ ◆ ⬩ ⬩ ⬩ ⬩ ⬩

AMARI

AFTER FOUR DAYS of tunneling through the mountains outside of Ibadan, our entry point finally opens up. Kâmarū steps away from the eroding stone, revealing the glistening water that fills the underground caves. As it ripples below, my stomach turns to rock. The other elders look to me, waiting for my command.

"Are they in there?" I turn to Dakarai. Behind us, he whispers his incantation, summoning a swatch of stars between his palms. Translucent images of the different villagers in their pyramid ahérés fade in and out between his hands.

The cave walls close in with every scene he narrows in on: the children swimming in the lake; the father and daughter preparing the dinner as the sun goes down; the line of people grabbing buckets of water from the village well.

Each innocent villager feels like a mine on the battlefield.

"There they are." I grab Tzain's arm as a translucent image of Mother and Inan appears between Dakarai's hands. Though the image is blurry from outside Ibadan's mountain range, I know their silhouettes.

They sit in a pyramid ahéré surrounded by military officials. It feels strange to watch them from afar. They're completely ignorant of what is about to come.

"We don't have long." My voice echoes against the cramped cave walls. "The soldiers patrolling the village change guard at sunrise. Once Nâo locates the path to Ibadan's lakes, we'll have to move fast to strike during their shift."

"Let's do this." Nâo slides her blue helmet over her shaved head. "I'm ready. Who's diving with me?"

Roën rises in the back of the group, no emotion on his face. Once we're in, he's our best chance of locating Inan's hiding place.

"I'll go, too," Tzain offers. "I know the village. I can help find them."

"Whoever goes with Roën will be stuck in Ibadan until Nâo comes back for us." I shake my head. "We need someone with magic."

"I'll go."

I have to blink, not believing my eyes when Zélie raises her hand. She hasn't said two words to me all week. I'm surprised she's even here.

"I remember the village," she says. "We'll locate the king and queen while you all make your way in."

"That works," I nod to her, but she doesn't meet my eye. "Everyone else, rest up, but be ready to move. As soon as Nâo comes back for us, we leave to finish this war."

The elders disperse in the little space we have. Only Jahi lingers behind.

"What about us?" He lowers his voice, nodding his head at Imani.

"Wait till everyone's asleep," I whisper. "Then head for the mountains."

A bitter taste fills my tongue when Jahi turns to relay my instructions to Imani. The Cancer's face falls as he whispers, but she glances at me and nods.

Relax, Amari, I coach myself. *It won't come to that.* We can beat Mother and Inan. We just have to stick to the plan.

I walk up to Zélie; her lips press into a tight line as she puts on her armor.

"Thank you." I smile. "You didn't have to volunteer."

"I'm not going to let my brother kill himself just so you can sit on your precious throne."

She brushes past my shoulder, not even seeing how deep her hatred cuts. Zélie joins Nâo as the Tider gives Khani a kiss. The two hug before Nâo steps forward.

The Tider moves in front of the entry point and the stretches her palms out toward the water as an incantation leaves her mouth.

"Èyà omi, omi sí fún mi—"

Tider blue light glows around her slender fingers, making the water foam as it twists into the air. Nâo jumps into the empty path she creates, motioning for the others to follow.

Roën pockets his blade, not even sparing Zélie a second glance as he jumps in. But Zélie hesitates in front of the entry point. Tzain lays a hand on her shoulder.

"Are you sure you don't want me to go?" he asks.

"It's okay." She rests her hand above his. "I'm strong enough to finish this war."

Tzain wraps her in his arms, squeezing tight before letting her go. I move to his side as Zélie jumps in, landing beside Nâo and Roën.

"Èyà omi, omi sí fún mi—"

Nâo continues her chant, manipulating the water around them. It closes above their heads, trapping them in a pocket of air that allows them to move freely through the underground lakes. Tzain frowns as he watches his sister walk away. His body tenses with each step she takes.

"You really think they can do this?" he asks, and I force myself to nod.

"They have to," I say. "They're our strongest."

But my nails dig into my palms as they disappear from our sight.

I know what I must do if they can't.

CHAPTER SIXTY-EIGHT

INAN

As WE SIT in the pyramid ahéré, my hand shakes around the bronze piece. With every second that ticks by, I feel the weight of the lives that hang in the balance. Mother sits across from me, no sign of all the blood that coats her hands. There's no trace of guilt on her face. If anything, she holds back a smile.

"Your Majesty, we've received word from the palace." General Fa'izah hands me a rolled parchment. "The *Iyika* are nearing Lagos's borders."

"Are our soldiers in position?" Mother asks.

"Every single one."

"Good." She smiles at the officers around the table. When her eyes land on Ojore, the ache erupts in my core. I can't look away from the burns on his neck. Burns she caused.

I don't know how she can smile at him. Speak to him. *Breathe* near him. I haven't been able to look him in the eye since learning the truth.

I don't know when I'll be able to.

"I need some air." I rise, avoiding Ojore's gaze as I make my way toward the door.

"Inan, we need to stay in here," Mother calls after me. "The *Iyika* could strike at any moment—"

"I'll be fine," I cut her off. I don't give her another chance to respond.

The moment I get outside, I break into a sprint. The mountain breeze chills the sweat on my skin. I wheeze as I try to take it all in. But when I hear the shout of Mother calling after me, I slip into the iron ahéré of Ibadan's military fortress, locking the door before she can see where I've gone.

Distance does nothing to alleviate the weight of her crimes. To erase the blood that my family has spilled. My boots drag against the metal floors as I think of the carnage yet to come. How many people must die to protect a stolen throne? How many of them have to be maji?

I have to stop this.

I shake my head, pacing the empty room. It doesn't matter if Amari won't take my concession. I have to end this fight on my own.

I clench my fist as the lock clicks and the door handle groans behind me.

"Mother, it's over—"

My voice stops at the sight of Ojore in the doorframe. He stares at me with an empty expression.

"I-I thought you were Mother."

The door groans shut in our silence. He steps forward and the lantern light spills across the burns on his neck. I look away as nausea rises in my throat.

"We need to call off the attack." I stare at the ground. "I was wrong. This war . . . we're taking things too far."

"Why won't you look at me?"

The ice in his voice freezes me in place. Hairs rise on the nape of my neck as he takes a step toward me.

"You don't have to feel bad, you know," his voice drops to a whisper. "Your mother clearly doesn't, and she's known the truth for years."

A rock settles in my throat as I look up. Ojore's lips curl back into a sinister snarl. I don't recognize the person who stands before me. It's as if the Ojore I know is no longer there.

"I couldn't stay here when the fight was in Lagos," he says. "I couldn't leave my soldiers to finish this war themselves. I was coming to tell you. I didn't expect to walk in on you and your mother celebrating the death of my family."

The tears trapped in his throat are more painful than Father's sword to the gut. I don't know what to say. The color drains from my face.

"It was wrong." I shake my head. "She was *wrong*. That's why I'm calling this off. Th-that's why I want to end this war!"

But as Ojore stares into the distance, I feel my words bouncing off deaf ears. "Do you know the things I've done for your family?" Tears well in his eyes. "The maji I've killed?"

"I know . . ." I put a hand on his shoulder. "Believe me, I *know*."

Zélie's face fills my mind and I picture the life she could've had. The life she *should* have had. If things were different, she might still live in these mountains with her family. The Raid never would've broken her home. She wouldn't have made the mistake of trusting me. She wouldn't have the scars on her back.

"All these years, I thought the maji were the enemy," Ojore says. "I blamed them. I hated *them*. And it was her all along!"

His voice turns dark and something shifts behind his eyes. He straightens up, hatred transformed to a new resolution. My blood runs cold when he removes his sword.

"I'll kill her," he whispers under his breath. "I'll kill her before she kills anyone else."

"Ojore, wait." I hold up my hands, positioning myself between him and the door. "Mother will answer for her crimes, I promise. But right now there are lives at stake."

"Move."

My throat dries as he raises his sword to my neck.

"*Move*," he growls. "Or I'll make you move!"

I stare at the sword in his hand before looking at him. There's no waver in his stance. No sign that he'll give me a chance.

"Ojore, this isn't the way."

"I won't ask you again."

As soon as the blue light sparks in my hand, Ojore strikes.

I dive to avoid his blade, my magic extinguishing like a flame. Ojore doesn't hesitate before attacking again. I lunge as his sword collides with the metal wall.

"I don't want to hurt you!" I shout, but a blind fury fills his eyes. I can't hold back.

I pull a dagger from my belt, throwing it at his thigh. But with a wave of his hand, the dagger halts in midair.

Dark green ashê surrounds Ojore's fingers as the dagger hangs between us.

CHAPTER SIXTY-NINE

ZÉLIE

"Èyà omi, omi sí fún mi—"

Nâo continues to chant as the hours tick by. Her melodic voice weaves over the constant pulse of flowing water, making her magic form a protective barrier around us. I inhale the algae-scented air as we move meter by meter, lanterns at our hips lighting the way.

"It doesn't feel real." Nâo's hands fall to her sides as the wall of water solidifies. The tunnel darkens the deeper we go, bringing us closer to Ibadan's lakeshores. "It's actually happening. We're bringing this war to an end."

I try to meet her smile with one of my own, but it hurts to pretend. The victory we've been fighting for is mere moments away, yet I haven't felt this empty since Baba died.

One more fight. I close my eyes. One more fight and I can leave this all behind. At least when this war is won, Tzain will be safe. Baba and Mâzeli will have died for something. *And I . . .*

I don't know how to finish the thought. Being this close to Roën makes my chest tight. But when this is over, I'll be free of him. I'll be free of every ounce of pain and guilt.

"Z, we're okay, right?" Nâo glances back at my silence. "No one blames you for wanting to run. We all lost something when Mâzeli died."

Don't be sad.

The boy's large ears fill my mind, another puncture to my heart. If he were here, he'd be running through the underground caves. He'd be itching to reach Ibadan's shores and end this war.

"I know we let you down," Nâo sighs. "But we need you. No matter what happens, you're still our soldier."

"You should know that your soldier is a coward," Roën retorts at our backs. "All *Zitsōl* wants is to run away. Don't expect her to fight for you when this is over."

My jaw clenches at Roën's snark as I turn. He meets my glare with a hollow smirk as he speaks.

"What?" he challenges. "Am I wrong?"

I narrow my eyes and get in his face. "What? I hurt your feelings and now you want to play games?"

"I just want her to know the truth." Roën shrugs. "I seem to be the only one who can see right through you."

Nâo slows to a stop, eyes flitting between the two of us. "Do you need to talk—"

"Keep walking," I bark. "Roën just wants attention."

I turn on my heel, putting my hands to my ears as he continues to shout.

"These idiots bleed for you. They die for *you*. And all you want is to run away and lick your scars—"

"What right do you have?" I whip around. "You left your home!"

"Because I had nothing!" he yells at me. "I had no one. You're going to *win* and you still have so many of the people you love! I don't feel sorry for you. Stop feeling sorry for yourself!"

My throat burns as I come to a stop, inhaling a shaking breath. The air tastes strange on my tongue. The cave walls start to close in.

"You don't get to judge me," I whisper. "I didn't ask for any of this!"

"No one ever asks, but you're here. You're here when so many people aren't!" Roën grabs his head as if he could pull out his hair. "You survived the Raid. The guards. You survived the wrath of a *king*. You're not a victim, Zélie. You're a survivor! Stop running away!"

I can't move in the wake of his words. They hit me deep in my core. Roën stares at me before exhaling a slow breath and pressing a fist to his forehead.

"Forget it." He drops his hands and walks past the two of us. "I'm just a mercenary. What do I know?"

"Roën." I grab my chest as my throat closes up. The stale cave air starts to thin. My head begins to spin.

"Slow down!" Nâo shoots out her hand, extending the tunnel of air as Roën charges ahead. "I don't know what's going on with you two, but we need to stay together!"

When Roën doesn't listen, Nâo curses, extending another tunnel of air. That's when I see it.

The tiny spark of red above his black hair.

"Roën," I call after him, but he doesn't turn back. My legs pick up speed as the scent of oil leaks in. My feet pound against the hard rock. "Wait!"

I'd know that burning scent anywhere.

"Roën, *stop!*"

I throw Nâo back.

The first fuse blows as he turns around.

CHAPTER SEVENTY

ZÉLIE

Boom!

BOOM!

BOOM!

It's like a line of dominoes falling at once.

The first fuse is only the trigger.

Dozens of bombs go off.

The gods pull the ground from our feet as the cave collapses in every direction. My body throbs with a vengeance as I tumble through the water and darkness.

"Roën!" I try to shout, but water swallows my screams. My ears ring from the string of explosions. I can't see anything.

Falling rocks slice through my skin. The madness only stops when my back slams against the hard ground. The collision knocks precious seconds of air from my lungs. I grab my neck as water fills my throat.

Help!

My throat burns as I choke. Before I can figure out which way is up, large boulders hurtle toward me from the cave ceiling.

I grit my teeth as one lands on my leg. The stone digs into my flesh, cutting through muscle as I pull. I open my eyes to darkness as the truth sets in.

No one's coming to save me.

This is it.

The realization makes my chest tight. I kick and I scratch and I claw, but my fingers only hit gravel.

I always thought my life would end in a flash. Now I feel each second that ticks toward my end. I press my free leg against the boulder for leverage, but the jagged stone cuts like a knife. My shin sears as the rock scratches against bone.

Let go . . .

The whisper rises from deep inside. Tears well in my eyes as my body sinks onto the cold floor.

There's no war after this. No more scars that'll never heal. I know the peace of death's embrace.

I've already tasted the freedom that lies beyond the pain.

Let go, I mouth the words, holding on to them as my lungs scream for air. I can almost hear Sky Mother's song when Mama's silhouette shines through the darkness.

It shimmers with white light, growing brighter when Baba's silhouette appears by her side. I lift my head from the floor.

Then I hear Mâzeli's voice.

"Jagunjagun!"

I almost laugh at the third silhouette that shimmers to life. He stands by Baba's side, ears still too large for his head.

I reach out my hand toward Mâzeli's glow, everything in me wanting to grab on. I can't bear the pain anymore.

There's nothing more I can give this world.

His light reaches out toward me, a hand pulling me into the beyond. But when it hits, my Second doesn't grant me aid and pull me to the other side.

He grants me a vision.

Time stills as the moments before the explosion push through the fog in my mind. I see the flash of red. I smell the scent of gas that burned my nostrils.

The ring of bombs go off behind Roën's head, exploding the tunnel walls and sending us into this abyss. I couldn't make sense of it at the time, but there were so many explosions. Enough to wipe out an army. Enough to wipe out *our* army.

No . . .

My head spins as the realization takes hold. We didn't just trigger an attack.

We walked right into a trap.

The truth is like another boulder falling onto my chest. We thought we held the advantage, but somehow the monarchy knew we were coming. They knew we would take this path.

If they set this trap below, what other dangers lie above? What traps have they set for our people marching past Lagos? The maji and diviners are nearly defenseless.

All of our elders are here!

"Nana—"

My body goes numb with dread as Sky Mother's song vibrates through my skin. Though Mâzeli's silhouette draws back, the warm embrace of death reaches for me as my lungs collapse. Fire burns as water rushes down my throat, suffocating me from within. It stings more than any pain I've ever known. More than my body can hold.

Everything inside me screams to give in. To fall into the blackness. To end the suffering.

But beyond the pain, I see the gap between Mári's two front teeth. The patch of discoloration around Bimpe's brown lips.

I see the faces of every Reaper I've yet to meet. I see my brother's laugh. I see Amari and the other elders.

The monarchy we must find a way to beat.

The pain is too much to take, yet the same agony spurs me on. The pain I've been so afraid to feel is how I know I'm still alive.

It's how I know there's still something inside me that can fight.

Ẹ tọnná agbára yin.

The tattoos on my skin ignite with golden light as I invoke the command in my head. As they heat me in the ice of the water, I allow them to amplify the little lifeforce I have left.

A silent scream escapes in bubbles as I roar. Though I have nothing left to give, I push with all that I am.

My leg sears as stone cuts to the bone, scraping the flesh from my shin. With a gasp, my leg breaks free. My arms start to move.

Water fights me as I kick off the lake floor, following that one command. Tzain. Amari. Roën.

If I die now, they don't stand a chance.

Live.

Every muscle in my body falls limp, depleted of all oxygen. But I lift a shaking hand, picturing every one of my Reapers.

A purple glow cuts through the darkness, rumbling as shadows twist from my fingers. They latch onto something above, pulling me up through the water.

As I rise, it all falls away. Every ounce of pain. Mâzeli's final words. Baba's smile. The chain they wrapped around Mama's neck.

I choke as I leave every scar they carved onto my heart behind and break through the water's surface.

Live.

I want to live.

CHAPTER SEVENTY-ONE

INAN

My ARMS FALL LIMP as the dagger hangs in midair. I don't believe my eyes. Ojore controls the metal with his hand.

He drops the sword meant for Mother's head as he turns the dagger on me.

"You're a maji?"

A snarl rises to Ojore's lips.

"I prefer the term tîtán."

He flicks his finger and the dagger goes flying. I dive out of the way as the blade pierces the iron wall at my back. Right where my head would have been.

I don't have a chance to rise from the ground before the plates under my feet transform. The metal slides around my ankle like mercury. Slanted columns shoot up from the floor.

I cry out as one strikes me in the gut. Another clips my jaw. A flat column hits my chest with such force I twist onto my back.

All the while, Ojore watches from the corner. A soldier shaking with emotion. His mastery is greater than any I've seen. Far beyond a normal Welder's capabilities.

"I hated myself," he whispers. "I hated what I had become. I thought magic was the problem, but it was *you* and your mother all along!"

I fling another dagger from my belt, but Ojore splits the metal before it can strike. The air rings as it breaks into thick needles. With a snap of his fingers, the shards pierce my thigh.

"You don't deserve the throne."

The agony is so great, I can only gasp. My body seizes as the metal works through my blood. With another clench of his fist, Ojore tears the armor from his skin.

It molds around his bicep, transforming into a serrated blade.

"You can't claim the right to lead after all you've done to tear this kingdom apart."

The metal beneath me shifts, wrapping around my wrists. I can barely see straight as he lifts me up, hanging me in front of him with metal restraints.

"You and your mother." He shakes his head. "You're a poison."

He melts my breastplate, lifting my undercoat to line up his blade with my father's scar.

"I intend to end the epidemic with yo—"

I thrust forward, driving my knee into his chin. A loud crack echoes through the room as Ojore's leg buckles.

The metal restraints dissolve as he stumbles and I crash to the ground. But when he lunges for me, a cobalt cloud shoots from my hand. The bones in my arm snap as my magic hits him in the chest, temporarily paralyzing him.

I drag my body toward the door as Ojore bares his teeth, fighting my hold. His body shakes as I try to escape.

"Help!" I shout, my voice hoarse.

Ojore roars like an animal, fists clenched as he rips metal plates from the walls. The iron sheets surround me as I crawl, sharpening into blades.

I look back, not recognizing the monster that wears Ojore's face. We did this to him. We poisoned him with all our hate.

Now we shall pay the price. I can't even pretend he isn't justified. He deserves retribution for all the blood on our hands. All of Orïsha does—

"Inan!"

A blast rips the fortress door from its hinges.

I look up as Mother lunges toward us and shoots out her hand, driving a column of earth up from the ground.

Ojore's eyes bulge as it punctures his stomach. The metal blades surrounding me fall to the floor, clanking with their impact. Ojore slumps forward as blood leaks from his gut, pooling onto the silver floor.

"Quick!" Mother screams. "Get the Healers! We need to retreat!"

Boots pound my way, but I can't see past the hatred frozen on Ojore's face.

He's dead.

Ojore's dead.

The realization hurts more than any wound.

CHAPTER SEVENTY-TWO

ZÉLIE

I WHEEZE AS I break the surface. I fight to breathe through my coughs. Unfamiliar mountains surround me. Pale yellow light shines from above.

I drag myself to the thin stretch of stones along the water's surface, shaking as I latch on to something solid. My throat burns as I cough, shooting water from my lungs onto the mountain stone.

Breathe, I command myself. Air has never tasted so sweet. I try to take it all in as I fight to think through the haze.

My mind spins in waves, but one thought breaks through the noise. Nâo was furthest from the blast. But the cave collapsed right above Roën's head.

If he's still alive, he needs my help!

Though I still choke, I inhale all the air I can. Another second is all I give myself before diving back into the water.

Ẹ tọnná agbára yin.

The moonstone's marks glow along my skin, lighting my way through the darkness. Only one life pulses through the water's depths.

One that grows dimmer by the second.

I'm coming!

My leg throbs. Crimson bleeds into the water with each kick. But the agony is a gift. It's like air to my lungs, reminding me to fight on.

My heart clenches at the sight of Roën's limp form. His lifeforce is faint, only centimeters from death. A cracked mask like the one we used to surf the blue whale hangs from his nose, giving him his last breaths of air.

I dive closer until I see the massive slab crushing his bicep, pinning him to the rocky floor. I brace my good leg against the stone, but it's far too heavy to roll. No matter how I shift, his body won't budge. We're running out of time.

Roën reaches out and squeezes my wrist as the last few bubbles float from his lips. Though he can't speak, I feel his command.

"Go."

No! I shout to myself. How many times has he pulled me out from under? Dragged me back to the surface when I thrashed through water? I won't let him drown. It's my turn to rescue him.

Èmí òkú, gba ààyé nínú mi—

Purple shadows spread like ink through the water as Roën's eyes roll back. My shadows push against the stone, but they're too weak. Too slow.

Roën's limbs start to float. There's only one way to break him free.

My heart slams against my chest as my shadows shift, wrapping around his arm. Another shadow spreads through the water, creating a serrated blade. I send a prayer to Oya and close my eyes.

My shadow slices through his shoulder as I use up my last breath.

CHAPTER SEVENTY-THREE

ZÉLIE

STAY WITH ME.

I kick with the little I have left, Roën's body tucked under my arm. His severed arm lies underneath the boulder.

My glowing tattoos light the rivers of crimson that leak from his gaping shoulder. I try to forget how long he's gone without air when we finally break the surface.

"Stay with me!" I shout as I push down on his chest. Water shoots out of his mouth. He chokes as it comes out.

His body seizes when I drag him to the thin strip of land. But I won't let him die on me.

I won't lose another person I love.

"Zélie." He forces out my name through shaking breaths. His stormy eyes dart in all directions, yet they can't seem to take anything in. He grasps at me with his remaining hand. He doesn't seem to understand.

"My arm. My a—"

"Just stay with me." I press against the wound, but warm blood still leaks out from between my fingers. His heart pumps at double the speed, rattling against his rib cage.

The shadows of my tourniquet fade with my waning strength. Roën's eyes finally stop at the moon above. His lips part as he struggles for breath.

"My mother," he chokes. "She would sing . . ."

"What would she sing?" With one hand still pressed on the wound, I rip off Roën's belt. Blood flows free as I tie it tight, a hand's length below his wounded shoulder.

"Roën, what would she sing?" I shout at him, not caring if anyone hears. His voice is little more than a rasp, but he hums a foreign tune that grows louder with every note.

"Huh-mmm . . . huh-mmm . . ." He fights to keep it up. His voice cracks like a baby bird's, yet I can hear the remnants of his home.

"Keep going." I fight my tears, slipping a long stone into the knot of the tourniquet. "Please, Roën. It's beautiful."

"Huh-mmm . . . huh-mmm . . ."

I use the rock like a lever and twist. Roën's belt almost snaps as it tightens, leather cracking before the bleeding stops.

"She would sing it." His eyes start to drift. "When it rained . . . it always rained . . ."

"Hey!" I slap his face. "Keep going. What would she say?"

He tries to speak, but no words come out. His pink lips turn blue before my eyes. The bleeding may have stopped, but his skin still pales.

It's not enough.

"Roën, please!" My heart rips as I cradle his head. His body is cold to the touch. My tears leak onto his face. "Keep talking. What would she say?"

"The thunder," he manages to croak, but his voice falters. Though it feels like I may shatter, I force myself to sing the notes.

"Huh-mmm . . ."

Roën reaches up his shaking hand and grabs my own.

"Just stay with me." I stroke his hair in between the notes. "I'll sing it as long as you want, but you have to stay right here."

He nods, but his breaths escape in rapid spurts. Veins bulge against his neck as he fights for air. For life.

"Roën, please." I move my bloodied hand from his hair to his cheek. Beneath his skin, his lifeforce dims, slipping away like grains of falling sand.

"*Zitsōl.*" He forces the word out through his final gasp. He grips me with the last strength he has. *"Home."*

Confusion racks me as his fingers fall limp. But when the meaning hits, my body turns to stone.

Home . . .

That's what it's meant this entire time.

"Roën!" I scream, but he doesn't move. His eyes won't open. His chest doesn't rise.

"Roën!" My shriek echoes. "Roën, please," I whisper into his hair. But he's not here.

He's gone.

Grief tears a hole inside my heart. My bloodied hands fly to my chest. Though there's air, I can't draw breath. But when my tattoos shine with dim light, I see a flicker of gold in Roën's heart. It's smaller than a seed.

Smaller than a tear.

As it fades before my eyes, I think of my *isípayá*: the gold tether of life intertwining with the purple. I thought Oya was trying to show me the truth behind the cênters and the source of their magic. But what if I was the purple light?

What if the gold was Roën all along?

"Oya, please." The tattoos on my skin flicker to life again. For the first time, they don't shine in gold. They shine with Reaper purples.

The glowing seed is the only sign of life in Roën's body, but it's enough. It still holds a remnant of life.

"*Ẹ tọnná agbára yin.*"

Particles of purple light crystallize before my chest. They weave together like my shadows of death, forming a broken, twisting thread.

I push though I can hardly keep myself conscious. The thread moves like a knife, piercing through Roën's chest as his body rises above the stone. I feel the moment it digs into his heart. My teeth clench as my own heart strains.

"Ẹ tọnná agbára yin," I gasp. "Ẹ tọnná agbára yin!"

The thread takes all that I have, though there's barely life to give. The world blurs out of focus as the moonstone's light dims.

Roën's body floats back to the ground and my body falls with him, slumping over his corpse. I press my ear to his chest. The blackness closes in.

Oya, please . . .

My vision goes first. Then my body hangs limp. Sound starts to disappear, but as it goes, I hear it. Soft like the ocean tides.

The fragile beating of his heart.

Now connected to mine.

CHAPTER SEVENTY-FOUR

■ ■ ■ ■ ■ ◆ ◇ ◆ ■ ■ ■ ■ ■

AMARI

FOR THE FIRST TIME since his death, I wish Father still lived. Chained up in the palace cellars. Somewhere I could talk to him.

As the sun breaks over the mouth of the cave, the voice in my head isn't enough. I need someone to give me answers. Tell me which path is right.

"We need to go after them!" Tzain breaks through my thoughts. Concern sharpens all the hard lines in his face. He doesn't beg to follow them as he has every hour. This time he states his command. "Something happened."

"Don't jump to conclusions!" I snap. I can't have Tzain unravel on me now. I'm already unraveling on myself.

What do I do?

What can I do?

What should I do?

With each passing second, our victory slips away. The future of Orïsha goes up in flames. We need to take Mother and Inan out now, while they're isolated and alone. If we can't do it here, we won't win this war.

You'll never beat her. You can't. For Mother, no sacrifice is too great.

Inan's right. I can't win unless I play their games. But can I really go through with this? Is any cost too great if it'll end this madness?

I think of all the villagers we saw in Dakarai's search; the children playing in the lake, the parents lining up at the village well. I think of what it will actually mean to wipe Mother and Inan from their earth.

I think of the fact that Zélie could be alive inside those walls.

In what world could I sacrifice her after everything she's done for me? Everything she means? She and Tzain are the people I love most in this world.

Who will I be if I sacrifice that love just to win the war?

"Look!"

I snap my head up as Kâmarū runs to the entry point. Khani screams as Nâo rises through the carved hole, water propelling her upwards.

She collapses onto the rock, blood and bruises coating her skin. My gut clenches when I realize that Zélie and Roën aren't with her.

"What happened?" Tzain rushes to them. "Where's my sister?"

"I don't know," Nâo says through her coughs. "There were explosions—"

Before he can hear the rest, Tzain takes off, sprinting toward the cave's exit.

"Tzain, no!" I scream after him. He can't go into the village. He doesn't know what's about to happen.

"Tzain!" I yell, but he sprints like a man possessed. Other elders follow his lead. There's only one way I can stop him.

"*Ya èmí, ya ara!*"

It's like ripping my own heart in half to wield my magic against the boy I love. Tzain grunts as the cobalt blaze strikes him in the back. With a lurch, he tumbles to the cave floor. His legs are frozen stiff. He'll never forgive me for this.

I shall never forgive myself.

"What are you doing?" he yells, and my resolve threatens to crack.

"You can't go in there." I clench my fist. "None of you can."

He bares his teeth, but the rage falls away as realization sets in.

"What did you do," he breathes. "Amari, what did you do?"

Everyone's questions begin to mount at once, drowning me in their chaos. Kâmarū realizes Jahi's absence first. Khani screams her sister's name.

Mother wouldn't stop.

I press my hands to my ears, trying to block out the noise. She would sacrifice anyone to win this war. How can I end it if I won't do the same?

"Amari—"

"Everybody shut up!" I scream as the seconds tick away. The sun rises higher and higher into the sky. I dig my hands through my curls.

Strike, Amari. Father's face comes to me. I don't need him alive to know what he would say. It wouldn't have mattered if it was his first choice or his last resort. It wouldn't matter if it cost him everyone he loved.

I will be a better queen.

My last words to him play through my ears. If I go through with this, I won't be any better.

But if I don't, I'll never get the chance to save Orïsha.

When the sun hits its mark the soldiers patrolling the village will change guard. We only have seconds before we lose it all.

They'll find us at any moment.

"I'm sorry." I whisper the words to the wind as I bring the horn to my lips.

My tears fall as the signal blares.

CHAPTER SEVENTY-FIVE

◆ ◇ ◆

ZÉLIE

I DON'T KNOW if it's possible to feel more drained than I do now.

My body drags like lead.

Every step pushes past death.

Roën still lies unconscious, his remaining arm draped around my neck. My own is hooked tight around his waist as I drag him forward.

"Almost there," I whisper to him and myself. I don't know how long we lay by that mountain lake, but when I opened my eyes, the moon still shone above. After hiking across the cold rocky trails, I see my old village glinting like a single star in the night. The pyramid ahérés rise a full kilometer away, creating their own mountain range around the lakes where Tzain and I used to play.

I thought coming home after all this time would only fill me with more pain. That I would only see the horrible night of the Raid. But in the mountains, I see the nights Baba and I laid outside our ahéré, counting the stars. I remember watching Mama and the Reapers chant on the highest peaks, cleansing the village of spirits under the full moon.

I feel everything I thought I lost. I feel my parent's love.

Despite everything that hurts, it's another reminder to carry on.

I push myself, moving despite how my legs shake. Ripped fabric bandages my shin, the only way to put pressure on my own wounds. I can

343

barely support my weight, let alone Roën's. His breathing remains shallow, but his heart still beats with mine. I pull strength from our connection even as it drains me to keep him alive.

I don't know how long we have before the connection eats through us both, but the command to live still breathes within me; a fire burning brighter than it ever has.

I don't want to run. I don't just want to survive. I want to fight.

I want to thrive—

Wa-ooooooooo!

My heart skips a beat as a horn rings through the air. I wait for Nehanda's tîtáns to descend. But the horn doesn't sound like any they've used before. In fact, it's strangely familiar.

It sounds like one of ours . . .

I lay Roën down as the winds change direction. The flutter of flapping wings fills the air. Black-feathered hawks fly overhead, invading the sky like a storm as the horn blares again.

I grab the nearest ledge, dragging myself up through their piercing shrieks and squawks. The hawks don't fly toward us. They run from something else.

I don't know what awaits me as I pull myself over the cliff, but when I see it, my hands fall limp. Above, the winds move in a violent circle. They pick up speed as they come together, a sphere of air creating a dome.

"What in gods' names?"

The enclosure touches down to the ground—a gate closing around Ibadan's borders. No, not a gate.

A barrier keeping everyone in the village locked inside . . .

Amari, what is this? I squint, searching for the glimmer of our colored armor. But all questions fade when I realize the true nature of this attack. Rust-colored clouds build in the distance.

The Cancer's gas climbs into the sky, rising a full kilometer into the air. It creates a wall within the dome of wind, just waiting to be unleashed on my helpless village.

"Amari, don't do this," I whisper, pleading from afar. There's a breath as the cloud hangs at Ibadan's borders, growing higher and thicker by the second. But when the horn rings again, the cloud surges forward.

The gas unleashes its attack, launching the wall of death.

"No!" I scream.

The cloud moves like a wave, crashing over everything in its path. Birds squawk as they try to escape, only to hit the rotating sphere of air and be thrown in another direction. One's wings fold as it's flung into the cloud.

The second it's hit by the gas, its body shrivels. It plummets to the ground.

"Run!" I scream at the top of my lungs, not caring who hears me. In the distance a few villagers exit their homes, marveling at the orange smoke.

I try to climb down from the ledge, but I only crash to the ground. There's no way my legs will be fast enough. I have to use my magic. I have to move like Mâzeli.

"Èmí òkú, gba ààyé nínú mi—"

Four shadows of death twist from my hips like ribbons as I wrap my arms around Roën. I think of the way Mâzeli flew through the jungle as my shadows shoot forward.

Rocks crack as they dig into the mountain stone. An instant is all I have before my body lurches through the air, propelled by my shadows like a slingshot.

I grit my teeth, clutching Roën's body as the world flies by. Mountains blur against the pale orange wall and I struggle not to inhale. As I'm propelled forward, the sky becomes the ground. I don't have much time to orient myself before my descent. Though my magic wanes, I push again.

"Jáde nínú àwon òjìjí re. Yí padà láti owó mi."

The wall of gas closes in as I swing through the mountain peaks with my shadows. Ibadan's village center nears. The last place the toxic gas will hit. Landing there will buy us time, but where do we hide? If Nâo were here, we could dive into the lakes, wait in the water for the gas to dissipate—

The well!

I hone in on the circle of granite rock as the idea takes hold. Baba used to walk me there every morning, letting my legs dangle over his strong shoulders.

As more villagers spill into the streets, I know it's our only shot. We have to get inside. Barricade ourselves and pray to our gods.

"The well!" I scream as the last shadow lowers me to the ground. "Get in the well!"

Feet thunder as the villagers follow my command. I drag Roën over the edge and hand his body off to those who've already climbed down.

"Come on!" I wave my hands as more people climb into the shelter. Hysteria transforms to honor as people push their spouses and children to the front. The wall of gas swirls like a storm, an endless orange cloud closing in from every direction.

There's not enough time.

No matter what I do, they won't all make it.

"Wait!"

The desperate plea rises above every other cry. I turn to find a woman with tears in her eyes. She pushes out her arms, frantic to save the baby in her hands.

The gas is only seconds away. The woman cries out as it hits the back of her head. Blood shoots from her mouth on impact. Her skin shrivels as it turns black.

I see the moment she realizes that she won't make it. The baby falls from her hands.

"*Èmí òkú, gba ààyé nínú mi—*"

It's the fastest I've ever seen a spirit transform. The mother's corpse doesn't even hit the ground before the incantation allows her soul to course through me, granting me new shadows, new arms. They reach out, catching the baby before it can hit the ground.

The shadows retract as I pull the infant to my chest before the spirits transform.

They block off the top of the well as the gas howls overhead.

CHAPTER SEVENTY-SIX

AMARI

I REMEMBER THE morning after the Raid as if it were yesterday.

You would think the sun wouldn't have risen, or the moon would've gone dark, but everything started exactly the same.

I awoke with a start, six years old and searching for the pleated lines of Binta's bonnet. My dreams had gifted me an adventure on the seas. I had to tell her everything.

"Binta, where are you?" My voice echoed against the gold decor and pastel pinks of my quarters. But when the door swung open, a tall handmaiden entered, a kosidán with thin lips and a sharp chin.

I sat with balled fists as she scrubbed my skin too hard. Pulled my hair too tight. Whenever I dared to ask where Binta had gone, the handmaiden pinched my arm. I broke free of her grip the first chance I got.

"Father!" I slid across the marble floors as I ran. I thought the handmaiden shrieked after me with rage. Perhaps it was actually terror.

I burst through the oak doors of the throne room, ready to make my case. But Father was still.

So unnaturally still.

"Father?" I stepped back into the hall. He always watched the sun rise over Lagos, but that day the very air held its breath around him.

In that stillness I knew something had changed. We would never return to a kinder time again.

All these years, I've wondered how he must have felt.

Today I feel it myself.

"*No!*"

Tzain thrashes like a wild animal, desperate to break my mental hold. I can't stomach the way he writhes. The tears and snot that drip past his nose.

"How could you!" His screams are like shattered glass echoing in our silence. "How could you?"

The toxic Cancer clouds begin to dissipate. Not even a single breeze moves between Ibadan's mountains.

I try to ignore the hollow pit in my chest. I won the war.

But at what cost?

Strike, Amari.

The world spins around me though my feet stay rooted in place. There's no going back from this. This is a strike Tzain and the elders won't forgive.

But I cannot allow that weight to break me now. We have our victory.

It's up to me to declare it.

"Let's go." I march to my cheetanaire, mounting its leather saddle. This is the moment that will spread throughout the lands. The story that shall birth Orïsha's future.

A new kingdom will rise from these ashes. A kingdom worthy of these sacrifices. But no elders follow my lead. They all stand still in shock. Shock I don't have the luxury to feel.

They'll understand in time.

Right now I must go declare the end of this endless fight.

I snap the reins of my cheetanaire, racing away before they can see me crack. I can't stomach the sound of Tzain's tears. The agony of his whimpers.

My hands shake beyond my control. I can't believe all the lives I took.

Inan. Mother.

Those soldiers. Those villagers.

Zélie—

No.

I push away the weight I could never bear. If Zélie were alive, she would've returned with Nâo. The monarchy killed her with their explosions.

Zélie's sacrifice allowed us to win the war.

That is the story we shall tell.

But as I approach Ibadan's borders, stories aren't enough. Even from afar, I see the blackened corpses that lie in the streets. Corpses that lie there because of me.

I picture Inan and Mother among the dead.

I picture my best friend.

Strike, Amari.

Father's voice fills my mind as the tears fill my eyes. Though I breathe, my chest stays tight. It feels like I'm being buried alive.

"Orïsha waits for no one," I whisper the words. "Orïsha waits for no one."

I will the words to be true as I ride through Ibadan's gate.

CHAPTER SEVENTY-SEVEN

ZÉLIE

When my eyes flutter open, I don't know where I am. It feels like I'm suspended in darkness. A light circles above my head.

The rough cords of a rope are wrapped around my chest before I'm pulled toward the light. The infant still screams against my neck.

"Pull her over the edge," a weathered voice instructs.

Firm hands latch onto my arms, pulling me over the side of the well. I shield my eyes as someone takes the baby from my hands and another bends to unwrap the soaked bandage from my bleeding shin.

"Allow me." I blink at the older woman who kneels by my side. She takes the white gele around her gray curls, using it to re-bandage my leg.

"You saved us." She shakes her head. "I can't thank you enough."

I close my eyes, trying to think past the pain. My mind throbs with a vengeance. I can't feel my legs. But the memories start to piece themselves together, bringing me to the well we used to escape. The shadows I channeled before everything went black.

"Roën." I clutch my chest, straining to feel him. His heart still echoes through me, but it grows weaker by the second.

"They're tending to him. They're doing the best they can." She points and I follow her hand to a pyramid ahéré beyond the well. Its stone doors are thrown wide open, revealing the village Healers and kosidán who huddle around his wounded form.

"I have to go." I bat her away, struggling to rise to my feet. I can feel his life within me, but his pulse is still too weak. The pressure is already building in my chest. The same crushing weight that hit before Mâzeli's death.

I don't know how long I can sustain the connection before his dying body kills us both.

"Zélie, please." The woman holds me down, forcing a cup of fresh water down my throat. She clicks her tongue. "Just as stubborn as your mother."

"You knew Jumoke?"

"I've never seen another Reaper move like that." She nods. "I thought she had risen from the dead." She sits back and looks out at the carnage. "Just when I thought the war would leave us behind."

Beyond her, I see the first body lying in the street. The man's red cap sits in the dirt. Blood stains coat his lips and nose. The whites of his eyes are now yellow. His dark skin has turned black, shriveled from the Cancer's gas.

A young girl escapes the well, falling to the ground the moment they remove her harness. She scrambles faster than her feet will allow, tripping over herself as tears fill her eyes.

"Baba!"

Her shriek makes my ears bleed. She falls onto his shriveled corpse, clawing at his stained robes. I have to turn away as another villager grabs her, pulling the girl away. Her screams are far too familiar.

Just like mine after the Raid.

Why? I hide my head in my hands, trying to understand. *What happened to our plan? Why would Amari launch this attack?*

Though body after body is lifted from the well, I'm surrounded by those I couldn't save. The young mother who saved her infant. The divîner who couldn't run fast enough.

"No . . ."

I turn as Amari walks into the square. Her hand flies to her chest. She crumples to her knees. At first I think it's the corpses in the street, but then I follow her gaze. My brows knit at the message painted on the mountain overlooking the village lake.

The red ink is stark against the mountain stone, dripping like blood. Other elders approach from the north, horror dawning as they take in the words.

WE HAVE YOUR ARMY.
SURRENDER OR FACE THEIR EXECUTION.

My heart collapses as I read it, suddenly understanding the monarchy's true target. These people were sacrificed in vain. We didn't get them.

The monarchy outmaneuvered us.

We've lost this war.

CHAPTER SEVENTY-EIGHT

INAN

THE STEADY ROCKING reaches through the blackness first. I blink open my eyes, meeting paneled wood. A constant creak rings through my ears, in harmony with the patter of paws. My body feels like it's been set on fire as the memories trickle back in.

"Ojore . . ."

His hatred sears into my core. It all happened so fast. So fast, it's like it wasn't even real.

One moment he was there, sharpened blades held to my neck. The next . . .

I didn't know Mother could strike that way.

"Oh, thank the skies." Mother rises from the front of the caravan. She sets down the parchments in her hand, moving to the side of my bed. She looks strange with the blood splattered across her face.

She places her palm against my head. "How do you feel?"

"What happened?" I croak. I attempt to sit up, but the pain is too severe. Mother keeps me on the bed, perusing her collection of glass vials to bring a sedative to my lips.

"It's alright, Inan." She strokes my sweat-soaked hair. "You can rest. We did it."

Her words carve a hollow pit in the little that's left of my heart. "We captured the *Iyika?*"

"Your plan worked." She nods. "The maggots who marched past Lagos put up a fight, but without their leaders they weren't a match for my tîtáns. We've captured every single one."

I try to feel the victory, the warmth spreading through my body. It's over. Done.

The war is won.

But tears rise to my eyes as I squeeze my gut. *Ojore* . . .

Skies, he was my oldest friend.

"Do not grieve him." Mother squeezes my hand. "Do not let that traitor twist your mind! After everything we did for that boy, you'd think he could show a modicum of restraint—"

"Restraint?" I yank my hands back, shooting up from the bed despite the agony it sends through my chest. "You killed his family. You killed *him!*"

Mother narrows her eyes, coldness sharpening her features. "He attacked the king. That foolish boy killed himself."

It's the last sword in my gut. I'm surprised when I don't feel blood. Ojore saved me more times than I could count. He needed me today.

But instead of backing him, I let him down.

I let Mother sacrifice him for the throne.

"He was right," I whisper. "We're poison."

"We are rulers, Inan. We are *victors!*" She speaks with such conviction. I hate how much I want to believe her words. To purge myself of this guilt. Remove this hollow pit in my chest.

"You did what was required of you. You stayed strong until the end. You won this war, and now you can rule your kingdom with grace. You can spread the peace you desire!"

She smiles at me, and in her expression, I finally see my truth.

I wanted to be the king my father couldn't be.

All I did was finish his work.

CHAPTER SEVENTY-NINE

AMARI

DENIAL IS ALL THAT I HAVE.

All that I am.

It carries me from blackened corpse to blackened corpse, to the message written on the mountain.

It doesn't take long to find the place Inan and Mother planned their attack. The tunnel she dug beneath the ahéré that they used to escape the village. While they drew our strongest warriors here, those we most needed to protect were left defenseless.

Behind me, maji crowd around Dakarai, watching the blurry frame that spreads between his hands. Almost a hundred of our maji and divîners sit in chains, bound inside a cell in the palace cellars.

Strike, Amari.

Father's words taunt me as I stare at the bodies on the ground. Their lives were meant to be a sacrifice for Orïsha. Instead their senseless deaths don't amount to anything.

Whether or not we concede, Inan has our army. We're done.

Because of me, we've lost this war.

"Zél?"

I look up as Tzain enters the village center, covered in dirt from his fall. He sprints toward her, the only motion in the square filled with dozens of bodies. His relief rips through my heart. If it hadn't been for Zélie's bravery, I would've killed more people.

I would've killed *her*.

"I thought I lost you." They're the only words Tzain can muster before he sweeps her into his arms. He shakes as he cries into her shoulder, squeezing her so hard it has to hurt her. Zélie closes her eyes and holds him tight. But when her eyes open, they lock onto mine.

My heart stops as Zélie pushes Tzain back. My fingers go cold when she limps in my direction.

"I thought you died." I take a step back. "When Nâo came back alone, I was sure you were both gone—"

She opens her hands and dark shadows of death shoot forth. Pain rips through me as they wrap around my body and my throat.

The moment I hit the ground, Zélie starts to charge. But before she can attack, her eyes roll back. Her shadows dissipate as she collapses in the dirt.

"Zélie!" Tzain runs forward.

Her body twitches with violent convulsions. Her lids flutter as the tattoos flicker on her skin.

"Get her to the ahéré!" A village tîtán steps forward. I back away as Kâmarū lifts her seizing body and carries her to a pyramid hut.

"Lock her up!" Na'imah shouts as they run.

Tzain slows at the Tamer's order. His eyes meet mine when Kenyon drags me to my feet. Instinct makes me want to cry out for help as the Burner binds my arms with a metal restraint, but I know I have lost the right.

Tzain's gaze moves from me to his village. To the bodies dropped by my command.

"I'm sorry," I whisper, but he flinches at my words. In him, I see what I've lost. The warmth I shall never feel again.

Watching him walk away is the final knife in my heart.

CHAPTER EIGHTY

ZÉLIE

"I DON'T UNDERSTAND——"

"She's overexerted——"

"We need more blood——"

Every voice sounds like it's spoken underwater as the world moves in fragments. One moment I'm on the ground. The next the wind grazes my back.

"What's happening?" Tzain fills my vision as he and Kâmarū lay me across a stone surface.

"I don't know." Khani puts her hands on my chest. "Her body's shutting down!"

"Roën." I fight to speak his name aloud. He seizes across the ahéré, his body convulsing with mine. I used the moonstone to connect our lifeforces. I used our strength to make it through the mountains. But without a blood sacrifice to bind our connection, neither of us can survive.

"Break it." Tzain puts the pieces together. "Now, before it's too late!"

I lurch as an ache cuts across my sternum. *I can't!* I try to wheeze.

I don't have enough power to break our connection. And even if I did, what would happen to Roën? I already lost Mâzeli.

I'm not giving up on him.

"He's dying!" Healers carry Roën's body from across the hut, laying him by my side. We're running out of time. My heart will die with his.

But I know what I have to do. Oya showed me in my *ìsípayá* on that fateful day.

If the first ribbons of light were Roën and I, then the next lie right here. Connecting to more lifeforces is how we buy ourselves time.

It is how we survive.

I latch onto Tzain's wrist, and his lips press together as he reads my eyes.

"What's going on?" Khani's gaze flicks between us when Tzain puts his hand over my own.

"She needs to connect another heart," Tzain says. "It's the only way to save them both."

"No!" Khani shouts. "That strain could kill all three of you!"

"Then use me, too." Kâmarū extends his palm. "The four of us can handle it."

"*Torí ifẹ Babalúayé.*" Khani grabs her temples, cursing under her breath. She extends her palm. "Gods, just do it!"

They gather around me, all placing their hands over mine. Their heartbeats start to bleed into my ears as their lifeforces appear before my eyes. I see the emerald glow of Kâmarū's ashê. The tangerine light of Khani's magic. Even Tzain's lifeforce surges through his blood, powerful in its white glow.

"*Ẹ tọnná agbára yin.*" I wheeze the sacred command and my tattoos ignite with purple light. All around me, Tzain's, Kâmarū's, and Khani's pulses thunder between my ears. It's like five drums beating at once, searching for the same rhythm.

Tzain grunts as his chest arcs toward the ceiling. His feet lift off the ground. Kâmarū follows next. Khani rises between both of them, screaming as she floats in the air. The three of them hover as the particles of light materialize before their hearts, the very grains of their lifeforce. They stretch forward like ribbons, weaving themselves together as they twist toward my heart.

"*Ẹ tọnná agbára yin!*" I fight through the strain, chanting though I can no longer breathe. Tzain wheezes as he grabs at his throat. Khani's eyes roll as her body shakes. Our connection is killing us all.

Oya, please. I close my eyes, pushing as the tether of life breaks through my chest. The ribbon of lights digs into my heart. My body burns as if my insides have been set on fire.

Tzain clenches his teeth. Veins bulge against Kâmarū's dark skin. I worry I can't sustain it all without a sacrifice—

The force that erupts knocks everyone back.

Tzain grunts as he flies into the far wall. Kâmarū trips over the stone tables and chairs in his path. Khani falls to the floor.

The world spins around me as I lift myself from the table. A foreign force pulses through my chest. Instead of two hearts, five beat as one.

"Did it work?" I exhale as Khani rises to her knees and crawls to me. Her hands still shake, but she lays her trembling palms on top of me.

"*Heal.*"

She doesn't even summon an incantation. With one word, her magic spreads through me like a spiderweb, deep orange light healing me from within. The muscles and tendons crackle as skin regenerates around my injured shin. The heat of her magic erases all of my pain.

"It's working." Khani releases a breathless laugh. She looks at her hands before running over to Roën. With one touch of her hand, his breathing stabilizes.

"For the love of Ògún . . ." Kâmarū's eyes widen as he lifts all the metal tables in the room with a single point of his finger. I haven't seen him work with metal once, but now he crushes his fist and the iron breaks apart, disintegrating into a cloud of dust that condenses in the air before him.

Kâmarū looks at his own iron leg before laying both his hands on Roën's bandaged shoulder. He sculpts the metal as if it were clay. Khani moves to join him.

My mouth falls open as their magic weaves together, working in perfect tandem. Metal tendons connect to Roën's raw shoulder as Kâmarū fashions an iron arm with shifting plates. Though Roën stays unconscious, his metal fingers twitch. I can't believe my eyes.

I've never seen magic like that.

I lay my fingers across his temples, fighting the knife in my throat. *This was it . . .*

Oya's vision.

It all started with him.

"Let's go!" Khani grabs my hand, leading me outside the hut. She stops before a corpse: the father whose red cap fell in the dirt. Her intent dawns as she kneels by his side, laying her hands over his heart. As she chants, I join her, weaving our magic together.

"Ara m'ókun, emí mí—"

The corpse glows as we summon the magic of healing and the magic of life. The man's wrinkled skin smooths itself again. His rigid limbs soften.

Clouds of orange expel from his mouth and blackened skin, floating into the air. His very body seems to vibrate under our touch, glowing with golden light—

"Ugh!" The man shoots forward, wheezing as he grabs his chest.

"Baba!" the girl cries out. She tackles him to the ground before he can rise.

Every gaze falls to us as Khani and I lock eyes.

With this kind of magic, we can raise the dead.

We can get our people back.

CHAPTER EIGHTY-ONE

ZÉLIE

EVERY TIME WE lay our hands on another shriveled chest, I wait for our magic to fail. But one after another, each corpse awakens, rising from the dead. I feel the most sacred gift of Oya beneath my hands, the holy magic of life and death. When the last body breathes again, I stare at the glowing tattoos on my hands.

No Reaper or Healer in history has ever been able to do that.

In our magic, I see the answer. What Oya wanted me to understand all along. If we use the moonstone to bind our lifeforces, we can save the maji from the monarchy's grasp.

We can still win this war.

I rise from the ground, marching toward the well.

"That's her," a young boy whispers. "*Jagunjagun Ikú.*"

For the first time, the title feels right. When I climb onto the well's edge, everyone stares as if I were Oya herself. The sun's rays dance like fire along my skin as I look at the crowd.

"I'm sorry." I meet every elder's eyes. "You all needed me before and I was too broken to show up."

"We're sorry." Na'imah steps forward, mountain winds blowing her curls. "You told us to leave Orïsha behind. If we had listened, our people would be alright."

Mutters of agreement follow in her wake, but I shake my head.

"We're the children of the gods." I lift my chin. "If someone's running away, it's not going to be us."

I think of all the pain our rulers have caused. The bodies they've sacrificed. Magic has never been the kingdom's problem.

The monarchy has.

"Eleven years ago, I stood in this very spot when Saran's Raid destroyed Ibadan. I lost my mother and my home. We lost our magic!" I lift my hands. "Today, Saran is dead. Our birthright runs through our veins. But in mere moons, the monarchs have brought nothing but death and destruction to our streets again!"

"*Mowà pęlu olú ọba!*" a villager yells, raising his tanned fist. His cry rings through my ears: *Down with the monarchy.*

"They've taken our magic. Our homes. Those we love most. No more!" I swipe my hand across my chest. "They are Orïsha's past. We are Orïsha's future!"

Cheers spread among the elders, a flame I cradle in my hands. I don't want their fire to die. I want to ignite a blaze.

"*Mowà pęlu olú ọba!*" I shout, and this time the chant spreads, echoing through the village crowd.

"There will be no mercy. No peace. No terms of surrender. We will connect our lifeforces and wield the power of the gods! We will march to Lagos and tear down its walls!" I remove my staff and raise it above my head, extending its blades. "We will rescue our people and make sure no monarch ever touches this land again!"

"*Mowà pęlu olú ọba!*" This time their chant escapes in a deafening cry. It makes me feel alive.

"*Mowà pęlu olú ọba! Mowà pęlu olú ọba!*"

My heart swells as the villagers join in, but a cold realization sets in as I stare at the elders. Connecting with Roën almost took me down.

Connecting to Tzain, Khani, and Kâmaru almost killed us all. Even as we stand together now, the pressure grows in my chest as our connection eats through us.

My throat dries as I remember what Mama Agba told us in the council room when she explained the great cost of making our own cênters. If we're going to join together, we need more than the moonstone's magic.

I need to sacrifice someone I love.

CHAPTER EIGHTY-TWO

ZÉLIE

The promises of my speech swell within me as I walk the mountain paths along the outskirts of Ibadan's village center. As the rows of pyramid ahérés end behind me, I think of every maji who's dedicated themselves to this fight. The life we'll need to sacrifice.

I can't give up Tzain and I can't give up Roën. There's only one other person I love, despite the way she has betrayed us.

Dread weighs down my legs, slowing my journey to Amari's cell. I don't know what to say to her. How I could ever forgive what she did.

Even though everyone she killed breathes again, she sacrificed them. She sacrificed *me*. She didn't care who she hurt as long as she got to sit on her throne—

"What do you mean it's over?"

My steps falter; I press my back against the side of a mountain before I turn the corner. The deep voice grates against my ears. I didn't expect to hear it again.

Harun? I crouch down, peeking around the ledge. The stocky mercenary stands with five other members of Roën's crew, all clad in black.

"You heard me."

When Roën speaks, my hand flies to my heart. He sits on a ledge behind them, exhaustion curving his body toward the ground.

366

The sight of him releases a pressure I didn't realize I still held in my chest. His cheeks are sunken and his voice is weak. But he's alive.

He's here.

"That's not going to work," Harun snarls, revealing his yellowed teeth. "Payment's already been sent. You can't stop what you've started."

Though the other mercenaries close in, Roën doesn't acknowledge them. He takes a flint from Harun's pocket, struggling to light it with his left hand. His metal arm hangs limp, the stillness only broken by the occasional finger twitch.

"You seem to have forgotten that I don't like to repeat myself," Roën says. "I don't care what's in motion. Put an end to it. Now." Roën reaches over to pull a cigarette from another mercenary's pocket. He sticks it between his teeth, but before he can strike the match, Harun smacks the cigarette to the ground.

"Did she neuter you before or after she cut off your arm?"

His words make my skin hot, but Roën only blinks. His muscles stay taut, like a puppet's whose strings have been pulled too tight.

"Serves you right." Harun shakes his head. "I shouldn't have to feed you lies for you to get the job done."

Roën blinks, a wave of understanding washing over his face. "You knew Nehanda was lying?" He lowers his voice. "You fed me wrong information on purpose?"

"You've gone soft," Harun says. "You're not fit to run this crew." He lights a cigar and sticks it in Roën's mouth. "Consider this a parting gift. You're out."

Harun tenses when Roën raises his hand, but Roën doesn't strike. He takes a long drag of the cigar, eyes falling closed as he exhales. After a long silence, he gives Harun a nod. Victory shines behind his enforcer's yellowed smile.

Then Roën strikes.

He moves like the wind, a viper snapping its prey. In one swift motion, Harun is facedown on the ground, Roën's metal hand pressed to his neck.

"Get off me!"

As Harun squirms, Roën smiles, taking another puff of his cigar. Then he removes it from his lips.

I flinch when he presses the burning tip to Harun's neck.

Harun thrashes like a fish washed ashore, but the more he flails, the harder Roën pushes. The other mercenaries stand frozen, unsure of what to do. In an instant, I understand the leader Roën's always been. The reason it took this long for his crew to attempt a rebellion.

"You've grown confident in my absence, Harun." He smiles over his enforcer's screams. "I like it. A few more years and I might even buy it."

He removes the cigar and takes another long puff, tipping his head back to savor the smoke. Harun's body falls limp with relief.

Then Roën presses the lit end to Harun's skin again.

"Now, I'm not asking you, because I never ask," Roën speaks through his teeth. "I said stand down. You hear me?"

"Yes!" Harun gasps between his screams.

"I'm sorry. I didn't catch that."

"We'll stand down!" Harun writhes. "We'll stand down!"

Roën flicks the cigar to the ground and rises back to his feet. Harun rolls on the mountain stone. Smoke rises from his neck.

"Take the crew," Roën spits. "I'm done rotting away in that cave. But if I catch so much as a whiff of you going against my orders, I'll hang you by your own intestines."

The ice in his voice makes my stomach clench. There's no bluff in his stormy eyes. No sign of the tender man connected to my heart.

The mercenaries drag their wounded leader down the mountain path. As they retreat, Roën clenches his teeth in pain. His mask of power falls and he doubles over, grabbing his wounded shoulder.

"You don't have to hide," he calls out.

"How did you know?" I ask as I step out.

He puts two fingers to his heart and taps. "It always beat faster when you came near. Now it beats harder, too."

I know the pull he speaks of. This close to him, it's like a caged hummingbird beats within my chest.

He sits back on his ledge and all I want to do is embrace him. But the cigar still smokes on the ground. The scent of burning flesh stains the air.

"What was that about?" I ask.

"Nothing." Roën removes the cigar from the ground and inhales. "Nothing now."

"You're really going to give up your crew?"

"I couldn't run it even if I wanted to." His eyes close when he exhales. "Compromised myself and my men the moment I fell in love with you."

He speaks the words as if it were a simple fact. As ordinary as the mountains around us.

"Don't worry," he says. "I don't expect you to feel the same after that display."

"I know you're a mercenary," I whisper.

"But you've never had to see what that means."

I step closer to him, considering what he says. On the warship, we stayed on his boat. During the ritual, it was an all-out war. In everything he's done to help me, I've been shielded from the truth we both know. There's no more hiding now.

The monster is out in the open.

"Back in the mountains, you told me about your mother," I say. "You said she used to sing. You hummed her song to me."

Roën lowers his head, but he extends his hand. I lace my fingers with his.

"Why then?" I ask.

"It was worth remembering." He shrugs. "She was worth remembering."

He looks up at me and I see the heart he pretends not to have. I can't hold myself back. Every objection quiets when I bring my lips to his.

His embrace sends a shiver through my skin as I dig my hands into his hair. His metal fingers are cold to the touch. He has a way of holding me that makes time stand still.

"*Zitsōl* . . ." He pulls away, touching the tear on his face. I look down and wipe my eyes. I don't even know when I started crying.

He rubs the spot behind my ear and I lean my forehead against his. One hand drops from his neck, stopping where his shoulder meets his metal limb.

"Does it hurt?" I ask.

"Only when I breathe."

"Always with the jokes." I shake my head.

"If you wanted the jokes to end, you should've let me drown."

I smile at him again, kissing his pink lips. "Next time I'll think twice before saving your life."

"As long as you're taking feedback, you should know I have my limits. If it's ever a choice between life and a certain appendage, I am requesting now that you let me die."

"My gods!" I push him back.

"What's that saying you have in your lands?" Roën tilts his head. "'Don't chop it till you try it'?"

"Next time I'll let you drown."

He laughs as he pulls me in, resting his hand on the small of my back. The smile falls away as the end of this war looms between us.

"I heard about your plan to save the world," he says. "When do you leave?"

"In a few hours."

"Okay." He nods. "I'll be ready."

"No." I pull away. "You need to heal!"

Roën clenches his teeth, grabbing his shoulder as he rises to his feet.

"Roën—"

"I'm going." His metal fingers twitch, still out of line with his intent. "*Zitsōl*, you are my home. You don't get to leave me behind."

CHAPTER EIGHTY-THREE

AMARI

I WILL BE a better queen.

My last words to Father return. A vow for the person I once was. A mockery of everything I've become.

I don't know if Father would be horrified by the actions I've taken, or if the depths of my descent would make him proud. I am no better than him.

If anything, we are one and the same.

Strike, Amari.

I pull at my hair, wishing I could pull his claws out of me as well. His whispers are like the bars Kâmarū crafted from stone, a prison I can't escape. For so long he was the scar on my back. The tyrant I had to vanquish.

How in the skies did I allow his ghost to become my guiding force?

I grit my teeth against the sting of bile that shoots up my throat. Though nothing sits in my stomach, it all comes up at once. I feel every ounce of pain. Every shriveled-up corpse. Despite everything I want, I'm just another monarch terrorizing this kingdom.

I'm the very monster I hunt.

"At least you finally look sorry."

I snap my head up; Zélie stands on the other side of the stone bars.

The mountain ledges cast half her face in shadow, but a light seems to shine from within.

"You're alright . . ." I prop my hands up, but she's so much more than that. It's like a new fire burns in her heart. My skin almost prickles from the heat of its blaze. .

"If you had known I was alive in the village, would you still have launched that attack?" she asks.

I shrink into myself. The truth carves out the last pieces of dignity I have.

"To win this war?" I close my eyes. "Yes."

I put my hand to my mouth, not knowing if vomit or screams will come out. "There's no excuse for what I did. I know you could never forgive me." Facing her now is like a sledgehammer to the heart. It forces me to face the reality I've fought so hard to hide.

I am the child of King Saran. The daughter of Queen Nehanda.

I was raised to win at all costs, no matter who gets hurt in the process.

"We brought them back." Zélie crosses her arms. "You don't deserve to know, but every person you killed breathes again."

"What?" I shake my head, unsure if I actually heard her. "They're alive?"

"Each and every one."

I stumble as the world falls out from under me again. Relief rips through the last parts of me that were still whole. I can't believe my ears. I can't stop the tears that fall.

"How?"

"We used the magic of the moonstone to connect. With our combined power, Khani healed their bodies. I brought them back to life again." She looks at the golden tattoos on her skin, seeing something I can't. "We're going to use it to attack Lagos and bring down the crown."

I rise, though my legs feel like water. "You'll be slaughtered."

"Not after we all connect. We're going to end this war and destroy the monarchy once and for all. Even Nehanda won't be able to stop us."

Strike, Amari.

Father's words shrivel in my chest. I don't know what to say. What I should feel. The throne is where this all started. Perhaps it's where this all ends. But the thought of the crown becoming nothing . . .

"You'll throw Orïsha into chaos." I shake my head. "The agony you'll cause—"

"Anguish and anarchy are far better than the tyranny we've known," Zélie says. "The future of Orïsha will no longer be corrupted by a crown."

She frowns and I see the pity in her gaze.

She thinks that's what happened to me.

I will be a better queen . . .

I release the vow I can never fulfill. I've gone beyond losing this war. I've completely lost the right to lead.

"When do you leave?" I ask.

"Tonight."

"After you connect?"

Zélie's mouth falls open, but no words escape. The purpose of her visit becomes clear.

"You need a sacrifice."

She rubs her arms and looks away, staring over the mountain's edge. The wind whistles in her silence, giving me the answer I seek.

It feels like the entire mountain comes down on me at once. Terror grips my chest. I struggle to draw breath.

But in my punishment lies a certain release. A chance I thought I wouldn't have. If I do this, I can make things right.

I can give them the power they need to save the kingdom.

"Alright."

Zélie whips around, shock in her silver gaze. "I haven't made a decision."

"You don't need to. I'll do it."

Speaking the words makes my heart lurch. My hands start to shake. But how else can I make up for all the pain I've caused?

"No." Zélie shakes her head.

"What other choice do you have?" I ask. "It has to be someone. Someone you love."

Though she keeps her face hard, her lips twitch with the emotion she fights back. It almost hurts more to know there's a part of her that still cares about me after everything I've done.

"Zélie, please." I grab the bars. "Let me make one thing right."

"I can't do that."

"You should not have to." A second voice speaks.

We look up as a distant thud comes near, the steady rhythm of wood hitting stone. My jaw drops when a cloaked figure emerges from the shadows, resting both hands on her cane.

"Mama Agba?"

The Seer looks between the two of us, sadness radiating from her heart.

"It is not your time, my child. Take me instead."

CHAPTER EIGHTY-FOUR

ZÉLIE

ANY RELIEF THE SIGHT of Mama Agba could bring quickly turns to despair.

"No."

"This is not up for debate." Mama Agba shakes her head. "Far too many children have perished in this fight."

"I said no!" I turn around. "I'll find a way. I just need time."

"You do not have time." Mama Agba grabs my shoulder, forcing me to face her. "Nehanda's already declared the end of the war. The maji she captured have mere days before execution."

"Mama Agba——"

"*Tí o ò bá pa enu ù rẹ mọ!*" She raises her cane above my head. "Shut up and listen!"

I flinch out of instinct, waiting for the smack of her staff. Mama Agba's nostrils flare as she sets it back down, using it to walk toward me. But when she nears, I can't meet her eyes. My throat burns with everything I wish I hadn't said.

"Look at me." She lays her wrinkled hand on my cheek. "Zélie, *look* at me. You are my heart. There is nothing you could do in this world that I would not forgive."

She wraps her arms around me, enveloping me in the smell of

sweetened tea. More tears fall as I breathe it in, savoring the scent of her love.

"I won't let you do this."

"You have no choice," she says. "Our people need you."

"They need you more." I squeeze the folds of her robes, thinking of all she built. All she saved. The maji would've died ten times over if it weren't for every effort she made. My entire family would've perished.

Mama Agba takes my hand in her own, quieting my objections with her touch. She doesn't speak as she leads me down the winding path away from Amari's cell. She stares at the clouds that pass over the mountain's ledge.

"Do you remember when I told you about my *isípayá?*" she asks. "When I ascended years ago, I saw myself kneeling on a mountaintop. Sky Mother welcomed me with open arms." She turns to me, mahogany eyes shining. "At the time, I thought I was peeking into the beyond. Now I see my vision was of you all along."

She kisses my forehead, using her robes to wipe my tears. She holds me as I sob, fighting the sacrifice she tries to make.

"I can't." My voice cracks. "I can't do this alone."

"You do not have to do this by yourself. You carry all of us in your heart." She takes my hand and lays it over my chest, lacing our fingers together. "We shall live in every breath you take. Every incantation you speak."

A smile spreads across her dark skin, crinkling the skin around her eyes.

"You are the children of the gods. You shall never be alone."

. . . . . . ◆ ◇ ◆ . . . . .

WHEN I REACH the mountaintop, it's so quiet my footsteps echo like thunder. The ten maji stand in a circle. Amari watches from behind Tzain, her arms still bound in metal restraints.

377

The elders bow as they step back, creating a single path. Their bodies align to form a perfect circle.

All that's missing is its center.

You can do this. I dig my nails into my palms as I walk forward. Pointed pillars close around us like a fence, circling the flat mountaintop. Beyond the red stone, the setting sun paints the sky in vibrant reds and burning oranges. It brings me back to the days when Mama walked this very path, preparing to lead the Reapers of Ibadan.

You carry all of us in your heart. We shall live in every breath you take. Every incantation you speak.

Mama Agba's promise swells inside me as I remember how the sunlight would shine through my mother's coils. Today it runs through my own, bathing my white hair in gold. I hold my breath as I step into the center of the circle.

Ahead of me, Dakarai moves to bring Mama Agba in, his round face somber. Pressure builds in my chest as her cane smacks against the hard stone. But every wall I have falls the moment I face her. It's impossible to fight my tears.

Mama Agba glides forward in a shining suit of armor, silver collar gleaming around her neck. Her silk cloak moves like clouds in the wind. Kâmarū has even fashioned her a glistening cane. Her white coils sit like a crown on her head.

She's never looked more beautiful.

"*Nana——*" Na'imah sings under her breath, starting Sky Mother's song. Her voice rings in our silence, a melody to accompany our grief. When the others join in, Mama Agba closes her eyes and rests her hands over her heart. She takes everything in before turning to Dakarai.

"My elder," Mama Agba addresses him, wiping the tears that streak his russet-toned skin. "You are the dream of our people. Never doubt what you can achieve. Trust the things you see."

Dakarai nods and wipes the snot from his nose. Mama Agba kisses his forehead and holds him tight before letting go. I expect her to make her way forward, but she walks to Kâmarū. She stops in front of each person in the circle, passing on words of wisdom. Even in her final moments, she guides us forward.

A Seer until the end.

"My brave boy." Mama Agba wiggles Tzain's ear. "You have grown into an even braver man."

She makes Tzain laugh through his pain. He wipes his eyes and grabs her hand.

"Thank you for everything."

She pulls him close, rubbing her hand up and down his back. "Take care of them. But do not forget to take care of yourself."

"Please don't do this." Amari's voice cracks with tears. She hangs her head when Mama Agba steps in front of her, metal restraints still clinking around her wrists.

"You are not your mistakes." Mama Agba holds both of her shoulders, making Amari cry harder. "Do not let one moment define or destroy you. The gods work in mysterious ways. Have faith in their greater plan."

When Amari nods, Mama Agba kisses her cheek. I try to prepare myself, but I can't when she turns toward me. A smile ignites her dark skin, bright like the sunset at her back. She walks with an unbreakable purpose, ready though I'll never be.

"My little warrior." Her eyes well for the first time. She raises my chin and squares my shoulders. "Not so little anymore."

"Mama Agba—" I try to speak, but I can't find the words. No matter how many times I tell myself I can do this, I'm not ready to rip my heart in half.

"Remember what I said." She wipes my tears and places her hand on my chest. "Every breath. Every chant. You fight with the heart of your father. The spirit of your mother. When this is over, you will fight with me as well."

She kisses my forehead, squeezing my hand tight. I hold her in my arms, doing everything I can to soak in her embrace. I try to memorize every wrinkle in her face. To inhale the scent of shea butter in her coils.

When I can hold her no longer, she bows her head and kneels. My own hand shakes as I grab hers and remove my dagger.

"Go ahead."

I bring the blade across her palm, creating a thin line of blood. It drips down her hand, glowing white as it falls. She exhales when I draw the sacred mark along her forehead with my thumb. I put her hand on my sternum as I whisper the command.

"Ẹ tọnná agbára yin."

The tattoos on my back start to glow as the blood magic takes hold. Mama Agba gasps when the first drop of her blood falls to the ground. It sinks into the stone, sizzling with smoke.

White light spreads from our center, cracking through the mountaintop like a spiderweb. When it hits the maji around me, ten disparate heartbeats fill my head.

Buh-bump.

Buh-bump.

Each claps like thunder. Their pulses summon the storm. Howling winds swirl around us as white particles of light form in front of each chest, every lifeforce being called forward. They hang like fireflies in the night, glowing brighter with my chant. Tethers form as they blend together, reaching toward my center.

"Ẹ tọnná agbára yin."

My tattoos glow brighter than they ever have as the particles condense. Magic weaves itself together like threads in a tapestry. My body strains as they hit my chest.

The force lifts me into the air and Mama Agba follows, rising above the stone. Her hands fall limp as her chest rises. The wind blows through her silk cloak.

"*Ẹ tọnná agbára yin!*" It hurts to speak the words. Blood magic spreads inside Mama Agba, glowing through every vein. It shines brightest when it reaches her heart. My chest aches as it breaks her apart.

Her complexion darkens, turning deeper than the night. Particles of light shine through her armor and silks, glowing like stars woven into her skin.

With her rise, the spaces between the different hearts draw to a close. Beat by beat, each pulse slows. They fall into sync with the sacred rhythm as the ancient command leaves my mouth.

"*Ẹ tọnná agbára yin.*"

With the final chant, the shine around Mama Agba becomes too bright. She lights up the night like a comet flying through the sky.

I don't feel the moment my feet touch back to the ground. My chest thunders with the force of a storm. Each pulse is like lightning in my blood.

The power of ten hearts beating as one.

I press my hand to my chest and look up, somehow feeling the pulse of Mama Agba's love. Though tears fall from my eyes, the sensation makes me smile.

"*Títí di òdí kejì,*" I whisper the sacrament under my breath. I grab her fallen cane.

I won't let you down.

CHAPTER EIGHTY-FIVE

INAN

I THOUGHT THAT when the time came, I would be riddled with doubt. Crippled by the pain in my gut. But as I stare at my reflection in Father's mirror, it's like every weight has been lifted off my shoulders. For so long I've struggled to do the right thing.

Tonight I leave my mark as king.

Knock! Knock!

Mother appears in the door, a vision in a gown tailored from gold. The rich fabric glitters with embroidered crystals and shimmering pearls. A giant gele catches the light on her head. From the flush along her cheeks, I can tell she's already had her fair share of red wine.

"You look beautiful, Mother."

She lifts her chin, swishing the flowing cape draped across her shoulders. "Have you finally come to your senses?"

"I understand." I nod. "You've only done what you thought was right."

Mother's mask of calm falls and her shoulders relax. In her amber eyes, I see the woman I love. It almost hurts more when she pulls me into a hug, holding me close.

"I know you don't agree with my methods, but I hope one day you will understand that everything I have done has been for you. By dawn, all your enemies will be gone. Nothing will get in the way of your reign over this great kingdom ever again."

I pat her back, inhaling her rosewater scent. Conviction radiates through her words.

It always does.

"I understand, Mother."

She pulls back and dabs her eye, drying any tears before they can fall. She reaches for the pitcher on Father's dresser and pours red wine into the crystal flutes, before handing one to me.

"The toast we should've had." She raises her glass in the air. "To securing the kingdom."

"To securing the kingdom."

Our glasses clink, and Mother is quick to take a generous sip. She knocks back half the flute before directing her attention to my attire.

"You look handsome in navy, but we need to match tonight." She points her finger. "The gold agbada should be in your closet. Efia tailored it herself."

"I appreciate your guidance, Mother, but it doesn't matter what I wear." I set down my flute and meet her eyes. "This is it. I'm dissolving the monarchy tonight."

Mother releases a high-pitched laugh, resting her pointed fingers over her heart. "Have you had too much wine?"

I shake my head. "I've just had enough."

Her fingers fly to her lips, but they do little to suppress her raucous laugh. She sighs and shakes her head.

"Just when I thought you'd matured."

"I have matured." I close the distance between us. "I see the truth now. We pretend that magic is the root of our pain when everything rotten in this kingdom begins and ends with us. There's no helping it." I clench my fist. "Amari proved that in Ibadan. This throne corrupts even the purest of hearts. As long as it exists, people will continue to tear this kingdom apart."

"I don't have time for your nonsense." Mother drinks the rest of her wine before setting down her flute. "You're still upset about Ojore. Stay here and sulk like the child you are."

She turns to the door, but her knees buckle the moment she tries to walk. She blinks as she stumbles forward, bracing herself against the wall.

"What's going on?" she asks, her words starting to slur.

I close the space between us, guiding her back to Father's bed.

"I worried you'd recognize your own sedatives," I say, lifting up one of her emerald vials. Mother stares at her empty flute. My own is still filled to the brim.

I see the moment she realizes her mistake.

"You rotten little m . . ." Her words slur together and her muscles spasm as she fights the concoction. The ground quakes, but only small tremors answer her call. They grow weaker and weaker until she can't summon her magic at all.

I straighten my collar as she fights to stay conscious. Even as her face falls slack, her lips curl into a snarl.

"I hope you enjoyed the gala, Mother," I call back to her as I walk out the door. "It'll be your last."

CHAPTER EIGHTY-SIX

· · · · · · ◆ ◇ ◆ · · · · · ·

ZÉLIE

No one speaks as we make our way down Orïsha's coast, sailing on a boat powered by Nâo's magic. There's no need when every heartbeat pulses through our throats. The ocean spray coats our skin as the salt-filled air whips around us. A new magic roars through our blood, ready to tear through Lagos's impenetrable walls.

Every beat. Every chant.

I hold on to Mama Agba's words as the tides of my old home draw near. With their melody, I'm back on Baba's boat, drawing out the fishing net. I think of him as I turn to the others, not wanting to see the ruins of Ilorin. After tonight, our kingdom will never be the same.

"We're close." I turn to the others. "We can hide out on these shores until sunset."

Then we'll strike, I think to myself. *We'll save our people and make the monarchy pay for all the pain they've caused.*

I picture Mári and Bimpe trapped with our army in the palace cellars; the rest of the *Iyika* waiting for their execution. I think of all those who stand in our way. Every tîtán who will have to die.

"Get some rest," I continue. "Prepare yourselves. There is no telling what will happen when we take that palace down—"

"Zél," Tzain calls, forcing me to turn to him. His arms hang limp. My brows knit and I follow his line of sight.

I walk to the front of our boat, not believing my eyes.

In the distance, a single ahéré stands above the tides.

Confusion mounts as Nâo redirects us from the shore, bringing us closer to the sight. The memories of Ilorin burning moons ago cloud my mind. I can still remember the way the scent of ash choked my throat.

The entire village sunk to the bottom of the sea. I collapsed with my home. Yet somehow, my hut still stands above the crashing waves, untouched by all that's followed since the day I was forced to leave it behind.

When we reach the reed ahéré, the elders wait as Tzain and I climb. It's like a dream.

A dream or a nightmare.

My old home sits on wooden planks, a single safe haven above the sea. There's no sign of the fire that burned it to the ground. No sign everything else that was lost. But staring at the home we shared with Baba is like finding a missing part of me.

I hold Tzain's arm as we walk toward it, waiting for the illusion to shatter. It doesn't make sense. Outside our ahéré, it's like the fires never happened.

Tzain drags his fingers against the doorframe and I find the lines Baba drew above the two of us. Each moon a new crooked line marked our changing heights. I always cried when my line couldn't beat Tzain's.

"I don't understand." My breath hitches as I walk through the doorway. The reed walls curve around me, reeds just like the ones Baba and I wove together with love. It's all here: the cotton cots, the agbön ball that sat in the corner. Even a black calla lily hangs in the window. The petals pass like velvet between my fingers, stems freshly cut.

The only break from my memories is the parcel wrapped in parchment that lies on my cot. A folded note sits on top:

I'm sorry.

It's like I'm drowning again. A gaping hole opens in my chest as the words Inan spoke to me moons ago return.

"When this is over, I'll rebuild Ilorin," he said. *"It'll be the first thing I do."*

Inan promised to bring back my home. I never thought he'd keep his word. My throat grows tight as I unravel the parcel's strings. I don't know what to make of the dozens of letters that fall to the ground.

Why? The question rings through my mind as they spill across the floor. I reach down to pick one up, bracing myself for the words written inside.

> *There are nights when you visit my dreams. Nights where I can forget.*
> *When I wake, I drive myself insane thinking of what could've*
> *been . . .*

My throat closes up and I throw the letter to the ground. *Walk away,* I command myself. But another lures me in.

> *All this time I thought I was choosing my kingdom over my heart. I was*
> *naïve. Too blind to realize that you were both . . .*

Tears drop onto the parchment, bleeding into its ink. How dare he try to crawl back into my heart after all the pain he's caused me?

I slap the letters away, wishing Kenyon were here to burn them to ash. But when one letter clinks against the ground, I lift my head. I open up the parchment and a bronze piece falls into my hands. I tilt my head as I lift it by its silver chain.

Then I remember the piece I gave him . . .

"What's this?" he asked.

"Something you can hold on to without killing yourself."

I placed the cheap metal in his hands.

He kept it all this time?

My tears continue to fall as I unfold the parchment.

> *I know this might end up at the bottom of the ocean. But as long as there's a chance, I have to write it.*
>
> *I have to try to make things right.*
>
> *I could apologize until the end of time and it still wouldn't be enough, but I'm sorry for hurting you. I'm sorry for all the pain I've caused.*
>
> *It's clear to me now that the plague of Orïsha has never been magic at all. It's us—Father, Mother, and me. Even Amari has been twisted by this throne. The monarchy poisons us all.*
>
> *As long as it stands, Orïsha doesn't have a chance. So I'm doing the only thing I can and ending it once and for all.*

I grip the parchment so tight, it nearly rips in half. I didn't even know ending the monarchy was something a king could do.

> *I don't know what comes next, but I know it's time for this reign to end. I will work till my dying breath to protect this kingdom, to be the man I thought I could be when I was with you.*
>
> *But should our paths collide again, I will not raise my sword.*
>
> *I am ready to end my life at your hand.*

"What is it?" Tzain stands behind me. I wipe away my tears, handing him the letter. His eyes widen as he combs over the words.

"He did all this?"

I nod, and Tzain rubs his jaw. "You two." He shakes his head. "Even when you crash, you intertwine."

I stare at the bronze piece in my hand, wanting to throw it into the ocean. I hate Inan for doing this. I hate the part of me that wants to believe he's telling the truth.

"What're you going to do?"

"What I have to." I shrug. "It doesn't matter what he says, what he promises. Our people are still behind those walls. I have to do whatever it takes to get them out."

A silence hangs in the air and I grab his hand, staring at all the parchment on the ground. "What're you going to do about you and Amari?"

Tzain's face twists as he winces. He holds back his tears, but I feel their sting behind my own eyes. Throughout all the pain we've endured, she's been the only one to make him smile. Even when I resented her to my core, I loved Amari for that.

"There is no me and Amari," he finally speaks. "Not anymore."

"Tzain, how you feel about her, that's not something you can just turn off—"

"She almost killed you," he interrupts. "There's no coming back from that."

He sinks onto the replica of his old cot and I sit by his side. I squeeze the bronze piece in my hand as I lean my head against his shoulder, listening to the crash of waves outside our window.

"Next time let's fall for a pair of siblings that don't come with a crown."

CHAPTER EIGHTY-SEVEN

ZÉLIE

WIND WHIPS AT MY HAIR as we stand on the hilltop overlooking Lagos. Storm clouds thunder above, releasing a pelting rain.

Lanterns bathe the capital in an orange glow. Specks of light twinkle from door to door. The palace shines brightest of all, safe behind the city's massive walls.

"Are you ready?" Tzain nudges me, and I nod as I take Lagos's strongest defense in. The silver barrier around the city towers thirty meters into the air, nearly twice the height of any tree in the surrounding forest. But tîtáns and cênters be damned. We shall not lose tonight.

We carry the might of the gods.

I feel it with every beat of my heart, every chant waiting on my lips. There's no stopping us now.

We've brought the war to them.

I turn back to Amari, still bound in metal restraints. She stares at the ground at a safe distance behind us, not even moving when I motion for Kâmarū to release her binds. Roën stands by her side, and we exchange a nod. I look back at Lagos's walls, bracing myself for what's to come.

"For Mama Agba," I call. "Mâzeli."

"Baba and Mama," Tzain joins in.

"Zulaikha and Kwame," Folake whispers.

We speak the fallen one by one, naming everyone the monarchy's taken from us.

"Fight for them all." I walk forward, tattoos igniting on my skin. Their purple glow flickers around my hands like a blaze, covering my body in twisting light. I close my eyes as it spreads over us all, concentrating on the sound of our twelve hearts beating as one.

Time holds its breath as our magic bleeds together.

Then I whisper the command.

"Ẹ tọnná agbára yin."

The pulse of energy that explodes makes the ground beneath us crack. Gravel and dirt float around our feet. Bark splits in the surrounding trees.

The world moves in slow motion, illuminated by the rainbow of colors flooding from our eyes and mouths. The power of the gods burns through our beings as we march down the hill.

Kâmarū and Kenyon step forward, powerful ashês glowing around their forms. An emerald light shines through the Grounder's skin as a red one burns through our Burner's.

Together they shove their hands into the ground and the earth vibrates at our feet.

With a clench of Kâmarū's fist, the entire ground lifts.

Kenyon follows, creating a wave of lava that spreads through the land.

Majacite mines explode, one after the other, mushrooming in clouds of black. The lava Kâmarū and Kenyon create churns through the earth. Black plumes of smoke shoot into the sky.

"Defenses ready!"

Alarms blare at our attack. The first wave of tîtáns charge as the majacite flies. But before the soldiers and gas can strike, Jahi and Imani lift their hands.

The air howls at our Winder's command as the Cancer transforms the majacite before our eyes. The black clouds turn orange.

The sweat on my skin chills as a violent gust curves around our backs, so powerful the trees snap in half. The golden soldiers fly back into the wall as the transformed poison blows into them. Blood shoots from their mouths and their skin turns black like the villagers in Ibadan.

"Don't let them through!" a tîtán screams.

Iron groans as muzzles take aim. Cannons light like fireworks along the wall. Bombs explode in our path.

The soldiers throw everything they have, but it isn't enough to slow us down. Kâmarū stops each cannonball with a wave of his hand. For every explosive Jahi blows away, Kenyon sends a firebomb back. We break through every defense until there's only one left: the soldiers themselves.

The legion of tîtáns run forward in droves, all glimmering in their golden armor. Dozens charge from every point across the wall, magic blazing in their hands. But with the power of the moonstone, I can feel their spirits like the falling rain.

I stretch out my fingers and close my eyes, reaching for the life running through their veins.

"Gan síbẹ̀!"

When I raise my hand, every tîtán freezes in place. They seize as I close my fist, ripping their spirits from their flesh. A smile spreads across my lips as they fall into the dirt.

Nothing stands in our way when we come face to face with the wall.

CHAPTER EIGHTY-EIGHT

◆ ◇ ◆

INAN

As I STAND on the dais in the throne room, my hands shake with the weight of what I'm about to do. With Mother subdued, the hardest battle is won. All that's left are the people in this hall.

Silver platters of food fill long tables, glistening with roasted hen and moín moín pies. Red wine flows like water among the merry crowd. Nobles and officers spin on the polished marble tiles.

Above, Father's seals are gone, wiping the palace of the vicious snow leopanaire. In their place, navy banners shine, sporting an embroidered cheetanaire that Mother designed for my reign.

Staring at the ryder, I think of the bronze piece I no longer have. Mother desired an animal that was less commonplace.

She didn't realize how soon these banners would fall.

I take in the palace one last time, feeling the weight of history that hinges on this moment. After today, Orïsha will never be the same. When the monarchy falls, chaos will sweep the lands.

But there will be a chance. I close my eyes. A chance for something to rise from the ashes. A vision for Orïsha that isn't corrupted by our past.

Music dies down as I raise my hand and stand before the throne. I reach for all the strength I have as I address the crowd.

"Thank you all for being here." I nod to the attendees. "This war has stolen so much from us. It's a joy to celebrate its end."

"All hail King Inan!" a lieutenant shouts from the back. People smile and lift their goblets. Pressure builds in my chest as I motion for them to lower their cups.

"These difficult times have brought equally difficult lessons. The end of this war gives us a chance to right our former wrongs. To confront Orïsha's dark history and make a lasting change. In searching for the best path forward, I was brought back to the legends many of us grew up without hearing. I'd like to share one of these legends with you now."

My throat dries and I swallow, wishing I had grabbed a goblet of wine. My fingers twitch around themselves, but there's nothing I can hold anymore. Nothing I can hide behind.

You can do this. I picture Zélie's face in the crowd. I imagine Ojore at her side.

For them, for Orïsha, I can do anything.

"In the beginning, there was nothing. Not until Sky Mother made it so. She gave birth to the gods above." I lift my hands. "The humans below. With the gift of life came her gift of magic, a power that allowed us to build this great kingdom. But in the beginning, the lands were governed by the clans. The people ruled over one another." I take a step back, running my hands over the sculpted throne. "We didn't have our first rulers until a group of maji abused their gifts. They lost their ability to do magic, but their actions established this monarchy."

The mood in the hall starts to shift, a storm brewing beneath the gentle rain. Quiet whispers pass from mouth to mouth. I catch questions of Mother's whereabouts.

"You've been called here to celebrate a new era, and a new era it will be. The downfall of Orïsha is linked to this throne. Countless people have paid its toll in blood." I raise my voice as the crowd starts to swell.

"I intend to put the affairs of this kingdom in order. Then I'm ending this institution altogether."

People rush toward the stage. Confused guards keep them at bay.

"You can't do that!" a noble shouts.

"The maggots have messed with his head!"

"Please!" I raise my hands. "I know you're scared, but in time you shall see this is what's best. With the proper support, we can build something better than the monarchy. An institution that serves all the great people of these lands—"

BOOM!

The rumble freezes us where we stand.

It doesn't ring like an explosion.

It roars like a lionaire.

Alarms blare as bursts of rainbow light flash in the distance, drawing closer by the second. It's then I see the hole in Lagos's wall. My eyes widen when the realization hits. The elders . . .

They've come for the people we took.

"Run!" I shout. "Leave the palace now!"

The hall erupts in hysteria as people push against one another to escape. Goblets clank against the marble tiles. Tables crash to the ground as people run past.

"Get to safety!" I yell. "The *Iyika* are coming—"

Screams ring as the throne room windows shatter.

CHAPTER EIGHTY-NINE

AMARI

BROKEN GLASS SPARKLES like diamonds, glittering as it arcs through the air. Jahi's winds carry our fighters over the chaos, bringing us to the marble floors. It's like waking up in a dream to land in the walls of my own home. I can't see past the mass of bodies fleeing the throne room.

"Attack!"

Zélie's command releases the storm. With a roar, the maji launch forward, unleashing their connected wrath. Imani levels a platoon with her rust-colored gas. Nâo turns barrels of wine into battering rams. Kenyon's blaze rips through the painted ceiling, burning through the banners that hold Inan's seal.

Magic tears through the throne room, destroying the beautiful cage. A pressure lifts from my chest when Kâmarū shoots forward, ripping the golden throne in half.

"They're holding them in the cellars!" Zélie calls back, pushing into the main hall. Nobles and guards get out of her way. Elders follow after her as she races toward the stairs.

I sprint toward her to help, but then I feel the ground shake. Behind me, Mother nearly tumbles down the stairs, unsteady on her legs. Her cape rips off of her neck, spreading across the marble steps.

"No!" she yells.

Mother's shriek is like a prison cell closing me in. Looking at her, I see myself. The path she set me on. I think of all the blood she put on my hands. The look from Tzain I'll never see again.

She clutches the wall for support, muscles shaking beneath her ripped gown. Horror fills her face as she takes in the scene, but it turns to hatred the moment she spots me.

"You." She bares her teeth, pushing her weight back onto her trembling feet. I raise my hand to strike, but she wrenches a chunk of marble up from the ground and shoots it at me.

My stomach clenches as the slab rams into my core. The impact knocks me into the wall, stealing the breath from my throat.

I've barely hit the ground when Mother hobbles forward, punching out a shaking fist up that glows with green. A pillar of earth crashes through the marble floors and hits me square in the chest. I wheeze as it collides, reaching for my lungs.

The impact sends me flying across the marble floor. My head spins when I crash to the ground, rolling across the cracked tiles. My vision blurs as Mother closes in. I raise my hand before I can aim.

"Stop!" I scream.

The blue comet twists as it flies from my palm. Time seems to slow as it shoots through the air.

Mother raises her arm to defend, but it gives her no protection. A smothered grunt escapes her lips the moment my magic hits her. Her amber eyes bulge. I push myself up from the ground, coughing up blood.

Strike, Amari.

I stumble toward her, rage washing over my pain. Father's voice echoes in my head, guiding me as I raise my hand.

Fight, Amari.

Magic burns as it builds in my palm, but then another voice fills my head.

No.

The simple word binds me in its grasp. It holds my magic hostage, forcing me to stand still.

"What're you waiting for?" Powders and paints streak down Mother's face as she taunts me. But I drop my hand, blinking as I step back.

"It's over . . ." The realization catches me off guard. I thought killing Father was the answer. It only turned me into a monster. "You've lost, Mother. The maji are taking over. The monarchy's come to an end."

"You spineless traitor!" Veins pulse against Mother's neck as she fights to break my hold. Her words slur together as she yells. "You're nothing. You're not powerful enough to destroy the throne—"

"You're wrong!" My shout echoes through the deserted hall. The portraits of old kings and queens stare me down. I look up at them, feeling the power in my blood. "If the past few moons have taught me anything, it's that I'm capable of great things. I know I can be better. I choose to be better!"

I release my hand and Mother's body falls to the ground. She wheezes as she hits the tiled floor.

"You have never been great!" she roars. "You will never *be* great!"

But as she shouts into the floor, I limp toward the cellar stairs.

Each step I take feels lighter than the last.

CHAPTER NINETY

ZÉLIE

"HELP!"

The muffled screams echo through the cellar. We sprint across its stone floors, thundering past curved arches and wide pillars. Cries swell through the underground labyrinth, guiding us deep into its winding tunnels. I search for the *Iyika* when I see Mári at the end of the hall.

"Elder Zélie!"

My heart skips a beat when she presses her round face between a row of iron bars. Bimpe runs up behind her, both of them locked in a cell.

I nearly trip over myself as I sprint to them. The maji of our sanctuary lie in chains, screaming for our aid. Hundreds of bodies fill the cell, packed so tight I can't see through to the back.

"Work quickly!" I shout. "Free them!"

We surge forward, using our magic to rip through the chains. Kâmarū disintegrates the links with one touch as Imani and Khani pull the maji free.

The moment Bimpe and Mári are released, I take them into my arms. I squeeze them tight as they sob, holding back my own tears of relief.

"It's okay," I soothe them. "You're safe now. I'm sorry I ever let you get caught—"

But feet fly past our cell and down the hall, stealing the air from my chest. The relief of saving my Reapers fades when I turn to see Inan.

His spirit pulls on me like an anchor, dragging me back to him. He sprints down the opposite hall, two soldiers at his heels.

If I'm going to liberate Orïsha from his tyranny, I must do it now.

"Follow Imani," I command. "I'm going after the king!"

My heart thrashes against my ribcage as I sprint after Inan. Victory lies in our hands. But it won't be secure until he's gone.

The words of his letters reverberate around me, growing louder the closer I get to him. I try to keep his poison from bleeding through my ears.

There are nights when you visit my dreams—

When it mattered the most I let you down—

All this time I thought I was choosing my kingdom over my heart. I was too blind to realize that you were both—

"Inan!" I shout when he sprints down another flight of stone steps. He stops in his tracks, tripping up the soldiers that run behind him.

"Your Majesty—"

"Go," Inan orders his guards.

The soldiers look back and forth between us. But despite the way they hesitate, Inan urges them on.

"This is between us," he tells them as he turns to face me. "Get out while you still can."

With no other choice, the soldiers run off, disappearing into the shadows. Their retreating footsteps quiet as they leave us alone.

"Go ahead." Inan's chest falls. He raises his hands in surrender. "I'm not going to fight you. Not anymore."

The vow in his letters hits me as I descend from the last step:

Should our paths collide again, I will not raise my sword.
I am ready to end my life at your hand.

He was telling the truth . . .
The thought makes my fingers numb. Tzain was right.

Even when we crash, we intertwine.

The bronze piece he left in my ahéré burns at my neck as I force myself to walk toward him.

"The treasuries are located in the catacombs beneath the royal gardens," he begins. "When the madness ends, take Tzain and someone you trust. Be mindful of how you distribute the wealth. And the military——" Inan stops himself, closing his eyes. "You already know you have to start over. But don't forget to clean out each fortress. Our majacite is stockpiled there. Lone soldiers will try to use it against you."

"What are you doing?" I stop him. "Why are you telling me this?"

"By tonight's end, everyone who knows those secrets will be dead. The only chance Orïsha has is with you at the helm."

His words hang in our silence. He's so calm.

As if he doesn't speak of his own death.

I swallow as I approach him, pushing past the pain in my chest. He almost gives me a smile when we come face-to-face.

"I'm glad——" his voice cracks. "I'm glad to see you again."

"Don't speak." My fingers tremble as I raise my hand, placing it over his heart. His lifeforce crackles like a fire, prickling against my fingertips. He tenses as I start to pull, ripping it away from him. Everything that's passed between us hits me as his life fades.

I see the moment our paths first crossed in the marketplace. Feel the shock it sent through my veins.

The vibration of his blade against my staff. The roar of the waterfalls. The knife that carved through my back.

The rush of his lips on my neck.

I feel everything I don't want to let in. All the ways he entered my heart.

"I'm sorry," he chokes.

"I know," I whisper back. Though I've fought for his death, this feels like I'm killing a piece of myself. Inan's breath stalls as I squeeze my hand. I close my eyes, unable to look as his heartbeat slows.

"Goodbye," I whisper.

He chokes in response—

"Zélie!" Roën shouts. I whip around as he barrels down the stone steps. A mask hangs in his metal hand. He sprints from a moving wall of white.

Confusion overwhelms me as Roën throws the mask to me, his body falling the second the cloud engulfs him.

I don't have a chance to put it on before the cloud of white takes me as well.

EPILOGUE

THE SEARING PAIN forces my mind awake. My head throbs as my lids flutter open, eyes only finding the dark.

The stench of vomit and urine fills my nose. My throat burns as I choke. I try to rise to my feet, but the moment I shift, I trip over chains.

What in Oya's name?

I wince, tumbling to the wooden floor. Thick metal unlike any I've encountered before binds my ankles and wrists. The chains rattle through the silence as I struggle to break their hold.

It takes a few moments before my mind returns to the cloud of white. The gas knocked me unconscious before I even hit the ground. My heart stops as the realization sets in.

I didn't get him.

We didn't win.

"No!" I shout, banging my fists against the wooden wall. My breaths hitch as I try to smash the chains binding me apart, desperate to break free.

We had them. *I* had them. Yet the monarchy stole the victory right out of our hands.

Somehow they've captured us, and I have no idea where they're taking us now.

"Inan!" I roar, though I don't know if he's close. I look around me, trying to see who surrounds me through the darkness. Dozens of silhouettes fill the cramped space, linked by the same chains. I think of Mári, Roën, and Tzain. How many of us escaped? How many maji lie with me in shackles?

The floor rocks and I lift my head to the thin rays of light spilling through the cell. I strain to free my body from its fog. I have to know where he's taking us.

Amari stirs as I step over her leg. I perch myself on her side and use her unconscious body to climb upward. My neck strains as I lift my eyes to the windowpane, but the sight makes the world fall away.

There are no dirt roads to Lagos's gallows. No charred jackalberry trees.

There's no Orïsha at all.

All that surrounds us is open sea.

As I stare at the never-ending waves in every direction, a coldness like I've never known freezes me from my core.

Someone has stolen us from our land.

And I have no idea where we're going.

Q & A WITH AUTHOR
TOMI ADEYEMI

You've always envisioned the Legacy of Orïsha as a trilogy and your meticulous plotting process is legendary. Did your vision for *Children of Virtue and Vengeance* stay the same, or did it evolve? Did anything surprise you during the writing process?

I spent a lot of my life writing without outlining my plot first, but I could never finish a book that way. It wasn't until I was around twenty—about ten to fifteen years into my writing journey—that I realized writing stories was a skill and plot was something that could be broken down and studied.

From that point onward, I've always plotted out my stories, but those outlines act like more a road map for me to get me from Chapter One to "the end." The story itself is constantly a surprise because it's always changing—characters that I envisioned one way end up only working the complete opposite way; entire plot lines and settings get scrapped; character arcs get revealed; the world-building does 4,000 180s until it all makes sense. I've been "discovering" the true story of *Children of Virtue and Vengeance* since the second draft.

As I answer this question, I'm on draft eight now and I *finally* know all of its pieces. So to make a long answer short, I make a meticulous outline, but the story is evolving until I am no longer allowed to touch it because it needs to be made into a book that other people can read.

With magic fully restored to the ten maji clans, *Children of Virtue and Vengeance* features stunning new displays of magic. Was there a type of clan magic that you particularly loved writing?

Tamer magic! Honestly, I can't wait for the movie adaptation because there is so much more magic than I could put on the page, but I love the idea of a magic focused on animals and a lot of my favorite Tamer scenes had to be cut. I also have a soft spot in my heart for Grounders, so I loved playing with that! And as a Reaper, I'm always partial to the insane things Zélie gets to do.

***Children of Virtue and Vengeance* features the return of many characters and introduces a few new faces. Was there a particular character you were excited about revisiting, or a new character you couldn't wait to introduce to readers?**

The secondary cast is so near and dear to my heart, and it hurts me that I can't show their full brilliance when there's already so much going on in this book! I think Mâzeli and Mári brought me the most joy to bring to life. As for getting to spend more time with characters from the first book, any scene that involves Roën becomes electric for me. #TeamRoën

You've shared many of your inspirations for *Children of Blood and Bone*. Did you find new inspirations for *Children of Virtue and Vengeance*?

I'm inspired by literally everything, but the heart of my inspiration is still *Avatar: The Last Airbender*. Book 2 of that series is my favorite sequel to date, so it was important to me that the characters continued to grow in depth and the plot around them was exciting and dynamic in the same way. Also whenever I was in a rut, returning to *ATLA* always helped me think about this second book in a new and helpful way.

You've talked in the past about not being precious with cutting out characters or plot lines that weren't serving the story. What didn't make it to the final cut of *Children of Virtue and Vengeance*?

Like two hundred pages worth of plot and setting and battle and banter and make outs and magic. The earlier drafts of this book was six hundred pages so yeah (lol), it's been a journey!

Your series is being developed into a movie. Have you already started dream-casting in your head?

Oh, I started doing that from before I even had a book deal! I think all authors do! There are a lot of specific actors and actresses I have in mind, especially with the Nigerian heritage of this story. I would love the cast and the people behind the camera to be full of amazing Nigeran actors and actresses. But one name I will give now is Idris Elba because I pictured him when writing all my King Saran scenes! That means he kind of *has* to do it, right? Like it was basically written for him, so if someone reading this wants to text him or start a change.org petition, like that's fine.

What can we expect from the final book in the Orïsha Legacy?

I know what happens, but *how* it happens and what that looks like will be a big process of discovery for me. I'm bringing to life a fantasy I have had in my head for almost a decade. I have to do a lot of soul-searching and research to get it right, but I'm really going to take the time I need to write the most magnificent ending to this epic trilogy that I can.